REBIRTH

AETHERFORGED

BOOK ONE • REBIRTH

LUKE CHMILENKO &

HARMON COOPER

Podium

All rights reserved. No part of this publication may be reproduced, stored in a retrieval system, or transmitted in any form or by any means electronic, mechanical, photocopying, recording, or otherwise without prior written permission from Podium Publishing.

This is a work of fiction. Names, characters, places, and incidents are either products of the author's imagination or used fictitiously. Any resemblance to actual events, locales, or persons, living, dead, or undead, is entirely coincidental.

Copyright © 2025 by Luke Chmilenko and Harmon Cooper

Cover design by Mario Teodosio

ISBN: 978-1-0394-6619-7

Published in 2025 by Podium Publishing
www.podiumentertainment.com

REBIRTH

CHAPTER 1

The Great Demonswar was not merely a clash of blades and spells, but a defining moment in the reshaping of the Valestra Kingdom. It was a war of survival, where monuments crumbled and alliances fractured. The echoes of its devastation still linger across our lands and at our borders.

—Henry Evo, Master Convoker, Clergo,
and former Chief Historian of the Great Library

Now is our chance, lads! Go!" Callum Stross shouted, his voice cutting through the chaos as he summoned the power of a great dragon. The spectral beast spiraled above him in a brilliant eruption of mana, its presence rippling through the battlefield.

With a roar, Callum and the dragon became one, their energies merging in a blinding surge. Transformed, Callum exploded toward a winged aetherbeast that was mere seconds away from releasing a blast of concentrated power from the back of its throat. With sheer force, he seized the sides of its beak and wrenched them apart, silencing the beast in a spray of energy.

The battlefield erupted with motion. A hulking manabound wolf, one larger than any warhorse, charged through the madness. Above, a magnificent gryphon swooped down, colliding with a demonic aetherbeast that had four sets of wings and a reptilian head. The wolf plowed through a cluster of smaller aetherbeasts as the gryphon soared overhead, the beast raining feathered mana arrows down onto an incoming flank of monsters.

The battlefield soon became a storm of claws, wings, and roaring magic with Callum and his allies at the heart of it, fighting to turn the tide. "We're almost there!" Callum blasted another aetherbeast with a surge of power. He yanked the monster out of the sky, broke its spine, tossed its body behind him, and took to the air with a pair of fiery wings.

Callum collided with a three-tailed aetherbeast and drove the monstrosity into the ground, leaving a crater in his wake. He paused for a second as he caught a glimpse of the towering Demon King, who hovered above the fray releasing bolts of energy at the pacted heroes.

Outfitted in his infamous blood-woven regalia, a demonic armor made of hardened mana, the Demon King cut away any pacted hero that neared him using an arm blade covered in blackened veins and marked by a bulging yellow eye. His long, tattered cloak beat in the air behind him as he broke through rank after rank.

Callum lunged forward, about to reach him, the Demon King mere moments away from—

"—*What do you think you're doing!?*"

Young Callum flinched at the thunderous shout that split the air beside him, the sheer volume of it causing him to let out a surprised yelp. His yelp quickly turned into a whine of pain as he felt something hard slap his hands, producing enough force that it knocked the Memorycore onto the bed.

"No . . . wait!" Young Callum cried out, his heart sinking as the vivid vision of the Demon King dissolved into fragments, leaving his head pounding with a blinding spike of pain. "Ow!"

"Serves you right!" came the same voice, harsh and unyielding. His father loomed over him. He scooped the Memorycore from the bed in one swift motion and slipping it back into its pouch. "I told you about chasing ghosts, son! Here we are working ourselves bloody for a harvest that . . . it's failed, you damn well know that." His father pointed a crooked finger out the window. "You've seen it yourself. We'll be lucky to scrape through winter. If that. But this Memorycore. It's the last of our family's crystal, and it's worth something. Certainly more than ghosts."

"What did he do? What happened next?" Callum asked. "Tell me more about the Demonslayer."

Callum knew the basics of the story, how his distant relative had bested the Demon King and his forces. But how? Against all odds, *how* had his ancestor done it?

"That part doesn't matter. The memory won't do anything for us now. These ghosts—"

"They're not ghosts! *Callum Stross, the Demonslayer.* You named me after him," Callum said as he slowly gathered himself, the rude disconnection from the Memorycore having scrambled his senses.

He still felt as though he could fly through the crackling sky, battling against the Demon King alongside pacted aetherbeasts. He would have done anything to be experiencing that kind of glory over picking himself up off a straw hewn floor with the musky smell of rotting wood filling his nose, *anything* not to listen to his father remind him of their crop failure, or for him to yet again tell Callum how tough things were for them now.

"Cal—"

"He was our ancestor. He—"

"—has been dead and gone for five hundred years and counting," his father said harshly as Callum's head continued to clear. "I named you after him because it is a strong name, and your mother liked it. That's it. And I knew this day would come, the day when we would have to sell another Memorycore. And I'd rather it be this one than any of the others."

Vision rapidly clearing, it was right at that moment that Callum could finally make out the dirt-covered, weather-beaten man standing a few strides away from him. Rhane Stross wore his age like a threadbare cloak, each wrinkle and scar a testament to his father's lifetime of hard work for scant reward. The older man looked broken, but Callum was still too young to fully understand why. His father sat, not at all bothered by the cloud of dust that wafted around him.

"It's been like this since your mother . . . since . . ." Rhane shook his head. "That doesn't matter. This right here," he showed Callum the pouch with the Memorycore inside, "this represents hope. Not because of some war, or what some ghost can tell us about the founding of our kingdom, but because it contains value in its mana. Selling a Memorycore like this to a shardcrafter will see us through winter. It will help us get the seeds we need in the spring, and it will keep food in our bellies over the summer."

"But why can't I see it one last time?"

"Because you don't need to chase this, Cal. You need to accept who you are, who *we* are, who we have become, and maybe, just maybe, our luck will change for the better. I have a feeling it will. Just you, me, and the farm."

"And our cats," Callum said, reluctantly coming to terms with his father's words.

"Yes, them too. I've said it before and I'll say it again—"

"It's better to look ahead than to look back."

"That's right. It's better to look ahead than to look back," Rhane said softly. "And looking ahead, I can feel our luck will change. I feel it in my bones. But for that to happen, we're going to have to let go of the past and all its misfortunes. We need to look forward, not behind. Can you do that for me Callum?"

Callum looked up at his father and met his eyes, staring into them for a long moment. Eventually, he let out a small sigh and let his eyes drop down to the ground. "Yes, Da, yes I can."

CHAPTER 2

Aetherstorms are more than a terrifying weather event. They are a violent echo of magic crossing the planet, a storm of arcane energy that brings chaos and life to everything they touch.

—Xander Callow, Master Channeler, Clergo, and famed Demonswar Historian

Ten years of relative calm ended abruptly as the sky darkened over the Stross family farm.

"Argh! No, not now! Not today!" Rhane exclaimed as he shielded his eyes with his hand. "Not right before the harvest!"

The crackle of purple-white lightning caused Callum to drop the sheaf of wheat he had just bound with twine, his father's words not yet having had time to sink into his mind.

What? No way! Callum thought as the darkness intensified, the ominous clouds swelling above as if they were living things. He squinted at the horizon as ink-black shapes billowed forward, their contorted forms illuminated by withered fingers of lightning that painted horrifying images across the sky.

It was a sight that all but paralyzed him, the approaching storm causing his mind to go blank with fear. Callum had heard storms like this and he'd even seen the edges of one on the horizon, but that had been it. Until today an aetherstorm had never hit Weatherby directly, nor the Stross family farm by extension.

"Come on!" Rhane shouted, the words prompting Callum to turn his head just in time to see his father holding a glowing yellow shard in his hand. Rhane slammed the second Empowerment of Deftness Shard into his chest, a grimace forming on his face as he looked around again, wind blowing through his darkened hair spattered with bits of gray. "We need to finish before it arrives!"

Quickly realizing what the man meant, Callum's hand found one of two similarly hued crystals in his pocket and pulled one of them free. Callum's father met his gaze once the crystal was in hand, then nodded before clasping the glowing shard to his chest, resulting in a bright spray of light. Callum mirrored the act without hesitation and the resulting light granted him an instant surge of energy as it flowed through his body. Reveling in the warm and soothing burst of power, Callum felt as if he'd caught a second wind, his body practically beginning to vibrate with pent up energy.

"Good! We need all the deftness that shards can give us!" Rhane called over an increasingly loud wind. "I'll finish here, you bundle and get it to the barn!"

Callum didn't need to be told anything else and promptly went to work, bundling and stacking wheat. "Is it really an aetherstorm?" he shouted over to his father.

"Yes, my boy, it most certainly is!" came back the answer, yelled to be heard over the rapidly growing wind. "But don't burn your thoughts worrying about that now! Just focus on saving what you can!"

Of course, that was easier said than done in the chaotic moments that followed. Callum was unable to help but flinch and glance out at the oncoming storm with every peal of thunder and lightning that split the sky. Despite that, Callum had a lifetime of practice and instinct to guide him, so much in fact that he was able to work even half blind without slowing down.

Once he had bundled as much as he could fit in the cart, Callum took off. He jumped at the sound of lightning and ran even faster until he reached the barn, where he added the wheat to the stack he had already been working on, the bases wide and stable, the sheaves stacked in a crisscross pattern.

He braced himself as a blast of wind struck the outer walls of the barn, the temperature suddenly plummeting as it brought a fierce cold along with it.

Cart in tow, he raced back toward his father, who meticulously cut away at the wheat as sharp rain lashed the two of them, the windblown droplets pelting them as if they were arrows.

Damn it, not rain now too! Callum cursed inwardly as the freezing cold water washed over him, its arrival accompanied by another brutal gust of wind that nearly overturned the empty cart behind him. Panicking as he struggled to hold onto the vehicle, Callum just barely managed to keep it upright until the wind passed, feeling his muscles scream in the process. *Forget just saving the crops, will the barn—or even our home—hold up under this storm?*

It was a question that he didn't know if he wanted the answer to, for he knew all too well that the threat that the aetherstorm posed was more than just mere weather. They were nigh cataclysmic events that changed the face of the world wherever they passed.

And that was because of what the storms left in their wake, something that neither Callum nor anyone else in their downtrodden village would have a hope of standing against.

Aetherbeasts, Callum thought as he arrived a short distance behind his father and practically threw himself at the ground to begin gathering wheat, all while his hands trembled with fear. *Aetherstorms bring aetherbeasts.*

"Good! The field is done!" His father announced after a few more frantic moments of work, the older man then dropping his scythe in favor of helping Callum bundle it. "Small favor the rain arrived when it did, it saved us from having half the harvest blow itself into the sky!"

"Y-yeah," Callum replied as he completed a bundle with shaky hands, partly in thanks to the cold rain and partly in thanks to his overactive imagination.

Maybe it won't be so bad, maybe we'll catch a break.

"Please give us a break," he said as he chanced another glance at the storm, giving voice to his thoughts. "Just this once."

Yet if the storm heard him, it certainly didn't show, the looming clouds continuing to darken as they billowed outward. The result left it looking almost more intimidating than Callum could take and he forced himself to look down at his work, only to have his hands illuminated by the flashes of violet lightning from above.

Faster, Callum thought as he continued binding wheat alongside his father. *We've got to go faster!*

Forked lightning continued to relentlessly split the sky as they worked, collecting and binding everything that they could find before tossing it into the cart. Callum had never seen his father work so hard or desperately, seeing the man's eyes alternate between focus and panic whenever a clap of thunder pealed above.

"Father, we've done enough!" Callum shouted as he grabbed the last handful of free wheat, desperation leading him to simply shove it into another already tied bundle and hope it stayed in place, rather than spend time binding it separately. "We need to get this inside!"

"Aye, it'll have to do!" The man, to Callum's immense relief, promptly agreed before sharply motioning in the direction of the barn. "Get the cart back! I need to grab the scythe!"

Callum almost told him to leave it, but immediately thought better, knowing not only how stubborn the man could be, but also how dire their situation had become. They were in such need that not only were they actively harvesting a field during an aetherstorm, but so pressed for resources that the loss of even one tool would set them back further, adding to the mountain of debt already crushing them. And the last thing Callum's father, Rhane, wanted was more debt.

Callum did what he was told and took off toward the barn once again, though this time as he ran he had to worry about his feet sliding across the thickening mud beneath him, the storm having dumped so much water in such short a time that the ground couldn't drink it fast enough . . . On more than one occasion, he nearly slipped and fell, yet each time he managed to stabilize himself as he raced toward the still open barn, entering it at a run, and stopping just short of where he dumped his earlier shipment . . .

"We made it!" Callum exclaimed with relief, feeling his lungs and body burning from his exertion. Taking a moment to suck in a deep breath of air, it wasn't long before he heard his father arrive, the older man breathing a similar echo of relief as Callum had the moment he was out of the storm. Yet even as he did, Callum couldn't help but notice something was off.

Why isn't he shutting the barn door behind him? Callum thought as he looked back at his father, who leaned heavily against the wall, his head down as he counted something out on trembling, wet fingers.

He looked up at Callum, water dripping from his chin. "I have to go to the village."

"You what?" Callum called over the booming thunder.

"Poor as we are, we are still nobles, Cal," Rhane told him. "That means that the people have to be taken care of. We . . . *I* . . . owe it to them for everything they've done for us over the years. I have to go back to the village." He pushed himself off the wall and approached Callum, placing both hands on his shoulders. "I have to help them."

There was a look in his father's eye that immediately caused a wave of guilt to wash over Callum and the fact that he himself hadn't thought of it himself. "Do you want me to go with you?"

A look of anguish filled his father's eyes. "No. The East Manor field. It's the last one. You need to—"

"You want me to take care of the East Manor field alone?"

"It's the smallest. You've done it before on your own when you were sixteen. You can do it."

"In an aetherstorm? You want me to handle the field in an aetherstorm," Callum said as he slowly realized what his father was asking.

The look upon Rhane's face told Callum all that he needed to know as he stared back at him, the whispered reply arriving a moment later. "I already sold the field, Cal. Sold it and all the others in the village in full. We're allowed some slippage . . . but with the storm . . . it's going to be bad. Bad enough that we can't risk losing anything if we can help it, even one as tiny as that one."

Callum's father paused for a moment as he held out the scythe he'd recovered from the field, waiting for him to take it. "I wouldn't ask you this unless there wasn't another way, Cal. If we don't deliver . . . well, that's it for us. For Weatherby."

Callum craned his neck to see around his father, the way the rain now came down in sheets. "Are you sure?"

"As much as I can be. I've seen a storm like this before. Survived it too. Figure we have about two hours before the bulk of it hits us. At that point, just take shelter wherever you are. Better if it's in a cellar." Rhane's voice quivered and he shook his head as if to get rid of a memory. "Yeah. We've got this. We have time."

The man approached Callum and placed a hand on his shoulder. The two of them exchanged a nod, nothing else left to say between them. "Good luck, Cal. I'll . . . I'll see you on the other side."

CHAPTER 3

*The bond between a farmer and their land mirrors the connection
between a pacted aetherbeast and an archmage. Yet, just as even
the finest farmers and crops can be spoiled by a poisoned soil, even
the strongest link between an archmage and their aetherbeast can
be tainted by the insidious touch of dark mana.*

—Reavis Find, Duke of Echospire

Callum arrived in the East Manor field at a run with the cart in tow, a
free hand already pressing his second and final Deftness Shard into
his body, feeling its radiant energy instantly race through him. As it had
before, he felt the magic it released banish the lingering cloud of exhaustion
that loomed over him, steadying not only his nerves but sharpening his
movements and granting him the speed and poise that he would need in
the hours to come.

"No time to waste!" he exclaimed as he let go of the cart and grabbed
the scythe within it before bringing it to bear upon the waiting wheat, a
task that on any other day would have been mundane and barely worth
his thought. Today, however, with the storm bearing down upon him, was
no such day, and Callum was readily aware of his movements as he carved
through the sodden field, making the most use out of every second he had.

Father was right, it's not that large a field, Callum told himself as he
swung the tool before him, the shard's empowerment allowing him to work
and move even faster and smoother than he was otherwise used to, which
by any other reckoning was already a blistering pace. Blessed by a lifetime
of practice and effort, all Callum had to do was watch his timing as his
darkly tanned arms swung the scythe before him, whatever pauses he took
being only to push away the drenched lengths of his sun-kissed hair when
they drooped too far into his vision. But aside from those brief moments of

respite, Callum needed no other rest as he frantically harvested the small, almost pathetic field, his broad shoulders and the strong muscles that powered them effortlessly taking on the task.

Are things really so bad that we even need a field this small to keep from going under? Callum asked himself as he worked, wishing—not for the first time—that he had a clearer view into what obligations his family owed the world beyond their village. Something that his father had been loath to properly explain to him, often telling him to just enjoy being young for another season.

That's something that has to change after this storm, he thought as the work of cutting the field came to an end, leaving him to collect what had fallen. It was a process that on any other day would have been a more delicate affair, yet the winds grew stronger and Callum quickly realized that he didn't have that luxury. He opted for simply scooping up armfuls of the sodden wheat and throwing them into the cart. Once he wasn't in danger of being caught out in the storm, he could fix the mess properly, but until then, he had to make sure that he had a mess to fix in the first place.

Aided by the empowerment still coursing through him, Callum piled the cart as fast and high as he dared, the wind mercifully picking that moment to take a break in its ferocity. Or at least by some manner of weather that he didn't even begin to understand, it did for the field he was in, for as he neared completion he caught sight of one of the family's scarecrows flying through the air in the distance.

As good a sign as any that my time here is about spent! he thought as he rushed around the now substantially overburdened cart, grabbed its handles, and began to pull it forward. For several ominous moments, Callum was worried he would fail to move the cart as he strained and strained, but to no avail. Right before he was about to give up, he felt the vehicle begin to inch forward, slowly at first, but quickly picking up speed as the wheels traveled down the gentle incline of the hard gravel path leading away from the field. That was all that he needed to start making headway to his destination.

That place in question being one of the outbuildings that surrounded the decaying remains of the Stross East Manor.

Callum had no idea what its purpose might have been in the glory days of his family's legacy, but for as long as he'd known it, the place had doubled as an all-purpose storehouse for all tools and crops needed to work the eastern half of their property. However, as the previous field had shown, that work didn't particularly encompass much as the eastern half of their farm had gradually turned largely barren over the last few generations making it generally unsuitable for farming. That was why, as Callum closed in on the storehouse, he was greeted by a particularly dilapidated structure that visibly suffered from a profound amount of neglect.

So profound in fact, that no sooner had his eyes landed upon it, than a violent gust of wind tore open a large section of its roof and yanked it up into the sky, the entire building shaking precariously in the process.

"What? No!" Callum exclaimed as he watched the disaster unfold before him with countless more fragments of roof and wood tearing away from the storehouse, all while the structure continued to rock side to side with a rapidly increasing amount of instability. Immediately realizing that his plan to wait out the storm in the place was as good as dead, Callum ground his heels into the stone path beneath him, trying to shed the speed that the cart had picked up, all while frantically scouring his mind as to where he could go next.

The other barns are too far and too difficult to reach in this weather with the cart, he thought in a panic while mentally playing over the journey he'd have to make to reach them. The paths between here and there were likely mud by now. *There's no way I'd be able to get the cart off of them. I . . . I need to find something closer. But the only thing closer than those barns is . . . is the manor.*

It was with that foreboding thought that Callum turned his attention past the still shaking storehouse and toward the towering silhouette of the building that loomed a short distance beyond it. Standing some three stories tall and seemingly carved from a single block of stone, the ancient Stross East Manor was an eerie, imposing thing. Of course, such an image was largely helped by the broken windows and thick black stains of ash and soot that decorated large swaths of its face, brought out by the fire that had gutted it nearly two centuries earlier. It was a place that, for as long as Callum had known, had been a dark spot for the Stross family, its history a particularly painful one, not only to show how far they had fallen from their ancient roots, but also because of the fact that the place had claimed a swath of his ancestors. A good many during the fire that brought the manor to its knees, and then a handful more over the decades that followed, thinking that they would be the ones to restore it.

Don't ever think about braving that place, Cal, his father had told him the day he'd finally been old enough to ask about the place. *It's a death trap and dangerous beyond reason. If something falling from above doesn't get you, then the rotted floor giving way or some hidden critter hiding inside almost certainly will. Two of your granduncles found out the hard way, and it broke your grandpa's heart for the rest of his life. Please don't do the same to mine.*

"I'm sorry, Father, but I can't think of anything else to do," Callum whispered as he made the only decision available to him, angling the cart to give as wide a berth as possible to the storehouse. However, if Callum thought that the day's trials were coming to an end, he was quickly proven wrong by the very last thing that any sane person wanted to hear at that moment.

That thing being a long, warbling shriek that split the sky above him, its pitch and volume all but instantly taking over the wail of the storm surrounding him.

W-what in the world was that? Callum demanded as he glanced up at the storm, barely able to contain the sudden terror in his heart. And for good reason he discovered when his eyes landed upon a spiraling twister that had begun to stretch across the sky directly above him, flashes of purple energy merged with streaks of gold appearing across it.

No . . . wait, that isn't a part of the storm, he realized a second later as the brilliant display of light started to take shape in the form of a large, winged creature.

"It's an . . . an . . . aetherbeast!" The words all but fell out of Callum's mouth as he watched the distant monster break free of the clouds, tearing through the air at what had to be incredible speeds. Yet as surprising as the abrupt appearance of the stormborn monster was, what truly pushed Callum's fear into outright terror was when he saw its massive wings draw in close to its body, which in turn sent the creature plummeting downward in a shrieking dive.

A dive that led directly to him.

Callum ran for his life.

There was simply nothing more that he could do at that moment. His only chance at survival, however slim, depended on him finding cover, depended on him reaching the East Manor before the still shrieking beast from above caught him.

Come on, faster! Callum shouted at himself as he ran with the cart still in tow behind him, fear mixed with desperation making it never occur to him that he should leave the cart behind. An unexpected combination that, in the end, was responsible for saving him. As he closed in on the manor, he couldn't help but glance up one more time toward the blazing, birdlike creature diving toward him and saw it begin to unfurl its wings to catch itself. It was a sight that instantly burned itself into Callum's mind, as the image of the colossal bird-shaped aetherbeast filled his vision, its entire body seemingly carved from living violet-and-gold lightning. Yet, even as it did, it caused an idea to bloom in his mind, the sheer simplicity of it allowing him to put it into motion before it even finished fully forming.

That idea being to simply fall down.

Of course, such a thing was a painful experience, as Callum discovered when he hit the ground at a full run, the impact instantly skinning his knees and arms. Even so, the desperate plan all but paid off in the seconds that followed. For when Callum fell, he had made sure to do so as straight as he possibly could so that the cart that he'd been pulling behind him overtook him, placing wheat and wood on the receiving end of the aetherbeast's talons rather than flesh.

With its shadow vanishing over him as quickly as it had appeared, Callum was rewarded with a near deafening shriek of frustration as the stormborn hawk yanked the cart into the air instead of him. Or at least it did so for a split moment, Callum saw as he snapped his head up just in time to see his family's trusty cart hurtle through the air and crash into the heavy doors that barred entrance into the manor, taking them both off their hinges in the process.

It . . . it worked? Callum thought as he watched a cloud of wheat fly every which way from the impact, taking him a moment to process exactly what he was seeing. Yet when realization finally arrived, he immediately slammed his hands down on the ground before him and all but forced himself back up to his feet, ignoring the scraped knees and bruises his fall had inflicted. *It worked! I need to go!*

Aided by the lingering magic of the shard that he'd consumed, it took practically nothing for Callum to regain his earlier speed as he raced toward the now-open manor entrance. Yet as he ran, he was reminded that his battle wasn't yet over, for a thunderous flash of lightning coupled with a loud shriek split the air above him. It was enough for a renewed surge of fear to shoot through him as he snapped his attention upward and saw the underside of the aetherbeast as it rapidly beat its wings to regain altitude and turn itself for another pass at him. An experience that Callum was loath to relive.

But instead of giving in to the fear that he felt brewing inside him, Callum used it to spark a new fire inside himself that saw the distance between him and the East Manor rapidly shrink until the next thing he knew, he was passing through its shattered entrance and beyond.

Screaming wind blew past him as he rushed in, the newly opened doors causing it to kick up a storm of dust, fallen wheat, and what Callum vaguely identified as spiderwebs, if only because of how they stuck to his face. But more than just the flying debris, the most important thing that Callum found inside the manor was the remains of his cart, or more specifically, his father's scythe lying amid its shattered wreckage, somehow having avoided being crushed. Moving without any hesitation, Callum rushed forward to snatch up the scythe, unable to help but feel relieved the moment it was in his hands.

It's not a real weapon, not like the swords I've trained with before when King Morninglade's guard came through the village, but it's better than nothing, Callum thought before realizing just how absurd the sentiment was. *Wait? Am I going to fight that . . . thing? That . . . monster? That's . . . that's insane! I might be a Stross . . . but—*

A loud crash accompanied by a shriek from above interrupted that thought and caused a spark of fear to flood back into Callum as his heart leaped into his throat.

It came from somewhere above, maybe the roof, or the upper floor? he thought while looking upward, discovering in that moment that he could see the remains of said upper floor, or at least the charred skeleton of it, which certainly wasn't enough to hold him, let alone the aetherbeast. *It's probably on the roof, then, which means that I need to find a way down. Somewhere far away and small enough that it won't bother wasting time looking for me.*

That was easier said than done considering the forbidden place he found himself in, one where he didn't know so much as a hint of its layout, let alone the dangers that it held. However, he didn't let that slow him down as he turned his full attention toward the room around him, pausing for a moment to take in all the details that until now he had no time for. Eyes dancing every which way, it didn't take long for him to piece together that the place had once been the manor's foyer, the burned-out remains of two grand staircases that had once led upward evident at its heart. On the sides of the chamber, minus the direction he'd arrived from of course, he saw several hallways that led further into the manor, or at least in the case of some of them, had once done so, some having long since collapsed or become blocked by debris.

"Damn it, there are too many options!" Callum whispered as a wave of indecision struck him, thanks to the sheer number of paths leading out of the chamber. However, that hesitation only lasted for a handful of heartbeats, abruptly brought to an end by the sound of another loud crash from above and a wailing cry from the aetherbeast.

Straight, deeper into the manor! he instantly decided the moment he heard the noise, his feet starting to move before the thought even finished. *If there's a cellar, there's a good chance it faces north, which means I need to get through to its far side!*

Armed with a plan, however tenuous, Callum sprinted through the remains of the foyer and down the hallway that loomed at its far end. As he did, he took painful care to keep aware of his surroundings, recalling his father's warning about the place and its general instability. Fortunately, no ill fate befell him in those moments, and he was able to cut a path through the hallway, needing only to navigate through a surface level of debris and dust that had accumulated upon the once pristine marble floor.

But while luck tilted itself in his favor for the journey deeper into the forbidden manor, it did not last forever, for right as the hallway began to end, opening up into another large room beyond, a violent and thunderous crash echoed before him. One that was so strong, he felt it in his feet as the entire manor around him groaned ominously.

Shit! It found a way inside! Callum thought as he not only ground to a stop but completely froze as the aetherbeast's screech ripped through the darkened chamber ahead, the space then lit by a flash of purple-gold light. *Oh, oh no—*

That fleeting moment of panic was all that Callum was able to register before the doorway ahead of him abruptly exploded in a near blinding blast of light as a familiar, hawklike beast dropped down directly before it. Shaking the ground as it landed, the aetherbeast didn't waste so much as a second before it whirled toward Callum, somehow having sensed exactly where he'd been fleeing to. Moving almost faster than Callum could react, the monster threw itself forward through the doorway at him, or at least tried to, its overeagerness combined with its too large body causing it to crash into the comparatively narrow opening, its snapping beak falling just short of reaching Callum.

A miscalculation that he didn't hesitate to capitalize on, despite the sheer terror rushing through him.

"Gah! Why won't you just leave me alone?" Callum shouted as he swung the scythe before him with every ounce of strength that he had. The weathered yet still razor-sharp blade connected directly with the side of the creature's outstretched head.

Whereupon against any expectations that Callum might have had if he'd had moment to think through his actions, struck not only as if it had hit something solid, but carved through the stormborn hawk's lightning-hewn feathers and flesh as if they were real.

It was an act that surprised them both, first, Callum, in the realization that he had wounded the creature, half of its face and beak falling away with his strike, and second, the aetherbeast, as it realized its prey was not as helpless as it had seemed. Immediately the creature's earlier overconfidence and eagerness transformed into pure, unadulterated panic as it screamed in agony and yanked itself out and away from the doorframe it had just trapped itself in, taking a substantial portion of the frame with them in the process.

That, in turn, caused a foreboding rumble and crunch to sound out from directly above Callum, instantly robbing him of any sense of triumph that he might have found in the moment.

That sounds bad! he thought while forcing himself to backpedal away from the retreating creature, his eyes leaping up as he caught sight of a rapidly growing crack in the ceiling above. *Really bad! It's going to collapse! I need to get—*

Before he could finish that thought, a bright flare of violet-and-gold light interrupted him and forced his attention back down to where he had last seen the hawk, its body rippling with power. Or more specifically, once his eyes could focus properly upon the creature, its mouth was.

Oh, he thought numbly as he took in the ball of lightning that the creature held inside its ruined maw. A ball of lightning that as soon as he finished taking in, launched itself directly toward him at an impossible speed.

Yet not one fast enough to beat the ceiling as it abruptly gave way and struck the orb mid-flight, turning Callum's world into an explosion of light, pain, and, eventually, falling.

CHAPTER 4

Just as dark mana can consume its user, inducing physical transformations and rotting the spirit, so too does this effect apply to aetherbeasts, who must draw upon even greater Mana Reserves to sustain their demonic forms.

—Tensan Faire, Master Convoker, Archon of New Albion

Callum felt himself fall through the floor as the manor around him seemed to come apart.

Yelling as his stomach launched itself up into his throat, he felt his back slam into something hard, only to instantly feel it break under his weight. That, in turn, caused him to continue his descent through the subfloor and into whatever awaited below it. Unfortunately for him, that level proved to be just as unreliable as the previous one, his impact on the charred wood only slowing by a tithe as he crashed through it too. Gasping as the wind was knocked out of him, Callum desperately flailed in an attempt to catch himself on something, but to no avail, everything around him simply giving way under the lightest pressure.

And then he finally came to a stop, his body crashing into hard unforgiving stone with enough force that it caused his vision to go white and all sense to leave him, if only for what felt like a split moment.

Ugh . . . what . . . where . . . where am I? He groaned as his body started to scream at him, telling him all the places where his back, his shoulders, and legs hurt, the combined sensation all but overwhelming him for a moment. Despite the sheer intensity of the pain upon its arrival, it was mercifully short-lived. Or, perhaps more appropriately, Callum's body simply stopped worrying about it in light of the new and overwhelming sensation that flooded into him.

That being a deep and profound cold unlike anything he'd felt before.

Oh, w-what now? he demanded as a nearly all-consuming shiver washed over his body, prompting a billowing cloud of mist to escape his mouth when he gasped. *W-why is—is—it so cold?*

Unfortunately, it was a question that remained in want of answer as Callum tried to get a better look at the chamber he'd fallen into, its size hard to gauge from the feeble light that bled down through the ceiling above. Or at least that was what it seemed like for the first few seconds until he pushed himself up into a seated position, and his eyes adjusted to the space. As they did, Callum realized that the darkness was not in fact complete and that there was a dull violet-gold glow nearby.

Wait, is that from the . . . he immediately started to think as a familiar wave of fear raced into him. Yet before the sensation could consume him, or he could even finish the thought, Callum spotted the source of the dim light, which appeared just a short distance away from him. *Is . . . is that my scythe?*

Appearing in the shape of a half-smeared crescent, Callum's eyes couldn't help but widen as he spotted the tool, which by some manner of fate had managed to stick itself upside down in a pile of rubble so that its blade pointed up.

And is that . . . blood? Aetherbeast . . . blood? Callum added after a second of staring, his eyes by then having adjusted enough to finally make sense of his surroundings. That is, until his eyes landed on a thick black smear across the floor before him that instantly set off a warning alarm in his mind.

Wait . . . is that . . . is that Corruption? he asked himself, instantly freezing the moment he spotted the tarlike substance, its appearance one that every would-be farmer was taught to spot the instant they were old enough to reason. *What in the world is it doing here? Better yet, how did it even get here?*

His heart began to thunder as he realized why the room looked the way it did. Callum scrambled to his feet and grab his scythe, using it as a makeshift lantern to check the floor around him. As he did, the violet-gold light that the blade cast allowed him to discover not one, not two, but three other tendrils of the black tar that snaked their way across the floor ahead.

By the hells, what is going on down here? he demanded, while desperately trying to remember everything he'd heard about the cursed substance, which had unfortunately been half a lifetime earlier. *What did Father and that book he gave me say? I remember something about Corruption being a kind of dark mana, one that lingers as it rots and devours all it touches. And that it's usually brought about by aetherstorms . . . but the storm above just started. This . . . this Corruption here looks old, and there's so much of it. Has it been under the manor all this time?*

Like before, answers were beyond Callum and any experience that he had, especially because the longer he looked at the corrupted tendrils of mana that snaked across the floor, the more disturbing things he noticed about them.

Such as the fact that they all appeared to be breathing, pockmarks of sucking bubbles appearing occasionally along their lengths.

I . . . I have to do something about this, Callum thought as he pulled his attention away from the sight and looked back around into the darkness. *But . . . what? I think I remember you're supposed to burn Corruption away, but—wait, is that what happened to the place? Did my ancestors find this all and—*

A sudden warbling wail from above interrupted Callum's thoughts, causing him to jump as his head spun in its direction. However, instead of finding some sort of creature waiting for him, all he found was the gloom-shrouded ceiling, his mind catching up a moment later.

It's the aetherhawk, it must have survived the collapse, he realized as the screaming wail repeated itself, this time allowing him to pinpoint that it was distant, far away. *It . . . doesn't sound like it fell down here with me. I guess that's good, all things considered. But . . . but that means I'm trapped down here. At least until I can find another way out.*

If there's another way out, he added after a second's thought, taking a deep steadying breath of the freezing cold air to steady his nerves. It worked. So he took another and another until the latent panic that had been building up in his chest had been pushed back to a manageable level, allowing him to think clearly.

Or, as his mind pointed out a moment later, *see* clearly.

For when the panic finally receded away from him and he was able to return to inspecting his surroundings, Callum noticed that all the tendrils of Corruption he'd spotted were headed in the same direction, regardless of which way they had grown from. A sign that he took to be an important one, given the little else that he could make out in the dark room.

Corruption needs to feed off of something to survive, he recalled as he took a step deeper into the room, careful not to touch or step on the Corruption in the process. *Which means that there has to be something here. Something either alive . . . or something with mana inside it.*

But what exactly that could be, Callum had no idea. His knowledge of magic was limited almost exclusively to the Attribute Shards that farmers used to help augment themselves to help manage their fields throughout the year. Which was why when Callum finally reached the object that the Corruption had grown toward, he found himself especially confused at what he saw.

Is that . . . an altar? he wondered with a frown as an ornately cut rectangle of stone appeared from the darkness before him. Beyond seeing a few glimpses of metal that adorned its surface as he held its scythe over it, Callum couldn't piece together any other detail, thanks to the fact that it was almost entirely covered in Corruption. *I didn't know that my ancestors were religious . . . but even if they were, why is there so much Corruption upon—ah, my light!*

Dimming without warning, the glowing aetherbeast blood upon the blade of Callum's scythe suddenly lost what feeble intensity it had managed to maintain up until that moment, plunging the room into even greater darkness. A change that understandably panicked Callum and instinctively prompted him to yank the tool back toward him. Yet, as he did, so too did the sticky blood on the tool's edge abruptly shift, falling off the worn metal all at once. However instead of splashing upon the altar, the violet-gold liquid instead froze in the air just above it, hanging fixed in place, as if caught by some invisible hand. Then, before Callum could even form a thought let alone react, the blood began to move, rapidly thinning out as it shaped itself into the outline of an eye.

One that unmistakably fixated itself upon Callum, causing a weight unlike any he'd ever felt to slam into him.

"W-wait, what is—" he started to stay as the sudden magic brought him down to his knees, making Callum feel as if he was about to be crushed into dust. Yet almost as soon as the overwhelming sensation settled upon him, it vanished, causing Callum to gasp in relief.

<The Reborn Heir arrives,> a voice intoned within Callum's mind, the words arriving at the same moment that the shape of the violet-gold eye began to melt, the blood that it had formed itself out of coalescing itself into a single tear-shaped drop. It hung there for a split moment before falling into the altar, not only vanishing from sight, but also plunging the entire room into darkness. *<Now receive what was kept in waiting.>*

The darkness lasted for what felt like eternity to Callum, yet in practice was likely only a few moments.

However, when the violet-gold light returned, it wasn't in the form of the single droplet that he had seen earlier, but rather a series of bright runes upon the altar. Appearing dim first, the symbols rapidly increased in intensity until Callum was forced to shield his eyes, letting out a surprised yelp in the process.

"Damn it, what is happening now?" he demanded, flinching away from the light as he regained his feet, yet as he staggered away from it he was hit with the realization of warmth. In fact, as Callum latched onto the radiant sensation, it was an order of magnitude better than mere heat. Rather it was as if a blanket made entirely of feathers had enveloped him and swept him off the ground, holding him gently and carefully in its embrace.

However, while the light soothed and restored Callum, even causing his wounds and bruises to fade, the reaction of the Corruption that covered the altar was anything but. As the light bloomed, Callum heard the Corruption begin to burn, the snap and crackle of something akin to burning fat reaching his ears a few seconds ahead of an acrid, rotting stench that invaded his nose.

Which was accompanied by an absolutely bloodcurdling scream that echoed from all around him.

"Aaah!" Callum shouted as the torrent of sound slammed into him, its assault enough that he dropped his scythe in favor of clapping both hands to his ears. However, whatever event he had accidentally set into motion was far from over, for all of the tendrils of Corruption that Callum had spotted, and several that he hadn't, caught fire in spectacular fashion.

<Don't . . . don't be afraid,> a voice, one vastly different than the previous one, suddenly called out to Callum. <You . . . are . . . safe.>

"What?" Callum demanded as the presence whispered into his mind. "Who are you? Where are you?"

Instead of getting an answer from whatever being that had spoken to him, Callum was rewarded with a loud mechanical-sounding click. One that, as he whirled in its direction, he discovered had come from the altar as the runes upon it flared with a renewed intensity.

And in turn, caused it to begin to open.

Callum watched in awe as the upper portion of the altar unfurled itself, opening as if it were some kind of stone flower, prompting a fist-sized prismatic crystal to rise, spinning, from within. It was all Callum could do but gape at the floating shard, his eye catching a silhouette of something within.

Is . . . is that an Aethercore? he wondered with sudden awe as he watched it come to an abrupt stop mid-turn.

<Brace yourself,> the first voice warned. <This will be . . . unpleasant.>

Without any further warning, the Aethercore launched itself toward Callum faster than anything he'd ever seen before, passing straight between his outstretched arms and plunging straight into his chest. Melding into his body as it arrived, Callum's mind exploded with a renewed burst of pain as he staggered and then fell backward under the core's metaphysical arrival.

Landing hard on his back, there was nothing for Callum to do but endure the blinding energy that surged through him in the moments that followed, the experience of the Aethercore melding with him several orders of magnitude greater than any mere Attribute Shard he'd used before.

<I am sorry . . . > the voice said, this time sounding somehow closer to Callum. *<Awakening is never a pleasant thing, let alone this quickly. But . . . but we don't have time to waste.>*

The apology didn't make Callum feel any better as what felt like liquid fire burned through his body, the moment seeming to stretch forever before abruptly coming to an end. Gasping as the torment ended, it was all that Callum could do but lay on the ground where he had fallen, his mind eventually catching up to what the voice had said.

Awakening? he repeated in his mind, the term one that every living soul in the lands of Antiqua knew full well. *Does that mean—*

There was no time for Callum to finish that thought before a torrent of knowledge and clarity rushed into him, stopping his thoughts cold. While overwhelming in its own right, the experience was far from an unpleasant one. Instead it was as if Callum had suddenly gained a whole new sense, one that revealed everything about himself and his state of being.

Soul Sense:
Status:
Health: Uninjured
Mana Reserves: Half-Full
Soul Heart Rank: Initiate
Soulbonding Capacity: 6 Powercores, 1 Aethercore
Attributes:
Might: 4
Deftness: 3 (+1)
Vigor: 3
Resilience: 3
Regeneration: 3
Mind: 3
Soulbound Cores:
Attribute: Empowerment of Deftness: +1 Deftness
Ability: Empowerment of Zephyr Strike
Ability: Inner Light
Support: Empowerment of Sustenance
Pact: Pact of the Radiant Fox

My . . . my soul, it's been Awoken, Callum thought with awe, the revelation far beyond anything he, a *farmer,* let alone one in his family's position could have ever let themselves expect. *But . . . how? That's only supposed to—*

The sound of movement nearby caused Callum's thoughts to abruptly end as he started, his head whipping to its source. One that he belatedly realized was attached to him, or so he discovered when his eyes landed on the vague outline of a small fox made entirely of light that was streaming out from his arm. Taking shape and gaining focus rapidly, the light that was the fox quickly grew brighter and clearer, reminding Callum of the aetherhawk that he'd fought earlier.

And that was because it too was an aetherbeast.

The creature was no larger than a small dog, its orange-and-white mana-hewn body touched by a radiant fire that moved like wheat in the wind every time the fox turned its head. The fox's eyes glowed an even brighter orange, the creature's dark pupils fixed on Callum.

"W-who are you?" Callum demanded, even though he knew exactly what it was. His soul had told him what the creature was. A *Radiant Fox.* One that he had pacted with.

Someone like me shouldn't be pacted with an aetherbeast! he thought fleetingly as the fox slowly looked up at him. *I'm . . . I'm just a farmer!*

But the fox didn't seem to care about that sentiment as it fixed him with a tired, confused look and did the last thing that Callum expected in that moment.

It spoke.

"We are . . . aetherforged?"

Callum's mouth dropped open as he stared at the fox, completely at a loss for words for what was happening. That is until he uttered an inelegant, "Aether *what*?"

It was a response that immediately deepened the confusion on the fox, leaving it looking particularly troubled. "How would I be released . . . let alone aetherforged unless . . . unless what? Ugh, I . . . I can't remember. Everything is just—"

The fox's body abruptly stiffened and an intensity suddenly flashed in its eyes as if it suddenly remembered something.

"My name is Fen, who . . . who are you?"

"You're . . . Fen?" Callum repeated under his breath, still not believing what was happening to him.

"Where . . . where am I? Where are *we*?" Fen continued without giving Callum a chance to reply, his head darting from side to side. "Wait, this chamber. I . . . remember it. I remember you. Quick, tell me, where is Callum Stross?"

It was a question that caused Callum to stare at the fox blankly, the words finally piercing through his mind. "You mean me?"

"You?"

"I . . . I . . . am Callum Stross."

The fox stared at him for what felt like ages, leaving Callum feeling as if he'd said something wrong. "I . . . I can feel in your soul now that we are aetherforged that you aren't lying. But . . . you aren't Callum Stross."

Callum didn't know in the slightest how to reply to that, his already profound confusion only deepening. So he tried a different track, if only in hopes of having things start making sense. "What . . . what does it mean to be aetherforged?"

The fox's head immediately canted itself to the side in confusion. "What does . . . It means that we are connected. Our souls forged together as one."

"You mean *pacted*." Callum replied as something finally made sense to him. At least as much as the tether he now felt deep in his chest binding him to the glowing fox could make sense.

"Pacted?" Fen repeated, his expression dropping back into confusion followed by a quick glance around the ruined chamber. A motion that, as before, prompted a spark of something to shoot through the creature and its attention to lock back onto Callum. "Wait, what year is it? How long has it been since the Demonswar?"

"What . . . year?" Callum asked, the simple question taking him aback. "Why do you—"

"Please, it's important," the fox replied, taking a step toward him. "I . . . I need to know."

"Uh, well," Callum started, unsure what to make of the reaction. "It's been five hundred ten years since the end of the Great Demonswar, and right now it's just about time for the harvest."

A look of incredulity dawned on the fox's face. "So it worked. That . . . that explains everything now."

But no sooner had Fen finished speaking than his head abruptly snapped itself to the side as if he'd heard something, lingering there for a second before snapping back to Callum, his expression now serious and fierce. "Can you fight?"

CHAPTER 5

Soulbound cores forge an unbreakable connection between the wielder and the essence of the core itself.

—Faylen Smigg, Master Convoker

Huh? Can I *what*?" Callum demanded, his eyes going wide at the unexpected question and danger it implied.

"Fight," Fen repeated as both his eyes and body flared with light, mana visibly swelling around him. "I thought that the Corruption infesting this place was completely burned away for the moment, but I was wrong. Quickly, up to your feet! We need to meet it together!"

"Wait, I can't! I don't—!" Callum started to shout, yet before he could finish, Fen's body exploded into a spray of orange-white light that rushed straight toward him. As it connected with him, Callum felt a surge of power shoot through him, enough to make his head spin. Now lightheaded, he watched with blurred vision as gold mana tinged with bits of black began to flow down both of his arms, forming into claws of light.

<*Keep a look out around you. Whatever is left of the Corruption has regrouped and is coming for us. If we work together . . .*>

The sudden urgency was all that Callum's mind needed to finally focus, his body practically launching itself up into the air as he moved. Muscles that just moments ago had been exhausted and bruised now responded with not only vigor, but a newfound strength as well, leaving Callum feeling as if he'd absorbed a small mountain's worth of Attribute Shards.

Is . . . is this what it means to be pacted? The fleeting thought crossed his mind a second before a flash of movement in the gloom ahead of him stole it away.

Ever since the altar had exploded with light and set fire to the Corruption touching it, Callum had lost all sense of the room around him, understandably distracted by the events that followed. Yet now as he looked, he saw the scorch marks of where the black tendrils of mana had lain, at least until they vanished into the gloom. The light emanating from his mana-hewn claws was not enough to illuminate the chamber. But as Callum discovered, as that flash of movement resolved itself into a horrid, misshapen creature, he didn't need to see the whole chamber in order to deal with the threat that lurked within it.

Especially since it seemed so keen on coming directly to him.

<It's an imp!> Fen announced the instant that the corrupted monster appeared, its high-pitched shriek cutting through the air as it charged Callum. *<They are fast, but dim-witted and frail! Let it come to us and use our speed to surprise it and strike with our claws!>*

Of course, that was easier said than done, Callum discovered as the bulbous, vaguely bat-faced creature closed in, its movements and four-legged stride so erratic that he almost tripped himself up on his own feet. But even with an untimely stumble to throw off his timing, Callum was to recover, reset his stance, and strike out at the creature, thanks to the newfound speed his body possessed. Catching the imp before it even showed a reaction to its impending doom, Callum's luminous claws all but wiped it from existence in a single swipe, its body catching fire the same way the other Corruption had earlier.

<A good start!> Fen congratulated from within his mind, his tone then quickly shifting back to seriousness. *<But be wary, there are more coming.>*

And there were, Callum discovered a second later as another flash of movement caught his eye, this time as three more imps appeared from the gloom, all of them charging directly at him. So fast in fact, that he didn't even have the time to feel fear or panic at their appearance, for they were right on top of him, their claws and teeth filling his vision.

"How is the Corruption alive?" Callum demanded as he scrambled to meet the creatures. "It was just . . . sludge before!"

<It was always alive,> Fen's voice told him. *<We just woke it up. Now worry about focusing on the fight!>*

And that is exactly what Callum did as one of the imps picked that moment to lunge toward him, but in a way that seemed far too slow in his eyes. Reacting quickly, Callum countered its lunge with one of his own, grabbing the small creature and throwing it into the nearby wall, causing it to splatter everywhere. He did the same to the second imp as it leaped for him.

<That does work . . . but the claws are quite a bit cleaner,> Fen chimed in with a vaguely disgusted note in his mental voice as a potent stench rose up to greet Callum.

"N-Noted," Callum replied as he turned his attention toward the final of the three imps, which didn't seem to care in the slightest about the fate that its two siblings had just suffered, choosing instead to lunge viciously toward him. Perhaps for good reason, given that its attack was faster than either of the two imps before it, prompting Callum to dodge backward to avoid it.

Yet no sooner had he done so than the imp shifted to follow him, shrieking loudly as it attacked again and again, each time Callum barely managing to evade it. They danced in a wide circle over the next few seconds that followed, Callum gradually finding his rhythm the longer that the exchange went on. That is, until something about the imp's movements clicked in his mind and allowed him to instead dart forward when it reared to attack, putting his claws directly into its face.

Thereby leaving him alone once more, the last of the shrieking sounds that the corrupted creature had made fading away as the radiant fire consumed it.

<Well . . . done,> Fen told Callum as the fight came to an end, the fox's voice suddenly sounding somewhat weary. <That . . . that should be the last of them, for now at least.>

With those words echoing through his mind, the light and power that had been coursing through Callum came to an abrupt end and Fen reappeared, a stream of mana pouring itself out from his body until the fox was once more looking at him.

"We must deal with what's left of the Corruption and absorb its mana," Fen stated without any other explanation. "Don't worry, I can manage it for us."

Trembling, Callum looked down at his hands, which had burned with a white flame just moments ago. "What did you just do to me?"

"We melded our powers and scoured the Corruption," Fen explained. "That's what an aetherforge allows us to do. Or what *pacting* allows us to do as you called it. I was the first one of my kind to do it, you know."

"The first?" Callum repeated, the fox's abrupt change in topics difficult to follow. "The first what?"

But even as the words left Callum's mouth, Fen was moving toward the remains of one of the imps at which he lashed his fiery tail, causing it to burst into flames. Oddly enough, Callum didn't feel any heat emerge from the conflagration, even if it did create enough light to be blinding for a moment. One by one, Fen repeated the motion until all three pools of Corruption disintegrated into motes of light that flooded into Fen. Only then, once the task was done, did the fox turn back to look at Callum, posing a simple, if hesitantly worded, question in reply. "How . . . how much knowledge do you have of the Demonslayer?"

Callum couldn't help but blink at the query, finding himself needing to take a moment to consider his answer.

"I, uh, I know who the Demonslayer is," he replied once he was ready. "That was his nickname. I mean, it was one the original Callum Stross went by."

"Yes, yes it was," Fen said, for a moment looking sad as his eyes dropped down toward the ground then back up to Callum's. "And it was way back then, in your forefather's era when we first learned how to bond with one another. When we learned how an aetherbeast core, an *Aethercore*, could meld with that of a human."

"You and . . . the Demonslayer?"

"Yes, the *original* Callum Stross, as you called him," Fen replied with a nod. "How much of your family's history do you know? Ancient history, that is. And its connection to magic?"

"I know some."

"Then you are aware of everything you gained during our pacting and your Awakening, yes? And that of shards and cores?"

"I . . . do, though it is all new to me in practice," Callum answered thinking back to what his newly Awoken Soul Sense had told him. He'd bound to his soul new cores, vessels of magic that would allow him to shape mana into useful practical effects and spells.

"Completely understandable," Fen stated simply. "Fortunately, your newfound abilities are relatively simple in nature and it shouldn't be all that difficult for you to understand them."

"Erm, and how exactly would I do that?" Callum asked, suddenly finding himself a little eager at the prospect. Sure, he knew about pacting, about what it took to Awaken one's Soul Sense and make true use of the magical shards and cores that the world revolved around, every living person did. But even so, his knowledge was incomplete, limited only to the scope that a farmer would need.

Any dream I had about being anything more than that, to be a true pacted, died when I was young, Callum thought with not a little bit of bitterness, especially in light of his current circumstances.

<By looking inward,> Fen answered within his mind, despite still standing before him. *<When you first Awoke, you should have gained a new . . . awareness of yourself. Soul Sense as it's called. It allows you to see yourself as you truly are. What you must do is recall that sense and dive even deeper into yourself, into our bond. It will show you what we are now capable of.>*

It was a confusing explanation for Callum, if at least to start. Yet even so, when he gave Fen's instructions even the smallest bit of thought and focus, he felt something within him all but instantly rise, the newly gained Soul Sense awoke once more.

Melded Shards:
Empowerment of Deftness—Time left—03:24
Type: Attribute
Grade: Common
Effect: When melded, this shard empowers its wielder, granting +1 to their Deftness Attribute.

That's the power of the shard I used earlier to help me clear the fields, Callum noted as he processed what his Soul Sense told him, suddenly remembering a fragment of something that he'd read earlier about those who had Awoken. Their inner senses allowed them to process and understand the states of their bodies in a clearer and more innate way than those without the sense. Or at least that was the general rule. Supposedly there were other simple spells that people could learn to do the same, but Callum didn't know them.

Regardless, Callum's success was exactly what he needed in that moment as he focused on the empowerment and saw that its power was rapidly beginning to wane. Something that he couldn't help but lament given how the day's circumstances had played out. That was because the shards worked as a currency and using them for their powers was something that people only did if they could afford to do so. Or if they were truly desperate and needed the magical empowerments that the shard contained.

Maybe . . . maybe now we won't need them at all now that Fen is with me, Callum thought hopefully as he pushed his focus past that fragment of knowledge and continued deeper.

Soulbound Cores:
Empowerment of Zephyr Strike
Type: Ability
Grade: Common
Infusion Requirements for Grade Increase:
0/10 Air Affinity Shards
0/5 Deftness Shards
Affinity Requirements: Air

Effect: When bound to one's Soul Heart, this core grants its wielder the ability to shape their latent air mana into that of a powerful crescent of wind, slicing apart all it touches.

Inner Light
Type: *Ability*
Grade: *Common*
Infusion Requirements for Grade Increase:
0/5 Light Affinity Shards
0/5 Mind Shards
0/5 Regeneration Shards
Affinity Requirements: *Light*
Effect: When bound to one's Soul Heart, this core allows the user the ability to rapidly heal wounds and restore stamina.

Empowerment of Sustenance
Type: *Support*
Grade: *Common*
Infusion Requirements for Grade Increase:
0/5 Vigor Shards
0/5 Resilience Shards
Effect: When bound to one's Soul Heart, this core reduces the wielder's need for food, sleep, or drink.

Pact of the Radiant Fox
Type: *Pact*
Grade: *Common*
Infusion Requirements for Grade Increase:
0/5 Fire Affinity Shards
0/5 Light Affinity Shards
0/10 Deftness Shards
0/10 Vigor Shards
0/5 Resilience Shards
Mana Affinities Granted: *Air, Fire, Light*
Meldform Benefits:
Attributes:
+2 Might
+3 Deftness
+2 Vigor

+2 Regeneration
+2 Resilience
Radiant Claws: *When melded with the Radiant Fox, the wielder gains powerful claws made of burning light, which can not only be used to attack its enemies, but also empower further, unleashing blazing slashes of fire and light a short distance before them.*

<Do you understand better now?> Fen asked once the information surging through Callum's mind came to an end. *<This . . . this is what it means to be aetherforged. It is a long yet rewarding path to walk. Though . . . I am sorry to say that my powers have waned quite considerably over the centuries.>*

"I . . . I think I do," Callum replied, despite still finding it hard to believe what had, what *was* happening to him. "We really are pacted . . . *aetherforged* to one another."

<That we are.>

Callum paused for a moment as he considered that and what it meant for his future. "What . . . what does that mean for me?"

"Ah . . ." Fen hedged, this time out loud as he stared back at Callum, looking hesitant for a split second before continuing. "That is . . . a little complicated to explain right now. But know that your forefather and I had a plan for my reawakening. A plan for what I, what *we*, needed to do when I Awoke. We need to find the archive that he was building in a city called New Albion. The Archive of Destiny."

Fen cocked his head sideways as the words left his mouth, looking momentarily uncertain. "That he built? And hopefully that city still stands?"

"It does," Callum replied with a nod, his eyes unable to help but widen at the implication that he would need to travel to the capital alongside Fen. A journey that he had never taken before.

"Ah, good. And I'm sorry," Fen replied. "It will take me some time to get used to how much time has passed since I was last awake."

"I could say the very same thing," Callum replied in as dry a tone as he could manage given the circumstances before pausing to take a deep breath and brace himself. He still couldn't believe what was happening to him, what *had* happened to him. Everything just felt so surreal. But even so, he wasn't out of danger just yet. He needed to either find a way out of the manor or a place that he could hide out until the storm was over. Fortunately, as luck happened, he had the perfect guide in front of him to help do that, or at least he thought. "So, where do we go next if we want to get out of . . . wherever here is?"

Whatever hopes Callum might have placed on the fox to have a solution to their situation, he was quickly disappointed when Fen's ears flattened themselves against his head in uncertainty.

"Um, I was hoping you could tell me that," he said sheepishly while glancing around the almost completely ravaged room, which admittedly looked quite worse for wear even when discounting the extra debris that Callum's arrival had brought. "I'm afraid nothing I see here strikes a chord with me. Either my memories are still too clouded from my sleep, or my cache was moved after I was sealed away."

"Oh . . . I . . . see," Callum replied in a suddenly weak voice as he remembered just how he had gotten here in the first place. "That . . . that might be a problem then."

"It . . . is?" Fen asked, uncertainty clear in their voice. "Why?"

"Because there was an aetherbeast that chased me down here," he blurted without any preamble. "A large . . . bird, a hawk of some kind. It came from the aetherstorm over the farm."

The words were enough to cause Fen to instantly freeze, his bright eyes widening in the first hints of fear he'd ever seen from the fox. "There . . . there is an aetherstorm over the lands here, *right now*?"

"It arrived today, but yes, it's right over us," Callum answered, his own fear growing to mirror what he saw in Fen.

"That is bad, very, *very*, bad," the fox said as he immediately began to pace, taking several contemplative strides before his head snapped back to Callum. "Quickly, tell me how the storm began and about the beast you fought."

Which is exactly what Callum did over the next few moments that followed.

As he did, he saw the small fox wince at a few explanations, as well as express a look of sorrow when Callum described the state of the manor they were beneath. But despite those initial reactions, Fen's expression remained otherwise stoic as Callum told his story.

"You're completely certain that the creature never made it this far, to this chamber?" Fen asked as soon as Callum finished speaking.

"Uh, as much as I can be," he immediately replied, unable to help but find the question odd. "I saw it come down from the storm and chase me into the manor. I can't see when it would have had a chance to be here before I fell into it myself."

"Good," the fox said with a relieved sigh. "That is . . . good, *really* good. It means that there is no chance that the creature could have been exposed to the Corruption and infected by it."

"That . . . that can happen?" Callum asked, his stomach suddenly twisting at the thought.

"Oh, yes," Fen replied as he bared his teeth in disgust. "And it is a terrible thing to witness let alone battle against. Not that it sounds like we are going to be able to avoid a battle anyway."

"Wait, you mean you want me to fight, *again*?" Callum demanded, the thought of doing so giving him a wave of confusing emotions. On the one hand, he would do anything to feel that power, that energy surging through him, from when he and Fen were melded. On the other, he felt he'd already pushed his luck far enough today.

"I'm afraid we must," Fen said simply, showing no reaction at all if he was able to sense Callum's thoughts. At least not until his expression softened as he looked up at him. "I . . . I understand this is a lot to take in. To believe. There is much that we must speak about. *So much*. But we will find time for that later, once we are safe. Right now, we must deal with the beast before it decides to vent its fury at your injury to it on the surrounding lands. From what you said . . . it seems like we are the only ones even able to do so, should it decide to rampage."

Callum's stomach immediately twisted at Fen's words, leaving him feeling as if he were going to be sick. But even so, he realized that Fen was right. There were no other pacted here in Weatherby, or close by for that matter. If the aetherhawk decided to attack the village, then no one would be able to stand up to it. No one except him.

Poor as we are, we are still nobles, Callum said to himself, his father's earlier words coming to the forefront of his mind. *And Weatherby is our responsibility.*

CHAPTER 6

The aetherstorm brought with it destruction, yet it also brought life. It is how the pacted aetherbeast came about so long ago, a human's timeless companion in the fight against Corruption and the Demonsrealm.

—Emilia Eadred, Mastress Weaver, Core Lectora, quoted in the foreword to the second edition of the pivotal work *A History of the Valestra Kingdom*, by Sir Berenwald Wulmar

Callum steadied his focus with a quick breath in. He felt empowered by what he had just been able to do with Fen, yet he had no idea what to expect of the monster he'd seen earlier, the hawklike aetherbeast with its storm-hewn body, wicked claws, and razor-sharp beak.

"Should I get my scythe before we go?" he whispered to Fen, who promptly replied in his mind.

<*No, not with the climb ahead of us. It served you well earlier, but it'll only hinder you now. Don't worry, however, you have me. Use my claws and the power that our bond has forged. There should be enough mana between us to see us through whatever the creature is capable of.*>

"I hope so," Callum replied wistfully as he turned his focus toward his arm and pulled on the power that was Fen within him. A second later he felt a strange twist in his core that came coupled with an intense fire spreading toward his hands, forming into a pair of sharpened claws made of light. *That will take some getting used to!*

Turning away from his newly formed weapons, Callum found the spot he had fallen from and looked up, seeing only a small gap in the ceiling with the rest of it being filled with precariously placed debris.

Hmm, that doesn't look all that stable, he thought after a moment, the beginnings of an idea coming to him.

<*Ah, good idea,*> Fen immediately replied in an approving tone that couldn't help but startle Callum.

"Eh, what is?" he whispered back, his mind going blank for a split second.

<*You were thinking to bore a path through the debris, yes?*>

"Uh, y-yeah with the new power I have, Zephyr Strike," Callum replied, once again feeling exceptionally out of his depth. "I . . . I just don't know how to reach for it."

<*You just do.*> Fen stated a little unhelpfully. <*You imagine the power in your heart flowing down to your arm and forming itself into an arc of wind. Don't overthink it.*>

Of course no sooner did the fox say that, than an aptly timed shriek and a hard thump on the ground above them sounded out.

"I'm overthinking it," Callum stated with a flinch as he heard the aether-beast make itself known yet again. "I . . . I need help."

<*Of course,*> Fen replied patiently, the words coming at the same moment that Callum started to feel something start to swell inside him. <*I can draw attention to what you must search for within yourself. Do . . . do you feel it now?*>

"I . . . I do." Callum felt a storm of energy suddenly appear within him, one that all but launched itself down his arms the moment that he turned his focus to it. Building faster than he could follow, Callum barely remembered to raise his arm in time as a vortex of air wrapped around his fist and promptly launched itself forward, burying into the debris above.

A move that, in turn, caused the debris above to all but vanish as the crescent of air buried itself into it, launching what it couldn't sheer apart up and away from him.

<*Well done!*> Fen exclaimed as the two of them stared up at the now-open hole, ignoring the cloud of dirt, dust, and lesser debris that rained down in response to his magic. <*Now up quickly, before the beast comes to investigate the noise we've made!*>

A loud screech suddenly echoed from the room around him stealing away any better reply he might have had, causing his head to whip around and spot a familiar creature lumbering down toward him.

Callum took in the stormborn hawk, noticing quickly that it was quite a bit worse for wear since he'd last seen it. Not only was its face and beak badly scarred courtesy of his scythe, but one of its wings looked broken, thanks in part to a long spear of stone that had thrust itself through its body, no doubt from the collapse it had caused earlier.

<I see it! And, fortunately for us, it looks quite injured!> Fen answered as the beast quickly picked up speed, charging directly toward them. *<Now be ready! Here it comes!>*

And it most certainly was, Callum discovered as he took the fox's warning to heart and braced himself to receive the aetherbeast's charge, rolling to the side the moment that it drew close.

<Good! Now attack!> Fen shouted as Callum regained his feet and slashed out at the beast with his burning claws, landing two sharp cuts upon its body. Callum saw a spray of lightning-charged mana erupt from the wounds as the creature backpedaled away from him, screeching in pain.

But that brief pause was all the respite that Callum could enjoy before the creature's rage-filled eyes narrowed on Callum and it struck back, unfurling its unbroken wing in a sweeping strike. One that Callum just barely managed to block, taking the strike directly upon his claws. Yet while the move was enough to soften the blow, at least when it came to not breaking said arms that he used to block the attack, the aetherbeast's strike was still powerful enough that it sent Callum flying off his feet a dozen feet backward, stopping only when he slammed directly into the room's stone wall.

"*Ugh!*" Callum grunted as he hit the wall and fell to the ground amid splinters and other debris. Yet even while the hit had been powerful, instinct quickly had him rising to his feet, ignoring the blood that dripped from his chin and the pain blooming in his back.

<I'll mend you as best I can!> Fen's voice called out in Callum's mind, the pain in his body abruptly starting to fade as a wave came of energy rushed over him. It was such a surprising feeling, and he could see the scratch marks on his arms from his earlier fall stitching themselves together until only pale, healthy skin remained in place.

Invigorated by the fact his wounds had been healed, Callum quickly turned his attention back toward the aetherbeast, which to his dismay, had started to glow once more as it conjured a ball of crackling energy in its maw.

"Oh, not again!" he said as his focus narrowed completely upon the monster, its body dimming as it poured more power into the sphere. It was enough to force Callum into action as he called upon the wind mana now inside him, creating and throwing a wicked crescent of air toward it as he broke into a charge.

Crossing the distance between himself and the creature in the blink of an eye, the crescent slammed directly into the growing orb before it could complete itself, causing it to snap violently out of existence in a way that prompted the beast to shriek with pain.

<Callum, be careful—> he heard Fen start to shout in his mind as he closed with the aetherhawk a pair of seconds later, the fox's words getting lost in the chaos as Callum slashed out with his claws, rending open two new gashes upon its face and neck. From there, everything turned into a desperate melee between him and the aetherbeast as the two of them attacked one another in a frenzy, any skill that Callum might have lacked in the exchange being made up for by sheer desperation and the power that his meldform granted him.

"Why. Won't. You. Go. Away!" Callum shouted as he leaped forward after a close dodge, his mind reaching out to conjure another Zephyr Strike, the blade of wind rushing out from his fist and slamming into the aetherbeast at point-blank range. A blow that finally made it buckle as its legs gave out from under it.

Yet even as it crashed into the ground, Callum didn't let up his assault, clawing its head twice more in rapid succession before bringing his fist back for a final finishing strike.

<Callum! Wait a moment!> Fen called out as he reached out to the wind mana within him one more time, sending it down toward his hand. *<You don't—>*

But as before, Callum was too far gone to truly hear Fen as the mana finished coalescing. For no sooner was his newfound power ready, than he brought his fist forward in an explosion of air that finally brought the battle to an end, the stormborn hawk letting out one final screech as the blade of wind took its head off its body.

"There . . . it's . . . done . . ." Callum muttered, suddenly feeling impossibly tired as he watched the aetherbeast's head and body fall apart into countless motes of multicolored light. A move that surprised him to no end, especially when they all began to move. "What? What is . . ."

Whirling with a surprising burst of speed, the various motes that were once the aetherbeast began to rapidly clump together and before Callum knew what was happening, all of them rushed toward him in a blur. Prompting a flinch as they arrived and then stopped before them, the next thing Callum saw were three shards floating directly before him, his Soul Sense reaching out, seemingly of its own accord, to touch each of them and give him a perfect insight as to what they were.

Empowerment of Mind Shard
Air Affinity Shard
Light Affinity Shard

Oh, they're . . . shards, he thought to himself, needing to stare at the floating crystals for a second as a wave of even deeper exhaustion slammed into him, rising up from within as he felt his and Fen's meld unbind itself.

One moment he was standing, and the next, he was falling as darkness overtook him.

CHAPTER 7

And so, with the Demon King's fall, the shadows that choked the land were lifted. The songs of a healed world rose to greet the dawn.

—Sylvia Fernan, poet

Callum awoke with a start, his eyes snapping open to see Fen standing right before him.

"You're safe," the fox said without any preamble, a thin smile appearing on his face as he beamed down at Callum. "You almost ran out of mana after that last strike. It's . . . it's probably best we don't let that happen often . . . if we can help it. Are you feeling well?"

"I . . . ran out of mana?" Callum repeated, his skull feeling as if someone had shoved a fist between his eyes, leaving it pounding with a rather urgent headache. But as Callum considered the fox's question, his Soul Sense once again acted of its own accord and knowledge flowed into him.

Soul Sense:
Status:
Health: Mildly Injured
Mana Reserves: Low

"*Almost.*" Fen corrected, Callum noticing only then that the fox was radiating less light than he had been moments ago. "It was . . . close. Too close."

"It . . . was?" Callum asked, as he tried to make sense of all that had just happened, his mind feeling as if it were drunk. Had he really fought and killed that monster? "That . . . is a bad thing then?"

Fen let out a sound as if he were being strangled. "Yes, it is a very, *very* bad thing. What does your Soul Sense tell you about your Mana Reserves?"

"That they are low," Callum replied, gradually starting to feel better with every moment that passed.

"Then perhaps this is a good time to mention that I can sense your soul as well, and when you fell, your soul considered it as critical. So critical that you almost didn't have enough mana for your body to remain living." Fen paused for a moment to allow his words to sink in. "It was fortunate I was able to grant you some of my own vital mana, but I do not have much to spare, certainly not as much as I'd like to possess."

Callum couldn't help but feel his stomach drop at the fox's words. "So I need more mana."

Unfortunately those weren't the words that Fen apparently wanted to hear in that moment. "I'm sorry. I know how much I have pressed you in this short time but . . . do you know what mana is?"

"Uh, well," Callum hedged as he slowly started to try and get up. "It's how I'm able to use Attribute Shards."

"Ah, yes, you're not wrong," Fen paused to let out a deep breath. "But that's not exactly what it is. You're a commoner."

Callum had managed to get halfway to his knees, leaving him staring at the fox rather strangely when his words came out. "Erm, well, technically I'm a noble, but that's just a title my family has retained from . . . uh, well—"

Callum's words prompted Fen to stop. "No, I don't mean a commoner in an offensive way, as to your social status. I mean that you are a common mana user in that you don't have a full understanding of it. That you haven't formally studied it."

Callum had no answer for that, leaving him to stare at the fox for a moment before simply blurting. "How do you know that?"

"If you had, then you would have known better than to put everything into that final strike of yours. You wouldn't have pushed it knowing that you needed to preserve what you had," Fen said as he looked up at him, his expression softening somewhat. "Don't get me wrong. It was brazen, brave even, but it was also telling, and it shows me that I have much to teach you."

"How am I supposed to think about mana levels when faced with something like that?" Callum immediately asked, feeling at a complete loss. "Anyone in my shoes would have done the same."

"Not anyone. Some people, *most people*, would have cowered. So in that regard, it was most certainly brave," Fen replied, his head cocking to the side as he spoke. "And I suppose in that way you are like your forefather. He was never one to cower, but he also engaged with a strategy. It is further proof, to me anyway, that you truly are the Reborn Heir, the reincarnation of the Demonslayer. Let's start there."

Reincarnation? Callum's breath hitched, his fingers brushing over his chest as he searched for some tangible proof of the claim. *But I'm me,* he thought, the words echoing in his mind. His heart thudded in his ears at the weight of Fen's declaration, the words pressing down on him like a mantle he hadn't asked to wear. Something stirred within him—unease, curiosity, maybe even a flicker of recognition he couldn't quite place.

Callum shook his head, forcing himself to focus: "Shouldn't we get out of here first?" he asked, his voice a little sharper than intended. His gaze darted up to the main chamber of the East Manor, which was several stories above. From there he glanced back to the shards that the aetherhawk had left behind.

"I suppose we should. But"—a crackle of distant thunder rang out from above—"the storm hasn't gone just yet, and you are in no condition to fight off another aetherbeast. We're safer staying here for a little bit longer."

"Long enough for you to tell me about mana?"

"I . . . suppose so," Fen replied, his form flickering in intensity as he spoke. A sign that Callum took to be worrying.

"Are you . . . okay? You . . . don't look that great either."

But all that Fen did was offer Callum a weak smile and shake his head. "I'm alive. I'm alive and our plan worked, that's all that matters. Now, the Demon King. Tell me what you know about him."

"The Demon King?" Callum blinked twice. He had heard the stories numerous times, mostly from the villagers but never his father, who made it a point not to dwell on the past. "The Demon King died in the Great Demonswar."

"And do you know who killed him?"

"He did."

"He?"

"Callum Stross, the Demonslayer, my relative."

The fox hopped into the air. "That's wonderful news!"

"You didn't know?"

"How could I know? I've been here since . . . since . . ." Fen's glee ended abruptly. "Yet I am back."

"You are."

"And I wouldn't be back unless . . ." The fox's brow furrowed. "Oh, what did he say? What were his words? I can't remember. I can see him saying them to me, but I can't remember them."

"Whose words?"

"Your namesake," Fen huffed. "We'll put a pin in that for now. Tell me more about the victory, tell me all you know, and maybe I'll be able to better explain mana based on what you tell me."

"I understand what mana is."

"You have a working knowledge of it, yes."

"Everyone uses shards these days, and some people use Powercores."

"What about pacted creatures like me?" Fen asked.

"Only nobles have Aethercores."

"Ah, that makes sense."

"But not all nobles. I'm a noble, and I do not."

"You do now."

Callum ran his hand through his hair. "I suppose I do."

"Then everyone has a working knowledge of mana, but that doesn't mean you know exactly what it is, and that doesn't mean you understand why it's so crucial to what we will need to do next."

It dawned on Callum in that moment what it would mean to be pacted.

Before, getting an Aethercore had been something he had only dreamed of. A person like him could use an Attribute Shard, they may even have access to a Powercore, but being pacted, having an Aethercore, was something for archmages and a select few, people who had gone through one of the academies, which were notoriously hard to enter.

"Well?" Fen asked once Callum didn't respond. "What happened back then?"

Callum suddenly felt as if he didn't have the details right. After all, he now spoke to an aetherbeast that had lived during that time. He decided to approach the history in a broader sense: "Led by the Demon King, the Cult of the Black Dawn shattered the Heart of Creation, causing massive aetherstorms. Even more aetherbeasts were born, good and bad, and magic was distributed to everyone through things like shards and the occasional Powercore."

"Yes. Shards are the building blocks of Powercores. There is, of course, more to the Cult of the Black Dawn and their leader, the Demon King. But later. Why did the Cult shatter the Heart of Creation?"

"To let demons into the realm using the chaos of the Heart's destruction as cover," Callum said.

"Correct, so you do know some. Good. Breaking the Heart of Creation gave more people magic, people like your forefather, the original Callum Stross, who used the power to lead a fight against the Demon King through me."

"You?"

"Me. I was the first pacted aetherbeast, the first true Aethercore."

Callum looked the fox over. "You were seriously the first?"

"That seems to be lost to the histories, hmm?"

"Lost," Callum said, only realizing then that he had never questioned this part. He did, however, recall the vision he'd seen from the rare Memorycore in his youth. "A dragon, a wolf, a gryphon, and a phoenix."

Now it was Fen's turn to be surprised. "How do you know?"

Callum couldn't tell if Fen was offended or impressed. "We used to have a Memorycore of the event, the final battle of the Great Demonswar. My father sold the last one ten years ago."

"Why would he do that?"

"Because our fields had all but died and we had no money for winter. He sold it for its parts, the shards that made up the Memorycore."

Fen looked at him incredulously. "The fields never did well because the building we're currently in was filled with Corruption. But I guess it makes sense."

"It was all we had—"

"Not that part. The part of you seeing the others through a Memorycore."

"Others?"

"The other aetherbeasts that pacted with the original Callum Stross," he said, his voice wavering. "And did you see how they did it? Tell me you saw that final, fateful moment."

"I did not. My father didn't let me view it. But I know it happened, I know that the Demon King was stopped, and the Heart of Creation was rebuilt in New Albion."

It was a moment before Fen spoke again. "Perhaps we will be able to view it someday. Anyway, moving on. Your working knowledge of mana will suffice for now."

"Nothing to add?"

"There's plenty to add. It is the essence of everything, for one. I am entirely made of mana. It's why my form appears this way." Fen showed Callum his tail, the ends of which flickered with mana. "It's why it seems like I'm a living water painting made of light, as your forefather once called me."

"Same with the aetherbeast we fought. It looked like that." Callum motioned to where it had been. Like the imps, the aetherbeast had since vanished.

"Correct, only darker, made of a corrupted mana. The shattering of the Heart of Creation, as you mentioned, caused massive aetherstorms. Aetherstorms distributed mana far and wide and it created creatures like me. *That's* how powerful mana is. It can create a living being out of thin air. Think of it like that.

"Mana is entirely what I'm made of, and a portion of what you're made of. When we meld, we are melding through this mana. And earlier, you pushed yourself far enough to use all of your mana and some of mine. That's how we could die. And we don't want to die. I especially don't want to die because I'm here for a reason."

"What's that?"

"I don't yet know how, and I don't yet know what we're going to do about it, but we need to reach the Archive of Destiny. That I know. And it seems like the Demon King has been reborn."

Callum felt the blood drain from him. "You're certain? How could you know that?"

"It's the only other reason I can think of for your forefather to seal me up and not let me join him on that final, glorious day. It was an insurance policy. *I* was an insurance policy. He must have feared what would happen if he didn't entirely seal the Demonsrealm or eliminate the cultists."

"You think?"

"I'm certain of it. Leaving me here was a safety measure, a backup plan. And you just happened to find me, the Reborn Heir."

But I'm me . . . Callum wanted to say. His life flashed before his eyes in that comment, everything he had experienced up until that point. If he was a reincarnation, if what Fen was saying was true, what did this mean about the decisions Callum had made? Or who he actually was?

"You shouldn't think of it like that," the fox said, interpreting Callum's thoughts. "A reincarnation isn't a clone. Your soul has some aspects that are similar to his and you just happen to share his name, which makes sense considering your lineage. But let's not get ahead of ourselves." Fen looked up to the opening above. "It's time to climb. We have things to do."

"Like what?"

"Aside from escaping from here, we need to get to the bottom of what's happening. How far are we from New Albion?"

"From the capital? A few days' journey. I've never been."

"Perhaps we should start there."

"Is that where we'll find the Archive of Destiny?"

The fox's ears twitched. "I suspect so. But before we do anything, we're going to need to get out of here. And unfortunately, I am but a pale shadow of what I used to be. Otherwise, I'd simply fly you up to the top. No," Fen said with a shake of his head, "we're going to have to climb. But don't worry. You're a strapping young man. How hard could it be? Grab the shards and let's go."

CHAPTER 8

Sundering, or breaking a Powercore down into its component parts, is something that only someone who has reached the Channeler Rank is able to do. This makes all Master and Mastress Channelers shardcrafters. Yet not all shardcrafters are pacted, as it is a law in the Valestra Kingdom that those who are not in service to the Crown must give up their Aethercore. Even so, they retain the ability to sunder, and many make a good living as local shardcrafters in villages and towns across the kingdom.

—Aaron Richknee, Master Shaper, Archon of Morefell

Without any stairs or even a ladder surviving the manor's downfall, and without the ability to do something magical like fly or hover, Callum and Fen were forced to improvise.

After pacing for a moment and considering his options, Callum got to work, his first act being to go back into the lower chamber and get his father's scythe. He knew how much Rhane liked that scythe, and he didn't want to leave it at the bottom of the East Manor. Nor did he want to come back to get it later.

Once the scythe was in hand, his next task was to try and find a way out, which was thankfully easy to manage now that Callum didn't have an aetherbeast chasing him. All he needed to do was pick, climb, and twist his way back down the collapsed hallway without falling far enough to make it into one of the adjoining rooms that had flanked it. Once there, it was a handful of gentle swipes from his meld form claws to clear a shattered section of wall until he had a hole he could squeeze through it, thereby putting him right by the remains of his cart, the wheat it had carried still strewn about.

Yet instead of focusing on the wheat, the whole reason for why he'd ended up in the house in the first place, the light coming through the broken front door was the thing that caught his attention. *What time is it? Could it possibly be morning?*

Callum took a step closer and caught a glimpse of something golden on the other side, prompting him to practically race out the door, expecting to find a soft morning sun over a ravaged landscape, what crops he hadn't managed to harvest being completely destroyed.

"No way," he said, his mind not quite processing what lay before him. *How long was I down there?*

The sun was indeed up. Somehow, an entire night had passed, and Callum didn't quite understand how. Yet the sun was covered by light gray clouds, not exactly the shining beacon it normally was. No, the gold he had seen from inside the East Manor was coming from the field, from the wheat itself.

Impossible . . . Callum felt gutted, his legs shaky for a moment.

All of the wheat had taken root again and grown back so quickly, so strongly, that it seemed like Callum and his father had done nothing in their rush to save the harvest.

He staggered forward, a wave of emotion coming to him. "What . . . what happened?"

<*Perhaps the Corruption was what was keeping your farm from reaching its full potential. By eliminating it, all the mana that had been stored in the soil was released at once, stirred by the aetherstorm.*>

"You think?"

"Was it like this before?" Fen asked after his form took shape.

"No, it has never been like this."

Callum was visibly shaken by the sight, to the point that his mind couldn't process it. The golden hue of the wheat was richer than anything he had ever seen before. As a breeze passed over it, the wheat seemed to possess a faint, iridescent shimmer, the stalks robust, the field stretching endlessly all the way to the barn and their home beyond.

"I have to find my father," Callum said suddenly, his mind struggling to make sense of what he was seeing. "He . . . he needs to know about this."

"Without a doubt." Fen twisted his head in Callum's direction. "Hmm, I forgot to ask, what's his name?"

"Name? Oh, it's Rhane."

"Rhane," Fen repeated with a nod. "I'll remember that. Now, do you have any idea where he might be?"

It took Callum a moment to answer as he considered the question. "The village, Weatherby. Or in our home. Let's . . ." He gathered his wits. "Let's start with home."

Once Fen had melded with him, Callum took off, a few of their barnyard cats scattering as he reached the front porch of their quaint home. He rushed inside to find Rhane lying on the floor.

"Father?" he asked.

Rhane blinked, squinting his bushy eyebrows at Callum for a moment. "Cal!" He got to his feet and patted his son on the back. "I was up all night after I returned. I checked everywhere I could. The rain. The destruction. I couldn't see you. I came back here to get a lantern and I slipped." He rubbed the back of his head. "I can't believe . . . I thought . . ."

"Are you alright?"

"My head? Yes, I'll be fine. I think. Or I won't but I'll just learn to deal with what comes. Callum, where were you, son? The wind. It was so strong! I was so worried! It nearly blew me off my feet. I couldn't even make it to the barn by the time I returned. It's all my fault. I shouldn't have told you to—"

"Father—"

Rhane buried his head in his hand and rubbed his eyes. "I thought you might be—"

"Have you gone outside yet?"

"Outside?"

"Look out the window."

Rhane walked over to the window, his mouth dropping as he tried to make sense of what he was seeing. "The fields. What . . . ? What happened?"

"Come on!" Callum ran to the door, his father stumbling after him.

Rhane cried with joy upon seeing the rows upon rows of gleaming golden wheat. He fell to his knees as he tried to make sense of it.

"How?" he finally asked, as a laugh escaped him, the sheer joy of the sight taking away years of wrinkles on his face only to instantly return once he locked eyes with Callum and asked again, "How?"

"You're not going to believe it."

<Please don't do a big reveal.>

"Meet Fen!" Callum raised a hand into the air and nothing happened.

"Fen?" his father looked around. "What's gotten into you, Cal?"

<I told you, no big reveal.>

"He's a bit shy," Callum said as he suddenly felt embarrassed. "I pacted. That's what I'm trying to tell you. I have an Aethercore now and Powercores. I—"

"You did what? Callum, what are you saying!?"

Fen took shape in a flash of blinding, fiery light. Rhane pressed back, and seemed to be seconds from bolting away when he stopped. "The storm. That makes sense. But a fox? That's a very rare aetherbeast to pact with."

"Fen is the first of his kind," Callum said, overcome with excitement.

"The first pacted beast?" Rhane asked. "That would mean—"

"Correct," Fen said, head held proud. "I was the first to pact with Callum Stross some five hundred years ago."

"Five hundred and ten years ago," Callum added.

"We'll round down for now," Fen said.

Rhane stood. "The Demonslayer. You pacted with the Demonslayer's Radiant Fox."

Callum almost told his father about the Reborn Heir part but decided against it. He could tell by the troubled look on Rhane's face that this was a lot to process. And it didn't help that Rhane had a lump on the side of his head where he had fallen, one that he kept rubbing.

His father glanced out at the field of golden wheat and back to Fen. "You did this?"

"Your crops? No, I don't really have that sort of power. The aetherstorm combined with the removal of the Corruption in the East Manor likely did it. At least that would be my best guess. My memories of how this works is a bit vague."

"You ended up in the manor?" Rhane asked Callum incredulously.

"Not willingly. I was harvesting the fields when an aetherbeast came down from the storm and I couldn't make it into the barn in time." Callum shuddered at the thoughts of the winged aetherbeast and his experience inside the place. "It was a nightmare and exactly as you said inside there. I tried to lose the aetherbeast and find a place to hide . . . but it caused a part of the manor to collapse and well . . . led me to Fen. He was asleep inside a room filled with Corruption. At least until we took care of it."

"If I may," Fen said. "I was sealed away there by the original Callum Stross as a security measure if the Demon King was ever reborn."

"The Demon King . . . reborn?" The mere mention of the possibility caused some of the color to drain from Rhane's face. "Impossible. The Demonsrealm was sealed. The Heart of Creation was rebuilt."

"You've seen it?" Fen asked Rhane.

"Of course, I have. The Second Heart of Creation is in New Albion. I visited years ago in search of . . . a cure."

"A cure for what?"

Rhane grew silent.

"For my mother," Callum told Fen. "That's the only reason he would have traveled that far."

"Correct," Rhane said as a bit of gloom caused his eyes to flicker. "But that is neither here nor there. The Heart of Creation is there."

"In New Albion? Huh." Fen sat and considered this as a light breeze picked up. "Then that's certainly a place we should visit."

"The Heart of Creation? Good luck getting in there. It is heavily guarded."

"I would assume so," Fen told Rhane, "but I meant New Albion, the capital."

"And enroll in the Great College, yes?" The grin that spread across Rhane's face was one Callum couldn't remember seeing before. "I think before we discuss that, we should have breakfast." He rubbed his head again. "It's been a long night."

"I can help—"

"No, I got it this time. Take a seat, Cal." His father motioned to the small, wooden table where they had taken all their meals for as long as Callum could remember. "I'll whip something up."

As his father cooked some potatoes and scrambled some eggs, Callum went over everything that had happened the last night. Thinking of the information he had been granted access to spawned it again.

Soul Sense:
Status:
Health: *Uninjured*
Mana Reserves: *Half-Full*
Soul Heart Rank: *Initiate*
Soulbonding Capacity: *6 Powercores, 1 Aethercore*

Once again, Callum found himself staring down at his hands, his thoughts spiraling. *Am I really a reincarnation? Of the Demonslayer?* The question lingered, heavy and unanswered. He recalled the brief image he had seen of his forefather through the Memorycore so many years ago. *But he was so strong . . .*

Rhane eventually brought breakfast to the table, and they ate quietly, both lost in their thoughts. It was Fen who finally broke the silence. "How would we get into the Great College?" his voice cutting through the haze of Callum's mind.

"Yeah, how would I do that?" Callum asked his father as he placed his fork down.

"You don't know? You're a noble, a noble who has pacted."

"What's that have to do with anything?"

"I agree," Fen said, "What does the fact we have aetherforged have anything to do with the Great College?"

"The Great College is the most prestigious institute in the Valestra Kingdom. Its main branch is in New Albion. To be admitted, you must be a noble, and you must be pacted." Rhane eyes flickered as he looked over to Callum. "Son. You are a noble. You are now pacted. I don't know what the other requirements are, but those are the main two."

"Are you certain?" Callum asked.

"Yes. I was a boy with boyhood dreams once too," his father replied dryly, letting a rare smile cross his face. "Regardless, the shardcrafter in the village will confirm. Griselda is from New Albion. She knew your grandfather and I remember them talking about the college before when I was young."

"It means we need to get to New Albion," Fen said as he turned to Callum, his next thought projected. *<It will likely lead us to the Archive of Destiny as well.>*

"What about the fields?" Callum asked. "If I go, who will help you?"

Rhane blinked a few times, as if it was hard to process what his son was asking him. "What do you mean?"

"Who is going to help you here if I'm gone?"

"Help me? Why, I can find someone to help me. I can hire someone with what we'll make from the sale of this wheat." He waved his hand toward the window. "This is what we've been hoping for, what *I've* been hoping for years. Our luck has finally shifted! Had I known all we had to do was crack open the East Manor, I would have done so earlier! Finally!"

"At least let me help for the day. I can go tomorrow," Callum said after Rhane quieted down. "With Fen, I should be able to work even faster."

"No. You have other things to do now. First, you need to head to the village and get a change of clothing. Yes," Rhane said as he stroked his chin. "The village should be first."

"Why?"

"Have you seen yourself? Your shirt is tattered and covered in blood. You need a bath as well, and there is a public bathhouse in the village that has water warmed by Affinity Shards."

"I could warm some water—" Fen said.

"No, no, you deserve a real bath, Cal. You'll go there," Rhane said as he pushed himself away from the table. "You'll need a notebook. What else? I really don't know. I haven't thought of the Great College in years. Ah, but I do remember something. When I visited, I believe they wore cloaks there. You'll need a cloak, one with a hood."

"Father—"

"A cloak, a change of clothing, a notebook, and a book bag. You'll need a better satchel to keep your spare shards. Better than the shoddy one you have at the moment. You'll need a haircut as well." Rhane looked his son over. "You look like a lion with your hair long and crazy, which you'll need to tone down. Nobles keep it a bit more trimmed up."

"Where am I going to get the money for all of this? I need the shards I received from the aetherbeast to unlock more of Fen's powers."

His father grinned at him. "What have I told you about rainy days?"

"That we don't get enough of them?"

"Yes, that, but about saving. I have a Memorycore I can part with," Rhane told him. "I've been holding onto it."

"A Memorycore of the Demonslayer?" Fen asked, his interest piqued, radiant tail swishing.

"No, of my late wife, private moments right around the time Callum was born. I had it made in New Albion. I've selfishly held onto them."

Callum froze, the weight of his father's offer suddenly unbearable. "I can't take that," he said, his voice barely above a whisper. Hesitation etched across his face. "It's yours. It's your memory of her."

"I'm aware of what it is, Cal," Rhane said with resolve. "But it is better for you to have the funds and prepare for your entrance to the Great College than it is for me to hoard the memory away. I haven't viewed it in years. Too painful. You know my thoughts on the past. Better to look forward than backward, because, if we're being honest, that is the only thing we can do. I've tried to take that to heart. Take the Memorycore to Griselda. She will gladly sunder the core and pay you for it."

"When did you last view it?" Callum asked.

"Maybe five years ago. No, six. Anyway. It's yours. I'll get it now."

"No. You should view it one last time," Callum said firmly, his eyes locking with his father's.

"Cal . . ."

"I'm serious."

After a long pause, Rhane finally cleared his throat, his expression softening as he nodded. "Yes, perhaps you are right. Perhaps I will have one last look at it. Wait here."

* * *

The wait gave Callum more time to gather his thoughts. He knew that he could speak privately to Fen, but so much had happened that it felt right just to sit there at the table, gazing out at the field of wheat.

Everything is about to change . . .

The door to the bedroom creaked open and Rhane stepped out, his shoulders heavy. His eyes were red-rimmed, yet no tears fell. He held the Memorycore in his hand, its faint glow casting a soft light onto his weathered fingers.

For a moment, he lingered in the doorway, but then he stepped forward with all the stoicism that Callum had come to expect from the man. "Here's the Memorycore, viewed one last time, just as you suggested." He glanced away from Callum and grunted. "You should get to Weatherby."

Callum only stood from the table once his father didn't say anything else. He stepped outside, once again taken aback by the fields of wheat. *I can't sell it*, Callum thought as he started off. *I'm going to have to figure out another way.*

Callum didn't know what this other way would be as he left the farm, aimed at the village of Weatherby. In the past, he had performed a number of tasks for the villagers, yet he had never been paid that much, never enough to cover everything he needed if he truly was going to head to New Albion.

"A bath, a cloak, a change of clothing, a notebook, a haircut, a book bag, and a satchel," he said to Fen, whom he assumed was listening.

<Yes, I agree with your father. Even if you've changed shirts, you can't go to the capitol looking so scruffy. You're the distant relative of Callum Stross, the Demonslayer. That will mean more there than it does here, especially at a college dedicated to the study of mana. Of course, we will try to keep that part under wraps, but I suspect it will get out considering your name.>

"But I can't sell the Memorycore," Callum said, giving voice to the thought that wouldn't stop running through his head. "They're my father's remaining memories of my mother. I, *we*, can't sell this."

<I suspected as much. Sell the shards?>

"That's the plan. I'll sell the shards I got from the aetherbeast instead. Surely, we'll get more."

<Surely. This is merely the beginning.>

"Affinity Shards are rare, but we're going to New Albion. There are bound to be more ways to earn shards there."

<Agreed.>

Callum continued on, over another lane and past Marnus and Marith Righam's farm. He started to see signs of the village ahead, from the rooftops visible over a hill to a pair of horses being led by a thin man who walked with a limp.

Signs of the aetherstorm's damage became apparent as soon as Callum came across a home that had been completely toppled. The roof lay in splintered fragments, the walls in crumbled piles of debris. The family was already at work, sifting through the wreckage with grim determination, while the dog sniffed around the rubble, occasionally barking at unseen disturbances in the ruins. Their daughter, a girl named Julyn, waved sadly at Callum, but she seemed to be the only one who noticed as he walked by.

Beyond, other signs of destruction came into view—fields ripped apart as if they had been attacked by giant claws, fences splintered into kindling, a toppled watchtower leaning precariously against a barn that seemed moments away from collapsing. The acrid scent of charred wood and turned earth was heavy in the air, yet another sign of the aetherstorm's raw, untamed power.

As he had expected, the Weatherby village square bustled with activity. People were gathered to claim things that had been blown around by the storm. Callum recognized a noble, Eli, seated at a table tallying damages alongside a few other village officials.

While everything seemed to be in order, some people were especially distraught and a few were injured.

Callum couldn't help but shake his head. *We got so lucky with that storm*, he thought as he reached Griselda the shardcrafter's shop, which was surprisingly intact. Aside from a few missing shingles, it was as if the aetherstorm had passed right over the building.

Callum entered and found the older woman seated on a stool in the corner napping, her legs stretched out in front of her and covered by a patchwork quilt.

"Griselda," he said softly.

She gasped awake and nearly lost her balance. "What? Who's there—?" Her eyes narrowed on Callum and instantly softened. "Ah, it's you. Rhane's boy, although you're no longer a boy, I suppose. I see you survived the aetherstorm." She pressed off the stool and hobbled over to the counter. After adjusting the red scarf that was wrapped around her head, she continued: "So, how may I help you?"

"My father sent me to sell some things." He got out the small bag of shards he had collected from the aetherbeast, which included the pouch with the Memorycore in it.

"Of course, he did. Everyone suddenly has shards to get rid of now that the storm has finally landed. Why do you think I was sleeping?"

"I don't know," he told her.

"Because people have been coming in and out of my door all day. But that is neither here nor there." Griselda's eyes softened. "Is your farm okay? Did it make it?"

"It's better than okay. We've never had a crop like this as far as I can tell." Callum slid the satchel over to her.

"Then why are you here, Callum?" she asked, spreading everything out on the counter. "Some shards and a . . . Memorycore. And your crop is fine?"

"Better than ever."

She settled her gaze on him. "Then I'll ask again—why?"

"Because . . ." Callum felt a sense of elation as he told her the good news. "I pacted."

"You what?" she asked, even more confused now. "How?"

Fen's voice echoed in his head: *<Don't reveal my origins! It is best we get to New Albion, discover the Archive of Destiny, and join the Great College before we start telling anyone about me. Keep it vague.>*

"The aetherstorm, um, an aetherbeast appeared and I pacted with it," Callum said, going with the easiest answer.

"Just like that?"

"Well, there was a struggle, but yes."

She mumbled something about Callum being a noble, followed by him being a strapping young man, before finally switching to another question. "And what kind of aetherbeast did you pact with?"

"Just a little fox."

<Hey!>

"A fox? Do you mind if I meet him?"

"He's a bit shy at the moment. But he's here," Callum said as he touched his chest. "Or here." He tapped his temple. "To be honest, I'm still trying to understand how this works, which is why I'm going to New Albion."

"For what reason?"

"My dad said that being a pacted noble will gain me entrance into the Great College."

Her eyes widened as she looked at Callum in a newfound light. "Rhane said that, did he?"

"That's right."

"And you're here to sell a Memorycore and the shards so you can get the things you need for your journey?"

Callum shook his head. "That's the part I can't agree with. These are memories of my mother. I don't want to sell them. I want to just sell my shards instead. Now that I'm pacted, surely there is something I can do in Weatherby to make a little money so I can cover the cost of the trip."

"You don't need money, Callum."

"I don't?" he asked.

Griselda placed her hands on the counter and leaned forward. "Let me tell you why."

CHAPTER 9

The total annual fund allocated to the King's Scholarship will be adjusted from Year 504 onward, a modification designed to accommodate changes in the student body and their evolving financial needs. Eligibility requirements remain the same, and the award distribution structure will follow a tiered system based on entry results, need, and private contributions.

—Decree announcing Great College academic changes as part of
the Provisional Restructuring

Callum still couldn't believe his luck. He now stood before Weatherby's public bathhouse, which was set in a large two-story building with a thatched roof. Steam curled from the wooden slats along the upper floor, and flower boxes hung from every window, their blooms faded and brittle with the first touch of fall.

"The King's Scholarship," he said with a shake of his head. "Who would have thought?"

<*It makes sense, really,*> Fen told him.

Griselda's words came to Callum: "Yes, I'm serious. You qualify for the King's Scholarship, which means you don't need to sell your father's Memorycore to me, and you shouldn't sell the little shards you have. Keep them. And I'll loan you some money to get you what you need here."

"You don't have to," Callum had told her.

"I owe it to your grandfather. We were friends, you know. We went to school together before I continued on to one of the Great College's lesser campuses. Now, as for getting to New Albion, you'll need to do that soon. There's a caravan heading out in the morning with most of the harvest that was handled before the aetherstorm came. It's crucial that it reaches the capital. You can join the caravan, and, once you arrive, I know someone you can stay with."

Even now, Callum couldn't believe her generosity. He entered the bathhouse and paid for a private room.

"And you are aware how it works, right?" the man that ran the bathhouse asked. His eyes bulged slightly. "Ah, it's you, Lord Stross's son. Sorry. It's been a terrible twenty-four hours, and I hardly recognized you with your haircut. I'm just glad the Fire Affinity Shards weren't stolen."

"Stolen? Why would someone steal them?" Callum asked.

"People get desperate. I used to live in Ontaria, on other side of the kingdom. An aetherstorm came through and there was terrible looting after. That's why I moved here to Weatherby, actually. Some places are never the same after an aetherstorm, and I'm not the type to stick around when the grass could be greener on the other side. Anyway, the room is yours. The water will be heated for an hour."

"This is nice," Callum said a few moments later as he stepped into a room covered in floor-to-ceiling blue tile. Water came out of a spout shaped into the face of a serpent, quickly filling a basin while he undressed.

<It seems that luck is quite a bit in our favor. A caravan, lodging, and another shardcrafter to ask questions, should we have any,> Fen noted.

"I'll take all the help we can get," Callum agreed as he considered the fox's words. "Though . . . we don't really have much in terms of shards to work with."

<Not yet,> Fen stated, his voice optimistic. <But that can change quickly.>

Callum knew little about shardcrafting and he had only ever used shards as quick power-ups, like the Empowerment of Deftness Shard he had used last night during the aetherstorm. He had heard that a person could create an actual Powercore out of shards, but he knew little of the process.

But that's a worry for later, he thought as he entered the bath, the hot water doing much to soothe his body and the lingering aches and pains that plagued him. Once his time was almost up, evident by a knock at the door, Callum used Soul Sense to see if anything had changed.

Soul Sense:
Status:
Health: *Recovering*
Mana Reserves: *Half-Full*
Soul Heart Rank: *Initiate*
Soulbonding Capacity: *6 Powercores, 1 Aethercore*

"My listing for Health says 'Recovering.' Is that okay?"

<It's fine, for now. The relaxing bath has helped to some degree, but you need to physically rest, even with your Empowerment of Sustenance core.>

"I'm guessing I'll figure out better ways to recover health in the future. I have Inner Light, too."

<Indeed. Even if we would prefer otherwise, it may come to trial by fire.> Fen laughed. *<That's always a good learning method. Come on, let's get the rest of the supplies you need.>*

For the rest of the afternoon, Callum crossed the village gathering new clothing, a book bag, a notebook, and finally a satchel with numerous pouches designed for shards and cores. The satchel crossed his chest, allowing for it to be concealed under one arm. Further concealing it would be the cloak that Rhane had insisted on, which Callum felt wasn't necessary but purchased anyway.

Soon, he reached the farm to find his father seated on the porch drinking from a flagon carved from bone, his favorite cup.

"He returns," Rhane said, "ready to head to the capital."

Callum looked out at the fields, about half of which had been harvested.

"Don't worry about them. I'll finish it over the next two days. How did it go in the village?" His father eyed him curiously. "Didn't I tell you to get a cloak?"

"I got one. It's in the bag," Callum said.

Fen appeared, the Radiant Fox coming to life next to Callum. The flash of mana nearly caused Rhane to fall out of his chair. "Ah, sorry! I'm not used to that yet!"

"Nor am I in controlling my reappearance," the fox replied, seeming a little contrite. "I'll work on it. In the meantime, however, we are ready."

"I can see that. How is the village? I should be asking how bad it is. I'm certain it's not good. I should have headed in today, but there has been plenty to do around here."

"Not great," Callum said as he took a seat. "But it will recover."

"I just wish we had the same kind of magitek they have in New Albion here in Weatherby. There hasn't been an aetherstorm there in . . ." Rhane trailed off. "I don't know how long."

"What is magitek?" Fen asked, suddenly curious. "That's a new term for me."

"They have this great monolith there with huge shards at the top. If an aetherstorm comes to New Albion, its power is absorbed and used for research and to fuel the Second Heart of Creation."

"Come again?" Fen asked, his ears pressing back.

"The Second Heart of Creation was rebuilt at the end of the Great Demonswar," Callum told him. "To seal the Demonsrealm. I've seen drawings of it in the village."

"You really have never been to New Albion, have you?" the fox asked Callum.

"I haven't. What's so hard to believe about that?"

"It's the capital of the kingdom."

"And it's far away," Rhane told Fen. "We have plenty going on here. Anyway, dinner. I warmed up the stew from the other day."

"And I brought bread to go with it," Callum said as he produced the loaf he had purchased.

"I already ate, but seeing as how you brought bread . . ." Rhane patted his hands across his stomach. "I suppose I could eat again."

Later that night, after Rhane was asleep, Callum snuck out of their home. He was careful of the creaking floorboard near the kitchen and the groove that he sometimes tripped over near the door.

<What are we doing out here?> Fen asked once Callum stepped out onto the porch.

"The fields. My father can't do it alone even if he says he can, and I want to test our power."

<Test our power? You need to rest. Until you learn more about mana, your rest will be crucial. The caravan leaves in the morning, and I suspect that it won't be easy to rest along the way.>

Likely not, Callum thought as he grabbed his father's scythe and the cart.

<You're serious about this?>

"I have you, don't I?" Callum asked once he reached the East Manor field. It didn't register with him until he looked at the building itself that things had come full circle.

<What do you mean?>

"You know what I mean. When we meld, my powers are amplified. So let's meld, I'll finish this field and the next one, and my dad won't have to."

For a moment, it felt like Fen wouldn't comply. But then Callum felt the sensation of change as it rushed through him, his Might, Deftness, Vigor, Resilience, and Regeneration instantly augmented.

"This is amazing—"

<It will be better in the future. Now, are you going to get started or what?>

Callum rushed into action, doing what he had done so many times before only now he was much swifter, his endurance allowing him to cleave through stalk after stalk with more focus than he could ever remember having before.

Once the cart was filled, all the wheat bundled, he raced toward the barn, deposited it in a neat stack, and continued, back and forth, late into the night.

Callum worked himself into a frenzy. He wanted to leave his father two parting gifts: the Memorycore and their fields fully harvested.

Exhaustion came a few hours later.

<I told you,> Fen said. *<You shouldn't use your power this way!>*

"I have to . . ." Callum stopped by the barn, splashed some cold water on his face, and pushed through it. Even as his muscles pulsed and the world dimmed around him, Callum found an inner strength that allowed him to finish what he had started.

All the wheat handled, he noticed a tingling sensation roll down his shoulder, his meld complete.

Callum stumbled back toward their home.

He stopped on the porch, collected himself, and quietly went back inside, where he placed the Memorycore in his father's wardrobe, in a pocket attached to a belt he occasionally wore.

He'll find it in the next day or two, Callum thought as he turned to his own bed and collapsed.

He awoke several hours later to the crow of a rooster. This was followed by the sizzle of eggs. Callum, who had fallen asleep in his clothes, got out of bed to hear his father speaking to himself in the other room.

As soon as he entered, Rhane looked over at Callum. "You weren't supposed to handle the fields yourself."

"I know, but I couldn't—"

"You should have rested. I could have done it."

"It's fine," Callum said as he took a seat at the table.

His father slid a pair of eggs onto a plate and handed it to Callum. "You really shouldn't have," he said as he took a seat in front of him. Rhane glanced up at the ceiling like he was trying to hold back his emotions. "You're going to do well in New Albion," he said, not making eye contact with Callum. "I just know it."

"I'll do my best."

"You always do, son. Finish your breakfast, and I'll walk you down to the caravans. I've got some things I need to do in Weatherby anyway." He finally glanced to the window and back to Callum, a grin on his face. "Like deal with this new crop that seems ready to go. Once I get it all sold, maybe I'll send some money your way."

"You don't have to."

"And you didn't have to handle the fields," Rhane said, leaning back. "So in that way, we'll be even. Now, finish your breakfast. You have a big day ahead of you, and I need to find the document that proves our nobility." He glanced at a cabinet near the door. "It's in there somewhere."

Not long after, Callum packed what little things he had for the journey and walked to Weatherby with his father. They didn't say anything to each other along the way, aside from Rhane mentioning that it was a beautiful day.

Once they reached the outskirts of the village, Rhane turned to him. "Don't forget to wear your cloak. It will distinguish you from who you once were."

"I still am who I once was."

"And it will make your father proud for the villagers to know where you are heading."

<He clearly wants you to put it on,> Fen said to Callum by way of their bond.

Callum stopped. He got the hooded cloak out of his bag and Rhane helped him put it on. He felt a bit foolish wearing it, and it sat strangely on his broad shoulders, built over years of fieldwork.

"There, that's better." Rhane picked up his pace, practically marching into the village as people stopped to gawk.

As his father shook a few hands, Callum quickly grew overwhelmed by the sheer attention. More and more people turned to him, even those that were waiting in line to assess aetherstorm damages. The sudden spotlight made him want to shrink back. But then he caught his father's steady gaze, the quiet pride, and something in him steadied.

"I guess this is it," he said to the nearest villager, a man named Gary. They clasped hands warmly, and from there, Callum moved to the crowds, shaking hands and exchanging farewells.

As he neared the end of the gathered crowd, one older woman placed a hand on his shoulder. "I would say something like 'don't forget where you came from,' but I know that's not like you, Cal."

"I won't forget Weatherby," he assured her.

They journeyed to the back of the village, down a winding road littered with debris. Chickens pecked at the dirt, and Callum heard a pair of dogs barking behind a wooden fence. Soon, the two reached the caravan, which consisted of seven covered wagons pulled by black and gray horses.

A pair of guards on horseback trotted over to Rhane to speak to him.

"Brock, Serg."

"Lord Stross," Brock, who wore loose-fitting armor tied together with strips of leather. His mustache, which draped far past his chin, had been braided. "Griselda has already informed us that your son will be joining us on our journey to the capital."

"Thank you," Rhane said. "It seems that our wheat will have to go on the next caravan. You all don't normally send seven wagons, do you?"

"No, we do not," Brock told him. "But with the aetherstorm, people need money, and we just so happen to have enough wagons to transport the first shipment."

Rhane's eyes jumped from Brock to his mounted companion. "And just two of you to guard it all?"

"We are capable, Lord Stross," Brock assured him. "There hasn't been a serious attack on a caravan in some time. And I'd be lying if I didn't tell you that everyone else more capable is off dealing with the aetherstorm, which has moved north. But we are prepared if so. I have a few tricks up my sleeves, and we have shards, as always."

"Good, in that case, I will leave you to it." He turned to his son, his hand now on Callum's shoulder. "Do your best, and try not to have too much fun." Rhane managed a firm smile, holding it together as best he could in that emotional moment. "Your mother would be so proud of you."

After a few more words, and a tight hug, Rhane turned away.

"Welcome, lad," Brock told Callum once his father was gone. "There will be a spot for you at the front of the caravan. I would put you in back, but some of the families already paid for their place there. So you'll be seated next to the driver at the front. Hope you don't mind."

"That's fine by me."

"Good. Like I told your father, if we encounter anything along the road, do not worry. Serg and I can handle it. Although, with that cloak, you are pacted, aren't you?"

"You could tell just by my cloak?"

Brock laughed. "No, I heard what people were saying in the village last night. And just between us, students at the Great College no longer wear cloaks. But it was nice of you to keep it on just to make your father happy."

The cloak suddenly felt heavy on his shoulders. "So I should get rid of it?"

"No, or maybe. I don't know. I didn't go to the Great College, and I am unaware of the traditions they have there. You should keep it on. It will get cold later once we take some of the mountain passes. There could even be snow."

"Really, snow? But it's barely fall."

Brock grunted. "And three days ago, Weatherby had nearly forgotten about aetherstorms considering it had been so long since the last one roared through. What I'm saying is the weather is unpredictable, so the cloak is good for that. Now, we are to do some last-minute checks. Head to the front and find your seat next to Thaddeus. In two days, we will be in New Albion."

CHAPTER 10

While theoretically, anyone could pact with an aetherbeast if their Soul Heart was bonded with an Aethercore, aetherbeasts are highly intelligent and selective, choosing only to bond with individuals they deem worthy through what was once known as an aetherforge but is now known as melding. Those of noble birth, who they believe possess the strength, mana, and purpose to wield their power responsibly, have been preferred since the Demonswar, especially as instruction and research have been established through the Great College and its numerous branches.

—A quote from *The Great College: Its History and Abandoned Campuses* by Sir Gideon Coldwell, Master Channeler, Clergo

Thaddeus, the carriage driver, wore a wide-brimmed hat that cast a deep shadow onto his face, the older man barely saying hello to Callum as he took a seat next to him. Aside from a deep grunt once the caravan started up, Thaddeus remained silent.

For the first hour or so, Callum recognized their surroundings. *That's where I used to get berries for Miss Barrowsly. And that is where I would sometimes go to watch the caravans come in . . .*

They continued northeast from Weatherby, through a forest gutted by the aetherstorm. Many of the trees had been cleaved in half, and there were still some sections that were smoldering. At one point, Brock rode ahead, a spiral of power radiating around the mounted guard's wrist as if he were poised to fire at something.

If Thaddeus thought anything of it, he didn't say anything, maintaining his focus on the space just beyond them.

<So commoners really can use magic?> Fen asked.

<*Was this not the same back then?*> he asked Fen through their bond.

<*Yes and no. I was just surprised that the guard can use cores. He's not pacted.*>

<*You don't have to be pacted to use a Powercore,*> Callum replied.

<*I suppose this will be one of many examples of how things have changed over the centuries as everyone's understanding of magic grew. Truthfully, now that we are discussing it, I don't really remember how things were when it came to commoners and their magic. Life was . . . messy then. After the Cult of the Black Dawn shattered the Heart of Creation, unaspected mana was everywhere, and the world had yet to finish reeling from its effects by the time I was sealed away.*>

<*I've heard you say that word twice now. Unaspected mana. That's just a term for mana, right?*>

<*Yes, perhaps an older term for it, such as* aetherforge. *We can call it mana, if you'd like.*>

<*But what does it mean, exactly?*>

<*Everything has mana. It's how that guard can use a Powercore. It's how the other cores are also used, even how we have bonded through an Aethercore, the core of my own soul and power.*>

Callum had never really thought about the other kinds of cores, especially Aethercores. He knew there were Attribute Shards and Powercores, but he had rarely seen Powercores in action.

Fen continued. <*There are Aethercores like me, which represent the essence of an aetherbeast. Then there are Powercores, which are classified into Ability and Support. Next are Attribute Shards, all of which tap into unaspected mana in their own ways. But even so, it's only by pacting with an aetherbeast such as myself can you truly modify other cores. That much I remember. There was still much debate ongoing as how to codify it remember, at what thresholds peo—oh, I suppose that answers my own question.*>

<*How so?*> Callum asked finding the discussion and resulting knowledge fascinating.

<*The guard has a Powercore, yes? Yet he isn't pacted. Meaning, to my best guess, that it can only operate at a fraction of its full power. Yet he can still use it. Perhaps to relatively decent effect if the core is strong enough. Tell me, can people still enhance and empower Powercores?*>

<*They can,*> Callum replied, needing a second to infer what Fen was truly asking. <*Though now we call it upgrading.*>

<*Ah, I'll remember that,*> the fox promised, before immediately following up with another question. <*And truly? The king would really let a commoner have that much power to himself?*>

<Shardcrafters can upgrade it, like Griselda.>

<Ah, now that makes sense. And here I was assuming she just stripped Cores of their bare essences and returned them to you.> Fen said, pausing for a moment in a way that Callum was starting to associate with deep thought. *<Hmm, let's say that you needed ten Empowerment of Might Shards to upgrade a core and you were able to somehow obtain them. You yourself wouldn't be able to fuse them into a Powercore, right?>*

<That's right. I would have to take all of them to a shardcrafter so they could combine them.>

<I see. I suppose that would allow for some level of control, while also allowing more freedom in the use of magic for commoners.> Fen mused before eventually replying with a mental sigh. *<Regardless, you will need to learn the skills of a shardcrafter while at this college. I would rather not have us beholden to anyone's whims if we could avoid it.>*

<I'll . . . try. I have a lot to learn,> Callum answered in the most diplomatic way he could manage. Even though he really wanted to say something along the lines of "I have no idea what I'm doing." Something that he had no doubt Fen already knew. *<Just a few days ago, I was planning to help my father with the harvest and get ready for the long winter. And now . . . well, you know what now.>*

<Now you've pacted with your forefather's Radiant Fox and are off to the city to receive the King's Scholarship and enroll in the Great College,> the fox happily summed up. *<Quite the turn of events.>*

<That is putting it mildly.>

<Perhaps,> Fen agreed, a few moments of silence passing by before he spoke once more. *<I was meaning to find a way to ask, but what happened with the Stross legacy? When I was last awake, the family was celebrated and growing quickly.>*

<Honestly, I wish I could say,> Callum replied, having wondered how long it would take for that topic to arise. *<Truly all that I know is that at one point in our history . . . our luck changed for the worse, and stayed so . . . well, until recently.>*

<Eh? How do you mean?>

<It's hard to explain, but I've heard stories that were passed down in the village. About freak accidents that occasionally claimed a member of the family. A fall while hunting, choking on a meal, or encountering an unexpectedly fatal allergy,> Callum explained as he recalled the various fragments of his family histories he'd learned over his lifetime. *<And that doesn't include those who died in the king's service, fighting skirmishes or battles in faraway places, at least in the days when we still had members who were pacted in the*

family. But of them all, nothing was more devastating than the fire that nearly claimed the manor. Supposedly it started late one night in the winter, about two hundred years ago. It was . . . bad. Really bad.>

<*Oh, Callum, I am so sorry,>* Fen said in a gentle tone as Callum paused for a moment to collect his thoughts. <*We don't need to talk about this anymore if you don't want to.>*

<*It's . . . fine,>* Callum replied, even if he appreciated the fox's concern. <*I never knew any of them. It's . . . just something that happened long before I was even born.*

<*But even so, it claimed almost all of the family that was left, with less than a dozen members surviving after that,>* he continued. <*Then, believe it or not, things only got worse after that as the fields started to lose their yields, which, in turn, forced much of the family to disperse. Supposedly there was one Stross somewhere in our lineage after that who nearly gambled the farm away but was stopped by my grandfather when he was young. Supposedly there was a chance that our curse could have been broken when my father married my mother, but her illness ended that hope before it could even begin.>*

<*Her . . . illness?>* Fen asked, his voice more hesitant and softer than Callum had ever heard it.

<*When I was young, she caught a wasting sickness no healer could explain, let alone cure,>* Callum explained, the years, the *lifetime*, since having turned that pain into a distant ache. <*It all happened quickly . . . one day she was there . . . a few days later, she wasn't.>*

<*Callum . . . I . . . I have no words. I am so sorry,>* Fen said, his words arriving with an all-encompassing warmth throughout Callum's body, almost as if the fox was attempting to give him a hug. It felt particularly comforting to Callum and the two of them shared in silence before Fen eventually spoke again. <*You and I both saw what was beneath the East Manor. Saw what still plagues me to some degree.>*

<*You mean the Corruption.>*

<*I do,>* Fen stated in a hushed whisper. <*If a sickness took your mother . . . then she might very well have come in contact with it. Based on what you described . . . it would explain much.>*

<*Such as why that fire might have started in the first place all those years ago?>* Callum asked, the idea coming to him suddenly.

But before Fen could reply, Brock abruptly returned and rode past them, Callum immediately noticing that the guard's wrist was no longer glowing with mana. He circled the caravan, spoke to the other guard, and then trotted up next to Callum's carriage.

"What happened?" Callum called over to him.

"Something was out there. Serg and I handled it," he said simply, shrugging as he spoke.

"An aetherbeast?"

Brock nodded. "Aye, after a storm like the one we just had in Weatherby, they're just about everywhere. Truth be told though, I hoped we'd be out of it by now. Startin' to look like the storm was bigger than I thought, which don't bring me many warm feelings." He grumbled a curse as he finished speaking, then spat on the ground before moving off to the side to resume his vigil.

Continuing from there, it took several more hours to clear the damage from the storm. A journey during which they added a few people to their caravan: those walking through the forest, loggers and their families, whose homes had been destroyed.

The caravan reached the start of a mountain pass just after sunset. Callum couldn't shake the tension he felt in seeing the path ahead, the way it curved into the mountains, an end nowhere in sight.

There has to be another route, he thought. *I never really asked much about going to New Albion, but if this is the only way, no wonder we never visited.*

The wagons continued on, the horses grunting with displeasure at the slope of the land. They came to a pass that would be too narrow for the guards to move alongside the caravans.

Brock returned and spoke to Thaddeus, the driver. "Gonna trust your judgment to set our pace here, Thad," he said to the man without any preamble. "I know we left Weatherby much later than any of us would've liked, but I've taken this pass at night before. Shouldn't be anything for us to worry about. Just plod on as best you can and know that we are just behind you."

"Aye," Thaddeus mumbled. "I'll manage it, not a worry."

"Good, man," Brock said, his eyes then shifting over toward Callum. "You, lad. You are pacted."

The words came out more as a statement than a question, eventually prompting Callum to reply, "Yes?"

"Even so, if something comes down to bother us, let us handle it. You need to get to the city."

"I . . . of course," Callum replied, unable to help but feel a little bit of anxiety at that responsibility, even if he knew it was likely unwarranted. After all, he'd killed an aetherhawk by himself already.

"Good!" The guard continued on, back and forth as the caravan pushed deeper into the mountains.

They reached a point at which Callum had no sense of where they were. The winding path they'd taken from Weatherby had long since vanished, replaced by jagged cliffs and uneven ridges that seemed to stretch endlessly into the sky. Clouds drifted lazily beneath them, clinging to the surrounding peaks and softening the rugged landscape. The air felt thinner here, crisp and cold. It felt as though they had been transported to another realm, a place untouched by human hands. The sweeping views from the heights were breathtaking to the young man, who had rarely ventured beyond his farm in Weatherby.

The caravan pressed on at a steady clip late into the night, their path lit by a Fire Affinity Shard hitched to Thaddeus's carriage, the warm glow of the light barely enough for them to see the end of the pass.

Just as Callum started drifting off, he was pulled from his sleep by an earthshaking explosion.

He blinked awake to find the world on fire all around them as Thaddeus bore down on the path ahead, his hat missing, his face pale with fright. They charged through embers, through another, smaller blast, and it was only once they reached a wider path that Callum got the wherewithal to speak.

"What happened?" he asked as he tried to look around to see the rest of the caravan.

All he could hear were screams. All he could see was smoke. Then, a great blue pillar of fire, one that seemed to have been cast down from the heavens.

"What's happening?" Callum asked, louder this time.

<There has been an attack!>

Fen's voice in his head only increased Callum's distress. "We have to do something!"

<Agreed.>

"There is nothing to do," Thaddeus moaned. "Brock and Serg will handle it. Or they will not. Our job is to get these crops to New Albion. This is what we are instructed to do if something like an attack happens. We have to keep going!"

"You won't help them?" Callum asked.

"I would if I could, lad! But I have no way to help. I have no Powercores, no Attribute Shards, and I hardly know how to fight. Either way, we aren't supposed to—"

"I'm . . . I'm pacted!"

"If Brock can't—"

Another explosion caused Thaddeus to jerk the carriage to the right, the horses coming to a sudden halt. Callum looked back to see a second pillar of blue flame.

"Would you at least wait for me?" Callum asked the driver.

Thaddeus puffed his cheeks out. "You can't be serious."

To show that he was serious, Callum hopped down.

"If something happens, we can meld," he told Fen, determination taking over.

Callum took a cautious step toward the smoke and fire ahead, his eyes straining for any movement. Muffled screams pierced the thick smoke, mingling with the restless snorts and heavy stomps of a horse trying to flee the chaos beyond.

"Five minutes," Thaddeus called to him. "Five minutes, lad. If I see anything come out of there and it's not you, Serg, or Brock, I'm out of here."

CHAPTER 11

Royal Decree: By the authority of His Lordship, the Honorable and Esteemed King Morninglade, Sovereign of the Valestra Kingdom, and in accordance with the Edict of Summer, Year 506, Weatherby shall be visited by New Albion's Barrack Lords at the start of the forthcoming week for the purpose of militia training and basic swordsmanship. Let it be known that all able-bodied citizens, both male and female, aged eleven to seventeen years are required by royal mandate to attend all sessions when available and sessions organized locally, as decreed under the Post-Demonswar Act of Martial Readiness.

—Edict of Summer, Year 506

Fen's Radiant Claws traced over Callum's arms as he melded with the aetherbeast. He lingered at the edge of the smoke, hesitating as another muffled shout pierced the fiery haze beyond. Callum strained to hear Brock's voice or the clash of swords, but the silence pressed down on him, heavy and foreboding as he prepared for the inevitable.

Callum crept ahead and tried to ignore his excitement in doing so. A form appeared in the smoke ahead, a man with his head wrapped: a bandit moving quickly with his sword drawn.

<Your claws, you can use them at a distance as well. Try it. Try a slash in his direction.>

Callum brought his hand back and drove it through the air in front of him, creating an arc of energy made of light and fire. His attack struck the bandit squarely in the side, instantly igniting his clothing. The man dropped his sword with a clatter and fell to the ground, his frantic attempts to smother the flames futile as the fire quickly spread.

Callum watched, a strange hollowness forming in his chest. He didn't know if it was the power coursing through him, or the adrenaline of the moment, but the sight of the bandit's desperate struggle seemed almost distant.

His pulse quickened as another figure emerged from the smoke, cutting through his thoughts like a blade. The new bandit was already too close, sword drawn, his approach a blur of movement. Callum's stomach dropped—he hadn't expected anyone to get this close. Panic flared, but his instincts took over as he readied himself to react.

As the bandit brought his blade around, Callum hit him with another burst of the Radiant Fox's fire. It ignited his sleeve, the fire quickly spreading, blazing with light as the man also dropped.

<Do you know how to use a sword?>

<Just basic military training!>

A shriek from the back of the haze came coupled with a rush of fire, one that had the word of several carriages crackling. It was as if a dragon had unleashed a burst of flame from the back of its throat, the fire blue and hot. Callum instantly moved away from it.

<That's no ordinary flame. Someone is using a Powercore!>

<Do you think it could be Brock?> Callum asked, realizing that he had no idea what the guard's power was.

<Possible.>

"Let's unmeld for a moment," Callum said. "To conserve power."

<Good idea. Distract whoever is ahead and I'll deal with them.>

Callum looked at one of the swords on the ground, the blade just within reach of one of the dead bandits. He picked it up and noticed that the leather grip was saturated with sweat.

Distract the bandit, he thought, although he didn't know what had released the flame. *I hope it's not an aetherbeast . . .*

Now with both hands on the sword, Callum brought it up and held it up as he had practiced before. He saw a quick flash of mana ahead, indicating that Fen was on the move.

With a deep breath out, he pressed forward, straight toward the origin of the plume of fire. His heart thrummed in his chest and his breaths grew shorter in anticipation of what was about to happen.

Callum came upon a terrible scene. The other caravan guard was dead and Brock stood in front of a group of some of the passengers at the back of the caravan, the man looking seriously injured from the bandit attack.

Brock fired a lance of power from his hand, yet it went wide, searing just over the head of a female bandit whose entire arm was covered in flames.

At first, Callum thought that the woman had somehow caught fire. But then he saw the way the flames moved, controlled, oscillating from her fingers up to her shoulder and back. Even worse, she seemed to be conjuring a new blast of mana-fueled fire.

The bandit turned to him, her eyes narrowing just as she was broadsided by a flash of light. She was struck again, this time from the other side as Fen circled once more.

For a moment, Callum just stood there with his sword drawn, watching in slow motion as Fen came around again, primed to strike their opponent a third time. He snapped out of it and rushed to Brock, who grabbed him by the front of the shirt. "Callum—"

"The caravan—"

"They're all that's left." Brock motioned toward the group of people cowering near him. Callum caught a glimpse of the man's stomach in the process, the way it landed in a gap in his armor, saturating everything with blood.

"What do I do?" Callum asked.

"Thaddeus . . . Is he?"

"He's waiting for me."

A plume of fire flared as the bandit unleashed a final attack, one that was thrown off its intended trajectory by Fen. The fox delivered a final strike, and the woman fell, yet the fire raged on, growing toward them.

A flash of mana poured into Callum, the sensation a sudden buzzing in his chest, so powerful that he dropped the sword he had picked up.

Empowerment of Might Shard
Empowerment of Might Shard
Fury of the Firestorm

Brock pulled Callum even closer. "Get these people to safety—"

"What about you?" Callum asked.

"Take this." Brock touched his chest and produced a glowing orb, a Powercore.

"I can't—"

"Take it, Callum! Get these people to safety, *now*. There are more bandits coming. I know it. I've seen this before."

Fen appeared, saw what was going on, and melded once again with Callum.

<*Grab the Powercore; we'll examine it later, same with the cores we got from the bandit. Let Brock know you have it from here. The man is dying, and I'm not able to heal him.*>

"Go, lad!" Brock yelled. "The fire is getting closer. Go! Leave me here. Go!"

"Are you—"

"Go, now!"

Callum motioned for the group of people to follow him. "Come on, we have to hurry!"

The carriage nearest to them exploded and Callum batted some debris away with his Radiant Claws. It was through that gesture that he noticed the change in his energy levels. He felt his strength waning and with his next step forward, simultaneously shielding the small group of survivors, it became clear—he couldn't hold out much longer.

Even so, even with the strain, Callum pressed onward. He made sure everyone was safe as he led them to Thaddeus's carriage, Callum melded and barely able to keep it together.

"By the gods," Thaddeus said as people pressed out of the smoke, a few of them coughing.

"The others are dead," Callum said through short breaths. "Brock too. He told me there would be more bandits. That we need to go. I can't just—" Callum turned back to where he had left Brock and stumbled.

"Get in the carriage!" Thaddeus told him.

"But—"

<*He's right. We can't go back. You need to rest. It'll help fuel your Inner Light power to heal yourself. We must retreat, Callum, as much as it pains me to say that. It's our only option at this point.*>

Once the people were in the back of the carriage, Callum climbed into the seat next to Thaddeus. The driver started up again, faster than he had been traveling before.

"What a mess," Callum said as he relived what had just happened. He could still see the fire in his mind's eye and hear people shouting. He also hated that they had to leave Brock behind.

"It's the way of our world," Thaddeus said with utter disdain, "and it's not the first time it happened on the trip to New Albion. The problem is the bandits are getting stronger. They have better access to Powercores now, where they used to just have weapons and the occasional Attribute boost. I used to only travel with one guard, Brock, but then he decided to bring another, and it still wasn't enough." He wiped a tear away. "It's a pity, leaving him back there. But I will explain what happened to the guards once we reach New Albion. Everything will be handled. They will come back for the bodies and, hopefully, the Crown will do what it can to better secure this particular road."

"Why wasn't it already secured?"

"Because this doesn't normally happen on this trail. When I said it happened to me before, I meant in Ontaria, leagues away from the mountains here. But the Crown will do something. They will send a party to deal with it and find the bandits. I promise you that. There's nothing we can do now aside from get to New Albion."

Callum stayed awake most of the night, barely able to think with the adrenaline coursing through him after all he had just witnessed. He finally started to grow tired once the sun came up, just as Thaddeus handed him a piece of bread.

"Eat, lad. We still have a day to go. I know it's been rough."

"It has," Callum said as he took in his surroundings. They were no longer in the mountains, and most of the trees in the area had bright red leaves, many of which had fallen onto the ground. He was just about to ask where they were when Fen spoke to him:

<The Powercores we got last night. Let's discuss them now.>

Callum took a bite of the bread and remembered the lance made of mana that Brock had fired out of the palm of his hand. He then recalled the most powerful of the bandits, the way her entire arm burned with fire that she was able to unleash.

<First, the bandit's Powercore, Fury of the Firestorm. We don't need this one. Examine it.>

Still chewing the bread, Callum used Soul Sense to examine the core's details:

Fury of the Firestorm
Type: *Ability*
Grade: *Uncommon*
Infusion Requirements for Grade Increase:
0/10 Fire Affinity Shards
3/5 Vigor Shards
Affinity Requirements: *Fire*
Effect: *When bound to one's Soul Heart, this core grants its wielder the ability to control a horizontal plume of fire.*

"Wait," Callum said, nearly spitting out his bread. "Why wouldn't we want that?"

<Because I am able to do something similar once you upgrade my Aethercore. It is much stronger than this. Imagine a blazing fire made of light that

can't be quelled by water. We can strip this core for its components at a shard-crafter. Look at the next Powercore, the one Brock gave you.>

Callum did just that.

Gift of the Luminous Lance
Type: *Ability*
Grade: *Common*
Infusion Requirements for Grade Increase:
0/10 Light Affinity Shards
0/5 Might Shards
Affinity Requirements: *Light*
Effect: *When bound to one's Soul Heart, this core allows the user to conjure a lance made of pure light to hurtle at an opponent.*

<This is good. You got two Might Shards from the bandit leader. I'll give them to you next time I take my form. We will still need more Light Affinity Shards to upgrade the lance, and we should upgrade my Aethercore before we do something like that.>

"And that will make us stronger?"

<Most assuredly. It will unlock new abilities and, I suspect, help with the effects of the Corruption I was subjected to for the last five hundred years.>

Callum stared off at the path ahead, as red leaves fell from the trees that surrounded them. "We can't let something like what happened back there ever happen again."

<Mark my words, Callum. Once we are stronger, there won't be much that can stop us. And we'll need every bit of that strength we can get to deal with the Demon King.>

CHAPTER 12

The silent guardian holds steadfast its ground, the Second Heart of Creation, a sight profound. Aetherstorms no more endure, no longer do they rend and obscure; New Albion triumphs, a city pure.

—Phaedra Stoneshield, poet

Callum wasn't the only one in the caravan who gasped upon seeing New Albion's incredible skyline. Set in a valley, one in which housing had crept up along its hills, the city's design was a seamless blend of ancient architecture and modern ingenuity. The grand jewel of the city was the Second Heart of Creation, which had been rebuilt after the Great Demonswar.

Erected at the center of the city, a monument to the history of the kingdom, the mystical tower of magic resembled a grand obelisk, reflective in nature with a slight sheen to it. There were others in the city as well, smaller obelisks rising from the landscape like thinly bladed daggers.

Callum got the small note that Griselda the Shardcrafter had given him out of his pocket. He read the name and address again. He would have to find it later that night. His first stop would be the Great College to see about his enrollment and the King's Scholarship.

He really had no idea what to expect, nor had Griselda known the practicalities as to how he would actually collect on the scholarship. Everyone seemed so confident, and he liked that about people from Weatherby. With the hardships they often faced, it was nice to rally behind something. The fact that it was him they were rallying behind made it all the sweeter.

After reaching the carriage stand and bidding farewell to Thaddeus, who was too busy updating a guard captain on what had happened in the mountains to point him in the right direction, Callum started off into the city, where he was quickly overwhelmed by the large buildings and sheer size of the seat of the kingdom.

It seemed that space was at a premium in New Albion, many of the homes cobbled together with little thought to how their structures would complement things like foot traffic. This created narrow lanes that branched off the main thoroughfares, lanes packed with people and merchants selling their wares.

<We're going to the shardcrafters, right? You have the address.>

"I want to see the Great College first," Callum said. "I'll find it."

He eventually came to a booth selling wheat in sheaves and raw grain in burlap sacks stacked on top of one another. "Excuse me," he told the woman who ran the place. "I'm looking for the Great College."

She gave him a withering look, her disbelief palpable.

Callan tried again. "Have you heard of it?"

The woman turned back to her balance scale, where she used a grain scoop to measure out some threshed and winnowed wheat grains. "Are you still here?" she asked when he wouldn't leave.

"Yes. I was asking about the Great College."

"Were you now? What does a farm boy like you want with the Great College?" Even though her words were harsh, the woman had a slight smile on her face, as if she were teasing him.

Do I look like a farm boy? Callum thought as he made sure the cape his father had insisted he buy was correctly on his shoulders.

"You really don't quit, do you?" the woman asked after measuring more grain. "It's easy to find. City center. White buildings." She pointed north with her grain scoop. "If you head that way, you'll reach the campus whether you like it or not. It's sprawling, takes up too much space, if you ask me."

"Thank—"

<Don't thank her. Just move on.>

"But—" Callum started to tell Fen.

Once again, the woman gave him a strange look. "Was there something else?"

Rather than reply, he turned in the direction she had pointed with her grain scoop. Callum was just stepping away when he bumped into a short man carrying a sack of goods.

"Watch where you're bloody going!" the man roared at him.

"Sorry!"

<Don't apologize. He ran into you.>

<Are you certain?> he asked Fen as he moved on.

<Just be aware of your surroundings. Things are much tighter here, and the people aren't as friendly.>

<I'm starting to notice that,> Callum said as they came to a square filled with people enjoying a variety of unique sights and sounds. All of the

activity was set around a grand fountain meant to look as if the statue was conjuring the water. There were minstrels and musicians on one side, and an old storyteller on the other, children seated all around him.

There were several guild halls around the square, Callum noticing one for weavers and another for masons, each adorned with their respective banners. A large public noticeboard caught his eye, one notifying New Albions of upcoming debates and craft demonstrations.

Seeing it all was dazzling, and Callum was still shocked at how many people were able to live and function in one place. *The square itself is nearly the size of Weatherby, and this is just one of many!*

He pressed onward, past a pair of jugglers drawing cheers and applause from a crowd feasting on pheasant legs and drinking from bone flagons. It was only once he passed the square that he realized he was on top of the hill. The road arced downward toward the Second Heart of Creation, and Callum was able to see what he assumed was the Great College and its enormous, walled-in campus beyond.

"It looks so old," he said as he stood at the top of the hill observing the alabaster-white buildings.

Something in front of the Great College caught his attention as a pair of archmages landed directly in front of the entrance. The archmages had the Morninglade crest on their shoulders, a striking emblem of their order that seemed to shimmer. Callum had glimpsed the interwoven arcane symbol a few times in Weatherby, its presence commanding a sense of awe and authority. He was about to turn away from them when their arms flared with mana that quickly spread outward, the pair scanning the streets directly in front of the famed academy. They conferred with one another and moved on.

<What are they doing?> Fen asked as Callum continued to observe them from his vantage point.

The two archmages stopped in front of a home, and just as they were about to knock, the back door exploded outward as a man clad in black took off running.

One of the archmages took to the air again. He landed directly behind the man as his hand morphed into a long whip and the crowd around them scattered. He struck the man in the back with a flash of light.

As the man in black fell, he conjured a rush of water out of thin air, which the archmage managed to bat away. The other archmage landed, her form changing as she summoned her pacted aetherbeast. Wings grew from her back, her hands morphing into talons that her assailant tried to hit with another water attack. She struck him down with ease and dropped a knee onto his back as her counterpart went about securing his wrists.

<Get closer—this may be important!>

Callum raced down the hill and cut through an alley, where he came upon the scene just as the two archmages were hauling the man off. Smoke boiled out of his ears. It formed into a wasplike aetherbeast that took off.

"Get it!" The archmage told his winged counterpart.

She flew into the air, but it was clear that she wasn't going to be able to catch it. The small aetherbeast disappeared as its host died, the man's head slumped forward, drool dripping from his lips.

The archmage, who was still holding the man looked up at Callum. "Stay right there."

Callum swallowed, not sure what he should do. He'd never been in trouble before with any sort of government official, and he didn't know how to react to the archmage's command other than to follow it.

The archmage approached. The man was a few inches shorter than Callum, but the way he bore down on him made Callum feel as if he were a giant. "What's your name?"

"Callum Stross, sir."

His counterpart landed, her wings filtering away.

"Come again?" the man asked.

"Callum Stross, sir."

The two archmages exchanged glances. The woman spoke this time. "You must be joking."

"I'm not joking," he said, not sure of the tone he should take. "It's who I am. From the family Stross."

"The noble family Stross?" she asked.

"Yes." Callum couldn't remember a time when he had been questioned about something like this. He also couldn't remember ever having to use his family's name in this way. In Weatherby, everyone already knew who he was. They called his father Lord Stross and Callum went by his first name, simple as that.

Fen came alive and appeared on the ground. "He speaks the truth. He is Callum Stross and we are pacted."

The look on the woman's face changed from skeptical to awestruck. "You're a Radiant Fox."

"I am."

"I've never seen one before. I was under the impression that there were only a handful."

"I was under the impression that they were all gone," the archmage next to her said.

"Yet here I am," Fen told the two, "here to enroll in the Great College. Unless there is something else, will you point us in the right direction?"

Once again, the two archmages exchanged looks. The woman spoke again: "The campus is closed due to our investigation. But you're not out of luck, yet. The final day for enrollment is tomorrow."

"And I would apply for the King's Scholarship that way?" Callum asked. As soon as these words left his lips, he regretted saying them, especially after throwing his family's name around. To seek charity upon entering the Great College now struck as some sort of shame, even though he didn't quite know why.

The woman looked back to Fen. "Return tomorrow. And stay indoors tonight. I don't know what that rambling madman was going on about, but it is best if we play it safe. Good luck."

The two archmages hauled the man away.

<Did you see the way he spoke to me?> Callum asked Fen once the fox had melded with him again.

<I did. And it further speaks to what I already know, the Demon King has returned. We must reach the Archive of Destiny.>

<Can aetherbeasts be that small?> Callum asked as he remembered the way the wasp had flown away.

<They can be many things, but there's not much we can do about it now, not in our current state. Are we finally going to go where we need to go?>

<Yes.> Callum got the parchment out again and scanned it:

Telluride—Belldrum District—Near the Alanther Inn
Tell him Griselda said "Two Stars"

Callum had wondered what the "Two Stars" part meant, ever since Weatherby's shardcrafter had given him the message. "I guess I'll figure that out now."

CHAPTER 13

Anyone who has access to an Aethercore, a pacted aetherbeast, can fuse shards into a Powercore. But sundering, or stripping a core of its parts, is something reserved only for those who have reached the Rank known as Channeler. A person who has reached this Rank, yet has given up their Aethercore, becomes a shardcrafter, of which there are many across the kingdom, some more trustworthy than others . . .

—Ines Meida, Mastress Weaver, Archona of Aveiro, and famed legal scholar

The Belldrum District was filled with large and small ceramics, which were used to transport certain goods across the entirety of the Valestra Kingdom. With the pots came discarded ceramic shards, some of which stood in mountains in the far-reaching district.

It had taken Callum another hour to find the place.

The people of New Albion were less than helpful, and he hadn't quite figured out how the public transportation system of carriages worked, mostly due to a reluctance to ask. He was by no means stubborn, but after asking a few people for directions and getting the cold shoulder, he decided to figure it out on his own.

It was an older man leaning on a crutch who finally pointed Callum in the right direction. "Across that bridge and to the east of the Great College," the old man said, his voice defined by a raspy whistle. "It should take you about an hour on foot. Lots of hills. And when you get there, lots of pots."

Now I just need to find the Alanther Inn, Callum thought as he began exploring the Belldrum District. He walked past numerous studios where people fired pottery and got another glimpse of someone using a Fire

Affinity Shard to do something he couldn't quite place. While there were rare people who used shards in the village of Weatherby, it seemed much more common in New Albion, something he noticed as he continued through the grand city.

He reached one of the city's smaller obelisks, which occasionally sparked at the top, gathering mana from the aether. These locations were heavily guarded by archmages as well as the king's soldiers, who stood behind shields as tall as a man, most armed with pikes. They were also joined by teams of archers, who were positioned on towers surrounding the structure.

<*I suspect the obelisks we've seen prevent aetherstorms from reaching New Albion. I wonder if we will encounter more across the kingdom,*> Fen told him.

<*I didn't know something like that existed.*>

<*Sometimes, it seems like your border village was in a world entirely of its own.*>

<*I guess that would be one way to describe it.*> Callum spotted a girl with auburn hair carrying a basket full of eggs. She looked friendly enough. <*I'll ask her about the inn.*> "Excuse me—?"

She turned to him, scanned her eyes over his cloak, and laughed.

"What?" Callum asked her as she moved on.

"Who wears a cape these days?" the girl sneered.

"Do what?" Callum asked as he instinctively touched the garment. "There's something wrong with it?"

"You are joking."

"I don't think I am."

"People stopped wearing capes years ago," she said. "Do you see anyone else wearing them?"

"It's not a cape, it's a cloak."

"And the difference?"

"I don't actually know," Callum admitted, "but my *cloak* has a hood."

"A cape with a hood, huh?"

<*This one is certainly vain,*> Fen commented. <*And who is she to judge your cloak? Her dress looks like a potato sack. Tell her that. Tell her it looks as if she's wearing an old potato sack that should have been discarded a decade ago.*>

Callum decided against following the fox's advice. "What about people at the Great College? What do they wear?"

"They have a uniform," she told him. "Why?"

"I'm planning to enroll."

"You?"

"Actually," Callum said, ignoring her laughter, "I'm looking for the Alanther Inn. You don't happen to know where that is, do you?"

"Why do you want to go there?"

"I'm looking for a man named Telluride."

The girl's face went pale.

"Is something wrong?" Callum asked after she didn't say anything.

"He's no longer there."

"As in, he doesn't live there or . . . something else?"

"He should have died, especially after that explosion. Come, I'll show you." The girl walked Callum to a different street, where he found three buildings blackened with char. Several of the roofs had collapsed inward, and there was a bunch of ash on the ground. Two men moved about in one of the buildings, removing debris, their overalls covered in soot.

"What happened?" Callum asked.

"That used to be the inn. He operated out of a space next to it. So, to answer your question, Telluride happened."

"He did this on purpose?"

The girl gave him a funny look. "What? No, I mean, I would hope not. He was likely experimenting with shards. He's a shardcrafter."

"I'm aware."

She gestured to the mess again. "And, well, you see what he did."

"How many days ago?"

"Three. I could smell the burned wood in the air up until this morning. It's finally starting to leave the area. Anyway, if you want him, you'll have to try Stadacona."

"Which is?"

"Another district. Actually, it's not a district. It used to be a town near New Albion, but it's practically a district now."

"Is it far from here?" he asked the girl.

"Not really."

"And you're certain he's there?"

"Yes."

"Can you . . . show me?"

She glanced from her basket of eggs back to Callum. "Seriously?"

"I'll carry your basket for you."

For some reason, this made her laugh. "You are a strange one. What's your name?"

"Callum Stross of Weatherby. Yours?"

"Weatherby, no wonder you're wearing a cape," she said, not bothering to tell him her name or say anything about his lineage. The girl motioned for Callum to follow her. "I'll show you where he is. I was heading in that direction anyway. And no, you don't have to hold my basket."

She guided him through the Belldrum District, occasionally pointing out landmarks and sharing bits of gossip about the people living in the various homes. They passed over a river; Callum would have been lost had it not been for the Second Heart of Creation, which was still visible in the distance. From his earlier exploration, he knew that if he headed toward the grand structure, even if it took him some time, he would eventually find the Great College.

The pair reached the area known as Stadacona, which had shabbier homes than the ones he had seen in the Belldrum District. Barnyard animals wandered aimlessly through the streets, and things seemed to move at a slower pace, even if it was slightly more crowded.

The girl jutted her chin to a structure that looked like it was a repurposed barn. "He's in there. Telluride."

"You're sure?"

"I'm certain. It's my uncle's place. That's who these eggs are for."

"You were coming this way all along?"

"Maybe," she said, the corners of her mouth lifting into a sly grin. "My uncle always had a sweet spot for Telluride, and he's letting him stay here while he figures out whatever it is he's going to do next. Good luck, and a word of advice."

"Yes?" Callum asked.

"If you really are going to go to the Great College, maybe lose the cape."

"*Cloak.*"

"Only the older masters wear them now."

"Are you sure?"

The girl raised an eyebrow at him. "Are you from here?"

"No."

"Then, I'm sure. Good luck, Weatherby." She turned toward a house nearby, leaving Callum standing in front of a barn alone.

"Did she really just call me Weatherby?"

<Apparently so. But she's gone now. And I wouldn't say good riddance because she did help us, but good riddance.>

Callum knocked again on the barn door. *Should I try the big sliding door?* he wondered, circling around to the other side. Finding no luck there, he returned to the original door and knocked again.

"Hello?" Callum called out.

The interior of the barn illuminated with what he recognized as a Fire Affinity Shard, the space lighting from corner to corner as the shard moved about, seemingly on its own. The light revealed a bearded man laying on some hay, curled up into a ball, an absent look on his face.

Callum rushed over to the man to help him up. "Are you okay?"

The man batted Callum's hands away and let out a deep moan: "What could you possibly want?"

"I'm looking for Telluride—"

"That's me. But you didn't answer my question. What do you want?" Telluride was a short, bearded man, who smelled slightly of alcohol. He had grayish-black hair, which was shaved on one side in a fashion Callum hadn't seen before. His clothes weren't as tattered as Callum would have imagined they should be, considering he was living in a barn, but there were stains on them and the ends of his vest were black.

"Griselda sent me. She said you could help."

He squinted up at Callum, who now stood over him casting a shadow onto Telluride's face. "Griselda?" he let out another deep moan. "Well, then I must ask, what could she possibly want?"

"Two stars. She said something about that."

Telluride laughed miserably. "Of course she would be calling in a favor at a moment like this. Look, lad—"

"Callum Stross."

Telluride peered at him again, as if he had heard the name before. "Come again? The only Callum Stross I'm aware of is one of the founders of the Great College, the Demonslayer. There's a statue there in one of the courtyards. I used to sit near it and study."

"There is?"

"Yeah, Callum Stross and his Radiant Fox, whose name I can't seem to place. It's in one of the inner courtyards that the public rarely sees. You know how it goes, a famous academy like that gets visitors and they try to keep some things from them. Like the statue." Telluride squinted at him. "That would make you part of the Stross lineage."

"It would, sir."

"Huh. Well, in any case, I can't help you. Or I can, but I'm not in the mood to. How did you find me?"

"A girl walked me over here. She said her uncle owns this place."

"Ah, that would be Florence. Was she a little bit of a monster?"

"What do you mean?"

"Did she make fun of you?"

"The entire way."

"Yes, that would be Florence, but she just likes to tease. I'm assuming if you showed up with her that you saw the damage."

<I'll take it from here.>

Fen appeared, which caused Telluride to crawl backward for a moment, his face riddled with shock that soon flashed into a smile. "An actual Radiant Fox?" he whispered. "Callum Stross and his Radiant Fox . . ." He ran his hand over his face. "I must be hallucinating." He rubbed his eyes. "What's your name?"

"Fen. And I promise you aren't hallucinating," Fen said. "We have been sent here by Griselda, Weatherby's shardcrafter. You are a shardcrafter, apparently."

"I am," Telluride said as he gathered his wits. "This is a lot to take in. First, the name, and now you, an actual Radiant Fox. Profound! Where's my pipe?" Telluride searched around in the hay, found his pipe, and lit it with a match. After a few puffs, he focused on Fen again. "Callum Stross returns with a Radiant Fox, of all pacted aetherbeasts . . . huh."

Fen didn't waste another moment as he got right down to what they needed. "Griselda made it seem like you would be able to provide room and board for us, at least until we are admitted to the Great College." The fox glanced around, his tail flickering lightly in agitation. "I don't know if that will be the case here, not that I'm opposed to sleeping in a barn for a day or two."

"There are two rooms through that door," Telluride said with another puff from his pipe. "Not as shabby as it seems, really."

"And do you have your supplies?" Fen asked. "Or were they destroyed in the fire that you caused?"

Telluride shook his head. "With respect, Radiant Fox, I didn't cause the fire. I am known to experiment, as we all are, but I am especially careful with Fire Affinity Shards. No, it was started by someone else. A bloody thief. They broke into my shop to steal shards. I tried to stop them and, in doing so, the place caught fire."

Fen looked at him skeptically. "Then you did start it."

"Technically, yes, but it wasn't part of an experiment, as I'm sure Florence likely claimed. People always think I'm experimenting, and I'm not. In fact, I let them think that because it generally stops the bloody locals of the Belldrum District from bothering me unless they have shard business."

"And what happened to the thief?" Callum asked.

Telluride shrugged. "They got away, to my knowledge, but I was able to tell a few of the Crown's archmages about them and they seem to know what they should be looking for."

"Do you think . . . ?" Callum asked Fen.

"But you have some of your supplies here, right?" Fen asked.

"I have what I need, if that's what you're asking. Why? Are you looking to trade something?"

"Perhaps. We have a Powercore that we do not need called Fury of the Firestorm. Are you able to break it down?"

"Any shardcrafter worth their weight in, well, shards, can sunder a core."

"I figured as much," Fen said as his tail settled.

"What do you currently have?" Telluride asked Callum. "Sorry for being forthright, but I've never seen a pacted Radiant Fox before."

"You don't know yourself?" Callum asked.

"Ah . . ." A knowing smile appeared on Telluride's face. "Yes, I am able to check your status if need be, but I'm of the mindset to ask someone so I can see if they're being honest with me or not. I hope you don't mind."

Callum used Soul Sense and read what he saw aloud: "Empowerment of Zephyr Strike, Inner Light, Empowerment of Sustenance, Pact of the Radiant Fox and my newest one, Gift of the Luminous Lance. Plus affinity to Air, Fire and Light Mana."

Telluride exhaled a big cloud of smoke that Callum was forced to wave away. "The fox came with all that?"

"Aside from the lance, yes."

"We have to register for the entrance exams tomorrow," Fen said, getting right down to it, "and I'm hoping that you can do something with the Fury of the Firestorm Powercore." He looked back at Callum. "Give it to him."

Callum touched his chest and withdrew the fiery orb, which he handed it to Telluride, who examined the core as if it were a precious jewel. "Yes, yes," he said, a red glow illuminating his face. "This could be something indeed. Let's focus on the shards you currently have." Callum nearly got the shards out when Telluride stopped him: "Use Soul Sense. You were given this power for a reason; all of us were. It's much faster. And don't bother reading them out loud to me."

"Right, sorry." Callum produced the shards he currently had on him, which included a single Light and Air Affinity shard, one Mind Shard, and two Might Shards.

"And now I want you to see what you need to empower your fox," Telluride said. "Read these to me."

With those words, Callum better understood the information presented before him.

Pact of the Radiant Fox
Type: *Pact*
Grade: *Common*

Infusion Requirements for Grade Increase:
0/5 Fire Affinity Shards
0/5 Light Affinity Shards
0/10 Deftness Shards
0/10 Vigor Shards
0/5 Resilience Shards

"Five Fire Affinity Shards, five Light Affinity Shards, ten Deftness Shards, ten Vigor Shards, and five Resilience Shards."

Telluride examined Fury of the Firestorm again, staring at it as if he could look right through it. "I will certainly be able to get the Fire Affinity Shards you need from this. I have broken down a similar core before and netted Deftness and Vigor shards. This is only a fairly common core, but it's a strong one, and it appears that the person was in the process of getting it upgraded."

"Really?" Callum asked.

"The core already has three Vigor Shards infused in it, which isn't bad." Telluride handed Fury of the Firestorm back to Callum. As soon as he touched it, the Powercore's details appeared before him.

Fury of the Firestorm
Type: Ability
Grade: Uncommon
Infusion Requirements for Grade Increase:
0/10 Fire Affinity Shards
3/5 Vigor Shards
Affinity Requirements: Fire
Effect: When bound to one's Soul Heart, this core grants its wielder the ability to control a horizontal plume of fire.

"Do you see it now?" Telluride asked as Callum gave Fury of the Firestorm back to him. "It has already been fused." Telluride's eyes darted to the next room. "Grab my shardcrafting table. It's there," he told Callum. "And give me a minute."

Callum stepped into a part of the barn that had been fitted with walls. It still had the high ceilings, but without those, it would seem like a normal foyer. He went into the first room to find a small table with grooves on it. He returned to find Telluride with his head slightly bowed, the man now seated cross-legged.

Fen remained near him, his ears alert.

Telluride stayed in his quiet seated position for another minute before he finally looked up at Callum. "There, place it there."

Callum set the shardcrafting table in front of Telluride. He realized now why it was so short. The shardcrafter was able to sit before the table, his knees beneath it, putting him in a meditative position while he did his work.

Telluride placed Fury of the Firestorm near the edge of the table. "Fusing will be something that comes in handy as you collect more shards."

"What about my shard pouch?" Callum asked, yet another thing his father had recommended.

"That would be handy as well because not all shards you find will have a core that they can be fused into. Plus, you can hold Powercores in your pouch."

"I see."

"Later, if and when you reach the Channeler Rank, you will be able to strip a core of its basic shards yourself, saving time. This is, after all, what a shardcrafter such as me primarily does. Sure, we buy, sell, and trade shards, but much of our work involves repurposing cores by breaking them down, known as *sundering*, and fusing things for people without access to that system. By pacting, you can now fuse. And . . . you know what? Watch." Telluride gestured to a grooved piece of wood on his table. "Put your shards there."

Callum placed his Air and Light Affinity shards and his Mind and Might Attribute shards on the table. The crystals had a slight glow to them and they were warm.

"Now, access your Pact of the Radiant Fox Aethercore. You will need to return to him, Fen," Telluride told the fox.

Fen vanished, and Callum, who now sat before Telluride, placed Fen's Aethercore on the table.

Telluride examined the core again. "Do you see where it says zero out of five Light Affinity Shards?"

Callum scanned the Soul Sense information:

Infusion Requirements for Grade Increase:
0/5 Fire Affinity Shards
0/5 Light Affinity Shards
0/10 Deftness Shards
0/10 Vigor Shards
0/5 Resilience Shards

"I do."

"You have one Light Affinity Shard." Telluride picked it up and showed the shard to Callum. "Watch." He pressed the shard into the Aethercore and it fizzled until it was gone. Callum looked at the core to confirm that it worked:

Infusion Requirements for Grade Increase:
0/5 Fire Affinity Shards
1/5 Light Affinity Shards
0/10 Deftness Shards
0/10 Vigor Shards
0/5 Resilience Shards

"I get it now," Callum said. "One out of five Light Affinity Shards."

"Yes, the shard is now infused into your fox's Aethercore. You have several shards remaining." Telluride swept his hand to the crystals Callum had placed on the table. "Do you have any Powercores that need a Mind Shard? Before you pull out another core, return the Aethercore to your chest. Always keep your cores close to your chest," he said with a slight chuckle.

Callum returned the Aethercore and Fen reappeared, the fox sitting near him, his tail lashing against the ground as Callum scanned the information for his Inner Light Powercore.

Inner Light
Type: *Ability*
Grade: *Common*
Infusion Requirements for Grade Increase:
0/5 Light Affinity Shards
0/5 Mind Shards
0/5 Regeneration Shards
Affinity Requirements: *Light*
Effect: *When bound to one's Soul Heart, this core allows the user the ability to rapidly heal wounds and restore stamina.*

"I have Inner Light," he said as he placed the core on the table.

"Yes, you do," Telluride said. "Infuse it. Try."

Callum picked up the single Mind Shard and set it on top of the core's surface, which caused an instant sizzle of mana as the shard disappeared. He checked his Soul Sense to see that the Mind Shard was now infused.

Infusion Requirements for Grade Increase:
0/5 Light Affinity Shards
1/5 Mind Shards
0/5 Regeneration Shards
Affinity Requirements: Light

"You still have three shards," Fen said, who now stood, examining what had happened. "Two Might and one Air Affinity. What about Zephyr Strike?"

Callum checked the Powercore:

Empowerment of Zephyr Strike
Type: Ability
Grade: Common
Infusion Requirements for Grade Increase:
0/10 Air Affinity Shards
0/5 Deftness Shards
Affinity Requirements: Air
Effect: When bound to one's Soul Heart, this core grants its wielder the ability to shape their latent air mana into that of a powerful crescent of wind, slicing apart all it touches.

"This one takes Air Affinity," Callum said as he pressed the crystal into the Powercore. He checked to confirm that the fusion had taken place and put the core back in his chest.

"Two Might Shards left," Fen said, excitement in his eyes.

"Yes," Telluride said, "then we can deal with the Fury of the Firestorm Powercore."

Callum took Gift of the Luminous Lance out of his chest. He placed it on the table and fused the two Might Shards into it. Once he was finished, he confirmed that they had been fused:

Gift of the Luminous Lance
Type: Ability
Grade: Common
Infusion Requirements for Grade Increase:
0/10 Light Affinity Shards
0/5 Might Shards
Affinity Requirements: Air
Effect: When bound to one's Soul Heart, this core allows the user to conjure a lance made of pure light to hurtle at an opponent.

"Wonderful," Telluride said. "Fusing isn't very hard, but you must be pacted to do it. If you ever get a core that already has shards fused into it, either someone who is pacted did it, or it was a shardcrafter. It isn't a skill provided to commoners."

"They must either be pacted, or they must visit someone like you," Fen said.

"Correct. And when they visit someone like me, the transaction is noted in a Fusion Ledger that only I have access to, which is connected to the World Ledger."

"And has it worked?" Fen asked. "Has preventing the general public from fusing shards into cores worked?"

"I'm afraid not," Telluride told the Radiant Fox. "There are those who will fuse or sunder a core for the right price." He tapped on the Fury of the Firestorm Powercore. "Ready for sundering?"

"Yes," Callum told him, the young man fascinated by all that was going on. *To be able to store shards in the cores themselves will make all of this so much easier*, he thought as Telluride lifted the Fury of the Firestorm Powercore.

"There are many ways to do this, but I prefer this method." Telluride turned his hand around and slammed the Powercore into the palm of his hand, shattering it into six crystals.

"A bit dramatic," Fen said.

"Yes, but people like a show, and I like to give them one." The shardcrafter placed the shards on the table. "Five Fire Affinity Shards and one Vigor Shard."

"For Fen," Callum said.

"Exactly," Telluride told Callum as Fen returned to him.

Callum produced the Pact of the Radiant Fox Aethercore and fused the five Fire Affinity Shards and the single Vigor Shard into it. The count updated immediately:

Infusion Requirements for Grade Increase:
5/5 Fire Affinity Shards
1/5 Light Affinity Shards
0/10 Deftness Shards
1/10 Vigor Shards
0/5 Resilience Shards

"Good," Telluride said as Fen appeared again. "You can now fuse shards, and you don't have to collect too much more to upgrade your Radiant Fox. You're going to need everything you can get, too."

"Why's that?"

"How long ago did you pact?"

"Just a few days," Callum told the man.

"You're going to be behind once you start at the Great College, but that's fine. At least you know how to fuse now." Telluride glanced around. "And as I said earlier, you're welcome to sleep in the other room for the night."

"How much do I owe you for breaking down the Fury of the Firestorm core?"

"You don't. You can pay me next time you bring in some core that needs sundering."

"That's kind of you, but—"

"No," Telluride told him, "it's *smart* of me. You're Callum Stross, a distant relative of the Demonslayer, and you have a Radiant Fox. That means something. I don't know what that is yet, but I'm sure it's important."

CHAPTER 14

May the wise carve their destiny with mana.

—Maxim of the Great College of New Albion

Callum stood before the entrance of the Great College, not sure where he should go next. He didn't wear the cloak that his father had had him purchase, glad he had left it behind at Telluride's home when he saw the flowing overcoats that the students wore as they moved in and out of a set of huge, black oak doors.

<Well, ask someone where intakes are supposed to go, get registered, and then visit the Archive of Destiny.>

<Who should we ask?>

<That woman there. The one with frizzy hair.>

Callum turned to her. The woman, who wore flowing robes the likes of which he'd never seen before, dressed him down with her dark eyes. She moved right past him.

<Smooth. This time, try to say something. Are you nervous around women or something?>

<What? No. It's just that everyone here in New Albion seems more reserved than they were in Weatherby.>

<Is that your way of saying that city people are rude?>

<In Weatherby, I could ask anyone and they would point me in the right direction,> Callum said under his breath as a pair of male students passed him, both looking fresh in their overcoats and new haircuts. "Excuse me—"

They continued and never turned to Callum. A carriage pulled up at the bottom of the stone steps that led to the entrance of the Great College. This was followed by a second and third carriage, guards spilling out.

The driver from the first carriage hopped down from his perch and opened the door for a woman with striking blonde hair that extended to the small of her back. She wore the same overcoat as the other students, yet hers was cast over silver armor that seemed out of place until Callum watched two heavily armored guards standing at the base of the steps approach the woman.

"Who is that?" Callum whispered as the guards joined her. She headed up the stairs and was just passing Callum when she turned to him.

"Are you lost?" the woman asked.

Callum cleared his throat. "No. Actually, I was looking for the registration office. I need to register and apply for the King's Scholarship."

The corners of her lips lifted. "I see. And no one has helped you?"

"I just got here." Callum scratched the back of his head. "Yesterday."

"It appears so. In that case, I can escort you there."

"Your Ladyship," one of the guards started to say before she cut him off.

"Yes, Sir Trindade, I will lead him there. I am heading in that direction anyway."

"You are?" Callum blinked twice. "I mean, sure, if you don't mind."

<*Get hold of yourself. She's clearly important!*>

Callum's eyes bulged.

"Come," the woman said as she started walking again, the two guards flanking her.

"Sure!" Callum trailed behind the woman until she called her guards off.

"Sir Trindade. I can handle myself," she said in an even tone.

"Yes, Your Ladyship," the guard said as he straightened up and allowed Callum to pass. "Mind yourself," Sir Trindade told Callum under his voice.

"Ah, yes," the woman said, not skipping a beat as he joined her. "You said you just arrived, yes?"

"I did, um, Your Ladyship."

She gave Callum a funny look as some of the students around them had started whispering among themselves. *She must be a really big deal*, he thought.

"And you are?" she asked once he didn't say anything.

"Callum Stross."

The woman stopped walking, forcing the guard on her other side to stop, and Sir Trindade behind them as well. She turned to Callum. "He is one of the founders, the first to have an Aethercore, the Demonslayer."

"Yes, that's him."

"And out of curiosity, what have you pacted it with?" the woman remarked, her tone casual, almost dismissive.

Callum hesitated until he heard Fen's voice. <*It's fine, tell her, but don't tell her who you are or who I am exactly. And certainly don't tell her my name!*>

"A Radiant Fox."

She seemed almost troubled by this development. "You have a Radiant Fox?"

"I do." Callum sensed by the look on her face that her own pacted aetherbeast was telling her something.

"Interesting," she finally said before she moved on, Callum noticing yet again that everyone they passed seemed to be staring at them. Anyone in their path also veered far around them, allowing the woman plenty of space.

Much to his surprise, the woman didn't say anything else until they came to a smaller building built into an inner wall. It had a thatched roof and there was a large, open window that would allow someone from inside to speak to anyone who approached.

"Princess Selene," said the man inside, who immediately hopped off his stool and stood upright. He fumbled with some papers at the desk. "I apologize for our sudden closing yesterday. As you know, there was a small breach that needed to be handled. But your paperwork is in order. I have it right here and was planning to have it delivered to your suite today. And please, Your Ladyship, do not hesitate to send one of your guards to pick up documents like this. You must be exceedingly busy."

Callum barely heard what the man was saying. *Princess Selene? The princess? King Morninglade's daughter!?* His jaw, which had dropped open, only shut once the princess turned back to him.

"Callum," she said. "You may register here. Goodbye." And with that, Princess Selene stepped around him and moved on.

Callum stood there dumbfounded until Fen spoke to him.

<That would explain the guards. But hey, at least you made a friend.>

<Did I?> he asked as someone tapped him on the shoulder.

Callum turned to find a portly young man with a mess of dark hair and light blue eyes. "Are you in line?" the man asked.

"Yes, sorry," Callum said.

The young man paused for a moment to watch Princess Selene continue on. "I see you met the princess."

"You know her?"

"I do, but she didn't see me this time. Or didn't acknowledge me, one of the two. She pacted with a bear, you know."

"A bear?"

"They are a very exclusive family of aetherbeasts that have pacted with the royalty since the end of the Great Demonswar." The man extended his hand to Callum. "I'm Quinn Vendrick."

"Callum Stross."

Quinn leaned in just a bit closer. "Did you just say you were Callum Stross?"

"I did, named after an ancient relative, you might know him as the Demonslayer," he said.

"Remarkable. And your pacted aetherbeast?"

"A Radiant Fox."

Quinn's eyes bulged yet again. "Amazing!"

Callum, who was quickly coming to understand that having Fen with him would create quite the commotion, moved the conversation along. "You?"

Quinn touched his chest. "A Darkmoor Cat."

"A cat?" Callum asked.

"Yes, a rather large one, if we are being honest, but we suit each other. Hey, have you ever noticed when someone has an animal that they resemble them in some way?"

Callum thought back to most of the pets he'd seen around Weatherby. Most had a purpose, like the cats on his farm, the rooster at Miss Barrowsly's place, or perhaps a guard dog. He was just about to ask Quinn for clarification when the man behind him spoke.

"Excuse me."

"Sorry!" Callum turned back to the man at the registration window, who peered at him through a pair of oval spectacles. "I'm here to join the fall intake and apply for the King's Scholarship."

The man looked at him incredulously. "You do realize it's the last day to join the intake."

"I do."

Quinn stepped up. "He's Callum Stross, well, not *the* Callum Stross, but he's named after him. There's a literal statue with his namesake in one of the courtyards here. I've seen it before, you know."

"I will need to see some paperwork," he told Callum, who produced the paper that proved his nobility through the ownership of the farm in Weatherby. It was renewed every ten years and had the king's seal on it.

"Is there a problem?" Callum asked as the man continued to scrutinize the parchment.

The registration attendant tilted his head slightly as he continued to look at the document. "May I see your pacted aetherbeast?"

"Right here?"

"Step inside."

Callum did just that, and was surprised to find that the small, thatched building opened onto its own private courtyard. There were statues here around a circular platform with runic carvings on it.

Quinn, who had followed them, stayed behind the registration attendant just in case he wasn't supposed to be there.

"Ready?" Callum asked Fen.

The fox appeared and the registration attendant nodded with satisfaction.

"I'm assuming that like a shardcrafter you are able to view what someone has pacted with, right?" Fen asked as his tail flared with light.

"Correct," the man said.

"Then why was this necessary?"

"Because I had to see it with my own eyes. It's not often we get an applicant with a Radiant Fox, one of such noble lineage too. You would be a legacy candidate had it not been for a law that changed qualifications long before my time."

"Is being related to the Demonslayer not qualifying enough?" Fen asked.

"Ah, yes, it should be, but it is now based on legacy in terms of your family attending the college. But I digress. I'm not one to get into politics during office hours. Come inside and I will start your paperwork." He turned to Quinn and said, "Were you here for a particular reason? I recall you were registered two days ago, a Darkmoor Cat, correct?"

"That's right. They asked that I get a signature from you stating I was offered the King's Scholarship but my family declined."

"I see. Then I'll sign that first," the man said as he led them all back in. He signed the document in question and gave it back to Quinn, who approached the door and then turned back to Callum.

"Good luck," Quinn said before departing.

The registration attendant summoned a simian aetherbeast, one with a curled tail made of mana. "I could use your help, Oscarn."

"Did he just show up randomly?" the monkey asked as he sat on the table looking at Callum.

"Yes, and he needs to apply for the King's Scholarship."

"Ah, I see." The monkey jumped to the ground and headed to a different table, where he sifted through some papers and found the document in question. While he did this, the registration attendant filled out a few things as he asked questions about Callum's origins.

He quickly finished up what he needed to do, handed Callum the paperwork, and folded his hands together on the table. "You will have trials that you will need to pass before you can collect the King's Scholarship. And I should tell you now: the scholarship isn't what it used to be. All the people that attend the Great College are nobles, who come from family lines that run all the way back to the Great Demonswar. Most don't need the scholarship, so those funds have been allocated in different ways."

"I understand."

The registration attendant smirked at him. "You will have to do something. But that isn't unheard of, and there are ways to make money on campus. Eh, I'm getting ahead of myself. First, you must be admitted."

"What will the trials consist of?" Fen asked from beside Callum. He looked up at the man expecting an answer.

"Another thing you should know: students don't normally go around campus with their pacted aetherbeasts out. While this isn't a military college per se, not like the Great Armament on the other side of the city, you will be part of the military if you graduate, and they have rules about revealing one's pacted aetherbeasts on a whim." He looked at his own pacted monkey. "Present company excluded."

"So don't go around with Fen out and I can earn shards and money later," Callum told the man. "Got it."

"Good. Once you finish here you will head down the path directly in front of the Outer Registration Office. That's where we are," he said as he pointed at a nicely drawn map of the campus on the wall. "The *O-R-O* as it is sometimes referred to."

Callum's eyes found the *X* marking his current location.

"You will start first with Attribute Trials. While all of your information is available through Soul Sense, Mastress Lucerne likes to have it officially recorded at the Aeternal Tabula. Over the years this has morphed into a physical challenge that helps determine if you qualify for the Great College or not."

"I have a question about that."

The registration attendant looked at Callum over the rim of his glasses and continued without giving him a chance to ask his question. "Once you have visited the Aeternal Tabula, which is marked on my map with the letter *A*," he said as he once again pointed at the map, "you will then go to the Ordelarium across campus, marked with the letter *O*, to join the combat trials. Note that you will pass the Vestige Arena along the way, which is *not* where you need to be at the moment."

"First the Aeternal Tabula, letter *A*, and then the Ordelarium, letter *O*," Callum said. It then dawned on him what the registration attendant had just told him. "Did you say combat trials?"

The man looked him over yet again. "Yes, also known as the Entry Duels. You didn't think entrance into the Great College would be easy, did you?"

CHAPTER 15

The Great College's Soul Pythia is a unique role that requires years of study. Many have spent time in the Badlands and count themselves among the Beast Masters who have permanently melded with their Aethercores. Soul Pythia are capable of frighteningly powerful usages of mana that defy worldly conventions, from mastery over pocket realms to reality creation. Their rituals remain unique, mysterious, and often misunderstood.

—Fletch Gellutad, Master Channeler, Clergo

Outside the registration office, Callum ran into Quinn, who seemed to be waiting around for him.

"Hey," Quinn said as he noticed the confused look on Callum's face, "did you get it all solved?"

"I think so? I was told that the Attribute Trials and Entry Duels are up next."

"Ah, yes, good, I figured as much. I already did mine yesterday. I might stop by for the Duels, though. It's always interesting on the last day."

"Anything I should know about that? I think I understand the Attribute Trials, but I'm a little less clear on the combat portion. This isn't a military school."

A shadow of doubt flashed in Quinn's eyes. "True, but it could be argued that most, if not all wars, are decided by archmages. So it's a big deal around here, is what I'm saying. The Entry Duels are supposed to be a blind test. They are meant to test your true abilities against unknown opponents, who just so happen to be your future peers. Your overall level will be ranked in a way that combines your ratings from your Attribute Trials with your performance in the Entry Duels. There's another thing."

"Yeah?" Callum asked.

"You know what? Let me walk you to the Aeternal Tabula. I'll explain. It's this way," Quinn said as he took the lead. "There's a reason that the guy back there mentioned this wouldn't be easy. Most people have already done their Entry Duels."

"What do you mean?"

"Anyone left is either a late entry, or they have purposefully waited until the end for the challenge aspect. It's been tradition for a while now for those who have already trained or gone to one of the preparatory schools to do their Entry Duels on the final day of registration. Mostly to show off their abilities."

<*That would explain why Princess Selene has just arrived. It also means you might have to duel her,*> Fen commented privately through their bond.

"Do you think I'll have to duel the princess?" Callum asked Quinn.

"I don't know. Like most everyone, she has already done her Attribute Trials, so that would mean the Ordelarium is her next stop. But truthfully, I have no idea who you'll have to face. It's possible you might have to."

Callum let out a slow breath at the thought. "She was wearing armor."

"Of course, why shouldn't she be? Though they have armor there for people who didn't bring any. Did you . . .?" Quinn started to ask, only for his face to split into a gentle smile as he saw Callum's expression. "I'm going to go out on a limb here and guess no. That you don't have an Armorcore."

"An Armorcore?"

"I can loan you mine."

Callum imagined himself in armor that would fit Quinn. The man was much shorter than him. It didn't seem like it would work.

"Oh, you think I'm referring to physical armor." Quinn laughed. "No, we don't wear that stuff unless we're going into battle."

"Princess Selene was wearing physical armor earlier."

"Yes, and she will likely put *this* over it." Quinn touched his chest and withdrew a type of core Callum hadn't seen before. "Here. Take a look for yourself."

Armorcore of the Lakestorm Leviathan
Type: Support
Grade: Common Wearable
Infusion Requirements for Grade Increase:
1/10 Water Affinity Shards
0/5 Light Affinity Shards
3/10 Resilience Shards
Affinity Requirements: Light or Water

Effect: *Made of hardened mana harvested from the aetherbeasts of the Deepsea Lakes, the Armorcore of Lakestorm Leviathan provides instant protection.*

"You can borrow this for the Entry Duels," Quinn said. "Just give it back to me once you're finished."

"What is it exactly?"

<I'm wondering the same thing. This wasn't something I remember having in your forefather's time.>

Callum noted what Fen said as Quinn spoke again, "The armor is essentially a shell of extremely dense water and light mana. When you call upon the core, it shapes the mana into the appearance of armor and can take a certain amount of punishment before it fades. It's *technically* not a replacement for real armor, but these kinds of cores can be truly helpful in a pinch, not to mention augment proper armor drastically. I'd normally say to try out the core here and see if it's a good fit, but that kind of spellwork is . . . frowned upon out in the open. Makes people nervous, you see."

"Quinn, I really appreciate your help, but . . ." Callum said as he searched for a way to reply to the man. ". . . you really don't have to. We just met and—"

"Oh please, it's fine," the other man said, waving away Callum's concerns. "For one thing, I don't mind at all, and for the other, it pays to have friends when you're in college. Or so I've been told. What better friend to make than someone who bears the name of the Demonslayer? If nothing else, it's good karma."

"I, uh, well," Callum started to reply before simply nodding in response, deciding to take Quinn's help for what it was. "Thank you."

"Not a problem at all." Quinn replied with a smile. "Now, things you should know. Because the core is still a relatively low grade, it will only be able to absorb a handful of strikes. It should stand up to about five relatively weak hits, or fewer strong ones. Moreover, if the armor is nearly spent, or you decide to do something truly foolish, like stand headfirst in front of a runaway cart, the armor will only blunt whatever is about to strike you, not stop it."

"I understand," Callum said, the explanation making perfect sense to him. "And what happens when it breaks?"

"In the case of this Armorcore specifically?" Quinn clarified. "It shatters. A bit dramatically, I might add. But it otherwise fades away harmlessly to both you and any of your opponents. Mind you, other Armorcores have different effects, so don't expect the same thing to happen should you find yourself up against one."

<Hmm. If what he says is true, then you need to get your own Armorcore as soon as possible,> Fen mused privately as Callum nodded and took the offered core from Quinn. *<It would be extremely helpful.>*

"That is good to know, I'll make sure to remember it," Callum replied to Quinn, feeling a rush of energy surge into him as he pressed the core into his chest and felt it meld into him. "Thanks. I really appreciate it, and the advice."

"Not a problem. We're almost at the Aeternal Tabula. Actually, you should be able to see it from here." Quinn gestured to a building ahead, one with a spiraled outer frame over dark stone that reflected everything around it like a mirror. "Good luck, Callum."

Callum watched him walk away. *<I still don't know anything about the rankings.>*

<I guess there is only one way we can find out . . .>

Callum looked up at a doorway cut into the stone and marked by a set of wide, jet-black steps made of the same reflective material as the outer walls. *<You're probably right.>*

Callum entered the Aeternal Tabula to find a pair of female students standing as if they were at attention, their hands behind their backs, both in long robes that draped to the ground.

The woman on the left spoke. "Your name?"

"Callum Stross."

She remained at attention as something flashed across her blue eyes. "This way."

The woman stepped aside and motioned to another door. She followed Callum through it, the two entering a room that resembled a small amphitheater with dark walls. A cylinder of light cut through the middle of the space and formed a pillar over a person hovering in the air, their legs crossed beneath their body.

Callum didn't know what to make of the person, whose facial features changed every few seconds from man to woman. They trembled slightly, yet they maintained a strict posture.

"This is the Great College's Soul Pythia," the woman said. "You may call her Mastress Lucerne. Please summon your aetherbeast now."

Fen appeared and the attendant tilted her head a bit as she took in the Radiant Fox. "I will let Mastress Lucerne take it from here." She bowed slightly and departed, leaving Callum with the woman whose face kept changing.

Callum watched for a moment, unsure of what to make of her constantly shifting features.

"Hello, Mastress," Fen said as he sat beside Callum. "We are here for our test."

The woman lowered her chin slightly to take him in. As she did, a beard traced across her face, her visage now that of a grizzled warrior. It changed again, settling on a woman with fair features and blonde hair like the two attendants.

"You are Callum Stross, descendant of the Demonslayer, and you," she told Fen, "are a Radiant Fox."

"That is correct," Fen told her.

"There aren't many of you."

"I would hope not."

"Right," she said as she looked him over once more. "You are here to have to be tested through the Attribute Trials. If you use Soul Sense right now, you will notice that your Soul Heart Rank is listed as Rankas Initiate. At this Rank, you are able to have six Powercores and one Aethercore. You will learn more about what to expect at each Rank later. The first test will be your Might and Vigor attributes, which are currently listed at four and three respectively and without melding. The second test will be on your Deftness and Resilience, which are both at three. This is the same for the final test on your Regeneration and Mind, also listed at three without melding."

"And then?" Callum asked her, still dazzled by the woman's strange appearance.

"You will be given a percentage on each of these attributes within their sets, each will be ranked, and the combination of these rankings will give us an overall rank that will be compared to your Entry Duels performance to decide on your entry into the Great College."

"So I could fail," Callum said under his breath.

Mastress Lucerne moved on without answering the question. "Are you prepared to begin the Might and Vigor Trial?"

"Here?" Callum looked around at the empty space. Beyond the outer seating and the calm of light coming in from the ceiling, there was nothing in the vicinity, and certainly nothing to test him.

"Aside from the Aeternal Tabula being a World Ledger, this building and the magitek that went into it allow for wondrous things, which includes portals to other locations. Please, take a seat. I will replenish Mana Reserves to their full capacity, and we will begin the first trial. With each trial, you will be ranked on a scale of F to S, with S1 being the highest ranking you can achieve, and F3 being the lowest."

"Understood."

"After each trial, I will tell you your ranking. At the end, I will compile all of your rankings to give you an overall rank. Nod if you understand, and please take a seat."

He sat and everything around Callum flashed.

His energy skyrocketed and settled. As his mind processed how quickly his power had shifted, his eyes tried to make sense of the newfound space. He was in the same large room of the Aeternal Tabula, he was certain of it, yet it seemed vast, like it had no end.

His eyes settled on a massive boulder where Mastress Lucerne had just been hovering.

"Callum Stross," said the woman, her voice radiating all around him now. "Your first task is to move the boulder into the circle. Good luck."

Callum looked from the enormous rock, which was easily his height, to a large circle carved into the ground about thirty feet beyond it.

Move it? How?

He placed his hands on the rock and put everything he had into his back legs. Callum pushed with all his might, even if it seemed like he was trying to shove a solid wall. He pushed until it became abundantly clear that he wasn't going to be able to move the boulder on his own.

"We need to Meld," he told Fen. "We can do it together, I'm certain of it. When we Meld, my strength doubles."

Light flashed all around Callum as the fox jumped into him, the two instantly melding.

Callum couldn't help but revel in the strength that the transformation brought, finding that he had missed the feeling in the short time since his last meld. Breathing out slowly, he looked down at his hands, which now bore Fen's familiar claws.

<*Well?*> Fen asked.

Callum had to do this right.

He had to prove he had what it took to enter the Great College.

Fen had returned seemingly from the dead, and they needed to access the Archive of Destiny. *I just need to move the rock*, Callum thought as he shouldered into the huge stone with newfound determination.

The boulder shifted as he put all his melded strength behind. It scraped against the ground, Callum putting even more force behind it. He pushed even harder, picking up his pace, ignoring the burning sensation in his calves.

<*Keep going!*>

Fen's voice was strained, a constant reminder of the Corruption that still plagued the fox.

Callum kept pushing the enormous boulder until he became numb to the process.

He was close.

His target was ahead and he would make it out of sheer strength and willpower. Even with the augmented strength from Fen, he could feel the strain, he knew that something of this size had likely challenged most of the intakes.

Or so he assumed.

Callum really had no idea. He had met two so far, Selene with her pacted bear and Quinn with his pacted cat.

Another thought came to him as he neared his target: *Are there other ways to do this? I defaulted to sheer strength. How else could I have moved it?*

With a final breath out, Callum breached the circle. He pushed the boulder inside and took a step back as Fen's powers faded.

He was covered in sweat now, his calves and thigh muscles firing. Callum looked up just as Mastress Lucerne spoke again, her voice all around him like it was being carried on a breeze: "The next part of this trial will begin now."

Let's do this, Callum thought as the landscape before him morphed.

The boulder faded and the ground pulled back like a rumpled sheet to create a vertical incline, one that soon resembled the slope of an impossibly tall mountain.

Mastress Lucerne's voice echoed all around him: "Your next goal is to get to the top of this mountain. You will be timed. Begin . . . *now*."

"It already started?" Callum asked, still catching his breath from moving the boulder.

<Let's go. We can Meld again. Or . . . > Fen appeared and stared up at the incredible climb. "There may be obstacles," he finally said. "Best to take it on foot first."

"Got it!" Callum began his climb as Fen returned to him. *How far, no, how high up is it? Is there a way to reach the top faster?*

He glanced around, yet all he could see was similar terrain.

Callum nearly slipped. He caught himself and continued his climb up the mountain, having to press his hands against the tops of his knees at certain points as his hike continued. He reached a point where the only way to progress would be to jump, grab onto a ledge, and pull himself up.

<Can you manage it without melding?>

<I think so,> Callum told the fox after he checked yet again to see if there was an easier way to make it to the top. Callum suspected being able to fly would make the challenge much easier. He had seen archmages in the

village do something like it before. And there had been the rare occasion where they passed over his family fields like shooting stars.

Without another option, Callum sent his power into his feet and jumped.

He grabbed the ledge and pulled himself up onto it.

<Not bad. But I fear we are just getting started.>

Damn it, how long has it been since we started? Am I already behind? Callum asked himself as he pressed on. He still had no sense of how high he would have to climb. There were no indications, no other mountains around him, no way to gauge how far he had gone.

Only that his journey seemed endless.

<We just have to keep going,> Fen said a few minutes later as Callum paused to catch his breath. All the farm work Callum did had certainly kept him fit, but this was a trial that was a world of difference from his life, especially once he saw that he would need to leap across a gorge to continue.

<I'm going to need you for this one,> he told Fen as he looked at the gap, finding it too wide for comfort.

<A good idea.>

The two quickly melded, and as they did Callum glanced back to the other side of the gorge. With Fen's power, he launched himself into the air and nailed his landing.

Callum peered ahead. *<We've got this,>* he said as Fen's power left him.

His next step caused him to tremble. Callum suddenly felt lightheaded, like he wasn't getting enough oxygen. He took a few deep breaths, his lungs never able to fill. *What's going on?*

<Are you alright?>

<I think the air is getting thinner,> he told Fen.

<Like a real mountain. But this isn't real. Or? I cannot tell. Truly remarkable.>

Callum sucked in a deep breath and took another step forward.

<Your forefather would have been enthralled to see where humanity has taken the act of aetherforging. Who knew an Armorcore could exist? Who knew that magitek could be capable of something like this if given the correct guide?>

<You mean Mastress Lucerne.>

<Precisely.>

Callum reached the next obstacle. He would need to reach the ledge above, nearly twenty feet up by his estimates. "There's no way." He moved to the right until he saw a better path, which would force him to leap over a horizontal break in the rocks that spanned six feet. "Do you think we can make it?"

<I know we can.>

Once melded, Callum took a few steps back and charged forward. He hurled himself into the air and landed as stones crumbled beneath his feet. He pressed on, jogging as lightly as he could until the stones stopped falling.

"That was unexpected," he said with a huff, his breathing starting to get truly labored.

It means that we are really starting to run out of time, he realized as he forced himself to push on. *Just have to keep moving.*

Of course, no sooner did that thought cross his mind, than he felt the ground beneath his feet rumble ominously.

He looked ahead just as Fen's power rushed to him. Callum dove to the right to avoid a tumbling boulder, one about the same size as the stone he had moved earlier.

"Oh, shit," Callum whispered as his heart settled. He kept his head up and continued his climb in anticipation of more boulders.

Another boulder came tumbling toward them, Callum just barely able to get out of the way. He noticed on the third boulder that they were defying physical conventions, the boulders appearing out of thin air and moving at speeds that made it impossible to tell how quickly they were going. Each boulder was faster than the last, and some of them changed their trajectory at the last moment.

He stayed melded to Fen, even if he could sense his power waning. It wasn't just the altitude or the way his muscles complained at his constant ascent. It was deeper, Callum noticing exactly where the exhaustion was coming from.

And that was his core.

Callum was certain of it. He could almost see his core depleting of mana as he reached another ledge and pulled himself up.

<Callum, focus!>

Callum shifted to the left just as a boulder crushed the ledge he had just hung from, bits of rock scattering all around him.

"Whew," he said, yet again wiping sweat as he pushed on relentlessly toward the top of the seemingly endless mountain ahead of him, his breaths soon becoming painful.

Every intake at this point barely filled his lungs, and when he did get a satisfactory breath, it felt as if he were inhaling needles.

"Come on," he whispered to himself as he put one foot in front of the other. "Come on."

The two words became his mantra as he trudged ahead. He soon encountered a pair of tumbling boulders, and Callum was forced to turn his body to the side to fit into a narrow space between them.

He sucked in a wheezy breath. "I hope . . . we're close."

Another horizontal ledge, followed by a vertical jump coupled with a set of even larger boulders finally brought Callum to his knees.

He couldn't walk any longer, so he crawled.

His eyes were trained on what he prayed was the summit, and Callum was crawling onward as Fen shouted encouragements in his head.

<We can do this,> Fen told him repeatedly, the Radiant Fox fighting through his own exhaustion. *<Don't give up now!>*

Then, a light.

Then, a flat surface, the first in what felt like hours.

Everything faded.

Callum found himself seated in the Aeternal Tabula, Mastress Lucerne hovering before him.

Gone were the slopes around him, the rocks at his feet, the impossible climb replaced by the circular room with limited seating and a pillar of light shining on the Soul Pythia. Even his exhaustion had waned.

Mastress Lucerne spoke and, as the words left her lips, Callum felt instantly rejuvenated, all the pain, exhaustion, and everything that he had felt weighing him down during his ascent simply being wiped away as if it had never been there in the first place. "Your time to complete the Might and Vigor Trial is twenty-nine minutes and sixteen seconds. Your Might has been ranked B1, the eighty-third percentile and your Vigor at C3, the seventy-second percentile. Next, your Deftness and Resilience attributes will be tested simultaneously. Good luck, Callum Stross."

CHAPTER 16

The importance of testing a potential student's base attributes lies in not only measuring their potential but understanding their character. Strength without control, endurance without purpose, or intellect without focus—true mastery begins with knowing where one stands.

—A quote from *My Time at the Great College: A Memoir* by Sir Gideon Coldwell, Master Channeler, Clergo

Everything around Callum shifted violently, the air twisting and warming as he was deposited into a cavernous space bathed in an eerie glow. Purple flames flickered along the walls, their light casting jagged shadows that danced along uneven stone. The ground beneath him was uneven, a mixture of stone and debris. He tensed, whispering to himself as he peered ahead into the dark. "Where . . . ?"

Mastress Lucerne's voice filled the chamber: "Your next task is to make it to the end of the labyrinth. You will be timed."

"I guess there is only one way—" Callum took a step forward and a spear fired out of the wall, passing directly over his head.

<That was clearly a warning. We should meld.>

"Let's do it," Callum said as he felt Fen's power spread over him. He was about to move on when he abruptly stopped, remembering something. "We can use the Armorcore that Quinn gave us here. Worst case . . . it'll save us from an unlucky hit."

<Good idea,> Fen replied, a note of approval flowing through their bond. *<I completely forgot about it after our last trial . . . We are fortunate that Mastress Lucerne restored our power. I can't imagine needing to press on after it.>*

"Neither could I," Callum muttered as he invoked the Armorcore of the Lakestorm Leviathan by touching his chest.

The hardened mana armor rippled over his form, stopping just before his clawed fingers. *Whoa . . .* Callum ran his hands over the armor, which was made of overlapping plates cast in a deep blue. The lamellar armor glimmered with light, and the more he stared at it, the more its magical nature became apparent as Callum noticed it was semitranslucent and that he could easily wear additional protection beneath the Armorcore.

He crept forward, scanning the wall for more traps. One of the stranger things about the hardened mana armor was that he couldn't feel it. It had no real weight to it, yet it appeared as if it should be bulky.

Callum was glad he wore it after he stepped on a tile and darts fired out of the walls. He moved to avoid them, the armor doing the rest as he raced forward to reach a pair of swinging blades attached to chains that dropped from the ceiling.

They swung in front of him, returned to the ceiling, and came down again. Another set of blades dropped and performed the same maneuver, moving in a pendulum-like motion. These were just a few feet beyond the first pair, the blades cleaving through the air just a hair slower than the first.

"Could we break them?" Callum asked as a third pair of blades dropped, followed by a fourth.

<We could certainly try. Use your lance.>

He conjured the lance, which sparked with energy as he stepped back.

Callum threw it at the first chain. Bright light filled the space as his mana lance fizzled out. The blades kept swinging as more were released, the new pairs even closer to one another than the first four.

The rhythmic swish and the soft clang of blades soon filled the air as they swung in hypnotic arcs, their polished surfaces reflecting deadly glints of light that made it harder to gauge how close they were to one another.

Focus on one at a time, Callum thought, which had been advice his father had given him frequently when he was first learning to harvest efficiently. He hadn't thought about that advice in a long time, but it came to him now as he stepped past the first set of swinging blades and reached the next one.

<Do you think you have it?>

"I do." He watched as the second set of blades moved at a different pace than the first. Callum passed through to the third pair, knowing it would become trickier as the blades grew closer to one another.

Sidestepping more swinging blades, Callum stopped in front of the fourth set with even more determination.

<Focus . . .>

What lay before him, if he could make it into the Great College, was an incredible opportunity, and that was without understanding the reason for Fen's return.

I can do it, Callum thought as he rushed ahead, able to clear three more sets of cleaving blades before coming to a halt in front of the last pair.

He ignored the swishing sound behind him and the way his heart beat rapidly in his chest as he examined the movement of the final blades. Fen said something to him, but Callum could barely hear the Radiant Fox, once again focused.

He watched the oscillating blades swing toward one another, nearly touch, return to the ceiling, and then come back around.

There was little room for error.

Here's my chance! Callum pressed off his heels as he dove forward and rolled through the cleaving blades. He cleared them and he pressed onward, deeper into the chamber lit by purple light as the blades continued to zip past one another behind him.

<Careful!> Fen shouted as cracks abruptly started to form on the ground, quickly rippling forward. Callum jumped just in time as the stone beneath his feet gave way. He landed and charged, his speed augmented by melding with Fen.

Callum leaped into the next chamber, the space circular in nature and oppressing with its low walls. He was immediately met by shadowy, snake-like monsters with horned skulls for heads. He tore into them without question, his melded claws able to shred their bodies in half, spraying blackened mana into the air as he fought his way deeper into the new space.

He conjured his lance and drove this through three of the imps, the magical nature of his weapon causing their demonic bodies to sizzle, the creatures screeching in agony. He followed this up by swiveling around and hitting an incoming pair with Zephyr Strike, which shredded their bodies, plastering the wall with dark viscera.

They soon overwhelmed him, all jumping for Callum at once. The onslaught sent him into a frenzy that was partially fueled by Fen as they beat back the horde. Callum was glad for the armor, but he was also noticing that it was starting to crack.

Please don't break, he thought as he swatted at another corrupted monster.

Regardless, he kept up his momentum, the strikes from the imps' tails and claws clinking off his armor as he fought on. He finally killed the last two using his lance.

Callum nearly fell to his knees, rasping, but continued on.

I have to keep going, he thought as he started to stagger onward, well-aware that he was being timed. But just as that thought was crossing his mind, he heard Fen's voice.

<*Don't rush ahead until you've at least caught your breath,*> he said, his words prompting Callum to stop cold. <*We survived one battle here, and surely another awaits us ahead. There is no sense for us to rush ahead desperately and arrive with no ability to take on what's next.*>

<*R—right, that . . . that makes sense.*> Callum replied as he took in another heaving breath and allowed himself a few seconds for his heart to slow its pounding. Then, only when he felt truly stable, he moved on into a large, amphitheater-sized room with a narrow path crossing it. He took the narrow path with extreme caution, all but expecting the ground to give way. It never did.

His lungs filled with air as he reached a new chamber, where channels were scattered across the ground next to stones that looked like they would slot perfectly into the grooves.

<*Easy enough,*> Fen said before he gasped in Callum's head.

Callum felt all of the mana leave him, as if his core were shriveling up.

Callum reeled at the sudden loss of power. Something had siphoned the mana out of the room, he was certain of it.

Which means I'm supposed to do this one on my own, he surmised as Fen's voice became so dim he could no longer hear it.

He jumped to the ground, flat on his belly as sharp objects fired out of the wall.

Without Fen's boost in power, he had to use his own strength to slot the stones into the correct grooves, each of which were about the size of a chair. Even worse, he had to do so while being fired upon by projectiles. Luckily, the stones provided cover and Callum was able to push his back into them, power coming from his legs.

A quick smile appeared on his face as he remembered a time on the farm when he had been forced to do something similar helping his father move stacks of wheat.

This certainly isn't easier, but it is definitely motivating me to finish the job, he thought as he fused the last stone into its proper groove.

Callum ducked into the next chamber as more of the sharp projectiles flew overhead.

<*I'm back!*>

<*What was that?*> he asked Fen.

<*Some sort of mana negation. Remember, this trial is testing your Deftness and Resilience, and I'm going to assume that both played a part in what you just did.*>

With a quick exhale he moved on, once again melding with Fen.

Callum entered a narrow space with a low ceiling, forcing him to crouch, and preventing any chance he would get to see what was in the next chamber. "Whoa!" he shouted as a great flame of mana spread into the space, painting the inner walls black.

Rather than retreat, Callum rushed ahead, bursting into the next chamber to find a cloaked elemental, the being twice his size with flames crawling up its arms.

A flash of wind blew it back into a wall, preventing the mana elemental from releasing more flames. Callum jumped toward it and conjured his lance in the hope that he would be able to spear it as he had done the imps.

But the mana elemental was much faster than Callum's previous opponents. The elemental whipped around the room, a trail of fire in its wake as it appeared behind him, where it delivered a slash that *shattered* Callum's hardened mana armor as he slammed against the ground.

Callum spun to the right and leaped back to his feet.

He jumped to avoid a fiery lash from the mana elemental and dove forward once the elemental tried again. Then he rolled, smacked into the wall, swiveled, and went for another lance.

<*Good!*> Fen shouted as the lance managed to clip the mana elemental in the shoulder, staggering their opponent. Fen seemed to fully possess Callum as the young man rushed forward and delivered a series of mana-charged claws that cut through the elemental.

The ground shifted to a forty-five-degree angle as the battlefield changed, Callum stumbling backward and the mana elemental able to regroup now that it had the higher ground. *Wasn't expecting that*, Callum thought as he hit it with another blast of wind.

A sudden tenseness came coupled with the ground shifting to the right, throwing Callum and the elemental off-balance. He pushed from the wall, jumped, and turned to deliver a devastating blow augmented by Fen directly to his opponent's cloaked face.

The mana elemental staggered backward. But then his opponent's shoulders flared as it began to split, two skeletal creatures made of fire ripping themselves from its form.

The first came for Callum quickly.

He dodged right and delivered a strike that dislodged a portion of the mana monster's spine. Callum jumped onto its body as it fell and lunged to the next skeletal elemental, which struck him with a bolt of fire.

It burned worse than fire, Callum shrieking as he hit the ground and rolled, hoping to put it out.

<Focus!> Fen shouted. <We can survive this!>

Callum did his best to ignore the burning sensation as he pushed himself back up.

He tried not to look down at his arms, fearing the worst. With everything he could possibly muster, Callum summoned a lance and thrust it forward just as the skeletal elemental came at him with its fists blazing with fire.

Callum jabbed the lance into his opponent and tossed its body to the side. He staggered onward, each step a battle against his failing strength, his body trembling from exhaustion. A shaky breath did little to brace his mind for what lay around as everything around him darkened, threatening to pull Callum under.

But instead of more obstacles he was greeted by a blazing light, suddenly back in the Aeternal Tabula, seated before Mastress Lucerne as if nothing had happened.

He looked up the Great College's Soul Pythia, who hovered before him.

She spoke after a momentary pause: "Your time to complete the Deftness and Agility Trial is fourteen minutes and twenty-one seconds. Your Deftness has been ranked C3, the sixty-eighth percentile and your Resilience at D1, the fifty-ninth percentile. Next, your Mind and Regeneration attributes will be tested simultaneously. For the final challenge, your Soul Sense will be temporarily reduced to Heavily Injured and your Mana Reserves to a critical state known as Hollowing. This won't be pleasant, but have no fear, it won't last long."

Callum gasped as he felt his core constrict.

His energy levels instantly fell away, and his shoulders slouched forward.

Fen's voice felt more distant now, the fox barely audible.

Callum tried for a deep breath, hoping this would bring some power back to him. When this didn't work, he looked up at Mastress Lucerne with as much determination and defiance as he could muster. "Ready," he managed to say.

The room around him was stripped away. Callum got to his feet in the middle of a field of wheat, not far from the East Manor.

How? He thought as a great aetherstorm appeared in the sky above.

Lightning tore the dark clouds apart as the storm rolled in, the wheat stripped from their stocks as they whipped all around him. Callum tried to get his bearings. He felt as if he hadn't eaten or slept in days, his power levels at an all-time low.

Callum's temples pulsed. It wasn't the same exhaustion he had felt in the previous trial—it was a crushing mental fatigue, as if his power had been hollowed out of his very essence, his mind raw and fragile.

<Focus on your core!>

"Like meditation? How am I supposed to meditate in the middle of an aetherstorm?"

<You must endure, Callum!>

Callum dropped. He brought his legs back into a seated position, just as he had seen from Mastress Lucerne. Eyes clenched shut, Callum lowered his chin and focused on his core. He tried to visualize an orb of power, and he imagined himself absorbing mana with it. Callum knew if he could pull this off with good marks, it would help him in the coming Entry Duel, which would pit him against another student.

Swallowing the exhaustion that rippled through him, ignoring the intense mana wind that constantly berated him, Callum steadied his breathing until he sensed a subtle change deep within. The sensation was somewhere between elation and the buzz he felt after waking up from a good rest.

He did this for another few excruciating minutes, minutes in which the world around him felt as if it would come apart at the seams as the aetherstorm touched down. Callum passed out, and once he came awake again he found Fen crouched before him.

<You did what you could,> Fen said.

Callum used Soul Sense to see that he was Recovering. He was about to relay this fact to Fen when he heard a bloodcurdling scream. He jumped to his feet and turned toward his home just as the aetherstorm ripped through the barn.

The scream sounded off again as he caught a man running toward his family home, trying to escape the storm. Callum felt all the blood drain from his body as he recognized his father's gait, the way the man ran distinct due to an injury he had suffered when he was about Callum's age.

<No!> Fen shouted as Callum staggered forward.

"It's my father—"

<This isn't real. It's a trick! You should get to safety.>

"I have to help him."

<No, you don't.>

"I have all this power," Callum said as he looked down at his own palms, which radiated with an intensely dark mana. "I have to."

<It's an illusion. They're testing you!>

Callum watched his father run into the house. He took off and fell over the hand grip of an overturned wheelbarrow. He hit the ground and pushed himself up.

<Callum, this is an illusion!> Fen cried in his head.

"No," Callum whispered as the aetherstorm struck his home. *No!* Angry rain lashed all around him and lightning riddled the sky with white-purple flashes, and Callum gaped in horror as the roof was ripped off his home, the wood stripped from the walls as the frame came tumbling down.

This isn't real.

And with those words whispered somewhere at the back of his desperate and increasingly broken mind, Callum turned away from the storm.

The East Manor.

There was a golden glow to it now, something that told him it was the way forward.

He didn't know how he knew this, but he moved toward it anyway, careful of his footwork this time as the wind raged around him. He was beaten back by hail and more sharp droplets of rain. Lightning hit a portion of the overgrown field to his right, igniting it in flames.

Even with the rain and the hail, the fire grew.

It spread all around Callum as he used every last bit of strength he had to race toward the East Manor. He could feel the heat now mixed with blasts of cold wind from the aetherstorm.

He turned only once, and in doing so saw a phenomenon he had never seen before as a firestorm took shape in the form of a mini tornado, one fueled by both flames and bolts of purple lightning.

It grew closer, to the point that the flames were licking at Callum's heels as he continued his epic sprint toward the East Manor.

"Meld!" he shouted to Fen.

<You hardly have any power!>

"Meld and jump!" Callum said through quick breaths as the flames grew closer.

An overwhelming sense of power rushed over him and he sprang toward the open doorway, his dive into the East Manor knocking the wind out of him as he hit the ground on his stomach, arms spread out.

Then darkness, followed by a flash.

Yet again, Callum was seated before Mastress Lucerne, the Soul Pythia hovering in a meditative posture, her facial features changing every few seconds. In the moment it took her to speak, Callum caught his breath. He knew that what had just happened wasn't real, yet it felt real, and his heart beat like it was real.

He clenched his eyes shut for a moment as the image of his father being crushed by the aetherstorm came to him.

It was an illusion, he reminded himself.

Mastress Lucerne, whose facial features shifted and settled again, lowered to the ground and stood. She motioned for Callum to do the same. "Your Mind has been ranked D2, the fifty-fifth percentile and your Regeneration at D3, the fifty-eighth percentile. Here are your full rankings for the Attribute Trials." A slate floated over to him, with the information etched into it:

Might: (B1)
Deftness: (C3)
Vigor: (B3)
Resilience: (D1)
Regeneration: (D1)
Mind: (D2)

"Our best candidates rank A1 to A3, and most fall from B1 to B3. Your overall ranking is C2, which means you will need to perform well in your Entry Duels. I'm afraid the institute doesn't accept students ranked D1 or below." Mastress Lucerne offered him an uncertain smile. "Good luck, Callum Stross. You may proceed to the Ordelarium."

CHAPTER 17

Royal Decree: By the authority of His Lordship, the Honorable and Esteemed King Morninglade, Sovereign of the Valestra Kingdom, and in accordance with the Edict of Year 500, the use, creation, or trade of Demoncores remains strictly outlawed within the borders of the kingdom.

—Edict of Year 500

Callum tuned back into Fen once he left the Aeternal Tabula. The Attribute Trials had dazed him to the point that he found it hard to focus. He forced himself to stand there for a moment to take in the sprawling grounds of the Great College.

What just happened? He thought as he rubbed the back of his head. He used Soul Sense to confirm that Mastress Lucerne had replenished his mana.

"Sorry," he finally told Fen. "I just wish I could have done better."

<*It's fine. I didn't expect any of that. And truly, Callum, your strength saved us back there. Still, we are only one ranking away from reaching the cut-off . . .*>

"I know, I know. I can't go below C3."

A grimace formed on his face. Getting anything below a C3 rank would give him an average *below* passing standards . . .

<*You won't go below. That same determination will surely aid us in the Entry Duels. I'm sure of it.*>

The Ordelarium wasn't hard to find. Visible across a large courtyard, the place was clearly designed for combat trials, the building shaped into a sphere that almost made it appear as if it were magitek. The polished exterior reflected the surrounding courtyard like a distorted mirror, and Callum was unable to see inside.

Callum started on the cobblestone path connecting the building to the Aeternal Tabula.

"Things really weren't looking good on that last challenge," he said, recalling how he had been transported back to his family farm, faced an aetherstorm, and was convinced his father was in distress.

<That's what they're for and, honestly, I'm amazed at the ways they have used mana since my time. Truly. Let's get to the Ordelarium and be done with it. We might even make it back in time to have a celebratory meal with Telluride. There is more I would like to discuss about sundering with him. I have a question I should have asked yesterday when he was going over shards with us.>

"Yeah? What's that?" Callum asked as he turned in the direction of the Ordelarium.

<He explained what to do once we get shards.>

"Store them in the appropriate cores."

<Yes. And only a shardcrafter can break a core down into its component shards through sundering. That is, until we reach a higher level. But I'm wondering if there is a way to use a shard that we've already stored in a core.>

"Wouldn't that be the same as breaking it down?"

<Likely. It could have helped us in the Attribute Trials, though. If, for example, we had been able to use our Mind Shard, or perhaps a Might Shard. But you are probably right. Just another reason to increase our Stage so we can sunder cores ourselves.>

"That's assuming that the tests would have even allowed us to use a shard that way in the first place," Callum said as he approached the front steps of the Ordelarium. He paused for a moment, watching as the Great College's vertical banners, all vermillion, beat in the wind. Yet again, he caught sight of the Second Heart of Creation in the distance, a constant reminder of the battle his forefather had waged, and its aftermath.

He was just about to step in when Quinn exited, a flash of excitement suddenly in his eyes upon seeing Callum. "How did it go?"

"It went," was all he could really say. *Then again, I hardly know what I'm doing.*

"Your ranking?"

"C2 rank."

Quinn puffed his cheeks out. "That's close. I won't lie to you there."

"What about you?"

"Attribute Trials, B1. Entry Duels haven't been announced yet." Quinn had described his summon as an overweight cat, but he clearly had something going on. He had done much better than Callum in the Attribute Trials.

"We trained for this, you know," Quinn said once he registered the concerned look on Callum's face. "I'm guessing you haven't had your Soul Sense tested before, have you?"

"I just learned that these tests existed an hour ago. Or maybe less? It's hard to gauge time in the Aeternal Tabula."

Quinn laughed nervously. "It sure is. You know, before you go into the Ordelarium, you should see something. It isn't far from here."

"See what?"

"The statue of the guy you're named after, the Demonslayer. Come on."

<I certainly want to see this!>

"Shouldn't I be—" Callum motioned to the Ordelarium's open doorway.

"Don't worry," Quinn told him, "they haven't started yet, and this will only take a few minutes, promise."

Callum joined Quinn as another question came to him. "You said earlier that some people wait until the last day to do their Entry Duels."

"Correct. It's more of a self-challenge thing. The fights will run from now through the night, so while you're technically at a disadvantage, as long as you can fight, you should be fine. I think. Can you fight?"

"Somewhat, sure," Callum said. He had been in a few fights, like the time he had wrestled with Lander Hayle for stealing one of his father's tools, and another when he took a punch defending a younger boy from a bully. Then there was his mandatory militia training, basic drills and sparring sessions over the last several years that gave him enough confidence to hold his own.

"To be clear: you aren't going to win the Entry Duels or anything. There are people in there that have been training for this their entire lives. You just want to make sure you don't get less than a C3 rank, so it averages with your Attribute Trials ranking and you get into the college. That's all." Quinn guided Callum around a hedge that had seating before it. And there, in the middle of the rest area, they came to a statue. "That's him."

<Oh my . . .> Fen said as Callum looked up at the statue.

It was carved out of a type of gray marble that had weathered over the years, making the original Callum Stross's facial features hard to make out. He was joined by five aetherbeasts. There was a fox around his shoulders, an enormous dragon at the base of the statue, a phoenix, and a wolf. Seated next to him was a gryphon, its majestic wings folded back, a hardened look on its face.

Callum experienced a brief flashback to the Memorycore he had seen as a child, its warmth filling him in a way he didn't expect.

<If only I could remember them,> Fen said as Callum felt a yearning to say something similar.

"The Demonslayer," Quinn said, "your distant relative. Not a bad statue, either."

"Do you happen to know the names of his pacted aetherbeasts?"

"I used to, but it's been a while. I think one was Killeas, I remember that—the gryphon. It used to be inscribed here, but as you can see, time has taken care of that," Quinn said as he swept his hand to the weathered text. "But you could probably find that information at the Great Library once you get access. Anyway, I just thought I would point it out. It's not very far from the Ordelarium, anyway. I guess I should stop holding you up, though. You do have Entry Duels to join. Don't forget to use my armor."

"Thanks again, for that."

"Really, it's not a problem," Quinn told him.

Once Callum was at the Ordelarium, he entered the grand building and approached a registration desk manned by a middle-aged man in armor. A scroll was spread out on the table. The man had the insignia for the royal army pinned to the collar of his undershirt, and he examined the scroll for nearly a minute before finally looking up at Callum. "You are late."

"I just got here."

"Like I said, you are late."

"I mean, I just did my Attribute Trials today, sir," Callum told him. "I arrived in the city yesterday, but the Great College was closed because of some incident."

The man continued to stare up at him with a pair of scorching blue eyes. "What's your name?"

"Callum Stross."

"Heh. In that case, you will enter through that room there—" The man paused as what sounded like an explosion rang out in the room beyond. "As I was saying, you will enter through that room there, and you will place a wristlet on. You have armor? If not, mana armor will be provided for you."

"I have an Armorcore, yes."

"Good, that will work. When you get into the next room, place the wristlet on your nondominant hand. The wristlet will have five bars. If you get struck five times, or take a hit to knock you out, you will lose your duel. You may also technically forfeit your duel, but it's rare that anyone does that, and it's highly frowned upon," he said, his voice almost completely flat as he spoke, having repeated himself time and again. "As for injuries after a bout, don't worry, there are masters there that will be able to heal you. Between duels you will also have your core restored to its current maximum capacity based on your Initiate Rank, which will make sure that each duel is done to the best of both parties' abilities. Any questions?"

"No, I think I got it."

"Good luck. The next round of matches will begin soon."

The next room had a single slab of marble in its center, the walls completely bare. A series of wristlets were arranged on the marble table, their elegant design more fitting for a jewelry store than their current setting. Callum approached the first one, a wristlet with a silver band.

I think they're all the same, he thought as he picked up a wristlet at random and placed it over his arm. It snapped into place and five glowing links appeared. Callum took another look around the empty space and continued through the next door. After traveling down a long hallway, he came to the true interior of the Ordelarium, the space much larger than he expected. There were numerous banners circling the top of the dome. Seated at chairs placed on high pedestals were several masters ready to judge the fights. At the center of the chamber was a large, circular arena, its floor a patchwork of smooth stone.

Callum glanced around at the other students and found Princess Selene, who stood with her head down, eyes locked on the ground. Since he didn't really know any better, Callum approached her. "Hi," he said as he took the space next to the princess.

Her eyes shot open and she turned to him. "Ah, it's you," she said, relaxing to some degree. "You finally made it."

"Yeah," Callum replied, suddenly realizing just *who* he was talking to and what he'd done. "I had to finish my Attribute Trials first. They were . . . something."

Selene immediately winced as Callum finished speaking and a look of sympathy appeared in her eyes. "Oh, that's right, you just got here. They . . . most certainly are."

Callum did a quick head count. There were twenty students, all of whom wore actual armor, ranging from sleek and minimal to heavily plated and ornate. Each suit seemed designed not just for protection but as an extension of its wearer's personality and magical abilities.

He suddenly felt even more out of place, especially when his gaze landed on a young man with dark hair and equally dark armor, its surface polished to a mirrorlike sheen. The armor's shoulder pieces lifted into menacing curved spikes, their edges glowing faintly with a fiery red mana. The young man radiated confidence, standing with an easy posture that belied the deadly aura surrounding him.

The man turned to Callum and his eyes flashed red.

"Don't let him get to you," Princess Selene said as Callum turned his attention back to the front.

"Who is that?" he whispered.

"Draven Blademark, the duke's son." Selene rolled her eyes as she spoke. "Don't let him get under your skin."

"How did his eyes do that?"

"He's a warlock-in-training."

<A what?> Fen nearly shouted in Callum's head. *<A warlock? Here at the Great College?>*

"Warlock?" Callum asked Selene at the unfamiliar word.

"Draven is a Demoncore user. More than that, he has a reputation for trying to intimidate newcomers."

It was the first time Callum had heard of such a thing. "And what is a Demoncore exactly?" He wanted to tell Selene that he had just learned about all of this just a few days ago, but he didn't want to seem too uninformed. "I'm familiar with Aethercores, Powercores, and Armorcores."

"With your lineage, you, of all people, should be familiar with *the* Callum Stross, the Demonslayer. What do you think he was slaying?" She gave him a playful look, one that spawned a grin on his face.

" . . . Demons?"

"Correct, which are demonic aetherbeasts pacted with those in touch with the darker arts, people like warlocks, people who use Demoncores. Draven's family have been pushing for years to legalize the study of these cores arguing that they will help ward off any of the demonic aetherbeasts that have been attacking cities as of late. It gets worse. Last year, the Geshwine Empire legalized the study and usage of Demoncores, meaning we may have a potential enemy that we do not understand on our border in a few years if we don't make efforts to learn now."

"I . . . I didn't know."

"Draven and people like him believe that by *not* using pacted demonic aetherbeasts or Demoncores, we are hurting our chances of understanding enemies who might. It's a sentiment that is gaining traction. It certainly has with my father," she said, a hint of disgust in her voice.

Fen spoke to him: *<The enemies that your forefather fought used demonic aetherbeasts and various Darkcores in the same way we can, only they had a darker aspect to them. Like aetherforged, I suppose the word Darkcore has been changed over time. We absolutely do not want Demoncores, or for that matter, warlocks, here at the college or anywhere in the kingdom. They have a way of corrupting that.>*

"Knowing one's enemy can't be the only reason as to why they would want to experiment with Demoncores," Callum said.

She fixed him with a scrutinizing stare. "Yes. Allegedly, you are able to increase the Grade faster with a Demoncore, if you are tuned into that sort of thing. I'm assuming you aren't because this is the first time you've heard of it."

"I've learned a lot in the last few days," Callum admitted.

A faint smile traced across Princess Selene's face. "I don't think I've ever heard of someone just showing up here without any knowledge of what they're getting into. You didn't go to a preparatory school?"

"No. I'm from Weatherby."

"Weatherby . . ." She squinted for a moment and finally shook her head. "I'm sorry. Is that on the border somewhere?" Selene tilted her head, as if something was speaking privately to her.

It must be her aetherbeast, Callum thought as she nodded and spoke again:

"Ah, yes, near the lands of Antiqua. I should know better. I really should. I may have to go there in the coming weeks. And I know that sounds disrespectful, the princess asking where your town is, but really—"

"It's more of a village, but that's fine. How are Demoncores formed? Can you tell me more about that?"

"Have you encountered Corruption?"

He nodded.

"Then you know more about Demoncores than you think. Corruption is the result of mana that has taken on darker aspects. Our aetherbeasts are able to clean it and convert it to mana that can augment our own reserves. If there's too much of it in the area, however, it can cause issues for an aetherbeast."

That would explain Fen's illness, Callum thought. "And to cure it? If an aetherbeast is afflicted with Corruption, then what?"

"I have read that there are certain ways to handle it, and if the aetherbeast is cared for, any residuals from the Corruption can vanish over time. This is nice, you know."

"What is?" Callum asked her.

"Talking."

"You don't normally . . . talk?"

"I do. But most of my days are spent with royal attendants, meeting dignitaries, and in my own head because, as you can imagine, all of that grows tiring after a while."

"That makes sense."

"If I'm being honest with you, the casual conversation we're having at this very moment is the first I've had in ages. I don't normally speak to people, and when I do, there are barriers involved." She shrugged nervously as she locked eyes with a tall and very tan woman who seemed hesitant to approach. "If I say anything that seems rude, I apologize."

"It's fine."

"I'm adjusting."

"I am too."

"Then we have something in common, Callum Stross. I wish you success in your Entry Duels."

"And the same for you," Callum replied, more out of politeness than any doubt that Selene would be able to handle herself.

The students grew quiet as a door on the opposite side of the arena opened. A group of men and women entered wearing black robes beneath black overcoats. The lapels of their overcoats were crafted from embroidered leather and while the men wore thick ties, the women wore brooches featuring dark jewels.

A man with a nicely trimmed white beard stepped forward, one hand behind his back and the other on a scepter. "For those of you who I've yet to become acquainted with, I am Master Patrjohn Granadam, the dean of the Great College. We hold Entry Duels each day during the entry trials. If you are here, you've already had your powers tested, and you are awaiting your official ranking. We will begin in five minutes. Master Cruedark, please announce our first candidates."

He stepped aside to allow a huge man to come forward.

Master Cruedark had black hair and a thick beard, his towering frame the closest thing Callum had ever seen to an actual giant. With massive, broad shoulders, and a battle-hardened face, he radiated strength and intimidation. He placed his big hands behind his back and spoke. "Callum Stross and Victrin Righexa. You will begin the trials. Please take your positions. The first to receive five strikes or be unable to continue loses."

Two sigils formed across from one another, their brightness waning as the masters all moved to their seats, leaving Master Cruedark standing alone before everyone.

"Well?" he asked when neither Callum, nor Victrin, a man with red hair, responded. "Please, come forward."

Callum and Victrin exchanged glances and stepped forward in the center of the Ordelarium. As Callum passed Princess Selene, she reached out to nudge him, whispering. "You've got this!"

As he took his place across from Victrin, completely uncertain about what to expect, Callum couldn't help but feel a boost from the princess's encouragement.

<We don't know what he has pacted with; nor does he know the same about us,> Fen said to Callum as he readied himself for the duel. *<Because*

of that, we should try to end this as quickly as possible and get our five strikes on him as soon as the bout starts.>

<Zephyr Strike, followed by my Luminous Lance? That should stagger him. We move in for the kill after that with our claws. As quick as possible. If you have to use our claws with range, do that as well.>

<Good plan.>

Callum nodded, and he noticed that Victrin did as well, and recognized that the man was also likely receiving instruction from his pacted aetherbeast. As they stood there waiting for a few more students to file in, Callum came to understand something else about their opening match: after their battle, people would likely know what they were pacted with. Same with the matches to follow. This meant he would be able to go into the second round more aware of what he was up against, which could give him an edge.

Until then, it was a battle against the unknown.

I just need to make it through Victrin.

A quick glance to his right and he caught Draven's red eyes again, the dark-haired warlock clearly judging him. Callum also spotted Princess Selene, who had both hands clasped together under her chin.

<Focus,> Fen told him. *<As soon as they give you the signal, we need to meld and move. You have to win this one so you can maintain your ranking. They haven't revealed how they will rank our performance, but I have a feeling that winning will be a good thing.>*

<Meld and move,> Callum repeated, *<got it.>*

Callum kept his arms at his sides, his fists clenched shut. Victrin did the same, the tall young man with his head bent forward slightly.

Victrin finally glanced up at Callum, his eyes a light green that made his pupils look small.

"Begin!"

As soon as the word echoed through the chamber, Callum summoned his borrowed mana armor and melded with Fen. The Radiant Fox's powers came to him, light extending down his hands forming into claws. He triggered a blast of wind, but Victrin was already on the move, racing to the left on all fours.

Victrin bucked his head back to produce an enormous pair of antlers, which shot an arc of mana at Callum that he wasn't able to dodge. It hit him and he felt his wristlet vibrate, indicating he'd been struck once.

He dove to avoid Victrin's next projectile.

A crackle in the air came coupled with several bolts of mana lightning, all of which stuck the ground around Callum. They surged forward and sent a jolt down his spine as his wristlet buzzed again.

Damn it, only three chances left! Callum thought as he conjured a lance of light. He hurled this at Victrin, who managed to bat it away with the glowing antlers that had grown from his forehead. Yet the force of Callum's attack destabilized him enough that Victrin actually fell backward.

<*Now!*>

Seizing on his opportunity, Callum bolted forward and jumped on top of Victrin. He delivered two quick slashes before Victrin was able to knock him off.

Back on his feet, Callum was just about to make another attempt when Victrin reached up to one of his mana antlers and detached it from his head. He stood, a dark look on his face as he held the enormous antler with both hands like it was a sword.

<*Don't stand there gaping at him, hit him!*> Fen shouted, prompting Callum to leap forward and do exactly that. However, despite his aggression, Victrin was able to bat the attempt away and counter with a swipe, one that Callum just barely evaded in turn. Playing for distance, Callum's first thought was that the man was going to chase him, but to his surprise, Victrin quickly changed his stance and drove his strange weapon into the ground instead. A move which sent a bolt of light racing across the ground faster than Callum could follow.

It was so fast that the next thing Callum felt was something hot lashing across his back, the suddenness of the attack causing him to stumble forward. His wristlet buzzed again, reminding him that he was on the verge of losing.

I can't let that happen!

Callum's left arm hung numb, the shock from Victrin's last move still coursing through him.

He rushed forward and stepped aside just as Victrin thrust his antler sword forward in an attempt to skewer him. Callum used his mana claws to cut into Victrin's shoulder. He circled around as Victrin tried to swipe at him with the antler. When that didn't work, he bucked forward with the antler still on his head, but Callum was able to deliver another quick claw across the front of Victrin's armor.

Callum conjured a lance of light and spun around. He pushed it forward like it was a rake and managed to drive it just past Victrin's exposed thigh.

"And that's the match!" an authoritative voice suddenly called out. "The winner of this duel is Callum Stross!"

I did it? He looked around at what felt like a sea of shocked faces. *I did it!*

Callum let out a deep breath as his meldform faded.

"Good work," Master Cruedark said from the sidelines in his deep voice. "Callum Stross, you have advanced to the next round."

Victrin came forward and offered Callum his hand. "You got me there in the end," he said, his grip firm.

"Whatever you did was incredible. Did you pact with a deer?"

"Close. That was Luther, a Lightning Elk. What are you pacted with? I couldn't tell."

"A Radiant Fox."

Victrin seemed surprised to hear this. "Huh. I've never faced one of those before."

CHAPTER 18

Weaponcores and Beast Masters have more in common than one may think. When the essence of an aetherbeast is infused into any object, the result is always formidable—a fusion of raw power and bound intent.

*—Henry Evo, Master Convoker, Clergo,
and former Chief Historian of the Great Library*

The first round of the Entry Duels left Callum nervous about what would come. He couldn't be sure what everyone had pacted with but there were some Aethercores that were obvious, like Victrin and his pacted elk, or the man whose lower half became serpentlike.

But it was still a lot.

There's so much more to this than I originally thought.

Callum was also shocked that he had defeated Victrin. He now understood what some of the students were capable of, and it was clear how hard they had trained.

Quinn's words proved to be true: this group of would-be students had waited until the very last day of the Great College's intake to compete against one another.

Some were friends.

A few even teased one another.

But most were entirely focused on the second round of fights, which began when Master Cruedark called a woman named Lynnafer Sunsouth, who had pacted with a badger. Callum knew this because she hadn't melded in her first-round duel but had wielded a manabound polearm while her badger went on the attack.

This was another thing he learned while watching her fight. Not only were there pacted aetherbeasts, but weapons could be bonded as well.

Princess Selene explained this to him after the tip of Lynnafer's polearm morphed into what looked like a goose, which came down on top of her opponent and snapped its beak.

"A Weaponcore," Princess Selene said after she registered the confusion on Callum's face.

"A what?"

"Like a Powercore, but it conjures a physical weapon."

Callum considered his Gift of the Luminous Lance ability—a weapon that burned brightly but lacked permanence, its form fading quickly. In contrast, Lynnafer's Weaponcore had the solidity of a real polearm, albeit one with a goose's head shimmering an ethereal glow. "We didn't have those in Weatherby."

Lynnafer waited for Master Cruedark to announce her opponent. "Godric Rush. Step forward."

A shorter, heavyset student took a step forward, his cheeks puffed out as he took his position across from Lynnafer. He finally exhaled and offered his opponent a quick smile.

"Focus, Godric," she told him quickly, and by her tone it was clear that the two knew each other.

In his previous fight, Godric's size had nearly doubled once he melded, the man able to call upon a pacted ape that was stacked with muscles and seemingly transposed itself over his form. The ape even produced its own head, which it kept next to Godric's as if they had sprouted from the same neck.

While he didn't seem agile, once he melded, Godric was an absolute force to be reckoned with. He had beaten his earlier opponent in a matter of moments by pouncing on him and beating the man down with his simian fists.

"This is a rather cruel match up, as they go," Princess Selene whispered as the two prepared to spar. Next to her, the same tall woman with tan skin who Callum had seen earlier leaned over and whispered something to the princess.

"Eh? Why is it cruel?" Callum asked, pulled out of the moment by the unexpected words.

"They grew up together. Trained together," Selene explained with a sigh. "They've probably been dreading this moment. Knowing that victory by either could result in the other being declined acceptance in the school."

If that was truly the case however, Callum couldn't tell. Lynnafer and Godric exchanged glances so unreadable that it was impossible to discern if they were thinking anything at all.

Master Cruedark stepped back, and once he was closer to the rest of the staff, the battle started up.

"Begin!" he announced, the two opponents springing into action.

Lynnafer struck the end of her polearm onto the ground, summoning her goose.

Rather than snap its beak at Godric, a ball of mana fired out of the goose's mouth.

As Godric, midmeld with his ape, moved to dodge her opening attack, Lynnafer's badger appeared and scurried toward the shorter man.

Now melded, Godric lunged for the badger, grabbed it, and tossed the aetherbeast before it could bite down. It flew to the left and hit a stone wall.

Lynnafer shrieked and called the badger back to her.

She slammed the end of her polearm into the ground, where it stood erect, the goose tracking Godric as he charged toward his opponent. The goose drove its beak into the ground, causing Godric to leap to the side to avoid being impaled.

Lynnafer melded with her pacted aetherbeast and produced a set of thick claws, her arms almost like clubs now as a nearly translucent trail of mana ran up her shoulders and covered most of her form.

Back on the attack, Godric swung at her, and she countered for his legs. Lynnafer tackled him and got the first hit in. He slammed a fist against her back, and she scurried away, her movement reminding Callum of the way Victrin ran on all fours.

In watching this fight, and the others he had already witnessed, Callum was truly starting to understand the primal changes that came when a person pacted with an aetherbeast. He could see hints of a badger in the way Lynnafer moved and of an ape in the way Godric jumped around and beat his fists.

This is how I would be if I had more time with Fen, he thought as Godric clasped his hands together and struck Lynnafer with all his power. He scooped her up and body-slammed her onto the ground, Godric now one strike ahead.

Lynnafer's aetherbeast separated from her as she hit the ground. The badger rushed toward Godric, jumped, and managed to bite down onto the side of his neck.

It was only as Godric veered toward Lynnafer's polearm that Callum understood *why* the badger had attacked in this way. It brought Godric within striking distance, the polearm able to quickly tap him twice, counting as two strikes on Godric's wristlet.

Lynnafer called her badger back to her and conjured a watery ball of mana, which swept forward into a wave that slammed down on top of Godric. It struck him several more times quickly ending the fight.

"Match point!" an authoritative voice suddenly called out. "The winner of this duel is Lynnafer Sunsouth!"

"That was well fought," Princess Selene said as Lynnafer approached Godric and offered her hand to him. He took it, and a few of the students observing clapped at their performance. After Lynnafer gathered her pole-arm, which subsequently vanished, the two returned to the ranks.

Master Cruedark came forward again. He looked the potential students over as he crossed his big arms over his chest. "Next we have . . . Callum Stross and Draven Blademark."

Callum couldn't help but wince at that announcement as he started to make his way up to the Rank, his mind racing back to what he had seen of Draven's power in the first round.

Draven had faced off against a woman with a clawed aetherbeast. There had been a darkness that accompanied him, which seemed to entirely cover the arena grounds. That was about all Callum had seen of it as the woman was quickly beaten in the fog that followed.

A glance back to Princess Selene told Callum all he needed to know about the fight to come.

She looked nervous.

<He has a fog ability. You know that. We do not know what he's pacted with, but whatever it is, it's fast.>

<Should I meld with you?>

<We can, and should, experiment with other ways of fighting later, but I think that will work best. Callum?>

A long pause followed, one in which Callum started down his opponent. *<Yes?>* he asked Fen as he noticed something akin to a humorous look behind Draven's red eyes.

<Do what you do best. The only way we win this is by brute force and adjusting to whatever he does. Do not let his fog ability intimidate you like it did the woman earlier. He's going to cast it. By the time he does, move in.>

<Got it.>

"Duelists ready," Master Cruedark called out, giving the pair a quick look before signaling. "Begin!"

Callum did exactly as Fen had suggested.

He activated his mana armor and swiftly melded. Callum surged toward Draven, Radiant Claws blazing. He managed to get a single swipe in as Draven unleashed a black mist, shrouding the battlefield in darkness.

<Keep on him!>

Callum rushed in again. He lunged for Draven only to find that his opponent was no longer there. He spun and swiped his claws again, the mist so thick now that he couldn't see more than a few inches in front of him.

He swallowed the panic he felt, fear that he would be lost in the fog forever. It was so thick. And the only sound he could hear was a slight flutter above him.

Draven dropped onto Callum and brought him to the ground. Even with his armor, Callum could feel the grasp of something talon-like on his shoulders.

"Huh, down already? I guess this will be easier than I expected!" Draven said, his voice cutting through the mist. He rushed back into the air, leaving Callum prone.

<Hurry, get up!>

Callum pushed himself up and summoned a lance of light, which sizzled in his hand as he tried to make sense of where Draven could be.

<He came from above. Point it that way!>

Callum did just that as Draven rushed in again. He managed to spear his opponent, stopping Draven mid-flight.

Seizing on his momentum, Callum struck Draven with a spiral of wind just as the warlock hit the ground.

Just a few more attacks to go, Callum thought as he prepared to strike again.

As he pulled his arms back to unleash another fury of air mana, Callum was bombarded by a wave of black feathers. They hit him so hard that he flew backward several feet.

Callum came back up and happened to see Draven hovering in the air again, his opponent once again obscured by the fog.

<He's bonded with some kind of bird.>

<Makes sense, I saw talons and feathers,> Callum said as he looked around him to see the sharp black feathers slowly fading.

<Keep moving; make it harder for him to pin you down!>

Callum recalled what he had already seen from Draven. *Attacks from above, flying, mist, sharp feathers. But, of course, there's certainly more.*

He didn't want to lose, but the people he was going up against had trained for this their entire lives. Just as Fen had said, the only way he would win would be through his own strength.

But how could he deal with an opponent that could fly?

Bait. I have to become bait.

This meant that he would need to stop moving. Callum paused there with his fists drawn, mana claws pulsing slightly as he awaited his fate.

It came with a sudden rush, Draven going for a horizontal strike that engulfed his body in the form of a bird. He slammed into Callum and landed on top of him, only to be flipped around as Callum got on top.

He sunk a clawed fist into Draven's face and was just about to send another in when Draven opened his mouth and released a deafening blast that blew Callum off him.

Once again, Callum hit the ground. Draven came forward and Callum kicked at him, landing another strike. A quick glance to his wristlet told him that this counted as a strike, that Draven had now hit him four times.

But I got him four times as well! Callum thought, quickly realizing they were even.

Whoever landed the next hit would decide the battle. Callum knew he couldn't let the warlock take to the air again—*not with the fog concealing his movements, not with the devastating precision of his dive-bomb attacks!*

The tension crackled in the air as Callum surged forward, power blazing through his limbs. Draven was just rising to his feet, his dark wings beginning to flare as he prepared to launch.

Callum couldn't give him that chance.

Fueled by desperation, Callum hurled himself forward with an explosive burst of speed. His strike was wild, unrefined, and poorly timed—but it didn't matter. His mana claw scraped across Draven's shoulder, landing another strike.

The fog swirled around them as Draven stumbled in disbelief, his wings faltering as Callum's heart thundered in his chest.

"And that's match point!" Master Cruedark's voice called out a second before the fog vanished. "The winner of this duel is Callum Stross!"

"What!?" Draven roared as the mist faded away. He glared at Callum and then pointed a finger at Master Cruedark. "That didn't count!"

But no sooner were those words out of his mouth than Draven quickly lowered his hand and bowed his head. "Apologies, Master. I . . . I was too heated after that duel."

Callum couldn't tell whether Draven was about to shoulder through him or shake his hand. In the end, the warlock simply stopped directly next to Callum, red eyes narrowing on him. "Consider yourself lucky." And with that, Draven stormed off, straight out of the Ordelarium to the gasps and quiet chatter of other potential students.

Still reeling from his fight, Callum joined the other students and was greeted once again by Princess Selene.

"That was a lucky hit." It seemed like she wanted to say more but then her name was announced. "My turn."

Selene took center Rank across from another female student who had yet to fully reveal her pacted aetherbeast.

The fight kicked off and the princess eventually won. Callum was too distracted by what had just happened to really pay much attention to the duel.

The way Draven had stared at him as he passed kept coming back to Callum, the power of the other man's red eyes. *He's a warlock*, Callum reminded himself, still not certain what to make of the term or what Fen had told him about them.

After a few more fights, the wildest of which saw a student conjuring a giant, manabound lion head that ignited everything around him, the third round of fights was set to begin.

"You're doing well," Princess Selene told him. "If you can win the next round, it will certainly help your rank. You've done well to hide what you pacted with, too."

"Really?"

"All you've shown anyone are your claws and a lance. Not a bad strategy. You seem unprepared, but that shows me, and everyone here, that there is a method to what you're doing."

Callum nearly laughed.

"What?" Selene asked.

"Sure, we'll call *surviving* a method."

There was a little more murmuring before Master Cruedark took center stage yet again.

As usual, he was all business, the big man not really saying anything other than pointing out the fact that there wouldn't be many more rounds left in the Entry Duels. "In that case," he said, his arms now behind his back, "Princess Selene Morninglade."

"Good luck," Callum told her as she stepped past, a hardened look on her face yet again.

Master Cruedark scanned the students yet again. "And . . . Callum Stross. Please, step up."

Callum hesitated until Fen spoke in his head.

<You knew this was a possibility, right?>

<I hadn't actually considered it,> he told Fen as he begrudgingly took a step forward.

Callum turned to Princess Selene, who seemed to be looking right past him, fixated on something directly behind him. He showed her his hands as if to say, *Sorry about this*, but she didn't respond.

<She has a pacted bear. You're going to need to move quickly, or she will overwhelm you. Remember, Princess Selene has been training her entire life for something like this.>

<I'm very aware,> Callum thought back.

"Duelists ready," Master Cruedark called out, his voice just barely fading from the air before he added, "begin!"

Callum melded at the same time as the princess, her bear form flaring up, the mana rushing off her shoulders and releasing a wave of force that cut toward him.

The force slammed into Callum so hard that he was tossed into the air. He plummeted to the ground, only for Princess Selene to meet him with an incredible swipe that hurtled him backward nearly twenty feet.

As everything flashed around him, Callum tried for his lance. He loosed it in her general direction, but by then, she was charging toward him, rushing on all fours.

Princess Selene hit the air, twisted, and came down on top of Callum. It was hard to make out her form now, the woman's face covered by an ursine appearance, energy rushing off her shoulders in waves as she struck him again.

<Move!>

Callum rolled and managed to push her off in the process.

He tried for Zephyr Strike, but his attempt went wide. The princess charged again and he dove to avoid her next strike. Callum jumped back again and again as Selene pursued him relentlessly, her blazing fast movements and the strength behind them birthing fear within him.

But as he avoided her next attacks, he slowly realized that his fear had nothing to do with her, and *everything* to do with some effect from her pacted bear. He kept seeing flashes of her aetherbeast, the bear twice as large as any he'd ever seen around Weatherby.

He knew what a bear was capable of, and that was a normal-sized one, not one hewn entirely from mana.

Selene rushed in again, the fear Callum felt growing stronger with each near miss. That is, until he managed to get a strike in.

It was a lucky one, just as he had had with Draven. Callum was able to hit Selene just as she overreached with one of her huge claws.

But while the hit muted the fear coursing through him, the change that followed from the woman was sudden and profound. She brought her arms back and slammed her hands into the ground, which conjured a flash that was followed up by a terrifying roar as she and her bear unmelded.

The bear lunged, its massive form barreling toward him with the force of an avalanche. Callum didn't dare slow down, running at full speed in the opposite direction. His breaths came in ragged gasps, his focus split between escaping the charging beast and regaining enough control to counter.

Just one clean hit, that's all I need! But his efforts faltered, and before he could regroup, a flicker of motion caught his eye.

The princess stood poised, calm amidst the chaos, her hand alight with shimmering energy. In one fluid motion, she conjured a gleaming dagger of light. *A Weaponcore*, Callum thought.

She hurled it into the air, the blade transforming mid-flight. It morphed into a sparrow of pure light, wings flaring as it zipped toward him with unerring precision.

"No!" Callum shouted, twisting to evade, but the sparrow was faster. It struck him square in the chest, the force of it driving him backward.

The battle was over in an instant. The bear stopped its charge, retreating with a low growl as the princess approached.

"Match point!" Master Cruedark's voice called out in its traditional fashion. "The winner of this duel is Princess Selene!"

Callum fell to his knees and looked down at the throwing knife, the wings of which had folded back into its form, indicating that it was a Weaponcore.

Princess Selene approached. She picked up her knife and it vanished. The princess blew a strand of hair out of her face and offered Callum her hand. "That was great," she told him, a smile forming on her face as she helped him up. "I won't say you almost had me, but you were closer than most."

CHAPTER 19

*Enough is known about Demoncores to surmise that they should
have no place in the future of the Valestra Kingdom. Over time,
usage of Demoncores will turn an archmage into a soulless husk
of their former self, and legalizing its practice will do the same to
our great nation.*

—A quote from *History of the Valestra Kingdom*
by Sir Berenwald Wulmar

Callum truly had no idea where he stood with the Great College of New
Albion. He knew he had ranked as a C2 in his Attribute Trials, and
he felt like he had done well enough in the Entry Duels to at least qualify
for admission. But he wouldn't know the results until the following day, as
Princess Selene had explained:

"Those that have officially been accepted into the Great College will be
announced tomorrow in the Selection Ceremony. Most people already know
if they've been accepted or not based on how well they did in the Attribute
Trials, and how well they think they did in the Entry Duels." She offered him
a crooked smile. "Don't look at me like that. I didn't design the system."

Callum thought of her words and their duel on his way back to Telluride's borrowed barnyard of a home. He was ecstatic, nervous, still coming
down from all that he experienced over the course of a single day. From the
Attribute Trials to learning of Armorcores, Weaponcores, *and* Demoncores
to the strange things he'd experienced with the Soul Pythia. There was just
so much.

He ran his hand through his hair and continued on, barely paying attention to the city and all the people around him. He reached the barn in the
outer district of Stadacona and finally stopped to catch his breath, which
only took a moment due to his natural stamina.

"You smell that?" he asked as he took a sniff of the air. "I think Telluride is cooking something." Callum took a quick look around. "Or someone is."

He entered the barn and followed his nose to a room at the back that had a stove in it. Sure enough, the shardcrafter stood before a big black pot stirring a meaty stew, his pipe on the table next to him. "You're back," the shardcrafter said without turning to Callum. "How did it go?"

"I don't know. I mean, I know how I did in my Attribute Trials, and I made it to the third round in the Entry Duels, but I won't know until tomorrow."

"Heh, I was wondering if they still did that for students who did their entry exams on the last day." He scooped up some wild green onions and dropped them into the pot. "How do you think you did?"

Callum sat at the table and drummed his fingers for a moment. "The Attribute Trials weren't easy. I had to do everything from pushing a boulder to facing a mental challenge in which my family home was burned down, my father inside."

"Harsh. Soul Pythia?"

"Yes. I've never seen or experienced anything like that before."

"If I'd known, I could have warned you but they change the trials every year. Not that knowing would have been better for you. Sometimes, going in blind for something like that is better."

Callum wasn't sure if he would agree to that, but also didn't have an answer in reply. So instead, he changed the subject. "What can you tell me about Demoncores and warlocks?"

Telluride stopped stirring the stew. "Oof, getting right down to it, it seems. What do you want to know about them?"

"Everything. I had to fight a warlock. I beat him."

"A warlock?" Telluride turned to Callum. "They are allowing a warlock to enter the Great College?"

"Princess Selene—"

"Come again?"

"The princess. She was there. She was friendly enough to speak with me while we were waiting for our duels."

That seemed to be too much for the man to take all at once, leaving him shaking his head and muttering, "How?"

"I met her yesterday," Callum explained with a shrug before explaining what Selene had told him.

"By the gods. In my day, that was something that would never be spoken about publicly. Do they not know?"

<Exactly my thoughts!> Fen said to Callum.

"Do they not know what?" Callum asked Telluride.

"Demoncores, the negative mana associated with them," the man replied, waving a hand as if physically searching for the words he wanted to say next. "About what they can do to someone's mind—they *must* know. It baffles me that they would play with fire in such a way."

"So there can't be a good warlock?"

"I suppose there *could* be a good warlock, and there very well may be for all I know, perhaps a Beast Master out there in the Badlands. But I've been out of the loop for some time now. Once you relinquish your Aethercores, not many friends or people tend to stay that interested in you afterward. But still. Or regardless, everything you've already learned about sundering, stripping a core to its component shards, and fusion in general, could be done with a Demoncore as well. It's the other influence that worries me." He went back to his stirring the stew and cursed under his breath. "Almost burned it."

"What other influence?"

"The corruption of the soul. Call it what you want—dark mana, negative energy, corrupted mana—but the power of a Demoncore can affect a mind over time. It can lead to spiritual and moral decay, something like a gradual decline of the user's social and ethical boundaries. Worst-case, they could become demonic themselves."

"Well, Draven had red eyes, is that a factor?"

"Red . . . eyes?" Telluride asked as he spooned some of the stew into a bowl and brought it to the table.

"I've never seen anything like that. His eyes glowed red. Everyone seemed to accept it as normal."

"That is because everyone there, anyone who would wait until the last day to do their Entry Duels, likely knows Draven. The princess certainly did. I am still surprised that you met her."

"Why?"

"No reason, really. It is strange to think about, though," Telluride said as he filled his own bowl. "You have come from the backwoods of the kingdom, near the border of the lands of Antiqua no less, to meeting the princess. In what? A week's time? Something like that?"

"Something like that."

Steam from his bowl of stew swirled upward, enveloping Telluride's face as he sat before Callum. "I would say you are lucky, but you have a fox, of course you are lucky. Care to join us, Fen?"

"Certainly," Fen announced as he took shape on the bench. "And Callum is right. We learned a lot today, I learned more than I expected as well. I'm interested to know more, and to learn how it may stop Corruption."

Telluride tasted his soup and smacked his lips. "Ah, Corruption. You said there was a lot of it in this basement back at the farm. It does have a way of desecrating the environment. And if you would like to remove the effects, which I'm certain you would, it could involve cultivation; but simply improving the bond the two of you have—in old parlance, your *aetherforge*—should suffice. I'll be honest, that part was never my area of expertise. There are numerous things one can study when they start understanding mana. I was fascinated by shards and cores. Shards and cores," Telluride mused as he ate more of his stew. "Not bad. Compliments to the chef."

"It's good," Callum said. "Much better than my dad's stew. He was never a cook. I usually cooked for him, actually."

"You can cook?"

"I can."

Telluride scratched his beard. "You may prove more helpful around here than I thought. Heh. But who am I kidding? You will spend most of your time at the Great College, where you will certainly have things to do."

"You think I will make it in?"

"I would let you in on namesake alone, but that's just me." Telluride wiped his mouth with a napkin. "They will be much better at teaching you how to meditate and other ways to cultivate at the Great College. Better than me. I'm honestly still shocked to hear the duke's son is a warlock *and* he has been admitted."

"We don't know if Draven will be there yet," Fen said. "He had his Entry Duels today as well."

"True, but his admission is assured."

"How so?"

"He's the duke's son," Telluride told Fen. "He is a legacy student. Same with Princess Selene. You said you made it to the third round. Who beat you? Did you get their name?"

"We were defeated by the princess," Fen said for Callum.

Telluride snorted a laugh. "Is that so? Not what I was expecting to hear. What was she pacted with? And Draven? You never said."

"Draven was pacted with some kind of bird," Callum said. "The princess is pacted with a bear."

Telluride puffed his cheeks out. "Wow. That's some Aethercore. I've only seen that a handful of times. They are powerhouses, the pacted bears. Pacted elephants are too."

"It was enormous," Callum said as he remembered the sheer size of her bear, how it had frightened him in a way he still didn't understand.

"The ones I know of are Pact of the Spiritbound Bear and Pact of the Bloodrot Bear. But there may be others out there. Did you see what hers looked like?" Telluride asked Callum.

"I did. It was terrifying, but it didn't seem demonic or anything. I'm assuming the Bloodrot Bear would be red?"

"A good assumption. In that case, the princess probably has a Spiritbound Bear, which would be Light and Life Mana Affinity. Not surprising, really. She is royalty. I would have been more surprised if it had been the Bloodrot Bear."

"Would that be more suited for a warlock?"

"No, not necessarily. Some names sound more terrifying than they are. But you are right to think that there would be a red energy associated with it. It's not always that way, you know. Our world is wild beyond the reach of man," he said a bit whimsically. "Anyway. Eat up, lad. Tomorrow's going to be a good day. I can feel it."

Callum woke up the next morning to a rooster crowing somewhere near the barn. It was the last thing he expected to hear in the city center, and he couldn't recall hearing it the previous morning. It reminded him of the rooster they once had on the farm in Weatherby, one that was particularly large.

I wonder if he was a pacted aetherbeast, Callum thought as he got ready for the day.

He was just leaving the barn when Florence, the girl who had once led him to Telluride's barn, arrived.

"Are you hungry?" she asked, showing him her basket of eggs.

"No, I'm fine."

"At least have some bread." She reached into the basket and pulled out a bread roll. "I see you're not wearing the cloak."

"No, I am not," Callum said. He had used it as a blanket the previous night, for which it had served its purpose better than he expected. "Thanks!" Callum stuffed the bread roll in his mouth and took off toward the Great College.

It had been hard enough to sleep. Now, he would finally learn the full results of his Attribute Trials and Entry Duels. Telluride seemed confident he would make it in, but a night of restlessly going over each detail, each part of the tests had Callum doubting himself.

<*And what if I don't get in?*> he had asked Fen in the middle of the night.

<*Sleep, Callum,*> had been the Radiant Fox's reply. <*We'll light that fire once the wood's dry.*>

<Not much longer now,> Callum told Fen as they passed through a small row of shops.

It was easy to see the Great College because of its spire, so he had decided to take a new route just to familiarize himself with New Albion.

Callum was glad he did once he saw a building with several men in robes standing out front of a building with a placard above the door that read emporium. The building was constructed of a smooth, dark stone that had crystal veins running through it, which set it apart from the wooden buildings around it. The building was clearly old, but it had been well maintained.

<What do you think it is? A shardcrafter?> Callum asked.

<More than one, apparently. Let's head inside take a quick look.>

<But we need to get to the Great College.>

<We've not even been up an hour yet, Callum. So long as we don't linger, we'll be there with plenty of time to spare.>

Callum stepped around some of the men out front, who drank from little cups of hot tea and discussed a variety of topics. He hadn't seen people doing something like this before in Weatherby. Generally, mornings meant work, not discussing the latest philosophical treaty or catching up on some event. Those things could happen during work, but there was little time to stand around.

Callum entered the Emporium to find several shops, their attendants getting ready for the day. He scanned the signs above each individual booth and saw that they sold Powercores and shards. The booths were arranged by the types of Mana Affinity.

As he stood there in the doorway, Callum realized that he hadn't received a full explanation on the types of Mana Affinity. He knew that Fen had an affinity for Air, Fire, and Light Mana, but that was pretty much it.

Air, Earth, Fire, Water, Light, Shadow, Life, and Death, he thought as he read the signs above the booths.

"We're not open yet," a man said as he pushed past him.

Callum bumped into a crate, which sent a rat scattering. The man, who wore a green cap, chased after it for just a moment, collected himself, and pointed his finger at the rodent just as it slipped into a hole in the wall.

"That should do it," he said upon killing the rat with a bolt of mana. A few of the shop assistants looked up at the commotion but no one said anything as the man swept it into a dustbin and took it outside.

The man in the green cap moved past Callum again. "How did you get in anyway?"

"Through the door?" Callum motioned to the open doorway.

"In that case, you can see yourself out the same way. Good day."

<*Rude,*> Fen said once they were outside, <*but this would be a good place to come back to. Especially once you get the King's Scholarship.*>

<*If I get it,*> Callum said.

<*Why wouldn't you?*>

<*I haven't been accepted yet. And even if I am, I need to send some back to Weatherby. Plus, I'd need to pay Telluride,*> Callum said as he moved on. <*But like you said, maybe we can light that fire once the wood is dry.*>

Callum arrived at the Great College and felt fortunate to spot Quinn Vendrick out front. The portly young man was accompanied by a tall, bronze-skinned woman, who wore numerous bracelets and necklaces. Her curly hair, parted to one side and tucked behind her ears, was threaded with beads. Callum recognized her from the Entry Duels, where she had often spoken with Princess Selene, but he had never learned her name.

"I was wondering when you would get here," Quinn told him.

"You waited for me?"

"You didn't seem to know your way around yesterday, so I figured you wouldn't know your way around today. How did you do in the trial?"

"Who's your friend, Quinn?" the tall woman asked after Callum returned Quinn's Armorcore to him.

"This is Callum Stross."

"Ah, you're the one she kept talking to yesterday." She gave Callum a funny look. "That name is a little on the nose. I remember thinking that yesterday when I heard it."

Quinn laughed. "It certainly is. Callum, this is Marcella Faite."

"Nice to meet you," Callum told her, not sure of the protocol as to how he should greet her. He had never seen a woman like Marcella before, but he assumed that she came from the southern part of the kingdom, where he'd heard there were beautiful, sunny beaches and everyone wore elaborate jewelry. "I'm from Weatherby."

She stifled a laugh. "Aveiro."

"How did you do?" Quinn asked Callum. "I should have stuck around to find out but I had to visit the Emporium and sunder a Powercore that my uncle gave me."

"I made it to the third round."

"Who did you beat?" Quinn asked.

"Victrin Righexa and Draven Blademark. Princess Selene beat me in the third round."

"She sure did," Marcella said as she shook her head. "She beat me in the fourth round as well."

"That's not too bad, really. And to defeat the Great College's first war-lock," Quinn said, with a laugh. One that sounded a little too nervous to Callum's ear. "You might have just made yourself an enemy."

"Hopefully not," Callum replied with a sigh, dreading the thought of having something else to worry about.

"But unless they are docking you for technicalities, I think you'll get accepted," Quinn assured him.

"What do you mean by technicalities?" Callum asked, his chest tightening at the prospect of yet another hurdle. "Don't I get scored based on how many rounds I won?"

"Not exactly, or at least not just that," Marcella said she played with one of her bracelets. "You are scored on your overall performance, the skills you showcase, and whatever else the instructors are looking for. But it's good you made it to the third round, and that it was Princess Selene that beat you. *Us.* She has been trained by actual Beast Masters from the first moment she could be. The instructors will consider that in our favor."

"I sure hope so," Callum said as he thought nervously about what lay ahead.

"Relax, no sense in worrying about it," Marcella stated before offering him a shrug. "Anyway, shall we get a move on and see? No sense in letting things stew."

"Yeah, might as well get it over with," Quinn agreed before turning toward the courtyard. "Good luck, everyone."

CHAPTER 20

There are eight known mana elements, all of which have corresponding shards. They are Air, Earth, Fire, Water, Light, Shadow, Life, and Death. These Mana Affinity Shards are required for upgrading both Powercores and Aethercores. You may be attuned to several through your pacted aetherbeasts, but it is rare to be attuned to all.

—A quote from *Mana Basics: A Guide to Mastery, 3rd Edition* by Jez Sageglow, Master Weaver, Core Lector

The anticipation was killing Callum as he took a spot next to Quinn. Marcella was on Quinn's left speaking to Lynnafer Sunsouth, the woman with the pacted badger and the strange goose-headed polearm Callum had watched fight yesterday. The only other person Callum recognized by name in the grand auditorium was Victrin Righexa, his first opponent in the Entry Duels, who had already greeted him.

<*I wonder where the princess is,*> Fen said.

<*I was wondering about that myself.*>

Callum looked up to a Rank framed by golden curtains. Above them, a dome of stained glass and metal cast multihued light onto the auditorium floor. Everything was gilded and there were statues at all the entrances featuring aetherbeasts.

It looked grand, but with nerves twisting in his gut and the overwhelming sense that he didn't belong, Callum could barely focus on the auditorium itself, no matter how majestic it was. The vaulted ceiling arched high above, adorned with intricate frescoes that seemed to ripple with faint mana currents. All Callum could do was stare straight ahead, his heart thrumming in his chest as he awaited the verdict.

I just want to get this over with, he thought as more potential students filed into the space. There had to be well over four hundred, much more than he had expected.

"Do you know how much longer?" he asked Quinn.

"It should be soon. But at least it looks like almost everyone is here." Quinn replied before shrugging. "Beyond that, I have no idea."

"What about the princess? I haven't seen her."

"That's because she doesn't need to come to something like this. She is a legacy candidate, like Draven."

"Ah, so she won't be here," Callum said, the opportunity for any further questions fading away as the crowd abruptly started to grow quiet.

A retinue of archmages in white robes with golden accents filed out onto the Rank. They formed a line and all took a step back as Master Patrjohn Granadam came out, along with Master Cruedark, the giant of a man who had run the Entry Duels, and Mastress Lucerne, the Soul Pythia responsible for the Attribute Trials.

Master Granadam approached the podium and looked out at the students. The bearded man gave them a firm smile and began speaking, "In this five hundred and tenth year since the Great Demonswar, it is critically important to remember our duty to the kingdom, to the Crown, and, for that matter, to the world and its other kingdoms, regardless of past rivalries. The Great College represents the best of our world. The names that you have heard from bards and famous children's stories; the statues you have seen in town squares; the heroes of our kingdom—all are graduates of the Great College. The enlightenment that we have all benefited from, the mana we share, is the gift that our college protects. I'm not one for long speeches, but I will say this: if you make it today, what you do at the Great College, and, most importantly, after, can and will have profound effects. As I look out at our future student body, I am reminded of the words of the late Master Ashwan, 'Go forth with purpose, in duty, and without fear.' Let us begin."

Callum expected him to produce a scroll, some parchment to read from. Instead, a faint shift of light fell across Master Granadam's eyes as he spoke a name. "Lynnafer Sunsouth, A2."

The potential students around Callum clapped.

Like she had trained for this moment, Lynnafer approached the Rank, chin held high and greeted Master Granadam. Upon congratulating her warmly, he gestured to one of the attendants at the back and the pair disappeared behind the curtain together.

<I don't like that they are going to read your ranking.>

<Nor do I,> Callum said as Master Granadam called another name.

"Artur Filin, A2."

A man with short dark hair brought his hands into a prayer position. After being congratulated by the potential students around him, Artur approached the Rank and was taken by an attendant to some unknown location. Callum watched as the first attendant, the one who had escorted Lynnafer, returned.

"Theogar Desde, A2," Master Granadam announced. A young man with long black hair and acne smiled at his friends as they patted him on the back. He headed up to the podium with a big smirk on his face.

It soon became clear that no one had ranked higher than A2. Callum understood this after more than a dozen students were called, all with the same ranking until Master Granadam reached the lower A3 ranking.

"Marcella Faite, A3."

"That's you," Quinn told the woman seated to his left. "Congratulations!"

As the students clapped around her, Marcella mumbled under her breath that she should have at least been an A2.

"A3 rank is still really good," Quinn assured her. "Really, Marcella. It's better than most."

"I was certain—" Marcella began before her friends pulled her along. A chorus of jangling jewelry accompanied the tall woman as she made her way to the Rank, where she was escorted to the back.

It went like this for another few excruciating minutes as Master Granadam moved through everyone who had ranked at the A3 level. Callum knew this wouldn't be him, so he remained patient but tense as the high-ranking archmage moved to the B1 rank.

<That won't be us either, I'm afraid.>

Callum winced at Fen's comment. *<No, it will not.>*

<But as long as we get in. That's all that matters.>

That's all that matters, Callum thought, echoing what Fen had told him.

But he knew there was much more to it than that. Callum's potential classmates were much further along than him. He had a lot of catching up to do.

After the B1s, Master Granadam started on the B2s, which included Godric Rush, the man who had pacted with some sort of ape and been defeated by Lynnafer Sunsouth. The crowd around Callum started to thin as the old master finished the B3-ranked students, and then moved onto the C1s, which included Quinn.

"There are still two ranks to go," Quinn told Callum. "Don't worry."

"I'm fine," Callum said, even though his palms were now sweaty to the point that he had to wipe them on the front of his pants. He felt like everyone was looking at him, even if there was still a large group of students yet to be called.

"I'll see you later," Quinn said.

Callum felt a new wave of apprehension as Quinn climbed the Rank, greeted Master Granadam, and was led away by a woman in robes. Gazing up to the ceiling and staring at the stained glass did little to calm Callum's nerves.

He felt even more apprehension as Master Granadam started on the students who had ranked at the C2 level. "Petyr Norwood."

A silver-haired student in front of Callum silently pumped a fist in the air. Callum recalled Petyr losing in the first round.

<*You did better than him.*>

<*I know,*> Callum told Fen.

<*Then you must be soon.*>

Callum didn't respond. Instead, he once again looked up at the ceiling, hoping to pass the time as Master Granadam called more names. This went on for another twenty minutes, which told him that the majority of the students had ranked C1 or below.

After the C2s, the master finally reached lowly C3 rank.

If I don't make it here, I'll have to say goodbye to my chance at entering the Great College . . .

There were about a hundred people left now, every one of them doing their best to hide their anxiety. The whispers and squirming in the crowd grew louder.

A lot of nobles were about to be let down, especially as Master Granadam pulled his hands together on the podium and took a long, hard look at those who remained. "Ahem, we have come to the end of our list. If you are not one of the three students I name next, I will remind you that there are other roles that you may fulfill for our glorious Valestra Kingdom that will not require your pacted aetherbeast. Some of the most influential members of our society have never made it as far as you have today."

<*This is it,*> Fen said as Master Granadam called a woman's name.

The woman, who stood off to Callum's left, nearly fainted. A friend stopped her from falling and ushered her onto the Rank as another question came to Callum: *What did he mean by not requiring a pacted aetherbeast? Will Fen be taken from me?*

He glanced at the exit.

Callum could go there now, perhaps use the woman taking the Rank as a distraction. He wasn't certain of his destiny, but he knew that he would need Fen in the future. He shifted slightly and bumped into the short lady standing next to him, who had her hands over her mouth.

"Sorry," Callum told her as Master Granadam called another name.

"Silvia Hareth, C3."

"That's me," the woman beside Callum said. "That's me!"

"Congratulations," he told the woman even as his heart sank.

Only one name left . . .

There were still over thirty-five potential students standing around, everyone started to accept the fact that it wasn't going to be them. Only a few stood there with confidence, assuming that they would be called.

Silvia took the Rank and nervously spoke to Master Granadam. Like the others, she was escorted away as the older man looked out at the crowd. "We have reached the final student for this year's intake. Some of you were very close, I will say that. But we have our quotas, and our ranking system is designed for students best suited for the type of education we provide here. With that in mind—" he cleared his throat "—sorry about that."

An attendant stepped forward and whispered something into his ear. This went on for what felt like an eternity as Master Granadam nodded, said a few things, and finally peered out at the group nervously awaiting his decision.

<Come on . . .>

"My apologies," the older man told them. "As I was saying, we have our quotas, and the Great College's ranking system is designed for students best suited for the unique and often challenging education we are able to provide here."

He paused one last time.

<Come on . . .>

"Callum Stross, C3, please join us as our last candidate."

<Yes! Finally!>

Callum felt his knees buckle. He quickly regained control and moved toward the Rank with his head bowed, the men and women before him parting. He took the steps, where he was greeted by Master Granadam.

"Callum Stross." Master Granadam bent closer so only Callum could hear him. "Some of the students might not fully understand who you are, but the administration is aware of your relation to the Demonslayer. Your forefather, some five hundred years ago, founded the Great College. But that is not why you are being accepted today."

"Understood, Your Lordship," Callum said, increasingly aware that everyone was watching him.

"While you did well in your Entry Duels, reaching the third round, many of the judges found your skills and performance lacking. You ranked C2 in the Attribute Trials and, after much debate, D3 in the Entry Duels.

This has been averaged to C3, which does grant you access to the Great College, but barely so. If we're being honest, there are people glaring at you right now who technically ranked better. What I'm saying here is that there is a lot you must do to catch up. Since you were in the lowest percentile, your first semester will see you on academic probation."

"Understood, Your Lordship. Please," he said just as Master Granadam was starting to turn away.

"Yes?"

"How would I improve before classes start? What can I—?"

Commotion from the audience drew Master Granadam's attention. A student with dark hair had started yelling at the staff who was ushering him out.

"Oh, bother," Granadam said. "There's one of these every year." He refocused his attention on Callum. "Over the course of the next week, there will be opportunities to improve yourself and better the skill set you already have. I suggest you seek those out. You will now join your admission advisor," he said as he swept his hand to the robed woman that stood there wondering what was taking Callum so long. "You may ask her further questions."

<And the King's Scholarship?>

"And the King's Scholarship?" Callum asked Master Granadam, only realizing then that he perhaps should have saved that question for his admission advisor.

"Ah, yes, if that is something you seek, then you now qualify for it. But it isn't a lot." Master Granadam offered Callum a quick smile. "In any event, you will need money if you don't already have some, but the scholarship should set you on your way. But I mean it this time, if you have any other questions, please address them with your advisor. And do remember that you'll begin the semester on academic probation. You don't have a lot of time to catch up to your peers, Callum."

CHAPTER 21

Established three centuries ago by King Edric II, the King's Forest is a sacred aetherbeast hunting ground reserved for the royal family, who open it once for the students of noble families who are set to join the Great College. Known for his strong connection with the land, King Edric II's tomb is located in the forest near the nobles' campsite.

—A quote from *Guide to Greater New Albion* by Ludvik Dash, Master Convoker, a pamphlet published 506 years after the Great Demonswar

Scanning the document given to him at the registrar's office only made Callum feel worse. His tuition for the first semester was covered, but that left him very little, certainly not enough to fund room and board for the remainder of the year.

<*We need money, and to do that we're either going to have to find a job, or get some shards and sell them,*> Callum told Fen as he headed back to Telluride's place. <*The only problem is selling shards means we'll lose out on power boosts.*>

<*We'll figure something out. We should probably start with Telluride. And next time you see Quinn, you should ask him where he's staying so we can reach him. He would probably know something like this.*>

<*Likely.*>

<*Or Princess Selene but getting an audience with her could be much harder.*>

Callum thought of the princess as he continued through the Belldrum District and its numerous pottery studios. He knew that she was in the city somewhere, likely in the castle that wasn't far from the Great College. *But really, she could be anywhere,* he thought, *she could be training.*

<*We need to start training as well,*> he told Fen as they waited for a man hauling a huge cart to move past them. He had clearly used a Might Shard, since the cart was filled with huge stones that a normal person, even a strong one, wouldn't have been able to move on their own.

<*I was thinking that too. I learned a lot watching the other students battle.*>

<*I tried to. It was all so overwhelming.*>

<*It was,*> Fen told Callum as he crossed a stone bridge guarded by two soldiers with enormous shields and halberds.

They came to the barn, where they found Telluride seated out front on an overturned pail, puffing from his pipe. "Well?" he asked as he looked up at Callum.

"I made it in. I should send a letter to my father," he said. "There's something else."

"Oh?"

"The King's Scholarship. Most of it covered tuition. There isn't a lot left for food or a place to stay. I was told there are dorms there, but they are expensive."

"Yes, they are, but worth paying for if you can afford one." A grin formed on Telluride's face.

"Yes?"

"If you are a noble, then you are technically entitled to visit the King's Forest between now and the start of the semester. It's tradition, actually, if one can afford the trip. The nobles usually travel together in a caravan of sorts and make a big show of it, especially those who have recently been accepted to the Great College."

"How far is it from New Albion?" Callum asked.

"One- or two-days' journey, depending on how fast you go. Nobles generally go there as a group to train, to get any shards or Powercores they might be missing, and, if we're being honest, to start the network that they will inevitably form by attending the Great College. In that way it's more of a glorified social event, and they do bring plenty to drink."

"And I could join?"

"You probably wouldn't be able to afford to travel with them, but . . . your old friend Telluride knows a way that you could get there. It won't be a comfortable ride, though. How familiar are you with the King's Forest?"

"Familiar?" Callum repeated, tilting his head the same way Fen did when he asked a question. "Until a few moments ago, I didn't even know that King Morninglade had his own forest."

The reply caused Telluride to laugh. "Yes, I suppose that is fair. And when one already owns a kingdom, what's another forest? The King's Forest is for certain ceremonies and the royal family's sole enjoyment. You mentioned Princess Selene last time we spoke. Well, I've no doubt she's visited multiple times. If you are familiar with the map, there is a village beyond the forest, one called Ridgebarrow. Quaint, really. I just happen to have a friend who is heading that direction in the morning. He was just here, right before you came, actually."

"And he would let me ride with them?"

"I don't think he will mind, no. But it might not be the most pleasant of rides considering he usually fills his wagon to the brim to maximize what he can carry on the trip. And you won't exactly get off at the King's Forest. But you will be closer, perhaps a day's journey if you head east. Kaelor will know the best place to leave you, and it just so happens that he owes me a favor."

"Which means I will owe you another favor."

"I'm not keeping track of the favors that you owe me yet, Callum. But maybe I should be," he said with a puff of his pipe. He laughed again. "You didn't tell me your final ranking."

"That's because I was barely accepted and am already on academic probation. I was ranked at C3."

"Hmm, a challenge." The man mused. "But you got in. So nothing else matters at the moment."

"A lot of people didn't. There was a ton of disappointment in that room, especially once I was called last."

"Ah, well, that never makes it feel any better, being called last, but like I said you are in and fit to make your future going forward. Truly that's all that matters now." Telluride toasted his pipe to Callum as if it were a mug of ale. "That and heading to Ridgebarrow and to the King's Forest from there."

"Do you really think I will be able to earn that much in the forest? I will need shards for the Powercores I already have *and* shards to sell."

"I wouldn't suggest that if I didn't think otherwise. You just need to get there, and I'm sure things will shake out from that point forward." Telluride stood. "I'm going to head to the pub that Kaelor usually frequents. Didn't you tell me you could cook? It sure would be nice to come back to a warm meal."

"Certainly," Callum said.

"Good, I'll be back in about an hour, and I will let you know what to do from there. Speaking of favors, the butcher down the way owes me some meat. You can use that."

"Will do!"

Callum went to work as soon as Telluride left.

He diced onions and a clove of garlic, which he simmered in oil and brought to a boil after adding a few other herbs and seasonings he found in the shardcrafter's kitchen. "He doesn't have any meat."

"There was a butcher near here."

"Good idea."

Callum left quickly, got a hunk of mutton from the butcher that still had the bone in it, and brought it back to the barn. He tossed this in the soup, and proceeded to slice some bread that Telluride had picked up that morning.

By the time the shardcrafter was back, Callum had the soup ready, along with the platter of sliced bread that he served with a thick hunk of butter.

"Huh, you really *can* cook," Telluride said after his first taste, the man's eyes just a bit glazed over now, indicating he had drunk an ale or two.

"I told you. And your friend?"

"Kaelor said it was fine. He's heading that way anyhow. He thinks you should go all the way to the town, rather than hop off before. If you do that, you might have a chance to go out with an adventurer party. Although, that won't bode well if you're planning to meet up with the nobles that are camping in the King's Forest, and the adventurer party wouldn't be allowed, anyway."

"So I should still get off early?"

"It's probably for the best, yeah. We'll pack some food in the morning just to get you started. Finding the camp once you get there won't be that hard. Kaelor told me that there's a trail marked by stone statues. The only risk is that it's not well-maintained or guarded, so there's a good chance you'll encounter something along the way." He took another bite of his soup. "But I suppose that's the whole reason why you're in the forest in the first place, isn't it?"

After a quick breakfast with Telluride the next morning, he packed a few things, including a blanket and other supplies he would need to camp.

Kaelor picked Callum up at the farm in a covered cart being pulled by a pair of donkeys.

"Good luck," Telluride told Callum, the two of them having said everything they needed to by this point. After a few words with Kaelor, the merchant set off, Callum seated beside him.

Kaelor didn't say much along the ride aside from asking him where he was from and telling him he had been to Weatherby once, twenty years ago.

But big as New Albion was, it gave way to a forest soon enough. They traveled through it for hours in relative silence, the bouts of quiet interrupted by the occasional bird and a little thunder. There were also guard stations, something Telluride had told him about. According to the shardcrafter, there hadn't been an attack on the route for years.

Callum could see why.

Not only were there common soldiers at the guard stations, there were also pacted mages.

Kaelor finally slowed after they passed over a small wooden bridge, one that had been well maintained.

"There it is." Kaelor motioned toward a path marked by a huge tree carved into the bust of a woman in armor. Vines had grown up over her form, and Callum could see stone steps and smaller stone statues in the distance, all with varying degrees of decay. The merchant glanced up at the sky. "It's going to rain. I can feel it in my bones, you know."

"I've heard my dad say something similar," Callum told him.

"You'll understand when you get older. Anyway, I really do think you should continue with me to Meadowglade. I know that Telluride said you can fend for yourself, but it's dangerous out there you know."

"I'm aware, but this is where I get off, thank you for the ride." Callum said as he hopped off the cart and turned back to Kaelor. "Really, I appreciate it."

"I was going to save these for later, but if you're set on going, you should take them." He reached into a compartment built into the side of his seat and produced a bag of fruit. "Just let me have one of the apples," he said as he quickly pulled out the aforementioned fruit and took a bite. "The rest is yours."

"You don't have to."

"I know, I don't. And your canteen is full? Hmm, did I already ask that?"

"No, you didn't, and it's fine."

"Alright, in that case, good luck," Kaelor said, giving him a wave before he continued on.

While Callum watched him ride away, he ate an apple from the bag. "I wonder why this path is here," he said as he gestured to the route.

Fen appeared and sat next to Callum. "It might be an alternate route to the camping grounds. It is strange that there isn't a guard station here. There were many on our way."

"I was thinking the same," Callum said with another bite of the apple. He took in the forest once again. Their path was lined by towering trees with thick, gnarled trunks, their intertwined branches partially obscuring the gray clouds above. "Is all of this the King's Forest?"

"You are asking the wrong pacted aetherbeast. I'm going to assume that the main road is for merchants and travelers, and anything jutting off of it is protected land. Shall we? Once you find a good place to camp for tonight, we can work in some training. Tomorrow as well."

"That's exactly what I need." Callum finished the apple and tossed what was left of the core onto the ground. They walked past the carved wooden statue and took a set of stone steps down to a long pathway that went for about fifty yards before it came to another set of stone steps. The path that continued was rough, with roots and bramble snaking across it.

Everything was ancient, like it had been built during the time of his forefathers. He didn't recognize any of the statues, not that he would. Callum didn't know much about the famous people of his kingdom aside from his namesake, and the people of Weatherby weren't all that religious. Dealing with crops year in and year out could have led to superstition, but it didn't. Most of his neighbors had been extremely practical.

His father was the same way, aside from his strange obsession with forgetting the past as if their luck had been tied to it.

Now, Callum suspected it was something else.

The Corruption that had been beneath the East Manor, certainly had something to do with what happened with his mother. And the corrupted mana that afflicted Fen.

He seems to be doing better, though. Is it something I'm doing? Callum thought as they came to a well atop a small, foliage-covered hill, where they found a pair of sleeping mats, evidence of a campsite.

Callum approached the mats and crouched in front of the ash of a fire. He grabbed a stick and sifted through the ash to find a single smoldering coal. He noticed a banner affixed to one of the trees. "Soldiers. But where are they?"

Fen moved ahead, the fox traveling to the bottom of a hill. He returned rapidly, his tail swishing sharply to the right. "We have a problem."

Callum, who was still crouched examining some of the things around the fire, looked up at him. "What is it?"

"Just come with me."

Callum joined Fen and soon discovered a pair of bodies, their armor charred, the flesh burned black.

"An aetherbeast did this?" Callum asked as his heart thumped loudly in his chest.

"That or a bandit of sorts." Fen sniffed at the ground. "But I think it might have been an aetherbeast." As he said these words, the clouds above opened, the rain so sudden that it caused Callum to jump back.

Fen tilted his head back and examined the trees, his ears going flat. "Do you see that?"

Callum brought his hand over his brow as he followed the fox's gaze. It looked like something had come through the trees and struck the two soldiers; the branches were all scorched.

"It must have taken them completely off guard," Fen surmised.

"What makes you say that?"

"Both of them still have their swords sheathed at their sides. Had they actually had time to react, they probably would have drawn their weapons. Check both blades and pick the one you like the best. We can bring it with us as evidence to show the people at the nobles' camp that there was an attack here. Or, even better," Fen said as he looked once again at the blackened branches, "we find whatever did this, and deal with it ourselves."

CHAPTER 22

If you can fuse it, fuse it. If you must store it for later, do so, but do so with the utmost care. Attribute Shards and Powercores carry great value in our nation and our world. Keep them in your sight.

—Nanna Gral, Master Convoker, Clerga

Soon, the rain became so strong that Callum had to take shelter under the sprawling canopy of an ancient oak. He was lucky that not all the leaves had fallen, the tree branches angled in a way that allowed him to stand there for a moment and watch the rain fall.

The rain was going to make camping difficult, but at least the path was clear. It cut straight through the forest and was occasionally marked by stone statues. Callum got the sense that the path was trimmed once a year, everything overgrown yet still visible.

As they continued on, he took a deep breath into his nostrils. *<I always liked that smell, rain. On the farm, that smell in the spring meant that we would have a better harvest.>*

<It was never easy for you.>

<No, but that's fine. Others have it worse.> He placed his hand on the hilt of his sword, but then he lowered it. By this point, he was more comfortable calling on Fen's power than he was using a blade. Aside from the aetherbeast that had landed on his farm or those he'd fought within the Soul Pythia, Callum had never encountered a wild aetherbeast. He really didn't know what to expect as he pressed on.

Callum often hunted with his father, a tradition that had started when he was a young boy and food was scarce. During those times, he was responsible for getting whatever animal they were hunting to run toward his father. He got very good at sneaking, a trait that he had lost in his teenage years.

But not fully.

Callum knew about tracking, and he knew how to move in a way that would keep him relatively obscured. Yet something else came to him as he lightly stepped around a tree.

There was a change in energy.

Before, Callum would have thought it had something to do with the weather. Perhaps it still did, but he thought now that it was something magic-related. He couldn't quite see it, and he had yet to fully understand it, but for some reason it made him think about cultivation, what little Telluride had said.

It also made him steady his breath.

Close to his target, Callum crept to the side of a tree that had grown around a large boulder. He stopped, his body flat against the rock as he spotted a giant boar. The massive, hulking creature had elongated tusks and jagged, electrified spikes of mana rising off its spine.

Is that . . . Corruption? Callum thought as he saw the boar rummaging around, leaving a trail of bubbling dark mana in its wake.

<Ready when you are.>

His opening attack came swiftly as he shifted past the stone. He started with a blast of wind, Callum melding with Fen faster than he could remember doing before. It was becoming more instinctual, his movements heightened as he rushed toward the aetherboar.

The creature took the brunt of his first attack as it swiveled toward him. As Fen yelled in his head for Callum to press the attack. He struck the aetherboar with his claws. He jumped back as the beast lunged for him, kicking up dirt, roots, and corrupted mana.

<I'll hit him from behind, you use your lance!>

Callum conjured his Luminous Lance, its radiant form crackling with energy. With a sharp breath, he pulled his arm back, his movements precise as Fen darted ahead, clearing his line of attack. Timing it perfectly, Callum hurled the lance, the weapon slicing through the air in a brilliant arc before grazing the boar and pushing it off course. The beast let out an earsplitting roar, its furious snort shaking the ground as it reared its head, eyes blazing with rage.

Seizing the opening, Fen unleashed a concentrated blast of wind that slammed into the creature's flank, sending it stumbling. Callum wasted no time as he sprinted forward, his hand summoning another lance. With a surge of determination, he drove the weapon deep into the manaboar's side.

This seemed to do the trick, the beastly boar letting out a death rattle as it slapped to the ground and faded in a flash of sizzling mana. Shards rushed toward Callum and appeared in the palm of his hand.

Empowerment of Mind Shard
Empowerment of Regeneration Shard
Shadow Affinity Shard

"Good," Fen said as he immediately moved to absorb the Corruption the aetherboar had left behind.

"Should I fuse the ones I can now?"

"Do it," said Fen, who had just finished absorbing the Corruption. "Best to do so as soon as you can."

Callum accessed his Inner Light core and quickly fused both the Mind and Regeneration Shards into it, just as Telluride had shown him. He placed the Shadow Affinity Shard in his pouch to keep it safe. "Done."

"There's more training to do," Fen said as the rain continued to fall all around them. The ground was growing muddier, a factor Callum knew he'd need to account for in future encounters. He was also sopping wet, but it didn't really bother him much until the wind picked up.

"I was wondering when you would start imparting all that knowledge of yours from years of combat," Callum said, which was meant to be something of a joke.

Fen, who had traveled just a bit ahead of him, spoke as he continued on: "My memory isn't as good as it should be. And remember, I didn't fight with your forefather as long as the others considering my placement beneath the manor."

"The others he pacted with, from the statue," Callum said, recalling the wolf, gryphon, phoenix, and dragon that had once accompanied the Demonslayer.

"Exactly. I don't know everything, but I've picked up a few things, especially from watching the Entry Duels. They sparked my memory—let's put it that way. One of those things should come into play soon enough."

"What do you mean?"

"I'm no ordinary fox, as you know, but I am still a fox—and we are very good at rooting things out. There are plenty of lesser aetherbeasts around, some corrupted like the one you just saw earlier, and others just remnants left behind by old aetherstorms. Right now, those remnants are exactly what I'm searching for."

"Can you smell them or something?"

Fen, whose body was composed entirely of mana, tilted his snout into the air. "I wouldn't describe it as a smell, more of a sense. You should be able to do it at some point."

Knowing how far he had to go to catch up with his peers made him feel small. *But at least I made it into the Great College*, he reminded himself, which was a feat that he would have never predicted even a month ago.

Fen crouched, the fox's ears erect. "Ahead. A smaller one; no, several. Stay here and be ready to hit them with your lance. There's a ravine." Fen pointed it out with his chin. "I'll run them into there, you hit them with your lance, claws, and Zephyr Strike."

"It won't be as strong if we aren't melded."

"No, it will not. But that's fine. We're trying new things, and if we master the art of hunting together, we will be able to pick up more shards and perhaps even a Powercore or two on our way to the nobles' camp. Are you ready?"

"Ready."

"Good."

Callum approached the edge of the ravine, which was slowly filling with water from the constant rain. The rain wasn't as heavy as it had been when they killed the boar, but it was still coming, thick enough to obscure the forest like a thick fog. It was also loud, the constant drumming of the rain on the forest floor making it hard to track things.

At least the aetherbeasts are easy to spot.

He imagined bolts of light exploding out of the mist-like rain ahead as the beasts funneled into the ravine. Callum just needed to be ready to conjure his lance. Although, now that he thought about it . . . *Zephyr Strike first*.

It had a wider radius, which would allow him to surprise whatever Fen chased out.

Callum focused so hard on the woods beyond that his eyes started to hurt. He wiped some rain off his brow.

They came fast.

There was a flash of light, and then large, rabbit-sized aetherbeasts hopped into the ravine, four in total. Callum went after them with bolts of wind. It felt strange using the power without Melding, but he got the hang of it as he sent gusts of wind into the ravine.

Much to his surprise, the rabbits dispersed and then rushed back together, where they formed into a larger rabbit, one about the size of the bear. The amalgamation tossed its head back and released a short beam of mana, which struck a tree next to Callum as he dove right.

Fen reached him and the two melded, Callum instantly feeling the change in his strength.

Ignoring the rain, and the way his boots sank into the mud, Callum jumped into the ravine just as lightning crackled in the sky above.

He hit the amalgamation with one of his claws, ducked, and then felt a new sensation as Fen took control.

<Let me show you how it's done!>

It was strange watching his body possessed by the Radiant Fox, who charged toward the amalgamation in a way that Callum would never have dared, running sideways along the walls of the ravine and twisting off of it.

The strike was magnificent, enough to stagger the aetherbeast.

<Watch this!> Fen dropped onto all fours and vaulted forward, moving with a speed that would have been entirely graceful if not for the sword sheathed at Callum's side. The blade slapped awkwardly against his thigh but stayed secure as Fen closed the distance. With two swift slashes of his claws, Fen struck the aetherbeast, leaped back, and finished it off in a single fluid motion using Zephyr Strike.

"That was . . . that was amazing!" Callum huffed as the mana faded, leaving two glimmering shards that surged toward his open palm.

Light Affinity Shard
Empowerment of Deftness Shard

Callum fused the Light Affinity Shard into his Pact of the Radiant Fox Aethercore. He did the same with the Deftness Shard he had received and checked the status of the core:

Pact of the Radiant Fox
Type: *Pact*
Grade: *Common*
Infusion Requirements for Grade Increase:
5/5 Fire Affinity Shards
2/5 Light Affinity Shards
1/10 Deftness Shards
1/10 Vigor Shards
0/5 Resilience Shards

I need more Light Affinity, Deftness, Vigor, and Resilience shards, he thought as he pressed the core back into his chest. "Remember anything else about fighting?" he asked Fen as the fox appeared next to him.

"I'll tell you when I do, especially if it helps us in some way." Fen jutted his snout toward the path beyond. "Let's continue. And be ready to confront the aetherbeast that killed those soldiers back there. I still haven't sensed it but that doesn't mean it isn't waiting for us on the path ahead. All the rain may help obscure it."

"Right. It has wings."

"Indeed. And we don't. Not yet, anyway," Fen said as he trotted ahead.

CHAPTER 23

The establishment of the Emporium to buy, sell, and trade shards and Powercores is one of the best things that happened for New Albion during the reign of Queen Liza Morninglade. Its proximity to the Second Heart of Creation makes its bond with the World Ledger that much stronger, and after tracking prices and trades for years, we have noted an increased value in shards that move through the Emporium versus through private shardcrafter establishments.

—Sir Garrick Mormont, The Crown's Royal Tax Collector

The next round of shards flowed to Callum after a trio of smaller aether-beasts, no larger than sheep, fizzled away.

Water Affinity Shard
Empowerment of Deftness Shard
Empowerment of Deftness Shard

"Nice," Callum told Fen as the fox appeared beside him. "We can add those Deftness Shards to your Aethercore and save the water one."

"And the more saved shards we have, the more we'll be able to trade in at the Emporium to get the shards we need."

"And money."

"And that. Eventually, if we get enough Attribute Shards, we can save them so you can use them in a pinch."

Callum fused the two Deftness Shards into the Aethercore.

"Shall we?" Fen asked as he turned back toward the main trail. It was much wider here, the stones cut into huge slabs that had been partially buried. Callum had once built a stone path for a neighbor. He knew the work that would have gone into something like that.

"I wonder how long ago they built this."

"Whenever it was built, they have really lapsed on the upkeep. I suppose the fact that the wild aetherbeasts roam this forest would prevent the Crown from adequately seeing to it, but it does make you wonder. Let's keep moving. There are bound to be more along the path, and we still have plenty of daylight."

"This is fun," Callum said.

"It is until it isn't. Remember, there's something hunting people out there, and we should both keep that in mind."

Later, as they reached a secluded grove with the canopy above thick enough to prevent rainwater from coming through, Fen got low to the ground like he was prepared to pounce. Callum held back, his hand naturally falling onto the grip of his sword, even though he knew it wouldn't do anything against an aetherbeast.

"Watch," Fen said, his snout aimed at the tops of the trees, which occasionally shifted in the wind blowing overhead.

I don't see anything, Callum thought as he tried to make sense of what Fen had spotted.

He gasped as an aetherbeast landed in the grove, the owl much larger than the ones Callum had seen back at the farm, its eyes blazing with power.

"What's it doing?" Callum asked Fen as the owl focused on them.

"Quick—!" Fen never finished what he was saying as the owl released a bolt of sizzling mana in their direction. It grazed Callum's arm as he dove right, the sting instant, like he'd placed his hand too close to a fire.

Fen charged toward the owl and hit the aetherbeast with a quick swipe from his claws. The owl took to the air, Fen's attack barely pushing it off its intended trajectory, which just so happened to be to canopy above.

"We need to meld," Callum said as the owl whisked through the trees, its progress marked by flashes of light.

"Agreed!" Fen rushed to Callum in a surge of light just as the owl swooped toward him.

Callum dove to avoid its talons. With his enhanced speed, he was back on his feet in a matter of seconds and was able to hit the owl with an amplified funnel of wind, his attack causing it to lose some of its shining feathers.

As it tried to get to cover, Callum conjured his lance and hurled it at the owl. It pressed through the aetherbeast's manabound body and pinned it to the ground.

"I think I got it!"

<With aetherbeasts, never count your chickens before they . . .> Fen wasn't able to finish his statement as the owl released a huge cloud of shadowy mana that immediately obscured most of the grove and was so thick that Callum couldn't see in front of him.

He instinctively moved backward and lost his footing on a limb. Callum hit the ground, pressed back up, and swiveled left as a flash of light illuminated the thick shadows. The owl released another bolt that seared past him, mere inches away from his head.

<We can heal later. Focus!>

Callum used his wind attack twice, which seemed to clear some of the shadowy mist. He still couldn't see the owl, but he was starting to understand the pattern of light it made as it moved through the darkness.

Summoning all his focus and ignoring the pain on his arm and neck, Callum conjured a lance and pitched it toward a spot just in front of the flash of light. It hit the owl, which brought it down for good, the shadowy mist dissipating.

Fen moved away from Callum and began absorbing the shadowy mana that radiated on the ground, looking much like the corrupted mana Callum had seen.

Shadow Affinity Shard
Light Affinity Shard
Empowerment of Might Shard
Shadowbreath of the Lightveil Owl

"I received an actual Powercore!" Callum told Fen as the information appeared before him.

Shadowbreath of the Lightveil Owl
Type: Ability
Grade: Common
Infusion Requirements for Grade Increase:
0/10 Shadow Affinity
0/5 Mind Shards
Affinity Requirements: Shadow
Effect: When bound to one's Soul Heart, this core grants the user the ability to exhale a cloud of shadow mana able to obscure most locations.

"Huh," Fen said as he too examined the information. "To use this adequately, you would need to have an Aethercore that grants you an affinity to Shadow Mana, another pacted aetherbeast besides me, because I can only use Air, Fire, and Light Mana. You could still try it, but it won't be as strong."

"That's right, like that one power I got from the bandit, that was sundered. He wasn't pacted with anything."

"Correct. Try to use it and see what I mean."

"Let me deal with these shards first." Callum pressed the new core into his chest. He fused the Empowerment of Might Shard he had received into Gift of the Luminous Lance and the Light Affinity Shard into Fen's Aethercore.

Once he was ready, Callum invoked the Shadowbreath of the Lightveil Owl Powercore as he would any other.

He felt an itch at the back of his throat, one that forcibly caused him to bend forward and release a small puff of shadow mana.

"Not very impressive," Fen told him. "But like I said, if you pact with something that will give you Shadow Affinity, it could be useful."

"I could sell it whole or have Telluride sunder it for its parts."

"Also a good option."

Callum glanced ahead, noting where the path picked back up. "Shall we?"

The fox stopped a few moments later, his tail lowering in agitation. "That's . . . strange."

"Do you sense something?" Callum asked as he moved to the cover of a tree. He was aware how strong aetherbeast mana could be. Perhaps the shade of a wet tree wasn't the best location, but at least it moved him off the main path.

"It's not that," Fen said. "It's something much stronger."

"Stronger than an aetherbeast? Like what?"

"I don't know. Can't you feel it?"

"How should it feel?"

Fen took a quick look around. "Is there a good place to sit around here without getting your pants wet?"

"I don't mind. I can sit . . ." Callum found a root that had grown out of the ground. "Here."

"Good. Close your eyes, see if you can feel it." Fen lifted his snout and bits of mana traced around it. He sneezed, bared his teeth, and went back to focusing.

"I still don't know what I'm looking for," Callum told him.

"As the Soul Pythia alluded, meditation is one of the ways to tap into it. I'm not an expert, and you have to remember that things have changed since my time. You will be learning at the College as much as I will."

"What do you mean?"

"That is the nature of your species, to learn and build upon that learning. Surely you didn't think that everything from my time would be the same now. At least I would hope not. Well, Weatherby might be the same," Fen said, a rare joke. "But that would make it an outlier. Now, I'm not qualified to teach you how to meditate, but I can tell you to close your eyes and see if you notice anything else."

Callum did just that.

The sound of the light rain came to him first, but it quickly faded into the background as he noticed something else, a pulse. At first, he thought he had discovered what Fen was sensing, but then he realized it was his own heartbeat.

He tried to focus even further until he noticed something else. That pulse that he was hearing was indeed his heart, but it was beating in unison to something else, a slight thumping in the distance. And once he noticed that, once he homed in on the sound, he felt a very subtle yet noticeable pull at his core.

"Yes?" asked Fen, who stood directly in front of him now, watching the young man.

"What is that?"

"I do not know, but whatever it is, it has a lot of mana stored within. I do not think it is the aetherbeast we seek, but I do feel that we may encounter it the closer we get to the source of that power. Maybe there's something else here, another reason why the Crown would forbid the general public from coming to this forest. Maybe they're hiding something."

"Wouldn't we get in trouble if we discovered it?"

"That I can't tell you. But I do not think they would let nobles come here if that were the case. It is rather curious, but I think we should follow it."

"And camp along the way?" he asked the fox.

"In a few hours, yes. Rest is important to your overall health and since we are pacted, it is important to mine. I have started to feel better though." Fen motioned with his neck for Callum to follow him. "I do not think I am at full health, even if I seem strong. But I'm closer than I was when you first discovered me." Fen traveled down a set of steps, leaping from stone to stone.

Callum caught up with him and they soon reached another area where there had once been a fire, the char evident on some of the pine trees that were interspersed through the forest. Callum had noticed more of these the further they traveled along the trail, the pine trees leaving their needles and cones behind.

Something new dawned on him. "This isn't from a forest fire," he said as he examined one of the trees.

"Oh?"

"Look. It's only on this ring of trees." Callum pointed at the trunks in question. "Like something whipped through here."

"It's here as well," Fen said as he trotted over to another ring of burned-out trees. "It has to be an aetherbeast."

"Do you think it knows we're here?"

Fen looked around again as more rain fell onto the forest. "This may be to our advantage but follow the fire damage. But first, I will return to you, your surprise weapon."

"You're certainly that," Callum said as they melded and he felt Fen's power wash over him.

Callum crept ahead. He noticed something else as he moved quietly through the damp forest. It was a sense of agility that he didn't normally have, Fen's influence.

This reminded him of some of the meldforms he had seen back at the Entry Duels, how some of the students turned primal in certain ways when they melded. Maybe that was what he was experiencing now, this instinct to adapt to the animal nature of a pacted aetherbeast.

What would a fox do? he thought as he reached another ring of burned-out trees.

He could always ask Fen, but there was something gratifying about discovering it on his own. Callum had always been that way to some degree. Not hardheaded, but determined, a person who found challenges rewarding. Add a bit of prudence and this perfectly described how his father had raised him.

If only you could see me now. It was a thought that reminded Callum that he needed to send a letter and hopefully some money to Rhane once he returned to the city.

He reached a set of trees with a clump of smoldering wood on the ground.

Whatever was causing this, they were close now.

Callum watched as manabound claws grew over his fingers, his power surging as he caught sight of a fiery aetherbeast with its back to him.

It had the body of a wolf and the head of an eagle, with wings large enough to lift its body. There was corrupted mana here, all around it.

<*Do it.*>

Fen didn't need to tell him how to strike as Callum raced forward and attacked the aetherbeast with his Radiant Claws.

The monster roared in response and released a puff of fiery mana as its wings flapped rapidly, spinning the creature. Callum had to dive backward to avoid a sawlike blade of mana that scorched several of the trees, before being put out by the rain.

He now understood what Fen meant by them having an advantage. The rain prevented the aetherbeast from attacking them with all of its power.

Even as the enemy aetherbeast tried to blow a huge fireball at them, the distance its mana-flames traveled was dampened.

He barely had time to process it, but Callum learned an important lesson. It was so simple that he wondered why he hadn't connected the pieces before—aetherbeasts were elemental in nature, even if they were man-abound. So water would disrupt fire, and he assumed there were other combinations that would work well together or clash in a fight.

There was only one thing he didn't quite understand, and that was the substance of mana itself, how he wasn't able to hit the aetherbeast with his sword, yet the rain affected its attacks.

Fire, water, wind, Callum thought as he struck the creature with a sharpened bolt of wind, blowing out some of the flames that had rolled onto its wings. Another attack caused it to fly into a tree, the wet wood smoking as the aetherbeast righted itself and lunged for Callum.

He slammed the creature to the ground with Zephyr Strike, revealing something else about the physical nature of these beings. One more attack at point-blank range put the creature down for good.

Fire Affinity Shard
Light Affinity Shard

"Nice," Callum said as he fused the Light Affinity Shard into his Pact of the Radiant Fox Aethercore. He placed the Fire Affinity Shard in his pouch and moved back to the main trail. "I figured something out, too."

<What's that?>

"I figured out more about how aetherbeasts interact with the natural world."

<What do you mean?>

"The way my sword won't hurt an aetherbeast, but it can still catch a tree on fire."

<But your sword would hurt an aetherbeast if it was a Weaponcore. We need to look into getting something like that.>

"I'll get right on that," Callum said as he closed his eyes for a moment. He turned toward the east. "This way."

<Yes, I agree. We still have a ways to go, and we will likely camp along the way, but the sooner we find the source of this disturbance, the better. You seem to have a sense of the destination so, by all means, lead the way, Callum.>

CHAPTER 24

By nightfall, Callum had picked up a number of shards from lesser aetherbeasts:

Light Affinity Shard
Light Affinity Shard
Empowerment of Vigor Shard
Empowerment of Mind Shard
Empowerment of Mind Shard
Empowerment of Regeneration Shard
Empowerment of Might Shard

He fused the Light Affinity Shards into Pact of the Radiant Fox; the Mind and Regeneration shards into Inner Light; and the Might Shard into Gift of the Luminous Lance.

Callum had also received shards that he intended to sunder to get the ones he needed to upgrade his powers. These included a Death Affinity Shard, an Earth Affinity Shard, a Life Affinity Shard, and an Empowerment of Resilience Shard, which he could also use if he needed a boost to his natural resilience.

Later that night, Callum and Fen came across a stony grove that seemed ripe with energy.

"Is this it?" Callum whispered. "Is this what you were sensing?"

<No, I don't think so. Those stones, they're all covered in corrupted mana.>

The boulders had a glow to them. That was the first thing Callum had noticed upon reaching the stony grove, which jutted off the main path he had been following. Yet now, he could see what Fen meant. There was something different about the boulders, something he would equate to a dark sparkle.

<I should get to work,> Fen said as he unmelded from Callum.

Yet as soon as the fox touched the ground, one of the boulders came alive, a great aetherbeast that resembled a bear lifting out of the ground.

Callum stumbled backward upon seeing the aetherbeast. While it had a body made of mana like others he had encountered, it also carried a thick layer of stone on its back. The bear lunged for him, smashed into the ground, and brought down a tree as Callum dove to his left.

"Fen!"

The fox's power rushed into Callum as the aetherbeast threw itself at him again. It sent an enormous set of stone-clad claws through the air as Callum rolled out of the way, his escape augmented by Fen's power boost.

He should have been crushed by the next blow, but instead he fell down an embankment, the rolling aetherbeast launching right over him.

<Lance!>

<On it!> Callum told Fen as he conjured a lance and hurled it at the aetherbeast. It managed to break some stones off its shoulder, but didn't do much more damage as the creature righted itself and turned toward Callum, eyes flaring with mana.

Callum was hit by a sweeping claw of mana. He was flung through the air, soaring high enough that he crashed into a cluster of wet branches on the way down. The impact was brutal—the branches scraped against his exposed skin, and the hard landing left him aching all over. Even so, he pushed himself up just as the aetherbeast charged again and twisted the armored part of its body at him.

Callum sidestepped the attack and hit it as hard as he could with a surge of wind.

There was some damage and a bit more stone crumbled away, yet the beast recovered quickly as it tried to swipe at him.

Callum moved away quickly as Fen separated from him. "I'll distract it. Head around back!" the fox charged at the aetherbeast, which roared in a way that sent a vibrational force twisting through the woods, dislodging leaves, branches, and some of the trapped water from the day's rain.

Callum nearly slipped, yet he kept his footing as he followed Fen's instruction. Breaking its armor seemed to be the only way to go, considering every time he struck it, the beast would turn in a way to absorb most of his attack.

Is there something else? Is there something I'm missing? he thought as Fen continued attacking the bear as best he could. It wasn't a fair match, that was for sure, yet Fen held his own as he jumped from rock to root, occasionally releasing blasts of mana at the aetherbeast as Callum got into position.

<*I'm here!*> Callum called to Fen as he tried to remember what he had learned in fighting this kind of aetherbeast. Princess Selene had melded with a bear, but she had come at him so quickly in their duel and with so much power that there wasn't much he could learn from that fight. What about her other duels that he had witnessed?

From what he could recall, Selene's strategy had continued throughout the Entry Duels. It had been one of sheer dominance, overpowering an opponent, which Callum knew was also a mental game.

Maybe it's not as strong as it looks, Callum thought, which went against everything he was witnessing as the bear again tried to smash Fen, who was racing toward Callum.

He felt Fen's power return as they melded again.

Callum hit the bear with a powerful burst of wind. Rather than simply follow up with another spiral of wind, Callum dodged left to avoid the bear, and sent everything he could conjure into his next attack.

It hit the bear hard.

The aetherbeast fell to the side, rolled, and struck a tree. The tree creaked and slowly fell onto the aetherbeast, breaking away even more of its armor.

<*What was that? That hit!*>

<*I sort of charged up Zephyr Strike. I don't know! You're supposed to be teaching me; I'm not supposed to be figuring this out on the go!*> Callum thought back as he peered ahead.

<*Do that again. Charge it longer. It makes sense. I remember now. Yes! You aren't fully in tune with your core, but there's something there. You can use it as fuel. It may exhaust you. But you have to try!*>

<*Got it,*> Callum said as he tried to put some distance between him and the aetherbeast. He fired another burst of wind at it, but this one didn't have the same power it had previously.

<*Focus, Callum! Pour your power into it. I'll try to help!*>

<Let's try the lance!> Callum said almost as an afterthought as he dodged another attack from the bear, which was growing increasingly rabid and violent. Something had changed; the creature was coming at him harder and faster, anger rippling off its form.

Callum jumped back and pulled himself up the embankment just as the beast slammed into it. He conjured a lance, looked down at the creature, and focused everything he had into what he did next.

The lance exploded through the air and drove deep into the aetherbeast, pushing through its armor and piercing through its chest.

The monster staggered.

Callum didn't let up as he summoned another lance, his temple pulsing, heart thrashing in his chest as he once again tried to conjure as much power as he could into his next attack.

The lance brought the aetherbeast down. The beast tried to rise again but Callum finished the job with a final strike. Shards raced toward him, followed by a Powercore.

Empowerment of Might Shard
Earth Affinity Shard
Light Affinity Shard
Charge of the Shatterlight Bear

Charge of the Shatterlight Bear
Type: *Ability*
Grade: *Common*
Infusion Requirements for Grade Increase:
0/5 Earth Affinity
0/5 Light Affinity
0/10 Might Shards
0/3 Resilience Shards
Affinity Requirements: *Light or Earth*
Effect: *When bound to one's Soul Heart, this core allows the user to summon the crushing power of the Shatterlight Bear.*

"That's a good one," Callum told Fen as he examined the core that hovered before him. "I can use the Earth Affinity Shard I already have and the one I just got for this core. Plus, I had the Resilience Shard, so I can pop that one in as well. The Light Affinity Shard will be for your Aethercore, and I can use the Might Shard to complete the requirements for the Gift of the Luminous Lance."

"You're that certain you'll like this new core? You haven't even tried it."

"The ability to ram into something like a bear covered in stone? I'm almost a hundred percent certain I'll like it."

Fen seemed to grin at him. "In that case, fuse it and then check your Mana Reserves before you test the power. You aren't injured, but I am sensing a dip in your power. That makes sense considering you can't cultivate mana yet."

"If only I knew how." Callum took the Resilience Shard from his pouch and fused it into the Charge of the Shatterlight Bear. He followed this up by using Soul Sense, the information appearing before him:

Soul Sense:
Status:
Health: Uninjured
Mana Reserves: Half-Full
Soul Heart Rank: Initiate
Soulbonding Capacity: 6 Powercores, 1 Aethercore
Attributes:
Might: 4
Deftness: 3
Vigor: 3
Resilience: 3
Regeneration: 3
Mind: 3
Soulbound Cores:
Ability: Empowerment of Zephyr Strike
Ability: Gift of the Luminous Lance
Ability: Charge of the Shatterlight Bear
Ability: Inner Light
Support: Empowerment of Sustenance
Pact: Pact of the Radiant Fox

"With the new one, I only have room for one more Powercore at my current Rank," Callum said. "And my mana levels are at the halfway mark. I didn't really think about them until you pointed them out."

"That's good and bad. Good that you have enough power to do all we've just done and only be on half a tank; bad that it isn't a bigger focus of ours. But I suspect rest will help some and, later, cultivation." Fen smirked at Callum. "You want to try out that new power of yours, don't you?"

"How could you tell?"

"Call it a fox's intuition. Come, let's see what it does." Fen hopped away from him, moving about ten feet out. "Try it on me."

"On . . . you?"

"I'll jump. It just gives you a target. And remember, we aren't melded, so you aren't at your full power anyway."

"Alright," Callum said as he focused on the fox. He triggered the new core and noticed a rush of brute strength come to him as he charged forward, his form hulking, bits of mana rippling off his shoulders.

As promised, Fen jumped out of the way. "Not bad. Now, try it with me."

Fen vanished; Callum noticed the change in his power level as the two melded. He attempted the attack again and noticed the sheer power that Fen brought to the table as Callum burst forward, mana flaring off his back as he executed a charged tackle.

He collided with the ground, yet Callum was cushioned somewhat by the transformation, and it didn't hurt too badly. He pushed himself back up.

"Nice."

<Nice, is right. That would be an excellent opening attack. Or a way to take an opponent off guard. It's a good one.>

Callum dusted himself off. The two continued chatting as he moved back toward the main path, on which he traveled for another thirty minutes until he found the perfect camping space.

"It's even dry," he told Fen as he looked up at a tree over the site, and the rocks that the tree had grown around, creating a space somewhat protected from the elements. Callum got out the cloak his father had insisted he buy and placed it on the ground as close to the stone and wood as he could get.

Soon, he had a small fire going, though he wasn't all that hungry because of his Empowerment of Sustenance Powercore. He ate anyway, mostly out of habit. Once he finished, he sat with his feet facing the fire, his hands on the cloak.

"Your cloak came in handy after all," said Fen, who was curled up near him.

"It did. I used to love camping, back when my father and I would go."

"Why did you two stop going?"

"The farm, mostly. It took a lot of work, and every year was harder than the last."

"Likely due to the Corruption."

"Definitely," Callum said as he relaxed onto the cloak. He yawned and was about to drift off when Fen grew suddenly alert, his fur sparking with mana.

"Callum! We need to hide—!"

Fen melded with Callum as he scrambled closer to the tree. A great sweeping sound above them caused the hairs on his arm to stand to attention. He instinctively reached for the sword, even though he knew that it would do little against the winged aetherbeast that soared overhead. He only caught a glimpse of it, but what he saw told Callum that the creature was massive, perhaps the largest he had yet seen—easily as big as the one that had come during the aetherstorm and attacked the East Manor.

It passed overhead and mana rippled in the air after it. The beast sped up and was soon gone.

<*That was it! It has to be the one that killed those soldiers.*>

<*Should we follow it?*>

<*Yes. No, wait, maybe not.*>

<*Yes or no?*> Callum asked after Fen didn't respond for a moment.

<*No. It seems to be heading in the same direction as we are. You need rest; taking that thing down is going to require a lot of power. So I think no, no, we don't follow it now. We will also be able to see what it does on the path ahead.*>

<*What if it's heading toward the nobles' camp?*>

<*The source of mana is between here and there, to my knowledge. If it makes it that far, I'm sure they will do something about it. There are more of them, you know. And they are nobles.*>

<*I'm a noble, too.*>

<*You know what I mean. I mean they have been training longer.*> Fen separated from Callum. "It's good to know what we're up against. And, if we do run into the other nobles, maybe that will make taking it down easier." The fox looked at the path ahead. "That said, I really want to go after it."

"I do too."

"But we have to be smart about this, especially while you're ranked at a lower Rank. Something like that could kill us before we do whatever it is we are destined to do. I'm certain the Demon King has returned. And doing something like chasing after an unknown, certainly powerful, aetherbeast when you are at half mana could stop us from ever reaching the point where we find out." Fen sighed. "As disappointing as all this is."

"And if it comes by again?"

"Hopefully it won't. Just try to rest."

"Really?"

"Really." Fen paced for a moment. "Every time I feel like we have the hang of this—that we are getting closer to understanding, or at least being comfortable with our pact—I learn more. But I guess that is to be expected considering how long it has been since I was last alive."

* * *

Callum tried to get comfortable again.

It took him a while to fall asleep this time, even with the soothing sounds of the forest and the exhaustion he felt from a day of fighting aetherbeasts. The next morning came after a surprisingly solid sleep.

Once he was awake, Callum used Soul Sense to see where his Mana Reserves were.

> **Soul Sense:**
> **Status:**
> **Health:** *Uninjured*
> **Mana Reserves:** *Steady*
> **Soul Heart Rank:** *Initiate*
> **Soulbonding Capacity:** *6 Powercores, 1 Aethercore*

"It says they are *Steady*. That has to be better than *Half-Full*," Callum said.

"But it used to say *Full*."

"Correct."

"And that is something we will need to ask one of your new friends, or one of the masters if we hold off until lessons start."

Callum didn't yet think of Quinn as a friend, but it made sense to consider him as something like that. And he didn't dare assume that Princess Selene would be a friend. There were others he had met, too, people like Marcella, but those had all been through Quinn. "Well, for what it's worth, I feel better."

"Good. I am feeling surprisingly good as well. Consuming the corrupted mana appears to be helping me. Perhaps that is something else we will learn about. I wish I knew more. I'm sure you do as well."

"It's fine," Callum said as he packed up his cloak. "We're learning together."

"I suppose we are." Fen stretched his front paws out as mana fizzled over his form. "In that case, let's continue. We will take down anything along the way, and hopefully procure some more shards and cores. That's our goal. The more we get, the better our chances will be, and the more we'll have to sell at the Emporium. I'll go ahead. Be ready to spring into action at a moment's notice. And if we do find the winged aetherbeast, we'll hit it with everything we have."

CHAPTER 25

Mana can certainly bind with metal; it can pact with any number of objects as long as there is resonance and the person fusing knows how to transform something inert into a living extension of mana. If done correctly, this creates more than just protection or force, it creates potential. But remember, just like a good stew, certain elements have a way of blending into oblivion.

—Arjun Bonjardim, Master Weaver, chef, and author of *A Fork in the Flow: Recipes of the Aether*

An injury came later that morning after they fought a few smaller aetherbeasts that resembled the imps Callum had once faced in the corrupted depths of the East Manor. He received another Shadow Affinity Shard from these battles, as well as a Deftness Shard, which he had fused into Fen's Aethercore.

It all started when they came across a stream that seemed innocuous at first. Callum even crouched near it to fill his canteen when a lynx surged out of the water slashing its claws across Callum's exposed arm.

Even Fen, who was a couple feet away, hadn't sensed their opponent.

The Radiant Fox hit the lynx with a wind attack while Callum conjured his lance.

He missed his first attempt and only got the upper hand once he was able to charge at the aetherbeast using his new skill. He slammed into the lynx, then hit the bank, and then fell into the water with it, where it was able to claw at him again.

The sting from its attacks left Callum reeling for a moment, yet the pain soon dissipated as Fen's power rushed over him. Now melded, he beat at the aetherbeast with his Radiant Claws, feeling increasingly primal as he lunged for the creature on all fours. The lynx tried to overwhelm him, but

Callum was much stronger now, and his wounds were already healing due to his Inner Light power.

He managed to lift the lynx and slam it on the shoreline, where the aetherbeast stayed for a moment, dazed by the attack.

Callum conjured another lance and drove it into the beast's body with both hands.

Empowerment of Vigor Shard
Water Affinity Shard

"That was rough," Callum said as he got his bearings. He looked down at his arm to see the wound was nearly healed. He didn't think it would have healed so quickly if it been deeper.

<We must both be aware of our environment. We forget sometimes, or at least I do, that many of these aetherbeasts are elemental in nature. They can blend in and surprise attack us.>

Callum placed the Water Affinity Shard in his satchel. He then pushed the Vigor Shard into Fen's Aethercore. "Noted. I was not expecting to get so wet." He wrung some of the water out from his clothing.

<At least the rain stopped.> Fen reappeared by Callum's side. "Have you sensed anything this morning?"

"You mean like changes in the aether?"

"Exactly." Fen lifted his snout. "It's a bit different today. Further away."

"Maybe I should have chased it last night."

"Maybe. But I am a firm believer that if we're going to do this, we need to do this with you at full health. The aetherbeast that flew over us last night was absolutely massive. We need to be prepared."

"Which elemental force do you think it uses?"

"We saw the way the trees were burned back there with the soldiers. But that doesn't mean fire is the only affinity it has. I have three, as you know."

"Fire, Light, Air."

"Exactly. So it could have more than one. I can say this, though, it will be different from any that we have encountered so far, even the harder ones to defeat. That means it's older. Maybe it has been in this region for a while. Maybe it will even talk to us. Some do, some don't." Fen turned back toward the path. "I'm guessing we will find out soon enough."

They fell into a spell of silence as they moved on, Callum still wet, yet also feeling invigorated from a night of rest.

There was certainly a thrill in it. The excitement of uncovering something so many understood about his world, yet was something he had only begun to grasp, was a feeling that had yet to leave Callum, and he didn't think it would go anywhere anytime soon.

Make it through this and start at the Great College. Even on academic probation, it's a better chance than I would've had staying in Weatherby, he thought as he moved a stray branch aside, releasing droplets of water onto the forest floor. With the rain came a smell that reminded Callum of spring, how nice it was to see the final snow melt away in the water return.

Later, after traveling through what felt like an endless ravine, they reached an open area that turned into the ruins of an old temple, a few of the pillars intact. More of the crumbled and moss-covered statues drew Callum's attention.

The Radiant Fox sat and examined the ruins. "See if you can sense anything."

Callum lowered himself to his knees so he could focus better. Dipping his head, he tried to calm his beating heart, to ignore the sounds of the forest, the birds, the insects, and the occasional sweep of wind that brought a scattering of wet leaves.

There.

It was faint but he could sense it now, this magnetic force coming from the ruins. He finally opened his eyes. "Something is in there. I can't tell if it's the same source I felt yesterday."

"The temple looks like it's much larger than it appears from the outside. Perhaps there are some lower chambers."

"The last time I went into something like that, I discovered you."

Fen hiked his tail up. "Then perhaps it is our destiny. Let's see what we uncover. The path continues around the ruins, so it should be easy to find our way back once we check it out."

"Sounds like a plan," Callum said as he got to his feet.

Fen melded with him again as he approached the entrance to the old ruins. The steps were too crumbled to easily make it to the top, but he was able to scale a large pillar that had collapsed onto its side and hop to the old stone doors from there.

Callum slipped through the opening, barely making it inside. Light coming from holes in the roof cast spotlights across the ground, illuminating the space.

"The interior is massive," Fen said after he had unmelded with Callum.

The two now stood in a large room carved from stone, with ceilings high enough for a giant to pass through. Various glyphs were etched into the wall, many of which were covered in moss and vines. Ahead, more light, proving that there would be additional openings to enter the large temple.

"I can't believe someone abandoned it," Callum said. "You would think that the Crown would celebrate a place like this."

Fen closed his eyes and tilted his snout toward the ground. "Perhaps it has been left untouched for a reason. The sensation is stronger now, you know."

Callum closed his eyes and took a deep breath into his nostrils, as if he could smell it.

This made Fen laugh. "You're funny."

"I'm trying. It's just so subtle. I don't know how you are able to do it."

"Well, I am completely made of mana," the Radiant Fox reminded him, "not that humans haven't been able to do some amazing things with Power-cores and pacted aetherbeasts. He nodded ahead. "It is much larger than I expected, but there could be something here."

"Like treasure?"

"I'm not exactly expecting treasure, but there is no telling in a place like this."

"But we need to get to the camp."

"We are making our way there, aren't we? I have an idea," Fen said as he glanced ahead yet again. "Try to keep up. It will be good for your natural stamina."

The fox took off.

As soon as he cleared the main room he jumped to a collapsed statue, and then to the top of a stairwell from there. Callum charged toward the statue hoping to use it as a springboard. He barely made it to the stairwell as it crumbled behind him.

He scrambled up, meeting Fen at the top of the room, which fumbled out into side entrances that led to balconies. "Not bad," Fen said. "And as you can see, there are more ways in. Meaning we may find something here, and I'm not talking about treasure. With all these entrances, I assume that anything like that has been looted by now. But you never know. Let's continue."

He jumped to the banister and trotted along it, Callum keeping at his side. They reached an entryway into the next space, where the walls had collapsed. Fen made it look easy as he simply jumped down to the bottom floor. It was going to be much harder for Callum.

"Umm . . ." He looked around and noticed that part of one of the banisters had fallen. In doing so, he spotted the collapsed statue of a man melded with a giant bear. It wasn't too big of a drop from the broken portion of the banister to the top of the bear, but the landing would be strange, especially because it was slightly curved in nature.

Callum went for it. He crouched, judged the distance, about five feet down, and made the jump. He landed, pressed forward onto his hands, and nearly tumbled over. "Ha!" he said as he caught his balance.

"Are you sure you weren't a monkey in your past life?" Fen asked.

"A tail would make this *so* much easier." Callum joined the fox and they were about to move into the next room when they heard a chortling. Naturally, Callum grew quiet. He pressed himself up to the wall and Fen melded with him.

<*There are at least two smaller aetherbeasts in the next chamber. Let's move on them quickly lest they alert others.*>

<*How could they do that?*> Callum thought back to Fen.

<*Just a hunch. Let's hit it!*>

Callum concentrated once more, watching as thick claws formed over his fingers, crackling with energy. He rushed into the room with all the intention of someone looking to clean up in a matter of seconds.

The creatures he encountered were certainly dark aetherbeasts, small ones, and there was Corruption all around them. Yet there was also something human about them, since the goblinoid aetherbeasts had big heads, long ears, and sharp claws.

Callum hit one of the goblin aetherbeasts on the right with Zephyr Strike, which sent it flying backward, killing it for good. The second goblin aetherbeast saw what had happened, hesitated, and took off.

<*Get it before it alerts more!*>

Callum conjured his lance and hurtled it at the aetherbeast just as it reached the end of the chamber. It fell and a shard rushed into his hand.

Empowerment of Vigor Shard

"Nice," he said as Fen hopped away to deal with the Corruption. Callum still didn't quite understand how that worked, but the fox seemed to be getting healthier by the day. *Absorbing the Corruption is helping his Corruption? Something like that?* he thought as he pushed the Vigor Shard into Fen's Aethercore.

"We got lucky," Fen told him as he finished up. The fox sat and looked ahead. "There will be more, I reckon, and it's better that we *don't* have to fight them all at once. By themselves, they seem easy."

"I killed the first one with a single shot."

"Yes, but we could easily be overwhelmed."

"At least they will drop shards."

"That's a good thing. If we take it slow and creep our way through the next chambers, we might be able to net a good many shards. And we'll be cleaning this place up along the way."

"Works for me," Callum said. "Let's see how many we can take out."

The pair ventured into the next chamber, which was much smaller. The entrance he needed to continue onward looked entirely collapsed, aside from a small opening.

"Do you think you can squeeze in?" Fen asked.

"I can try." Callum removed his sword and passed it through first.

He got on his belly and pulled himself through the opening. It was tight but he soon reached the other side. This was a much smaller chamber than the last, indicating that they had reached the area where the people who ran the abandoned structure may have lived.

There was actual carpet here, but it was frayed beyond recognition, and Callum was not able to make out any of the images it had once depicted. "Is that an actual treasure chest?" he asked as he approached a chest that was already opened, the contents removed.

"Looks like it."

Callum peered ahead. "Where does this lead?"

They heard a sudden crash in a room beyond followed by a shriek. Callum readied himself and moved toward the sound. His father had mentioned that this was one of his unique traits.

"You're fearless," Rhane had once told him. *"If there's a fire, you'll run toward it, not away."*

"Why would I do that?" Callum had asked at the time.

"I already told you why, son. Fearlessness is a gift and a curse, but it's hard to get fortune's attention without taking a few risks."

Now, as Callum rushed into the unknown, he did so with his father's words in mind. He felt his power heighten as he melded with Fen. Callum came upon a pair of goblinoid aetherbeasts that sprang out at him, as if it had been a trap all along.

He swiped his Radiant Claws at the first and took a big chunk of mana from its form in doing it. The other jumped for Callum and bit onto his leg. Just then, a third dropped from the ceiling, and a fourth appeared, crawling across the stone above.

Callum's first move was to summon his lance, which he spiked at the aetherbeast that had yet to drop onto him. He used his new Shatterlight Bear ability to plow through the one in front of him, killing it. This also dragged the aetherbeast that had clamped down onto his leg into the fray, where it got trampled.

A blast of wind finished the next one and the shards came.

Empowerment of Vigor Shard
Earth Affinity Shard

"Could always use more shards," he said as he focused on healing his leg.

Strange, Callum thought as he fused the Vigor Shard into Fen's Aethercore. The Earth Affinity Shard went into his new Powercore. "Every little bit helps," he said as he peered ahead into the dark.

There was less light here, much of the ceiling intact. Yet there was still a slight glow, something he assumed had to do with the mana that was naturally in the air here. Callum was certainly starting to notice this the further they journeyed into the ruins.

The next corridor was wider, and there were actual suits of armor lining the walls.

Amazing, Callum thought as he cautiously moved past them. He kept glancing ahead, toward what he knew was the source of power. Yet it continued to remain at an unknown distance. There was Corruption here as well, which Fen had already started to absorb when the fox stopped.

"Watch out—!" Fen bounded toward him as one of the suits of armor came alive. It swung a massive greatsword as Callum, who instinctively drew his own blade.

Callum jumped back. He looked down at the sword in his hand and then up at the suit of armor fueled by Corruption in front of him. He knew how to use a sword but this was different, and his opponent was massive, easily two feet taller than him with a greatsword the length of a broom.

As Fen melded with him, it became clear what Callum needed to do. "Armor first, then deal with the suit of armor."

<*Do it!*>

Callum charged at the manabound suit and struck it with his sword.

The strength when melded Fen was noticeable, even if it hurt his wrists. His agility came into play as well as he dove under a sweeping strike and hit the suit again from behind. Callum was able to knock away the suit's right pauldron. This revealed more of the aetherbeast within, light and dark mana fizzling from the new opening.

Now with an opening, Callum rushed his opponent and cut off one of its manabound arms with his sword. Doing so, however, brought him very close to being struck by his opponent's massive sword.

Even more astonishing was his enemy's ability to maintain its footing and handle the enormous weapon single-handedly, lurching toward Callum in an unsteady arc.

It slammed the blade into the wall and managed to hit some of the stone decor of the chamber, which caused dust to fill the air.

Yet now Callum saw his true opportunity in the opening provided by the missing pauldron.

Still holding his blade, he used Zephyr Strike to hit his opponent from a distance. It stumbled and Callum blasted it again, causing it to fall onto its side and lose more armor.

Callum seized on his advantage as he charged forward, lance forming in his spare hand. He batted the soldier's sword away and then hit it with the lance. The explosion of mana and armor that followed caused Callum to fly backward.

He smacked into a wall, the wind knocked out of him as he received more shards.

Empowerment of Mind Shard
Death Affinity Shard

"That was something . . ." Callum said as he slowly caught his breath. He fused the Mind Shard into Inner Light and pocketed the Death Affinity Shard.

Fen, who now stood a few feet in front of him absorbing Corruption, looked back to Callum. "I was unaware that mana could do something like that, but I suppose it would make sense if there's such a thing as pacted weapons and armor. We'll have to be careful. It might make whatever we encounter ahead even more treacherous."

"The winged aetherbeast?"

"Yes, I sense it is close. I also sense that we are closer to the—"

They heard a scream. It was distant, but whatever it was, the scream was clearly human.

Fen returned to Callum, the fox jumping as mana rushed all around him. <*Let's go!*> Fen said, but Callum was already charging ahead.

CHAPTER 26

All who have pacted begin at the Initiate Rank, in which they are able to have six Powercores and one Aethercore. The Conjurer Rank brings this up to nine Powercores. At the Wielder Rank, they are able to have fifteen Powercores and two Aethercores. The Channeler Rank brings this to twenty-one Powercores. The Shaper Rank allows for twenty-four Powercores and three Aethercores. The Weaver Rank, thirty Powercores and four Aethercores. And finally, the Convoker Rank, thirty-six Powercores, and five Aethercores. Powerful? Indeed.

—*On the Nature and Simplification of Mana Reserves* by Renova Dreagis, Mastress Shaper, Archona of Ridgebarrow, Soul Pythia

Callum should have been able to easily handle another ambush from goblinoid aetherbeasts. Yet the room he rushed into—so close to the sound of the screams he'd heard—had giant holes in the stone flooring, causing him to plummet to the depths below.

"A dungeon," he said as he noticed rusted metal bars beyond.

<Looks like it!>

A trio of the aetherbeasts surged through the openings above before he could figure out anything else about his new location.

Callum struck one down with a huge swipe. He followed this up with a close-range wind attack on the second aetherbeast before slashing at the third with a series of quick, clawed jabs.

Mana fizzled around him, leaving a single shard that flew into his hand.

Empowerment of Might Shard

Callum was about to fuse the Might Shard into his Charge of the Shatterlight Bear when he decided to hold off. *I might need it later*, Callum thought, knowing that he could consume an Attribute Shard like he had back on the farm.

<You can get up there,> Fen said as Callum looked up at the ceiling that was partially collapsed. *<I'll help.>*

With a well-timed jump, Callum would be able to jump from a big chunk of the wall to a partition that would allow him to climb up. He glanced at the metal bars of what he now realized was some kind of holding cell, not exactly a dungeon like he had originally thought.

Callum calculated what it would take and went for it. He made his jumps and was able to pull himself back into the chamber where he'd just been ambushed.

<They're tricky, these particular aetherbeasts. But weak.> Fen stopped speaking as they heard more sounds ahead. These were followed by a crash, one that made the ground shake.

He picked up his pace, paying careful attention to the floor and any other potential traps. Callum didn't come across any more, but he did run down a long hallway where vines from outside had broken through, creating an additional obstacle.

A sudden brightness ahead signaled he was almost outside again.

He rushed toward the light and skidded to a stop as it opened into a battleground that had once had a dome over it, where he found three people battling the winged aetherbeast he had seen the previous night.

Callum immediately recognized the trio.

He nearly shouted their names as he stopped. Instead, he ducked behind a partially crumbled wall and focused.

"Quinn and Marcella look injured," he whispered, referring to the young man who had let him borrow his Armorcore and the tall southerner whom he had only met once. Princess Selene was also there and, from what Callum had just seen, she was losing pretty badly to the aetherbeast.

Her ursine aetherbeast wasn't with her, which told Callum that she was likely melded with the bear. But she had also looked like she was losing the fight, trying her best to protect Quinn and Marcella, yet being overwhelmed each time the winged monster swooped at her.

<Surprise attack?>

<Definitely. I'll need my Might Shard.>

<Yes, good call. I sneak around, distract it, you rush in and jump at it with your lance. I'll join you. We kill it.>

Callum grunted a response as he took the Might Shard out. He felt an instant surge in strength that he knew was compounded by the fact he was melded with Fen. Given the design of the space, with the stands beyond likely once reserved for royalty, he had a clear vantage point of the battle below. If Callum timed it just right, he could make an epic entrance, seize the moment, and, most important, kill the aetherbeast.

But there was room for error here. And unmelded, Callum was less agile.

Marcella, who hovered over Quinn, yelled something about *Harold*. Callum glanced around the partially crumbled wall to see an aetherbeast like a blue heron appear and try to attack the winged monster, which had all the makings of one of the most terrifying aetherbeasts he'd seen yet.

With numerous long necks and sharp beaks, as well as a double set of wings tipped with pointed feathers, the demonic aetherbeast slapped Marcella's summon to the ground. It had been a last resort, clear from the way Marcella yelped and Princess Selene threw everything into her next attack, charging at their opponent on all fours.

<Go!> Callum told Fen.

The Radiant Fox took off toward the other side of the arena. He had to jump down to the battleground below, but the aetherbeast was so distracted by Selene's attacks and Marcella was busy protecting Quinn, so no one seemed to notice.

Selene shouted as the winged aetherbeast hit her with an incredible blast of mana-infused wind, which sent her flying thirty feet backward. She hit a wall and broke through it, bricks crumbling after her.

The monster turned to Marcella.

Once again, Harold, her pacted heron, bolted forward only to be swatted aside as the aetherbeast narrowed all four of its sharp beaks at Marcella.

Callum saw his opening.

Even if the creature was sparking with dark magic, the impossibly large monster now had its back exposed. Callum noted the spot just between its double set of wings that would pierce the creature's body.

The aetherbeast was about to drive its four beaks down onto Marcella when Fen appeared. The Radiant Fox shot forward, right at its face, then Fen jumped like he was going to take the brunt of the monster's attack.

Instead, he zoomed past the aetherbeast just as it shifted upward, its wings spreading wide, the opening on its back as clear as ever as Callum jumped in the air, sizzling lance in hand.

Fen melded with him moments before Callum landed the strike, his lance pressing through the aetherbeast's body and out the front.

The creature let out a terrifying shriek as it fell, its body instantly dissolving into a bubbling pool of dark magic. Callum landed on his feet, head down, trembling both from the attack and the fact that he had pulled it off.

The shards came rapid-fire, along with a Powercore:

Empowerment of Resilience Shard
Empowerment of Regeneration Shard
Air Affinity Shard
Air Affinity Shard
Light Affinity Shard
Veil of the Gravewind Hawk

You have reached the Conjurer Rank.
Your Powercore capacity has increased to nine.
Your Attributes have all increased by one point.

Elation rushed through him as Callum turned to Quinn, who was on his back gasping for air, badly injured. "This should help!" He produced the Regeneration Shard he had just received.

He was familiar with the power of these particular shards. While he had been too young when his mother passed, Callum remembered his father telling him they had tried the shards, and for a while, they had helped.

"Give this to him," he told Marcella as he handed her the shard.

"Where did you come from?" she asked, shocked to see him.

Callum pointed to the top of the stands.

"I know that," she snapped as she pressed the shard into Quinn's chest.

Quinn started coughing as the life returned to him. He blinked a few times as his gaze settled on Callum. "You're here?"

Callum was already turning away. He rushed over to Selene, who was pushing herself out of the rubble. She should have been crushed beneath the fallen stones, but her pacted bear had shielded her.

"Are you—"

Selene slapped Callum's hand away. She then realized this was rude and let him help her up. "Sorry," she said as she dusted off her armor. "Where did you come from?"

"Marcella asked me the same question. I'll explain everything. Are you good?"

Selene examined her armor once more. She moved her elbows and knees. "I think so, yes."

The princess joined Callum to walk back over to Marcella and Quinn, both of whom now stood. Quinn fiddled with his hands. "Sorry," he told the two women.

"How could you have known? That thing could cloak itself," Selene said.

"Did it drop its cloaking ability?" Quinn asked Callum.

"Ummm . . ." Callum accessed Soul Sense.

Veil of the Gravewind Hawk
Type: *Ability*
Grade: *Legendary*
Infusion Requirements for Grade Increase:
0/10 Shadow Affinity
0/10 Light Affinity
0/10 Deftness Shards
Affinity Requirements: *Light and Shadow*
Effect: *When bound to one's Soul Heart, this core allows a mage to vanish completely. Consuming either Shadow or Light Affinity shards prolong the concealment.*

"I did," Callum informed Quinn, who still seemed a bit shaky.

"And its Grade?"

He glanced again, eyes widening. "Legendary." This was the first legendary drop he had received. Everything else, to his knowledge, had been listed as Common.

"Nice," Quinn said. "And your Rank?"

"I just reached the Conjurer Rank," Callum said.

Selene stepped up. "We should *all* be at the Conjurer Rank by now."

"Speak for yourself," Quinn told her. "Ahem, respectfully, Your Ladyship."

"You know you don't have to talk to me like that."

"I know, but it's fun."

"What's it mean?" Callum asked. "Moving from Initiate to Conjurer. I see my Attributes all increased by one."

"It means the capacity of your Soul Heart has increased," Quinn said. "Allowing for a number of things, from more powers to increases in your natural abilities."

"That's the best part about that first one, the power increase," Marcella said as she brushed her hand over her armor. In doing so, she shot a glance to Callum that he interpreted as the southerner wondering *why* he wasn't wearing armor.

"Moving from Initiate to Conjurer is easy," Selene said. "Most of our classmates do so before entering the Great College. From Conjurer to Wielder requires more focus on the other aspects associated with being an archmage. But when you do make it to the Wielder Rank, you can have two pacted aetherbeasts. Some people even make it in the first semester. That's what I'm hoping to do."

"I think I understand," Callum told them. "But the Legendary Grade. What's that mean exactly?"

"It is all about effectiveness," Quinn told him. "I don't remember the breakdown—"

"Yes, you do," Marcella said. "If anyone knows the exact numbers, it's you."

"I know them for the Initiate Rank. If you're at the Initiate Rank," he said, still catching his breath a bit, "a Common Powercore operates at one hundred percent; Uncommon at ninety percent; Rare at seventy percent; Exalted at fifty percent; Sublime at thirty percent; Legendary at fifteen percent; and Mythical at five percent. So it's probably a bit better than that. Also, I should say that this only applies if you have affinity. If you don't have affinity, then it's basically a flat ten percent."

"At the Conjurer Rank, a Legendary Powercore operates at twenty-five percent, if you have affinity. So not great," Selene said. "What's the description say?"

Callum read it to her: "When inserted into one's Soul Heart, it allows a mage to vanish completely. Consuming either Shadow or Light Affinity shards prolong the concealment."

"I haven't heard of a Powercore that can have its effects prolonged by using a shard," Quinn said, surprised. "Interesting."

"And you need Shadow or Light Mana to use it, yes?" Selene asked Callum.

"Both, apparently."

"That's odd too," Quinn said. "Often, if you have just one of the required manas you can use it."

"Not always. It is a Legendary Powercore," Selene reminded him.

"You have a fox, right?" Marcella asked Callum.

"I do."

"And I'm guessing by the wind and light I saw that you're not wielding Shadow Mana."

"No, I'm not. He's a Radiant Fox."

Marcella looked from Princess Selene to Quinn. "She doesn't have Shadow Mana, but you do."

"Shadow and Water, all Darkmoor cats are that way because their origin, believe it or not, is near a swamp that has a mana spring in it. Even though cats don't like water," Quinn said.

"So I could sell it at the Emporium, then," Callum said.

"You could," Marcella said. "But you should test it first. Even if it won't operate at its full capacity."

"It's worth a try." Callum pressed the orb into his chest. He looked down at his arm and noticed that there was a very slight change in its visibility, like he was looking at his arm in the corner of a room that has a bit less light.

"I can totally see you," Marcella told him, "Just in case you're wondering. Trade it."

"I'm with her, trade it," Selene told him. "You never know when you'll get your second pact, and if you need something like that, then you could just buy it. You need to be at the Wielder Rank to actually use two Aethercores, but these things do have a way of finding you. Like my bear, Ecaris."

"Or your Legion Guard, Sir Trindade," Quinn joked.

"Please. At least he didn't come with us."

"He threatened to," Marcella told her.

"He follows you around like a pacted aetherbeast, that's for sure."

The princess turned to Quinn and tilted her chin up slightly. "Maybe I *will* ask that you refer to me by my proper title." Selene laughed. "Kidding. As for now, we could continue on toward the spring, or chicken out like Draven."

Fen spoke privately to Callum. *<That must be mana I noticed in the air. Ask about the spring.>*

Yet upon hearing Draven the warlock's name, Callum had other questions. "Draven was here?"

"He was with us," Selene said, her tone sharp. "The coward took off to 'get help' the moment we were attacked. With his pacted raven, he can actually fly, so it's all too easy for him to disappear when things get tough." She squinted up at the darkening sky. "Now that it's getting late, who knows if he'll bother coming back for us at all."

"Well, now that the farm boy from Weatherby has rescued us," Marcella said, "I think we're just fine."

"Yes." The princess continued adjusting her armor. "I suppose we are."

<Ask about the spring.>

"Right," Callum said as he naturally placed his hand on the hilt of his sword.

"Is that a Weaponcore?" Quinn asked.

"No, nothing like that. I picked it up off one of the dead soldiers. The Gravewind Hawk aetherbeast was the one that killed them. I'm still sort of new at this," he said awkwardly. "I figured a sword would help me, and it really hasn't. Well, it did help me at one point in the ruins, but not the way that I would have thought. I just need to pry something open."

"We will alert someone once we get back to the camp," Selene said. "I'm afraid the King's Forest isn't as protected as it should be, but there are reasons for that. One of them being a push by the dukes that sit on the High Council. Politics, I know," she said to Marcella, "I promised I wouldn't get into it, and I won't. In fact, that sword may help illustrate the point as to why we need better maintenance and protection here."

"You mentioned this spring. What is that?" Callum asked all of them. "I mean, I know what a spring is, but . . ."

"A mana spring." Once again, Quinn's eyes lit up with the light at the fact that he was going to be able to explain something to someone. "So, an aetherstorm, have you ever experienced one in person?"

"I have. It's how I met my fox," Callum said.

"You should introduce your fox to us. I'll introduce my cat. Wait. Let's hold off on introductions. I was trying to explain something. So, an aetherstorm. What is it exactly? Well, some would tell you that it's an accumulation of magical energy that has become erratic. You know, like an actual storm. And like an actual storm, there's a core, only it doesn't always move with the aetherstorm, it's sometimes left behind creating a mana spring. And that is what we're after here."

"A mana spring? What will happen there?"

"Another good question—"

Marcella snickered at the way Quinn spoke.

"Just let him finish," Selene told her.

Quinn nodded appreciatively at the princess: "For one, we can drain the spring of its power. This can help with a number of things. You'll want to use your Soul Sense skill while you are there if you want to see it in action, but basically, it will fill in the gaps we are missing to upgrade our various cores. The only problem is that it does so randomly, meaning we don't know exactly which holes it will fill. But it beats collecting shards individually or buying them."

"Tell him the best part, Quinn," Marcella said.

"Ah, that. A mana spring can quickly amplify the size of your Soul Heart through its sheer power, meaning it's an easy way to reach the next rank. It's why they're highly sought after."

"And it's here?" Callum took a quick look around, as if there was something he was missing.

"You can't feel it?" Marcella asked.

"No, I can. I mean, I could feel something before."

"We don't have far to go, I can tell you that," the woman said as she turned in the opposite direction of the ruins. "Let's find it, shall we? And in the meantime, let's meet your fox."

"Wait, let me introduce my cat first," Quinn said. "Tuck, say hi to everyone. Well, you know Harold and Ecaris but say hi anyway."

An overweight cat appeared, its fluffy tail brimming with magic. He strutted ahead, turned, and bowed gracefully at Callum. "A pleasure," the cat said.

"And this is Harold," Marcella told Callum, not to be outdone. Upon saying this, a blue heron sparked into existence. It flew in a circle around their heads and landed on the ground next to Tuck.

"Why, hello there," Harold said in a deep voice.

"Ecaris." Princess Selene stepped aside as her pacted bear appeared, the beast enormous in stature. Even on all fours it was taller than Selene. "She's a bit shy," Selene told Callum after it had been a moment. "Go on, say something."

"Hello," Ecaris finally said.

Tuck laughed. "No, I'm not going to make that joke."

"Which one?" Quinn asked, excitedly.

"Something about a cat getting a tongue. Never mind. We're here on serious business. The mana spring."

"We're not far away," Harold told Tuck, "but there is still one yet to be revealed."

Fen appeared in a flourish of wind and light. "Hello, all, you may call me Fen," he said as the mana settled.

"Greetings." Tuck jumped onto Quinn's shoulder.

"Harold, see how much farther we have to go," Marcella told her summon. "And if you see Draven, um, don't."

"Don't?" the heron asked.

"Don't let him know where we are. He doesn't deserve to utilize the spring after running away like that."

Princess Selene didn't say anything, but it was clear from the short nod she offered Marcella that she agreed. They continued on, moving to a courtyard that had once held a fountain covered in aquamarine tiles.

As they walked, Quinn and Marcella questioned Callum, who maintained that he had nothing to do with the original Callum Stross. For her part, Princess Selene was mostly silent.

"Like many pacted aetherbeasts, we met *after* a storm," Fen told the pair. "Since Callum was of noble lineage, we decided to give the Great College a try, but only after a shardcrafter in Weatherby recommended it."

"That's such an inspiring story," Quinn said, which wasn't the first time he had relayed something like this. "And even if you are on academic probation, you will be fine. They just do that to scare you."

"We will learn quickly."

"You saved our asses today," Marcella said. "That has to count for something considering we are with the princess."

"I don't have power over the administration, you know," Selene said. "But I suppose you could say that my father does have some influence. Still, I don't think Callum will need my help proving that he has what it takes to be in archmage from the Great College."

Callum nearly tripped at the thought of the princess complimenting him. "Thanks," he said. "I'll do my best."

Harold returned, the heron gracefully spiraling directly into Marcella, melding in a flash. "Not much further now," Marcella announced.

As they came to a small meadow covered in blue flowers, Fen melded with Callum and then fused the shards he had picked up from the Gravewind Hawk into their appropriate cores. He fused the Empowerment of Resilience Shard into Charge of the Shatterlight Bear, the Air Affinity Shards into Zephyr Strike, and the Light Affinity Shard into Fen's Aethercore. He had a collection of unfused mana shards as well, one Fire; three Shadow; two Water; two Death; and one Life Affinity shard, which would give him something to trade with the others after he saw what the spring was capable of.

They stepped into the meadow and the air grew electric. The blue flowers Callum had just seen grew in size, as if they were blooming, their petals breaking off into tiny nodes.

"Access Soul Sense," Quinn said as he threw his arm to the side and took in a big breath.

Next to him, Selene did the same. Marcella sat cross-legged, her gaze on the ground.

<What are you waiting for?> Fen asked. <See what the spring can do.>

CHAPTER 27

*An aetherstorm brings with it destruction, but like a great forest
fire, it also has the power to create life.*

—Ines Meida, Mastress Weaver, Archona of Aveiro,
and famed legal scholar

Callum sat near Marcella and instantly noticed the sensation of magic rushing into him. It reminded him of the feeling of butterflies in his stomach, only these butterflies were much larger, all funneling in a spiral at once and brimming with power.

"Focus on one core at a time," Quinn said as Callum tried to get settled.

Callum focused on his newest ability, Charge of the Shatterlight Bear. Where he had once had three fused Earth Affinity Shards, this number jumped to five. He received an additional Resilience Shard and five Might Shards. This meant that he now only needed Light Affinity and Empowerment of Might shards to upgrade the ability.

He shifted his attention to Gift of the Luminous Lance, which gained two Light Affinity Shards, leaving Callum needing just eight more to upgrade the ability.

"It really is too bad we can't choose which shards the spring gives us," Quinn said. "And none of us are anywhere near the Channeler Rank, so we don't yet know how to sunder."

"That's what a shardcrafter is for," Marcella said.

"I know. But imagine discovering a spring like this and being able to sunder shards and move them around. I'm just saying, that would be next level."

Callum next focused on Empowerment of Zephyr Strike, one of the cores that had come with Fen. He gained a whopping seven Air Affinity Shards, but zero Deftness Shards.

Empowerment of Zephyr Strike
Type: Ability
Grade: Common
Infusion Requirements for Grade Increase:
10/10 Air Affinity
0/5 Deftness Shards
Affinity Requirements: Air
Effect: When bound to one's Soul Heart, this core grants its wielder the ability to shape their latent air mana into that of a powerful crescent of wind, slicing apart all it touches.

"I just think it's sad people use springs to make money," Marcella said. "Imagine coming across this and just selling off all the power granted to you."

"People come from different circumstances," Quinn reminded her.

Callum nodded in agreement, but he didn't say anything as he turned to Empowerment of Sustenance, where he received five Empowerment of Vigor and five Empowerment of Resilience shards, which gave him enough shards to trigger the upgrade he needed. "I received an upgrade!" he announced to the group.

"Nice," Princess Selene said. "Keep going."

Callum focused on his Inner Light ability. This received two Empowerment of Mind Shards, and two Light Affinity Shards from the spring.

Inner Light
Type: Ability
Grade: Common
Infusion Requirements for Grade Increase:
2/5 Light Affinity
5/5 Mind Shards
1/5 Regeneration Shards
Affinity Requirements: Light
Effect: When bound to one's Soul Heart, this core allows the user to rapidly heal wounds and restore stamina.

This left Fen's Aethercore, which received one Light Affinity Shard, five Empowerment of Resilience Shards, and three Empowerment of Deftness Shards.

Pact of the Radiant Fox
Type: Pact

Grade: Common
Infusion Requirements for Grade Increase:
5/5 Fire Affinity Shards
5/5 Light Affinity Shards
7/10 Deftness Shards
5/10 Vigor Shards
5/5 Resilience Shards

"Oh, great," Selene said, her tone not at all matching the serious boost in resources they had just received. Callum looked up at her to find the princess scanning the sky, an annoyed look on her face. He soon realized what had bothered her when Draven landed alongside several royal guards, including Sir Trindade, Princess Selene's Legion Guard.

"Princess—!" Sir Trinidad said as Draven stormed past him, the warlock's face filling with anger.

"What the hell happened?" Draven pointed a finger at Callum. "And why is he here? You didn't come with the caravan!"

"I made my own way through the forest," Callum said.

"You're not supposed to—"

"He's a noble just like you and me, Draven," Marcella said dryly, as if she had put up with his temper before. "Not only that, he's the one who turned the tide of our fight against the aetherbeast. You know, the one you ran away from."

"I didn't run away!"

"More than that," Quinn said as the redness in Draven's eyes intensified. "Callum saved us. I'm not ashamed to admit that. The aetherbeast was powerful. It had clearly visited the spring." He gestured to the meadow around them. "Callum came at the right time."

A pulsing vein appeared on the side of Draven's head.

<He's acting like he wanted it to happen, like he wanted them to be defeated by the aetherbeast!> Fen growled. *<Do not trust the warlock.>*

"If all of that is true," Draven finally said, "then you should have saved some of the spring's resources. How selfish of you all to drain the spring completely."

"We had no way of knowing if you would come back or not," Princess Selene told him flatly. "You sure left quickly, if I recall. Do you remember?" She took a step closer to him. "You sprouted wings and flew just as quickly as you could. The aetherbeast couldn't even get its opening attack off before you were gone."

"That's . . . that's not true!" It was clear by the way that Draven tensed up that there was more he wanted to say, yet she was royalty, and he had been raised to know his place. "That is not how it played out, Your Ladyship," he finally told her with all the vitriol of someone cursing at a stubborn animal.

Marcella laughed. "Poor little warlock. He got scared and flew away. Why should he have access to the spring?"

"You watch your tongue," Draven told her.

A whoosh of wind was followed by a tremor.

Master Cruedark appeared and the plants around all seemed to push away from the man for fear that they would be trampled. A large hammer rested over one of his shoulders, the Weaponcore nearly as long as Callum was tall. "Is the aetherbeast handled?" he asked, either not noticing or not acknowledging that the standoff or the way Draven stood, fists clenched at his sides.

"The aetherbeast is handled," Sir Trindade said. "Most importantly, the princess is safe. For the record, I would like to note that I advised *against* letting her go off on her own without my protection—"

"Enough," Princess Selene told him. "You should be prepared for this by now. And you are already aware of the upcoming Royal Excursion."

"Your Ladyship, I know you have a powerful meldform and you have trained for moments like this, but you must remember that your acceptance to the Great College is tradition, not necessarily a reason for you to do the sort of things a typical archmage would do. You must be aware of the capabilities, and you are pacted, so you should certainly improve them, but excursions such as this . . ." Sir Trindade trailed off once he noticed the sour look she was giving him.

Master Cruedark cleared his throat, and he was imposing enough that everyone turned to him as he placed the bottom of his hammer on the ground. He set a hand on the grip. "What happened? Tell me everything."

Quinn spoke fastest: "We were tracking the spring and were attacked by a Gravewind Hawk. Draven flew away to get help. We tried to hold it off, but it overpowered us with a wind that produced daggers. I was hit. Marcella tried to protect me while Selene—"

"Princess Selene," Sir Trindade corrected him.

"Sorry. Princess Selene tried to stop, and that's basically when Callum appeared."

"And how did you kill it?" Master Cruedark asked.

"With my lance," Callum said.

"A Weaponcore?"

"No, a Powercore."

Quinn took it from there. "He jumped off the stands as his fox created a distraction. He melded midair and took it down using a lance. After that, we continued on and found the spring. That's it."

"Did you, now?" Master Cruedark turned to Callum. "And how did you get through its natural armor?"

"I didn't even know it had armor. I just saw an opening between its wings and aimed for that."

The big man looked Callum over. "Your performance in the Entry Duels was middling, and your results in the Attribute Trials were just enough to pass. And yet, you managed to take down a Gravewind Hawk—one of the more formidable and fearsome aetherbeasts in the King's Forest. It makes me wonder if perhaps you weren't showing your full potential during the Entry Duels."

Callum shrugged, unsure what he should say.

"I really do think he's learning as he goes and, I don't know, maybe sometimes that's the best way to figure something out. But who am I?" Quinn laughed nervously.

"Callum showed great promise today," Princess Selene told Master Cruedark. "I believe the Entry Duels were his first time fighting in his meldform."

"Not my first time," Callum said. "The first time was on the trip from Weatherby to New Albion. My caravan was ambushed by bandits. It's where I got Gift of the Luminous Lance," he said, not going into further details."

"So he got lucky," Draven spat. "Moving on. We should probably return to camp—"

"We will in due time," Master Cruedark told him with finality. "First, you," he addressed Princess Selene, "while you are permitted to go out on your own, in a scenario like this, you should have left with Draven."

"I can't fly," she said.

"I can fly you," Draven told her, a grin on his face. "You know that."

"And leave us behind?" Marcella asked. "We would've been slaughtered. I should note I can fly too, but I decided to stay and fight. Ironic, really, considering—"

"I would have returned," Draven started to tell her before he was interrupted by Master Cruedark.

"And you, Draven, you shouldn't have left without her. It is incomprehensible that you would do such a thing knowing her status, how crucial she is to the sanctity of our kingdom especially with what is happening with the Geshwine Empire."

"But I—"

"I'm not finished," Master Cruedark said to Draven. "Both of you have important roles to play in the future, especially with your two houses joining together through marriage."

Through what? They're to be married!? Callum let the mere thought fall to the side as he tuned back into what Cruedark was saying.

"I don't know why you left her behind but it is certainly something of concern, something that will need to be discussed with both of your houses. When we return to camp, the two of you will go back to New Albion."

"Good," Sir Trindade said. "It is best that the princess is there anyway."

Selene tilted her head back slightly, clinched her eyes shut, and tried not to groan. It was clear that she had been handled this way before and she didn't like it.

"And now, you," Master Cruedark told Callum. "You, young man, have shown yourself to be quite adept and fearless. You deserve a reward, but I do not know yet what that reward may be. I suspect looking at you that there are some options, however. We will figure that out at the camp."

"Is he still on academic probation?" Quinn asked Master Cruedark.

"This has nothing to do with that, but his performance here will be noted." He lifted his hammer back to his shoulders. "Unless you are capable of flying," the big man said as he glanced at Draven and Marcella, "gather around me."

Callum approached Master Cruedark, Quinn at his side. They were joined by Princess Selene, Sir Trindade, and the other members of the retinue that had traveled with Draven. A wave of energy swirled around them as the big man maintained his stoic pose, hammer resting on his shoulder.

<That's one way to do it!> Fen said as they catapulted into the air, the movement so sudden that Callum could hardly process it.

One moment, they were standing in the meadow, somewhere in the King's Forest. The next, they were lowering toward the nobles' camp, which spanned a small stretch of land surrounded by orchards.

There were numerous tents here, all bearing noble seals. While Callum knew what they were, he didn't recognize any of them.

He recalled a few that had passed through Weatherby, one of a lion on two feet, the other of a pair of black swans, but it was all new to him. And he was too distracted by the fact that he had been teleported to realize that this was part of his legacy, that something had gone wrong in his family's timeline to separate him from this.

Quinn turned to him once they had settled. "Strange, right? I've only traveled like that a few times."

"What kind of Powercore is that?"

"You would have to ask Master Cruedark," Quinn said quickly as Marcella tapped him on the shoulder.

"What now?" she said.

Quinn laughed at her question like it was some inside joke between the two of them. "I'm wondering that as well."

"Once Draven is here," Sir Trindade told Master Cruedark, "Her Ladyship and the duke's son will return to the city. Much safer there."

Master Cruedark's big hammer fizzled away, confirming to Callum that it was indeed a Weaponcore. "We were supposed to be out here another two days."

"The princess's life has been put at risk—"

"I was fine, Sir Trindade," she told him.

"I have been granted the King's Authority, approved by the Council of Duchy, to call this off, and I believe that will be the only way to salvage this. You can stay for the night," he told Master Cruedark, "but everyone should head back tomorrow."

"As you wish." Master Cruedark turned to Callum, the grim look on his face softening to some degree. "You may come with me."

Callum started to question the request and then stopped himself. "Sure."

"Marcella and I will be over there," Quinn told Callum as he started to step away. "In the tent marked by the seashell. Well, when she returns from her flight. It's her tent, but she shouldn't be long." Callum followed Quinn's finger to the tent in question, which was yurt-like and tied off by an intricately designed blue rope.

"Got it." Callum was about to follow Master Cruedark when Princess Selene approached him.

"Thank you, again," she said, a troubled look on her face.

"It was my pleasure, Your Ladyship."

"Just Selene. You don't have to call me by my title," she told him, which drew an irksome glare from Sir Trindade. "I look forward to seeing you next week when school starts."

"You do?"

But the princess didn't respond. She stepped away, and Master Cruedark motioned again for Callum to follow him.

Uncertain of what the combat master wanted, Callum followed in the huge man's shadow as they headed toward the opposite end of the campground.

CHAPTER 28

Armorcore grades work the same as any core, its ranking directly affecting the amount of protection and power it affords. When one's enhanced defense is fueled by one's Mana Reserves, it becomes imperative to intuit your levels and overall Mind, Regeneration, and Resilience. This begs the question: How does one feel the energy, or lack thereof, that threads the entirety of our world?

—Oliven Ladas, Master Convoker, Magistor of the Fire Wyrm, and
Dean of the Great College from Year 400–431

Once Callum arrived at Master Cruedark's enormous tent, the large man motioned to one of the nearby apple trees. "Grab two." With that, he pushed through the flap of his tent and stepped inside.

"I hope I'm not in trouble," Callum said as he looked up at the apples.

They were a bit high for him to jump and grab, so he used wind attacks and his amplified claws to bring several down. He used the bottom of his shirt to gather them and then stepped inside the huge tent. He found Master Cruedark seated on the ground with several Powercores before him.

The big man's bushy eyebrows lifted as he saw how many apples Callum had procured. "I asked for two."

"I did know how to get them down."

Cruedark let out a sudden laugh. "You're a funny one." He gestured with the tip of his beard toward a basket on a side table. "Put the extras in that basket there. And bring me one. Take one for yourself as well."

After the extras were in the basket, he handed an apple to Master Cruedark, who took a bite out of it. Realizing that the large man wanted him to do the same, Callum bit into his apple and was suddenly met by a blast of crispness that he wasn't expecting. This was followed by a deep sweetness. "These are good."

"They are. And I will gladly eat the rest that you *picked* as well. Now, as to why you are here." He took another bite of the apple and chewed it slowly before speaking again. "I have Armorcores here. And I would like to give you one as a reward. Now, are you familiar with your Rank limitations and the effects on a core's Grade?"

"I am," Callum said, recalling Quinn's explanation about how he would only have access to a certain amount of power depending on his current Rank, which was Conjurer, and the Grade of a Powercore and the affinities granted by his pacted aetherbeast.

"Good. And you have a Radiant Fox, which means you've been granted affinity to Air and Light Mana."

"And Fire," Callum said.

Master Cruedark looked at him curiously. "Your Aethercore has given you access to three affinities?"

"Is that not normal?"

"No, it is not. Many only give access to one. It is uncommon for them to give access to two affinities, and very rarely do they give access to three. I would ask to meet your aetherbeast but we can do that later. So, Light, Air, and Fire. That would be these four . . ." He took a huge bite of the apple and placed the rest of it in his lap as he sorted through the Armorcores in front of him, the glowing orbs hovering into the air. "You may choose which one you feel suits you best."

Callum focused on the first Armorcore.

Armorcore of the Wind Banshee
Type: *Support*
Grade: *Uncommon Wearable*
Infusion Requirements for Armor Increase:
0/10 Air Affinity Shards
0/5 Might Shards
0/10 Resilience Shards
Effect: *Made of hardened mana harvested from the mysterious Palemoor wind banshees that call the cold north home, Armorcore of the Wind Banshee has a chance to redirect the residual mana of an opponent's strike back at them.*

<*That's not a bad bonus effect,*> Fen said. <*Redirecting residual mana, even if it doesn't happen every time, it is certainly something worth noting.*>

<*Definitely,*> Callum said as he turned to the next orb, which had an orange glow to it.

Armorcore of the Plume Parrot
Type: *Support*
Grade: *Common Wearable*
Infusion Requirements for Armor Increase:
0/10 Fire Affinity Shards
0/10 Might Shards
Effect: *Made of hardened mana-feathers harvested from Plume Parrots that call the southern islands home and are known for their unique purple flames, Armorcore of the Plume Parrot will increase the Fire Affinity damage of any Powercores you may possess.*

<*Also not bad, but you don't currently have any Powercores that utilize Fire Affinity.*>

<*You're right, the ones I have are either Air,*> he said, thinking of Zephyr Strike, <*or Light.*>

<*Yes, your Luminous Lance and Shatterlight Bear Powercores. What's the next one?*>

The next orb was bathed in light strong enough that Callum had to look past it when viewing the core.

Armorcore of the Brightflame Falcon
Type: *Support*
Grade: *Rare Wearable*
Infusion Requirements for Armor Increase:
0/10 Fire Affinity Shards
0/10 Light Affinity Shards
0/10 Might Shards
0/10 Resilience Shards
Effect: *Made of hardened mana-feathers of the endangered Brightflame Falcon, this armor grants a pair of brightflame wings when in use. It will provide scorch damage if your enemy comes in contact with the armor.*

"This one is really good," Master Cruedark said. "But you should note that its Grade is listed as Rare, meaning it would only operate at 85 percent of its true power at your current Rank of Conjurer. Also, the wings do not allow you to fly; instead, they are used as additional protection by shifting forward to protect your body."

"And the scorch damage?"

"Yes, Light-Fire damage." The big man's beard lifted into a toothy grin. "But there's still one Armorcore to check out."

Armorcore of the Flash Ferret
Type: Support
Grade: Common Wearable
Infusion Requirements for Armor Increase:
0/10 Light Affinity Shards
0/5 Resilience Shards
Effect: Made of hardened mana of the Flash Ferrets known to light paths along the Western Barren Steppe, this has a slick factor to it that can repel certain attacks.

<Repelling attacks is certainly something that could be useful,> Fen said.

Callum looked up at Master Cruedark. "And you're sure I can have one of these?"

"Do you currently possess an Armorcore?"

"I do not."

"Did you save the next in line to the throne of the Valestra Kingdom?"

"I just did what needed to be done, what anyone in my position would have done," Callum told him.

"That's a very noble thing to say, and often, if we're being honest, nobles aren't as noble as they think they are. This reward is the least I can do. Not only did you save lives, you saved me from having to deal with officials who might not be too happy that I agreed to let Princess Selene venture out with the others. She is the first from the royal family to have attended our college in quite some time, and certainly the highest ranked one. What I'm saying here is that I'm still getting used to what it is going to be like with her around. And in that regard, you have helped me. So I'm going to help you. Choose one."

Callum looked the shimmering orbs over again.

He ruled out Armorcores of the Plume Parrot and the Flash Ferret. He agreed with Fen that the Plume Parrot wasn't useful at the moment because he didn't have any Fire Affinity Shards. He could see himself using the Flash Ferret Armorcore, even if it had a weird name, but the other two were simply better.

The Wind Banshee would allow him to redirect residual magic. He had noticed some of this in the fights already, mana splashing off certain attacks. To be able to aim that back toward an opponent would certainly be helpful. And the Brightflame Falcon Armorcore provided additional protection through its wings, as well as scorch damage.

"It's between the Wind Banshee and the Brightflame Falcon," he said to Fen and Master Cruedark.

"Yes, those are very good options. You will not experience the full potential of the Brightflame Armorcore until you reach the Wielder Rank, but I don't think that will matter too much. If it were higher ranked, perhaps Sublime or even Legendary, then it might not be worth it. That said, even if it is just a chance, redirecting residual mana has turned the tide of many fights. Believe me."

"I don't doubt it." Callum scratched the back of his head. "Which would you choose? If you were me, and you were new to all of this, and you didn't have an Armorcore, which would you choose?"

"That's a good question. Since you seem to be the type that will get into things even I can't fathom at the moment, added protection may be a better option. Plus, scorch damage is no joke. Now, you should know that not every enemy you encounter will feel the effects, especially depending on their affinity, but it is useful, and it looks fierce."

"What do you mean?"

"When you use this Armorcore, it makes it appear as if your body is covered in a nearly translucent flame, which it is. Have you ever seen someone on fire? I would hope not, but if you have, you would know that it creates a certain visual. So I'd choose that one. Brightflame Falcon," Master Cruedark said with a firm nod. "Especially knowing what I think I know about you."

<What's that supposed to mean?> Fen asked Callum.

Rather than ask the same question of Master Cruedark, Callum reached out to the Armorcore of the Brightflame Falcon. He pressed the orb into his chest.

"May it provide the protection you need," Master Cruedark said solemnly. "And as I tell my all students, go ahead and check to make sure that everything is in place. You should do this every time you add a new core."

Callum quickly accessed Soul Sense. He noted that his core capacity had changed along with his Attributes. He also saw his new Armorcore listed as Support.

Soulbound Cores:
Ability: Empowerment of Zephyr Strike
Ability: Gift of the Luminous Lance
Ability: Charge of the Shatterlight Bear
Ability: Inner Light
Support: Empowerment of Sustenance
Support: Armorcore of the Brightflame Falcon
Pact: Pact of the Radiant Fox

"It's there," he told Master Cruedark.

"Indeed it is. I'm glad you stopped by, and I'll be sure to meet your Radiant Fox later. For now, it's rest time." He yawned. "And you should probably join your friends."

Callum left the tent feeling elated.

My first Armorcore, he thought, wishing for an opportunity to test it out.

Fen seemed to have the same idea. <*We really need to give it a try. Perhaps after we meet with your friends?*>

<*You really think that they're my friends now?*> Callum thought back. It wasn't something that he had fully considered. Everything had come at him so quickly since arriving in New Albion that he hadn't really given friendship much of a thought.

<*I believe so, yes. You could ask them.*>

Callum laughed. "I'll get right on that," he told the Radiant Fox as he found the large tent that Quinn had pointed out earlier. "And we will see about testing my new Armorcore. Something tells me it would be better to do it out here than it would in the city."

<*I don't disagree there.*>

The smell of something delicious reached Callum's nostrils as he slid the flap at the front of the tent aside. He found Quinn and Marcella seated on pillows eating from bowls of stew, bread on a cutting board in front of them.

"Callum," Quinn said, a grin forming on his face. "You should get a bowl. The food tent is two doors down."

"We don't have doors," Marcella reminded Quinn.

"Noted. Grab some stew and join us."

Callum placed his bag down and found the food tent, which he had failed to notice on the way over because of the way the tables had been set up along the south side of the tent. There were a few other nobles here, only one of whom he recognized. Lynnafer Sunsouth, who had a pacted badger and a Weaponcore that morphed into the head of a goose, offered him a short nod but didn't say anything else as a cook spooned stew into her bowl.

Callum grabbed a stone bowl, got some stew and a spoon, and headed back to the tent.

"Really not bad," Quinn said as he smacked his lips.

"Then go back for another bowl."

"I've already been twice," he told Marcella.

"You're asking me to go back for you, aren't you?"

"I don't want to seem like a glutton . . ."

Callum sat and had his first spoonful. The stew was nice and warm, but it wasn't very hardy, and it wasn't as good as the stews he'd had in Weatherby.

"I'll be back," Marcella said as she gave in to Quinn's request. "Actually, before I go, what about Master Cruedark?" she asked Callum. "What did he want to see you about?"

"He gave me an Armorcore. Let me choose one, actually."

"Really?" Quinn asked, a piece of bread sticking out of his mouth. He sensed Marcella's scowl and quickly finished his bite. "That's amazing. What kind?"

"Armorcore of the Brightflame Falcon, if that means anything to you," Callum said. "It grants a pair of brightflame wings that act as armor."

"So you can't fly?" Marcella asked as she adjusted her bracelets.

"No, I cannot."

"Too bad. Flying is fun. It's an easy way to get around."

"I'm sure it is."

"Anything else the Armorcore can do?" Quinn asked. "I'm guessing if Cruedark had it, it must have been good. I'm also surprised he didn't give you a Weaponcore. I thought surely that was what he was planning to do. You all saw his hammer, right?"

"How could we not see it?" Marcella asked.

"I wish I knew what else it could do."

"Actually, this armor is sort of like a weapon," Callum said. "It has scorch damage."

Quinn was clearly impressed. "I've only ever heard of that, never really seen it in action."

"It's funny you mention that," Callum said, "Fen and I were hoping to test it out a bit later. "

"We should definitely do that," Quinn told him. "But after more stew."

Marcella groaned, but she left the tent to get another bowl for Quinn.

Later that night, under a clear, cool sky filled with stars, the three quietly slipped away from the nobles' camp. The trio headed into the orchard, keeping to one of the lanes, where they came upon a couple of apples that had fallen from the tree.

"They are really good," Callum said. "Cruedark had me eat one."

Marcella picked one up and examined it. "I was unaware that we could eat them."

"You didn't know?" Quinn asked her. "What did you think they put in the bread pie two nights ago?"

"I knew they were apples, but I didn't know they were from the orchard." She replied with a shrug. "Guess if they knew they were here, they wouldn't have needed to pack them."

Callan didn't have a chance to ask her what she meant as they came to a small clearing. There were numerous wooden buckets around and open barrels, a staging ground likely for the workers who would collect the apples. This wasn't something Callum had done before on a farm, but he could imagine what it would look like, and he assumed that they had tools that would allow them to reach the apples at the tops of the trees.

Tuck, Quinn's pacted cat appeared. "Well, I'm certainly ready for a demonstration," he said as he sat near Quinn and began licking his paw. This image struck Callum as odd, considering the cat was completely made of mana.

Beside him, Harold appeared, Marcella's heron waddling for a moment before adjusting his wings.

<I would join them,> Fen told Callum, *<but we have business to attend to.>*

"I really can't wait to see this," Quinn said. "Armorcores are always interesting."

"Let's see how it goes." Callum was just about to summon the armor when Quinn stopped him.

"First, do it unmelded. Then do it with Fen."

"I didn't even think about that," Callum said as he felt Fen's influence start to cascade down his arms. This stopped immediately, which told him that the Radiant Fox agreed with Quinn's suggestion.

Callum refocused and the armor took shape over his body. There was a flame-like nature to it, and it was certainly bright, but it didn't have the wings that he had expected. He looked down at his arms, which he was still able to see through the hardened mana armor. Callum extended his hand in front of him and noticed how bringing his hand into a fist drew small, fiery spikes over his knuckles.

"It looks fierce," Marcella said. "Let's see it melded."

The change was immediate as the armor flared on his shoulders, thickening as it rushed over his body. A sharp helm formed as a pair of enormous wings took shape on the back of his arms. Unlike bird wings, these were bat-like in design—nearly translucent and faintly glowing. At least it seemed that way as Callum looked over his shoulder and tried to observe them.

"I'm going to try something." Marcella picked up one of the apples. "Don't block. Or, at least, don't consciously block. Or do. We'll try to see how this armor works."

She took a step back and Harold rushed toward her, the two melding to increase her might.

Marcella hurtled the apple at Callum, and just as the apple was about to hit him in the chest, his wings flashed around him like they were forming a quick cocoon, protecting Callum from the strike.

The apple hit the ground, half of it sizzling.

"Impressive," Tuck the cat said with a purr.

Quinn's eyes bulged. "Scorch damage is awesome. But I'm going to guess that it won't be great on your Mana Reserves."

"I didn't even think about that," Callum said as he once again examined the bright flames lifting off his arm. "It wasn't listed."

"Mana consumption is never listed, but its overall limitations are aided by Resilience, Regeneration, and Mind. You could fuse a shard as well."

"Mana consumption is supposed to be something that you can intuit," Marcella added, "the listing when you use Soul Sense is accurate, but it doesn't paint the entire picture."

Callum sent his arm in front of him again, watching as bits of flame fizzled away. He tried to sense any change to his Mana Reserves, but was unable to do so. *I'm not there yet*, he thought, which made sense considering his lack of training. *But I will get there.*

He comforted himself with this thought, a sudden clarity washing over him as his new Armorcore melted away. Standing there with Marcella and Quin, Callum was struck with an inexplicable sense that the choices he made now, and the lessons he learned, would shape events of great importance in the future.

CHAPTER 29

*While it may appear to merely be a tool of combat, a Weaponcore
is a living conduit of mana, aetherforged to become a dynamic
extension of its master's will. A seamless union of material and
arcane, heart and soul iron, a Weaponcore is a vessel of bound
potential that gave our kingdom the proverbial edge in the Great
Demonswar.*

—Geneva Wraithstorm, Mastress Weaver
and famed Weaponcore Smith of Aveiro

The first thing Callum did upon returning to New Albion was make
plans with Quinn to meet at the Emporium that afternoon.

"Believe me," Quinn assured him, "you'll get better deals if I'm there."

"Why?" Callum asked as his eyes drifted to a hawk flying overhead. He
had spent enough time in the forest over the last few days to notice things
like the wildlife that still existed in the kingdom's largest city.

"Like Marcella," Quinn nodded to the woman, who had already stepped
away and was talking to another student, "my family only recently became
noble. That's how we got to know each other, actually, as kids. New nobles
tend to stick together."

"And how will you get better deals? Are you good at haggling, or
something?"

"No, and I'm glad not to have to haggle. I'd be terrible at it. I know
I'll get better deals because—and this is not a brag— my family became
noble through the real estate it owns here in New Albion, including the
Emporium."

"Your family *owns* the Emporium?" Callum asked as he remembered
the building he had seen and all its booths. There had been more shards and
cores than he could have ever imagined.

"Partial owners, yes. But I don't get a discount or anything. We don't run it like that. But they don't overcharge when they see me, like they often do other Great College students. They'll offer and pay me a fair price for a shard or a core, and they'll let me see any rare finds they might have. I can't really blame them either," Quinn said, leaning in. "Only nobles can attend the Great College and most are wealthy. It makes sense to overcharge, or at least mildly increase the price."

This statement reminded Callum that he wasn't like the other nobles. Coming from humble beginnings didn't do justice to his upbringing on a wheat farm in one of the kingdom's outermost western towns. A farm that, despite all their effort, rarely had a good harvest.

"What kind of rare finds?" Callum asked.

"Well, Demoncores, for one."

<That's so incredibly dangerous, a merchant selling a Demoncore!>

"They're still illegal," Callum said.

"Need I remind you we have a warlock amongst us now?" Quinn asked, referring to Draven. "And the Crown seems to think—or at least they're being persuaded to think—that maybe it's time to relax the restrictions placed on these particular cores."

"I've been wondering how that is even possible, how Draven is even allowed to use Demoncores."

"Well, his father is one of the most powerful dukes in the nation, one who sits on the High Council, meaning that he can skirt around them because he knows all the Magistors, and they wouldn't dare prosecute Draven. I also think that it is somewhat of a test, to see how a warlock would benefit from an education at the Great College. Anyway, we'll see about that later. And who knows if a merchant at the Emporium actually has something like that, or not."

"Right."

"And tomorrow, we'll check out the Dueling Grounds. That's always interesting to see," Quinn said.

"Yes, that should be interesting," Callum told him, remembering this was Marcella's suggestion on the carriage ride back to the city. "I don't really know anything about New Albion."

"Then we'll make a point to show you around tomorrow, or I will. Marcella will come too, but I'm from here, she's not, so in a way she'll be shown around as well." Quinn seemed to grow excited with this plan. "I'll be a tour guide, and then . . . then it all begins." He motioned in the direction of the Second Heart of Creation, his elation dampening to some degree. "First day of class."

"Are you coming or what?" Marcella called over to Quinn.

"Yes," he grinned at Callum. "See you later."

<He's quite nice,> Fen told Callum as they headed back in the direction of Telluride's barn.

<He is. And getting the best price on the shards we collected will help us cover tuition, room, and board. Everything. Plus, I will hopefully be able to upgrade your Aethercore.>

<That would be ideal. I am still shocked they are talking about relaxing the restrictions on Demoncores.>

Callum nodded. Fen had said similar things to him before.

<It's utter madness, but desperation can cause humans to act erratically, especially with an Empire on the border that isn't playing by the rules. With the increased power of aetherbeasts and the destruction they have wrought, the Crown is looking for a solution. But warlocks? Surely, there has to be a better solution than that. It doesn't help that the first warlock we meet is a powerful coward.>

<I don't get that part.> Callum admitted. *<Draven was incredibly strong in my fight against him in the Entry Duel. To flee like that and leave the princess behind? If anything, you'd think Marcella would have gone. She can fly with Harold.>*

<I find that part suspicious too. Why would you send one of your better fighters? Why would he volunteer to leave? This is what I mean by a powerful coward. There's more going on here than what is on the surface. I don't know when we will get to the bottom of it, especially if the Demon King has resurfaced, but it is certainly something we should be wary of.>

"Agreed." Callum stopped as a horse-drawn carriage passed in front of him. A pair of children looked at him from the back, both dirty but happy. They reminded him of the children of Weatherby.

I need to send a letter to my father, he thought once he reached the barn. *And some money, too.*

He entered the barn to find that Telluride was gone, yet there was a faint smell of pipe smoke in the air, which told Callum that he hadn't left that long ago. After changing into the only other set of clothes that he had and running some water over his face, Callum washed his first set of clothing and hung it to dry outside.

He was about to leave when he remembered something.

"I keep forgetting to eat," he told Fen as he entered the kitchen and grabbed a loaf of bread. He found some lukewarm butter, which he smeared over one of the sides. He knew this was because of his Empowerment of Sustenance, but it was still important that he ate. *Otherwise, I'll be tapping into Mana Reserves . . .*

After leaving a quick note for Telluride telling him that he had returned to the city, Callum checked the shards he currently had, nine in total. He also had Veil of the Gravewind Hawk, which he could either sell or sunder for parts via a shardcrafter.

He didn't yet know what he would do, but Callum wanted to come out of the Emporium with two things. The first was an upgraded Aethercore. And the second was enough money to send some to Weatherby and also have some for the semester. If he was lucky, he would also get a new Powercore now that he could use more at the Conjurer Rank.

With this in mind, Callum headed out into the night, taking the same path he had the last time he walked by the Emporium. He reached the sprawling complex to find Quinn standing out front. "I came a little early."

"I did too." Callum rubbed his hands together. "I'm excited to get started."

"It's always a good time in here." Quinn gestured to the building, which had people from all walks of life heading in and out. The king had several guards posted here, and Callum also noted that there was a pair of arch-mages as well. "Before we go in—"

"Yes?" Quinn asked.

"I don't have any Attribute Shards, just Mana Affinity. Is one worth more than the other?"

"Yes, and you are in luck," Quinn said as a woman stepped around him, "because you have the one that is worth more."

"I also have one core that I'm not going to use."

"The Gravewind Hawk, right?" Quinn asked, his voice just a little quieter this time.

"That's right. Should I sunder it or sell it as is?"

"A core like that will be worth more as is. It's not a Demoncore, but a power that allows you to vanish completely certainly is close. I know who to see about it. Just follow me." He waved Callum in, heading past the first several booths and then under a doorway that had the head of a deer hanging above it.

They entered another room where several dealers spoke with students and collectors about shards, and then into another space that was much smaller and had only a few booths displaying a handful of cores.

<And down the stairs we go,> Fen said as they headed down the spiral staircase and into a basement where a smartly placed stained-glass window allowed light to seep in.

"Quinn?" a woman asked. She wore a scarf wrapped around her head and she sat on the ground, her cores before her in the same way that Master Cruedark had arranged his Armorcores.

Are they from the same region? Callum thought as the woman traced a pair of yellow eyes over him.

"Birchwen, this is Callum," Quinn said. "A friend. He has something you might be interested in."

"Oh?" Birchwen asked as she pushed her scarf off her head, revealing a much younger woman than Callum had thought. By the way she had been hunched over and the fact that he couldn't see her face, only the glint of her eyes, he had assumed that she was older, yet she seemed close to his age.

Callum took a quick look around.

There were a few other sellers in the dark space and a handful of customers. He didn't know the protocol for taking out something like this. It was much less intimate than what he had experienced back in Weatherby with Griselda the shardcrafter.

Birchwen laughed. "Is your friend going to show me what he would like to sell or not? Please, sit."

The two sat in front of her on a pair of thickly cushioned square seats. "Here," Callum said as he produced the core from the pouch his father had told him to buy.

The orb floated over to Birchwen, who caught it in her palm. She examined it for a moment and Callum caught a glimpse of the Gravewind Hawk soaring deep within the orb.

"Yes. I will take this." She looked up at Callum. "What price are you asking?"

Quinn spoke for him: "Your best offer. No sense in haggling. You know what this is worth if you sunder it. Gravewind Hawks are quite uncommon."

"They are, and you're right," she said as she set the orb down and turned and produced a wooden box sealed by an iron clasp.

Callum suddenly had doubts. Should he keep it? What if he later had access to Shadow Affinity? He wished now that he had been able to stay longer in the King's Forest, where he would have had the chance to get more shards and cores.

But surely there's other places that I can do that. Quinn would know.

This thought eased him to some degree. This wasn't the last transaction like this he would be forced to make, and right now he needed shards and funds.

Birchwen smiled at Callum. "Or is there something else you'd like to trade for it. Perhaps some shards you desperately need."

"Hold on a moment." He used Soul Sense to view Fen's Aethercore. *Just three Deftness Shards and five Vigor Shards needed to upgrade.*

He also quickly reviewed Gift of the Luminous Lance, Zephyr Strike, and Inner Light, and it was clear that he could use a good number of Light Affinity Shards, and Empowerment of Regeneration Shards for Inner Light, and more Deftness Shards for Zephyr Strike.

He skimmed over his Charge of the Shatterlight Bear, Empowerment of Sustenance, and his new Armorcore. *I need too much to upgrade these; I should focus on the others, specifically Fen's Aethercore and Zephyr Strike, meaning I need eight Deftness and five Empowerment of Vigor shards.*

"We can trade shards upstairs," Quinn told Birchwen as Callum was about to speak. "We brought this Powercore to you because I know that you know its true value."

"You didn't bring the core to me, your friend here did. I do know its true value, and you should at least hear me out."

Quinn's brow furrowed. "I suppose you're right."

Birchwen grinned at Callum. "You want shards, yes? You could use more Powercores, right? You want money? What if there were a way to get all three?"

"I have Mana Affinity Shards I want to trade as well."

"Good, now we're getting somewhere," she told Callum. "Let me see what you have."

Callum produced the shards and placed them in a small leather tray, which he handed to her. "That's all of it."

"See?" Birchwen said. "That wasn't so hard. Three Shadow, one Fire, one Life, two Water, and two Death. Plus the Gravewind core."

"Yes," Callum said.

"And your affinities?"

"Fire, Light, Air."

"Ah, good." Birchwen opened a box with circular indentations in it. Callum noticed a glow to the box and an etching on the front that looked like a flame with air swirling around it. "These are common and uncommon. I'd say one of these three would be ideal for you with your current affinities." She tapped three of the orbs, which glowed as they slowly rose into the air. "Two Powercores, and one Weaponcore. See for yourself. You can advise him however you'd like, Quinn, or, you can consult your pacted aetherbeast."

Sear of the Blazing Gale
Type: Ability
Grade: Uncommon
Infusion Requirements for Grade Increase:
0/10 Fire Affinity

0/10 Air Affinity
0/10 Might Shards
Affinity Requirements: *Fire and Air*
Effect: *When bound to one's Soul Heart, this core allows a mage to conjure a fire-infused wind capable of scorching the battlefield or forcing enemies into a tight spot.*

Halo of the Dawn
Type: *Ability*
Grade: *Common*
Infusion Requirements for Grade Increase:
0/10 Light Affinity
0/10 Resilience Shards
Affinity Requirements: *Light*
Effect: *When bound to one's Soul Heart, this core creates a protective barrier that also increases mana regeneration with each upgrade.*

Weaponcore of the Tempest Fang
Type: *Accessory*
Grade: *Uncommon Weapon*
Infusion Requirements for Grade Increase:
0/10 Air Affinity
0/10 Vigor Shards
0/10 Might Shards
Affinity Requirements: *Air*
Effect: *When bound to one's Soul Heart, this Weaponcore allows a mage to conjure a nearly invisible swirling wind sword capable of cutting through enemies.*

<*These are good,*> Fen said. <*All could be useful.*>

"You don't have a Weaponcore, right?" Quinn asked Callum.

"No, I do not."

"The halo one would be helpful, especially later, once the regeneration power is stronger."

"It would," Callum said. "And the Sear of the Blazing Gale would be incredibly useful."

"You know," Birchwen began, "your Gravewind core is worth quite a lot. I could see it being worth all three of these cores."

But I need money, Callum thought. *And I want to upgrade Fen's Aethercore and Zephyr Strike. . .*

Birchwen shifted a little, revealing a set of jingling bracelets that stopped at her wrists, similar to the ones Marcella wore. "Let's try this. You said you needed shards. What shards do you need?"

"I need eight Deftness and five Vigor shards."

"Let me see about that." Birchwen produced a bit of parchment paper and made some scratches on it.

<I think you should go with the weapon,> Fen told Callum. *<Get enough money for this semester if you can, the weapon, and the shards. Or we can have Telluride sunder something else and get shards that way. There will definitely be more opportunities to get shards in the future.>*

"Well?" Quinn asked as Birchwen continued jotting down some numbers.

She finally stopped. Rather than say anything, she handed the scrap of parchment to Quinn.

<Is that a bill of sale?>

Callum leaned in to see that it was one, with a sum written down that was much more than he expected from the Gravewind Powercore, especially if he was going to get the Attribute Shards he needed alongside a core.

"This is a great offer," Quinn said. "You'll get the shards you need for your upgrades, one of the cores, and some money."

"The Weaponcore," Callum said. "That's the one I want."

"I had a feeling that would be the one. It should serve you well, for now. But I'm making this offer to you on one condition." Birchwen looked him over with her yellow eyes.

"Yes?"

"You return to me first whenever you have more high-Grade cores to offload. I have a feeling this could be the start of a very fruitful relationship."

"Deal," Callum told the shardcrafter.

CHAPTER 30

The abandoned campuses of the Great College, once bustling with the brightest minds of their era, now serve a different but no less vital purpose. These once-esteemed halls of learning echo with the clash of aetherbeasts and difficult expeditions, ensuring the legacy of the College endures into a new era.

—A quote from *Valestra's Legacy* by Sir Trevor Bierce

I know a place we can test it," Quinn said as he led Callum through the streets of New Albion. "We're students now, remember? We have access to the training grounds."

Callum, who still couldn't believe his luck, caught up with Quinn as they rounded a corner and reached one of the Great College's enormous gates. It was here that Callum, yet again, came to understand just how large the campus was. It seemed like they were on a small hill, and he could see many buildings beyond, and more gates.

"I didn't notice those ones last time," he told Quinn.

"Ah, those." Quinn turned to him. "The Great College is famous for a number of reasons. Aside from graduating some of the best archmages in the kingdom, there are a lot of . . ." He squinted for a moment as he thought of the right word. "Mysteries. Let's call them that. Mysteries and links to abandoned places."

"Links to where?"

"To abandoned campuses. Do you remember the way Master Cruedark portaled us to the nobles' campground? It works like that, these lost campuses utilized for certain types of training. You wouldn't know unless you truly explored, but there are aetherbeasts and other mysterious things there as well."

<*The Archive of Destiny?*>

"What about the Archive of Destiny?" Callum asked, repeating Fen's words.

"That's in the Great Library," he said as he pointed to a square building notable for the spires that rose around it. "You won't have access, though, until class starts. They were remodeling it over the summer. I know because my family provided a storehouse for some of the books during the process. I was so lucky to get to read a few. Anyway. Follow me."

Quinn led Callum down the hill, past a circular seating area, to an enormous door situated on a stone square. The door was etched with runes and other symbols Callum didn't quite recognize. He all but expected the door to slide open on its own when the exact opposite happened.

The door vanished, leaving just an arch to pass through.

<*What kind of magitek is this?*> Fen asked Callum.

Quinn spoke again, as if he'd heard Fen's question: "Pass through the door and you will be provided a space to train or test a new Powercore. It's not a type of magitek that I claim to understand, but we are safe when we are in there. I do know that. See you on the other side."

Quinn stepped through the doorway and Callum followed. They appeared in a strange space that reminded Callum of an open field but also felt like an illusion. Above, the once dark sky now had a hint of green and gold to it that soon shimmered away.

"What's first?" Quinn asked. "Testing your new Weaponcore or upgrading?"

Callum took another look around. He turned back to see the doorway was still there, that he could leave at any time. "Cores."

He upgraded Zephyr Strike first by pressing the new shards into it. This changed the Powercore's rating from Common to Uncommon.

"Ready?" Callum asked Fen.

<*Always.*>

He accessed Fen's Aethercore and pressed the shards into the orb, which fizzled for a moment before settling. Callum used Soul Sense and immediately saw the changes:

Pact of the Radiant Fox
Type: *Pacted*
Grade: *Uncommon*
Infusion Requirements for Grade Increase:
0/10 Air Affinity Shards
0/10 Light Affinity Shards
0/10 Deftness Shards

0/10 Might Shards
0/5 Resilience Shards
Mana Affinity Granted: *Air, Fire, Light*
Meldform Benefits:
Attributes:
+3 Might
+4 Deftness
+3 Vigor
+3 Resilience
+3 Regeneration
+1 Mind
Radiant Claws: *When melded with the Radiant Fox, the wielder gains powerful claws made of burning light, which can not only be used to attack its enemies, but also empower further, unleashing blazing slashes of fire and light a short distance before them.*
Radiant Inferno: *When melded with the Radiant Fox, channel pure radiant energy into flames that create a white-hot fire capable of melting through armor and dispelling darkness. The flames burn brighter than natural fire, blinding enemies with their intensity.*

<Oh my . . .>

"Well?" Quinn asked Callum excitedly. "What are the changes?"

"My Meldform benefits improved by a point and I received a new ability called Radiant Inferno." He read the description to Quinn.

"That sounds amazing. We have to try it. But first, what will your stats be if you are melded?"

"Let me check." Callum started to do the math in his head when Quinn spoke again.

"Meld, then check."

"Right." Callum felt a sudden surge of power as he melded with Fen. It was definitely different than it had been before, Callum shaking with intensity for a moment. Once again, he used Soul Sense: "Might, eight; Deftness, eight; Vigor, seven; Resilience, seven; Regeneration, seven; and Mind, five," he told Quinn.

"That's incredible. You know, they say that for every three to five points, you double the power of a normal person." He whistled. "I really need to upgrade my Aethercore."

Tuck, his pacted aetherbeast appeared. "You really do," the cat said as he took a seat.

"Why don't you just buy the shards that you need?" Callum asked Quinn.

"Aside from the fact that I sort of want to earn them, your Aethercore is tied to your Rank. What I'm saying is for Fen to move to the next Grade, you would need to move to the next Rank. Even if you collected all the shards, it wouldn't do anything. Aethercores don't work the same way as Powercores, Armorcores, Weaponcores—you get the idea. At your current Rank, you can have a Legendary Powercore, like I told you back in the forest, but it comes with a massive cut in potency. Aethercores are different. You can't upgrade them past your current Rank."

"Makes sense."

"It does. Now, your sword. I'm dying to see it. And you should definitely test this new power you got from your Aethercore."

Callum invoked the Tempest Fang. A grip took shape in his hand, one with a knuckle guard bound in mana. The blade extended from there, curved in nature and made of wispy wind that constantly changed its form.

Quinn's mouth dropped open. "That looks crazy. I knew a wind sword would look wild, but that's awesome!"

Callum sliced the sword through air as if he were attacking with his Radiant Claws. It produced a trail of mana-fueled wind that cut forward about ten feet. Recalling some of the training he had done with the local militia back in Weatherby, Callum moved into a sword stance and performed a few strikes.

Every time he did, he felt a surge of wind as the blade changed. He turned to Quinn. "You don't have a Weaponcore, do you?"

"I keep meaning to get one, but no, not currently. Why?"

"I wanted to see what it felt like to strike another weapon."

<Perhaps I can help.>

<Sure,> Callum told Fen. *<Join us.>*

The Radiant Fox took shape. He was larger, like he had grown several inches in each direction. There was something else different about him as well. Callum had noticed before how he had a hunch, likely from the Corruption. This was straightened out to some degree, Fen looking healthier than he had ever seen him.

Fen hopped to a space across from Callum.

"Ready?"

"Ready," he told the fox.

Fen flicked his tail; Callum blocked the energy attack with his new wind sword.

"It's amazing," Callum said as he looked down at the blade again. He lightly lowered his hand through the wind and noticed that it wasn't hard and he was able to press his fingers through the blade portion.

"Your own Weaponcore can't hurt you," Quinn explained. "It's not like a normal weapon."

"I can see that. Fen? Let's test Radiant Inferno."

The fox raced toward him and the two melded again.

"I think I will step back," Quinn said as Callum began to charge. "Come on, Tuck."

"Right," the cat said as it hiked its tail up and pressed back.

With his free hand, Callum conjured a ball of white-hot fire, which he lugged in front of him. It grew with radiance and exploded a few seconds later.

"It's like a . . ." Quinn ran his hand through his hair as he tried to think of a way to describe it. "Sort of like a fireball, but if it doesn't hit something, there's a delay, and then it explodes. That's awesome."

<*This could be very useful depending on the fight,*> Fen said.

Callum looked down at his new Weaponcore, glowing with intensity, wind twisting around it. He brought the sword to the ready and cut through the air again, feeling its power. *It will be very useful,* he thought.

By the time they finished in the training ground, Callum was tired. He parted ways with Quinn and headed back to the barn that he shared with Telluride. The shardcrafter was already asleep, yet he had left some stew for Callum, which he gladly ate.

Upon waking the next morning with plans to join Quinn and Marcella, Callum found a note from Telluride:

Callum,

I saw that you returned yesterday. We certainly need to catch up. I'm afraid I've been called to the hamlet of Echospire for the day, and I might stay the night there. If I'm not back tonight, I should be by the morn!

Good luck, and have fun exploring New Albion!

Telluride

"I'd better let him know I might be late," he said as he scratched out a reply on the bottom of the parchment.

He responded that he would be back late as well and then left in the direction of the Great College, where he met Quinn and Marcella. Marcella was playfully teasing Quinn about the outfit he had chosen.

"It's not winter yet," she told Quinn as Callum approached.

"Not winter? You're wearing clothes more suitable for Aveiro," he responded.

Marcella did a small spin and lifted her arms. She wore light blue fabric draped from her wrists to her waist, the flowing material evoking a graceful impression of a bird's wings in motion. Despite its elegance, the design allowed her arms to move freely. Her look was further adorned with intricate jewelry—dangling earrings and a long necklace that cascaded down to her navel.

Quinn was the exact opposite, the portly young man dressed in a pressed pair of brown pants and a matching jacket. His outfit reminded Callum of the clothing the tax authorities wore when they came to Weatherby.

Rather than tell Quinn this, Callum merely smiled at the two of them. Marcella looked him over. "Weren't you wearing that yesterday?"

"It's clean," he said, which was true. Aside from the cloak, Callum had brought two sets of clothing, and he had washed one before meeting Quinn the previous day.

"In that case," she said, looking him over again, "I can already see our day shaping up."

"We were going to go watch the duels, right?" Quinn asked Marcella.

"They've been canceled. I'm staying near there, remember? I walked by this morning while they made the announcement."

"I thought you were going to live in one of the dorms."

"I'm planning to, yes, but there are some changes that I wanted so I have to wait for them. Like the drapes," she told Quinn as she lifted her arms, the fabric trailing after her wrists.

"You are looking more like Harold by the day," Quinn told her, referring to her pacted heron.

"He did compliment my outfit," she said as she did another spin. "What do you think, Callum?"

"It looks like it would be nice near the ocean. But I've never seen the ocean," he said, "so I don't really know."

"You've never seen the ocean?" Marcella looked at him with sadness in her eyes. "Really? Right, Weatherby is nowhere near the sea. But I figured you would have made a trip at least once. Never a summer holiday in Aveiro?"

"There's a lot to do on the farm in the summer, especially leading up to harvest."

"I'll bet," Quinn said, who seemed eager to get a move on. "So, if we're not seeing the duels, what are we doing?"

Marrisa answered: "Well, for one, our dear Callum Stross—who isn't the famous Callum Stross from so many years ago but is shaping up to be pretty famous after his actions in the King's Forest—is in need of some new clothing. If I remember correctly, over breakfast you said that he got some money yesterday."

"I need to send some back to Weatherby, to my father and a shard-crafter who helped me out," Callum said. "I should do that before I buy anything."

"You can do that tomorrow," Marcella told him as she started down the steps. "And you are in luck. Sale season started today. With me as your stylist, and perhaps your lead negotiator, we should be able to get plenty of clothing. Because really, Callum, really."

"What?" he asked as he caught up with her. That was one thing he had already noticed about Marcella—she moved quickly when she walked, leading Quinn to exert himself as he kept up.

"Fashion isn't important, especially with all the things going on in the kingdom. It's not important to our studies, and it isn't going to make a real difference on the battlefield. But we live in a world where people make assumptions based on the way you look. So while you may be a humble farm boy capable of great things, like saving us, and you are technically noble, people are going to see you and think otherwise. In that regard, it is of the utmost importance. Especially if you expect to be seen with the princess."

<*She has a point. It is best that we blend in. Though considering her outfit, she might not be the best one to show us how. But with Quinn's sound advice, I think that this could work out.*>

"As long as it's comfortable," Callum said, after listening to Fen.

"You don't think my wings are comfortable?" she asked as she flapped them slightly.

Quinn laughed. "You can be over the top, you know that?"

"This is considered modest in Aveiro," she told him as they rounded a corner and came onto yet another wide road, one that had been blocked off.

Callum soon saw why as they reached an open-air market. It was lively and colorful, with striped blue tents and booths arranged in neat rows, ropes crisscrossing overhead and strung with fluttering tassels. "This is amazing," Callum said as he looked at the shadows the suspended ropes had traced across the ground. Various smells came to him as they traveled deeper into the market, from the strong scent of fresh leather to grilled meats.

Marcella certainly stood out. More heads turned to look at her than Callum had ever noticed before. Not only was she tall and pretty, but the colors she wore were unlike anything usually seen in the capital of the kingdom. She got a few compliments but mostly stares.

"How about this?" She asked as she came to a booth with a lime-green outfit with yellow stitching.

"You have to be joking," Quinn told her. "Don't you know what these are for?"

"No," she said.

"It's a celebration later in the year where everyone wears bright clothing and parties in the streets. You haven't heard of Gildentide? The idea behind the holiday originally was that the bright clothing would help make the winter shorter, but it is now a three-day event that is mostly drunken revelry. Anyway. He can't wear this." Quinn grinned at her. "But you could wear that," he said as he motioned to her outfit.

"I can't help it if I look beautiful." Marcella tilted her chin in the air and moved on, people parting in front of her.

"You get used to her," Quinn told Callum as she moved ahead.

"She's fine. But I don't know about the green outfit," he said.

"Don't worry, I will let her pick things out and I will subtly do what I can," Quinn told him with a little laugh. "She's not the first southerner to show up here wearing strange clothing. In fact . . ." He nodded to a pair that were just passing by. "Can you tell where they're from?"

The man and woman both wore light-blue clothing, the woman with a skirt that had been cut into long slits that danced over her feet.

"Aveiro?"

"Or thereabouts, yes," Quinn said as Marcella motioned for them to catch up.

The three turned onto a new lane in the market, where they found clothing that was more suitable for the big city. This included a few sets of trousers that were loose enough that Callum would be able to move freely in them. The trousers could also be cut off at the knee, which reminded him of the pants he would wear in the summer in Weatherby. There were shirts as well, but the pants were the only thing that they picked up from the lane.

"You'll have your new Armorcore, but you also wear regular armor at some point," Marcella told him. "And you'll need things to wear underneath it. You should get ahead of that now."

She helped him pick out a few more things and waited with an annoyed look on her face as Quinn sorted through her selection, picking colors that were more appropriate.

"You really are no fun," Marcella told Quinn after they had finished shopping. Callum now had several outfits, all monotone colors.

The three stopped by a tea shop with outdoor seating set in a circle around a small fountain. "Let me get it," Quinn said as he motioned for the two of them to take a seat.

Once he was gone, Marcella leaned toward Quinn. "You are lucky, you know. Quinn is a nice guy, a good person to know, even if his fashion sense is questionably bland. Because of Quinn, I now know the princess. I can't believe that," she said, as she glanced around like someone could hear her. "We're sort of friends. Or we are friends. I don't know. But we've had private meetings a few times now, ones without Sir Trindade around." Marcella relaxed a little more. "It has all been so sudden."

"What does your family do?" Quinn asked. While he knew that she was a new noble, he didn't know much about the tall woman that sat in front of him wearing avian-inspired clothing.

"Shipping. Aveiro is by the sea, after all. That is one of the reasons I know Quinn, because his family owns warehouses and, well, new nobles have to stick together, er, new nobles and ancient ones like you. Don't," she said as Callum started to speak. "I don't want to hear that you're just a simple farm boy from Weatherby."

Callum thought of his farm, his hard upbringing, the cold winters he'd experienced with his father, and all the sacrifices they'd had to make. It didn't seem like he had anything in common with someone that considered themselves noble.

Quinn returned with tea and pastries on a tray. Soon, the three were talking again about the King's Forest and Callum's epic jump in which he had speared the Gravewind Hawk.

"I'll never forget that," Quinn said. "You appeared out of nowhere. What a vision."

Later, the three had dinner at a pub. Callum felt great on his walk back to Stadacona, his new clothing neatly folded in a leather bag Marcella had insisted he purchase.

Callum knocked but Telluride didn't answer.

He procured the large key the shardcrafter had given him and unlocked the side door. The space beyond was dark—deep and unnervingly still, as if it swallowed all light. Stepping inside, Callum let the heavy door creak shut behind him, the sound echoing ominously in the silence.

"I guess he's not back yet," Callum said as he peered into the darkness.

CHAPTER 31

The Second Heart of Creation stands as a testament to our rejection of demonic aetherbeasts and the Corruption of Demoncores. May its very presence guide us for all eternity.

—Branscombe Joule, poet

Callum placed the leather bag of clothing he had purchased on a side table near the entrance of the barn. He was about to light a lamp when Fen shouted in his head.

<Watch out!>

The fox melded with him, and they rolled to the side as a bolt of red energy seared right past Callum's head.

He summoned his Armorcore as a demonic aetherbeast surged out of the darkness, its progress lit by wispy bits of crimson energy. The beast swiped its claws at Callum, who blocked the attack with his forearm as his new Weaponcore took shape in his hand.

The monster screeched as it leaped backward, a part of its enormous claw ignited by the scorch damage from Callum's armor.

This gave Callum a glimpse of the monster, which had a crustacean body and numerous smaller legs that all trailed back into a tulip-shaped stinger.

<A demonic aetherbeast!>

Callum charged at the creature using a boost from the Shatterlight Bear. The monster tried to pierce him with the thick stinger, which was strong enough to smash through a table.

Splinters of wood hit the air as Callum dove, rolled, and came up with his Tempest Fang at the ready. He swatted away the creature's stinger and then hit it with a blast of light energy using his Radiant Claws attack.

The aetherbeast came at him with another stinger, which broke one of the barn's support beams, bringing down wood and supplies that had been stored in the rafters.

Dust filled the darkened barn as Callum summoned a surge of wind. It was much stronger now, his attack was able to blow the demon backward, where it slammed into another support beam. More debris fell from the rafters as Callum beat back its stingers, which were becoming increasingly sporadic in spawning from the tail end of its body.

The monster scurried up the wall and dove for Callum, twisting in the process.

It brought with it a surge of reddened mana that fired over Callum's head and into the open kitchen, destroying the table. Pots and pans tumbled down, clanking against the ground as Callum raced to the right and sliced through another of its stingers.

He followed up with a quick twist that sent a spiral of wind toward another stinger, yet his attempt was blocked by the creature's thick claws. It bashed through another support beam, bringing down a portion of the ceiling, some roof tiles slipping through and cracking against the ground.

They would have buried Callum and perhaps killed him had it not been for the wings on his Armorcore, which rushed forward and swept the tiles out of the way creating projectiles.

The debris flew through the air as Fen shouted, *<Use Radiant Inferno!>*

<Got it!> Callum jogged backward a few steps to avoid the demon's rapid-fire attacks.

Without looking at Soul Sense, Callum knew his energy levels were dwindling. It was a feeling deep within his core. The sudden surprise attack, the power needed to fuel his armor and sword, the sheer strength of the demonic aetherbeast, Callum knew without a shadow of a doubt—*I have to end this now!*

It was instinctual, just as he had noticed back in the training zone. Callum intuited when it was time to release the plume of light, which blew the demonic aetherbeast backward.

Much to his surprise, another blast came from his right, the blue mana exploding a portion of the monster's armor. Callum hit it with his Tempest Fang, spun, and then impaled the creature with his lance.

As the dust settled and what was left of the rooftop creaked, he turned to find Telluride, a hint of blue glowing around his hands and slowly fading.

"I'm sorry," Callum said. "Your barn . . ."

Telluride's shoulders relaxed to some degree. "Definitely a demonic aetherbeast . . ."

The thought of what Telluride had just said sent a chill down Callum's spine. "Do you think a warlock did this?"

"Only warlocks can summon aetherbeasts like this and force them to do their bidding. Think about it: Any aetherbeast you work with will have to be pacted, meaning you will have its Aethercore. This is different." He gestured to the corrupted magic now boiling in the place where the demon had just been. Fen separated from Callum and approached the Corruption, then began absorbing it.

"Do you think it was Draven?" Callum asked as he tried to make sense of what had just happened.

"The duke's son? We have to be careful before we make accusations like that, lad. He isn't the only warlock in our world, you know. His father, Duke Blademark, is trying to legitimize Demoncores and warlocks." Telluride kicked his foot against some of the rubble. "Attacking you would be counterintuitive."

"Counterintuitive unless they were certain that he was related to the Demonslayer," Fen said.

"Yes, a fair point." Telluride stroked his hand over his beard.

"Why? Did they have something against the original Callum Stross?" Fen asked.

"Not to my knowledge. They would, however, have an interest in protecting what they are trying to promote, Demoncores, summonable aetherbeasts unlike any the world has ever seen before. You see, the fact that one must pact with an aetherbeast, and there's a limit to how many one can pact with, has a natural way of keeping order. Even a Convoker is only capable of bonding with five Aethercores."

"But being able to summon demonic aetherbeasts to do one's bidding—"

"Is something else entirely. You see?" Telluride asked Fen. "So while I'm not accusing the duke, I am saying that they may have a vested interest in preventing someone like you from meddling in any of their affairs. After all, what do you think your forefather would say, hmm?"

"The Demonslayer wouldn't agree with that," Fen said as he finished absorbing the corruption. "My memory of him is blurry at best, but things were set up the way they were set up for a reason. This attack, this attempt to murder you, tells me that we may be getting closer to the truth than we thought. This is why we must access the Archive of Destiny."

"At the Great Library, yes," Telluride said. "It is a mysterious thing, that. But before you can even think about that, you need to find a place to stay."

"But where?" Callum asked, feeling distraught as he looked around at the barn.

"The Great College itself, at least for you. I would like to see a demonic aetherbeast try to attack you if you lived in a dormitory there, especially with all the wards protecting the place."

"A dorm?" Callum hadn't even given thought to the idea.

"Yes, where a student should actually stay, not a barn."

"I have money," Callum said. "I got some from my excursion in the King's Forest, from selling shards."

"I was wanting to ask you about that. Your excursion, not the money part."

"But I wanted to send some back to my father and to Griselda."

"I'm going to go out on a limb here and say that both your father and Griselda would want you to get settled first. Visit the campus tomorrow—classes are starting then, yes?—and get set up in a dorm. You can worry about money later. There will be plenty of opportunities for you to gain more now that you're getting a better handle on what it means to be archmage."

"What about you?"

"Me?" Telluride laughed bitterly. "I have a place I can stay, where we both can stay, tonight. You can catch me up on what happened in the forest along the way."

"And just leave the barn like this? In ruin?"

Telluride turned away. "It's not going anywhere."

"I can help rebuild it."

The shardcrafter paused as he considered Callum's offer. "That is mighty kind of you. If you have time, then sure, by all means. But your studies need to come first. I'm actually giving out sound advice for once." He laughed at himself as he motioned for Callum to follow him. "Well? What are you waiting for? It's been a long day."

No matter how hard he tried, as he followed Telluride away from the barn, Callum couldn't shake the lingering tension. It seemed like the shadows came alive with every corner they turned, and Callum was reliving the experience of being ambushed, how he would have certainly died had it not been for Fen's sudden reaction.

He jumped as they passed a tannery from the sound of someone sliding a wooden door open, and almost melded with Fen.

<Easy,> the fox told him.

"Sorry," Callum said under his breath, before nodding and continued on.

Ahead of him, Telluride walked with his hands crossed behind his back as if he were going on a casual stroll, his unlit pipe perched on his lip. He didn't seem disturbed at all by the attack at the barn, not in the way that Callum was.

Then again, he wasn't there at the start of it, Callum thought as they reached a tavern that seemed to have been fused into the side of an ancient wall.

"I'll be just a moment." Telluride gestured to a pair of seats around an overturned barrel.

Callum took a seat, his eyes scanning the buildings around for disturbances. That edge. He couldn't quite shake it no matter how hard he tried. It didn't matter if it was the breeze or someone passing by, he felt jumpy, like there was another ambush coming.

<I just need to rest,> he said to Fen.

<I agree, that might help. But you need not worry with me around.>

The words should have been comforting, yet there was a deficiency that Callum felt and not acting on his own, not checking the place. It was irrational and he knew this, but it was also a reminder that he had a long way to go.

After about ten minutes, Telluride emerged from the tavern with a pair of pints. "I guess you shouldn't be drinking, considering you have class tomorrow." He shrugged. "Looks like I get two, then, while they prepare our rooms." He took a drink from the first pint, considered the taste, and comically took a drink of the other before nodding. "This will do."

"Let me pay for it."

"Certainly not. The innkeeper here owes me a favor. We won't stay for long. Besides, it's the slow season now that school is about to be in session. Business will pick up again once the fall festivals start." He sat across from Callum and took a drink from one of his pints. "So, the King's Forrest, what happened?"

Callum explained how he had explored on his own for a while gathering shards before eventually venturing through an abandoned ruin, where he came across the princess and two others fighting an aetherbeast.

"So you saved the day," Telluride said after Callum had explained his strategy, using Fen as a distraction while he prepared to pierce the monster.

"And then Draven finally showed up," he said, before detailing how the warlock had brought back Sir Trindade, Master Cruedark, and a few other guards.

Telluride seemed to have the same question as Marcella, "Why didn't he stay behind and fight?"

"I don't know. He's not weak or anything."

"That's strange. You'd think he would want to show his true power in front of the princess. They are betrothed, you know." He took a big drink from his pint. "People are always talking about it."

A pang of unease tightened in Callum's chest. "I'm aware."

"Yes, his father, the Duke Blademark of Karna, grew up around King Morninglade. This is common knowledge. Their children have been promised to each other since they were babies. Perhaps that is one reason he didn't stay and fight. Maybe he didn't want to show how powerless he actually was, although that seems like a strange thing to want to do, especially in front of his future wife." He took another drink from his pint. "Curious. All of this is curious."

Later that night, Callum tried his best to get a good night's sleep. He kept tossing and turning, stirring every time he drifted off because he felt that something came in from the shadows. It was like a nightmare that would never end, this thought that things could change so suddenly.

"I could never fathom something like this a month ago," he said at one point as he stared up at the dark ceiling of the tavern, all but expecting the ceiling to come alive.

<*But you are getting it now. Your only course of action is to get stronger and be ready for the next attack. I have returned for a reason. It is your destiny, as much as it is mine. We will be more careful going forward.*>

With those words, he finally drifted off early in the morning, only to awaken to Telluride knocking at his door. "Callum, you're going to miss your first day at the Great College if you don't hurry!"

CHAPTER 32

The core curriculum of the first semester at the Great College is the foundation upon which future mastery is built. By focusing on combat, history, Manavitality, and Elemental Mana and its principles, the curriculum ensures that a student has all the tools they need to harness their abilities responsibly and effectively.

—Master Weaver Patrjohn Granadam, Magistor of Gilded Radiance and current Dean of the Great College

The new clothing Callum had purchased fit but was uncomfortably tight, something he noticed as he hurried toward the Great College. He spotted Quinn and Marcella on the steps, each holding a piece of parchment in their hands.

Marcella gasped when he joined them. "What happened to you?"

Callum ran his hand through his hair. A student approached quickly from his right and he swiveled to her, jumpy as ever.

"Hey," Quinn said after the other student moved on, "what happened?"

"I already asked him that." Marcella looked Callum up and down. Gone were her flowing, birdlike robes, replaced with the same dark clothing that everyone at the Great College wore. Yet there was a twist, Callum noticed as he took her in, a lightness in the stitching that made her clothes look custom. Jewelry and a couple of dark flowers pinned to her lapel also made her stand out, but less so than she normally did.

Quinn looked pretty much the same as he had the previous day, though portly young man had a fresh shave and his cheeks were just slightly red.

"I was attacked last night," Callum blurted out. Just uttering those words made it feel as if a weight had been lifted off his shoulders. "Last night, when I got back to the barn—"

Marcella's expression turned incredulous. "You were attacked *in a barn?*"

"I had been staying in a barn, yes."

Her eyes bulged slightly. "You make it really hard not to call you farm boy, you know that, right? But seriously, why were you staying in a barn? You should be staying in a dorm here."

"I'm not . . ." Callum was about to say that he wasn't rich, but didn't want to lead with that. Instead, he pivoted. "It looks like I'm going to have to find a dorm anyway. I mean, I guess I could stay with Telluride—"

"Who?" Marcella asked.

"At least let him finish what he's saying," Quinn told her.

"Telluride is a shardcrafter, the one I have been lodging with in the barn. Now, we're staying at a tavern," Callum said, lowering his voice.

"No one can hear you," Marcella told him. "But I get why you're being secretive, the whole attacked thing. What were you attacked by? A thief? Some bandits?"

"Not exactly. It was a demonic aetherbeast," Callum said, figuring he would just come right out with it.

Marcella exchanged glances with Quinn. "See? I told you."

"You are really him, aren't you?" Quinn asked Callum point-blank.

"Umm . . ." Callum gulped, not prepared for this line of questioning.

Quinn gestured toward the campus. "The statue. The real Callum Stross. The Demonslayer. You're him."

"I'm not him—"

"Related to him, that's what I mean. And now you were targeted by a demonic aetherbeast." He turned his head, an indication that his aetherbeast was speaking to him. "Or . . . so it seems," Quinn said.

Marcella continued in a conspiratorial tone, "They know. They have been putting pressure on King Morninglade for some time now."

"Who? The Duke of Karna in his push for legalized Demoncores?" Callum asked.

"That, or the Cult of the Black Dawn. Ugh."

"Let's not speculate," Quinn told Marcella.

"I always trust my gut and you know that."

"How much do you know?" Quinn asked, returning his focus to Callum.

"About the cult? Not much. About Demoncores, just what Telluride said about the duke and his relationship with the king. Not to mention Draven and the princess."

Marcella's fist tightened around the parchment in her hand. "I keep hoping that it won't go that way, that things turn out differently for her."

"We all hope that," Quinn said, "but these kinds of politics are messy. And they can lead people to do strange things. I'm not saying that Draven or the duke had anything to do with the assassination attempt, not directly, but they have been secretly pushing for Demoncores for years. We literally have a warlock in our class, something unheard of even five years ago. And one could argue that they are doing it with good reason, particularly with the intensity of the aetherstorms lately. Then there are the tensions with the other kingdoms, especially with the Geshwine Empire relaxing their previous ban on Demoncores."

<The bleeding idiots! Consorting with demons? It's a crime in every sense of the word, and it won't do anything to dampen the power of aetherstorms or the rise of the Cult. If anything, it will make the cult even stronger!>

"Fen is saying that legalizing Demoncores will make the cult even stronger," Callum said.

"Which may be one of the reasons someone tried to deal with you early," Marcella told him. "They have access to family trees via the World Ledger. That would also mean some royals know, like the princess. I'd assume she knows. Other nobles would know too, like Draven, or Victrin, whose mother is the Duchess of Ontaria. So someone knows. And more people are going to know soon if you keep doing things like, I don't know, saving the princess."

"I didn't—"

"Callum, you literally came out of nowhere and jumped toward one of the most terrifying aetherbeasts I've ever seen. You melded and pierced it with your lance. People are going to find out about that."

"Not if you don't tell them."

"I have a big mouth," she admitted. "And it was impressive. Quinn has told people too."

"I didn't tell anyone."

She playfully patted him on the shoulder. "You told Godric over breakfast. I was there, remember?"

"That's because he was telling me a story about his pacted ape and how once jumped over the head of a pacted gazelle in a sparring match near Echospire."

"My point remains. People will know. So that means you need to come to grips with this," Marcella told Callum. "And you need to get into a dorm tonight. The campus is protected by wards. Even though it can be a strange place, it's much safer here."

"She's right," Quinn said. "Attacking someone in public is one thing, but if they did it while you are on campus, it would likely lead to the law against

Demoncores staying in place for another hundred years, especially because you are a descendant of the Demonslayer. Don't forget there's a literal statue of your ancestor just over there," he said as he motioned toward one of the numerous courtyards.

"I don't even know where to begin," Callum admitted. "I don't have my schedule, I don't know where to go, everyone seems to be ahead of me in some way, and even if I knew how to get a dorm, I'm afraid it might be too late anyway."

"And that's where your friends come in," Quinn said as he handed Callum a piece of parchment. "Here is your schedule. I went to the trouble of getting it for you. Lucky for all of us, our first class is a combat class with Master Cruedark."

Callum scanned the parchment and saw that this was indeed the case. He also had a history course, a class on something called Manavitality, and one on Elemental Mana and Its Principles. It seemed like a light schedule. "Just four classes?" he asked.

"Oh, they'll keep us busy," Quinn assured him. "Believe me. Come on."

As they walked past the Ordelarium, vermillion banners beating in the wind around its entrance, Marcella assured Callum that she would help him get a dorm: "I told you they were renovating mine. To do that, they also have to renovate the room next door. And it's currently unoccupied. The only real problem is that they will not be ready until tomorrow. But I can handle all that as long as . . ." She turned him. "You were going to send money home, right?"

"I was. But I think I need to do this first. There is something else I have to do as well. I have to help rebuild the barn that was destroyed last night."

"Maybe we could do that together," Quinn said.

Much to Callum's surprise, Marcella agreed: "I've never done anything like that, but I'm sure I can help, and Harold can be useful. I don't know about Tuck," she said, referring to Quinn's pacted Darkmoor cat.

"Cats are useful in their own way," Quinn told her as they traveled down a pathway lined with enormous statues.

The statues cast shadows onto the cobblestone, enough to remind Callum of the way it had felt beneath the canopy of the King's Forest. For a brief moment he missed being out in the wild, even if it had been dangerous. Even creeping through an unknown ruin, he had not felt the same tension as he did in the city now, knowing that he was a target.

Fen is right, he reminded himself. *I have to be ready for things like this.*

This thought seemed to do the trick as they passed through an archway and came to an open space with wide platforms beyond that rose like pillars into the air. The new student body was gathered there, all in their overcoats as Master Cruedark stood before them, his big Weaponcore hammer resting across his shoulders.

Callum scanned the crowd to find Princess Selene standing off by herself, arms crossed over her chest. She was in a different set of armor, this one much bulkier, with an intricately detailed gorget extending upward from the chest plate, shielding her neck and throat.

He was starting to wave at her when he sensed a presence behind them.

Even in his exhausted state, Callum turned with the idea that he may have to fight. His intuition wasn't right just yet, but it wasn't far off as Draven stepped through the arch.

The warlock's red eyes fell on Callum and lifted in surprise. This quickly morphed into a scowl, as if Draven were angry to see him alive. He sulked over to a group of nobles, none of whom seemed to notice the way that Draven had looked at Callum.

<*That was obvious.*>

<*It was,*> Callum told Fen. <*Do you think he knows something?*>

<*Hard to tell. He might still be upset about the way you saved Princess Selene back in the forest. I agree with both Telluride and Quinn that we shouldn't jump to conclusions here, even if there are some that seem obvious. And believe me, I'm gritting my teeth as I say this. I despise demons and anyone wanting to pact with one.*>

Princess Selene turned to Callum, Marcella, and Quinn. The hard look on her face softened as she flashed a smile in their direction. True to her nature, the smile quickly became something more professional, her brow lowering some. But she seemed generally excited to see them as she approached.

"Are you ready for round two?" she asked Callum.

"Am I going to fight you today?" he asked her, almost jokingly.

"That's not really up to me." She motioned to Master Cruedark, who stood stoic as ever. "But from what I know about the first day of combat class, there is some sparring."

"Well, I have an Armorcore and a Weaponcore now."

"Do you?" she asked. "Good." Princess Selene turned to the others. "Quinn, Marcella."

"Princess," Quinn said. "You missed a fun time yesterday. We went to the outdoor market to do a little shopping."

"I was wondering where Callum got his new clothing."

"I helped pick his new stuff out," Marcella told her. "Well, at least he went with some of my suggestions. Perhaps I'm a bit too colorful for the north."

"If only we had the colors of Aveiro here," Princess Selene said as Callum looked beyond her, spotting Draven glaring at the four of them.

As the princess continued speaking with Marcella and Quinn, assistants joined Master Cruedark at the front. After speaking with him, the assistants moved into positions around him and cast their hands over various portions of the training ground. Energy rippled outward from their palms, igniting large circles on the ground that flared with runes before settling.

It's some sort of barrier, Callum thought as he imagined what it would be like to fight within the ring. Each of them was certainly large, about fifty feet in diameter, but with the way that aetherbeasts moved, especially when melded, it would be a tight space.

He tuned back in to what his friends were talking about as Quinn revealed to the princess what had happened. "Last night he was attacked by a demonic aetherbeast," Quinn said as he gestured toward Callum.

"Oh?" She turned back to him, something flashing across her eyes. "I was wondering why you look like you haven't had any sleep."

"Hard to sleep after that," Callum admitted.

"Do you know what kind of demonic aetherbeast it was?"

"How would I? I'm not good with any of the classifications," he told her. "But it had claws and armor like a lobster, or something like that. Crustacean. And numerous stingers that kept regenerating, and it was strong. It seemed to be able to melt into the shadows. That was how it ambushed me."

"What about now? Where are you staying?"

"He should be staying here," Marcella told Princess Selene, "but he doesn't have a dorm. The one next to mine should be open soon, which means—"

"I'll stay at a tavern tonight," Callum told Selene.

"You absolutely will not," she said with all the firmness of someone who had commanded people since she was a child. "My quarters have additional guest rooms. At least a dozen."

Callum gawked at the fact that there would be such a large space on campus for a single person. But then he remembered Sir Trindade and the other attendants he had seen with the princess. They were likely for them.

"I can't," he started to say.

"Must I order you?" Selene asked, a grin lifting her cheeks. He still couldn't quite see her mouth due to her armor, but it was clear she was smiling at him. "You will not stay at a tavern tonight. And you need to eat something. Have you eaten?"

Callum blinked a few times as he thought about what he had done that morning. "Actually, I haven't. I didn't sleep well and I woke up late. So I rushed here."

"You can't be serious."

"I didn't want to be late," Callum told her.

"Well, regardless, you will stay with me tonight and move into your dorm tomorrow. I will have Sir Trindade arrange everything. You have some stuff there at the tavern, right?"

"I do."

"I will also have your things delivered from the tavern. Just let me know which one it is," she said as she returned her attention to the front.

Master Cruedark stepped forward and grunted, which seemed to quiet everyone in a matter of seconds. "All of you have now been ranked based on your Attribute Trials and your Entry Duels. This is a very academic way to better understand where you are in relation to your peers. It is human nature, after all, to compare oneself to another. But there is much more to combat than rank. That's not to say that your Aethercores, your Attributes, and the powers you possess don't play their role, but one's total power can never be separated from one's true abilities, the kind that show themselves when a person is put to the test. What I'm saying here is that an S3-Rank and a C3-Rank might have more in common than they think. And the C3 could very well be stronger in an actual fight."

A few of the students murmured at this suggestion.

"Don't believe me?" Master Cruedark asked. "In that case, several demonstrations are in order. We will see collectively how they go. There are seven combat rings." He scanned the students, his eyes with a hint of light to them. "Callum Stross. You will be in this ring here. Let me see . . ." He scanned the students again. "Draven Blademark, you will join him. In the next ring, Marcella Faite and Quinn Vendrick. The ring beyond that," he said pointing the end of his beard toward a ring near one of the arches. "Silvia Hareth and Lynnafer Sunsouth."

At about this point, Callum could no longer focus on Master Cruedark's instructions. He was already jumpy from last night's ambush, but to be the first selected and to go up against Draven again put him on edge.

What is Master Cruedark even thinking?

<We beat him into the ground last time. You're stronger now.> Fen said. *<Much stronger. If anything, the warlock should be afraid of what we have in store. I think your teacher is trying to prove a point. He is pitting high-ranked people against those ranked lower.>*

Callum glanced around again and noticed that this seemed to be the case. He didn't know everyone's ranking, but he had seen some of them fight, like Lynnafer Sunsouth with her pacted badger and goose-headed Weaponcore.

With this in mind, he stepped into the combat ring, where Draven already stood, a sour look on the warlock's face.

Callum looked at the barrier and noticed that it was semitransparent. He had sensed something when stepping through the barrier and had a feeling that it would stop him from flying out of the ring.

"Look at you," Draven said so only Callum could hear. "It seems like our farm boy just woke up."

Callum ignored him as he stood across from the warlock, arms down at his side. He went over what he would do in his head, first melding, then activating his Armorcore, and then going with his Weaponcore. While he had improved since they had last fought one another, Callum could also see that something was different about Draven.

It was in his eyes. They remained red, but there was a fiery darkness to them now. Callum knew that Draven was rich and, while he would be limited with what he could do because of his Rank, that didn't mean he couldn't go out and buy the strongest and best Powercores that money had to offer.

Whatever happened next, Callum was certain that this wouldn't be the same fight as in the Entry Duels.

"I know who you really are, or at least who you are related to," Draven said. "But that doesn't mean anything now. You're nothing but a backwoods noble."

<So he knows. Push him on it. See what he actually says.>

"Then you are aware I was attacked last night, right?" Callum asked.

Draven didn't flinch. "I know nothing about your personal life, only that you are a backwoods noble, a farm boy related to the Demonslayer. Not that this little detail matters anymore."

"You are aware that a demonic aetherbeast tried to assassinate me last night, right?" Callum asked again, barely able to hide the edge in his voice.

Draven shrugged this comment off. "Attacks happen, especially to a fish out of water, such as yourself. It must be strange to see what you could have had, to see how a real noble lives, and to know you will never have any of it. You'll never live up to the legacy of your family, and, if you're lucky, you'll be sent back to Weatherby to be the archmage-in-residence, or maybe a lowly shardcrafter, where you can wallow in whatever it is your poor family can scramble together." Draven spat at Callum's feet. "Pathetic."

Callum responded by rushing forward and shoving the warlock backward. He hadn't melded, nor had he activated his Armorcore, yet he was strong enough to force the duke's son to the ground.

"Not yet," Master Cruedark said, his voice booming to the point that it seemed to shake everything around them. "We will begin when I say so and after I explain the rules of this engagement."

Draven got to his feet, teeth gritted as he narrowed his gaze on Callum. It was faint, but the warlock now had a red aura covering him, the mana flickering like an angry fire. "You're going to regret that, farm boy," he seethed.

CHAPTER 33

Traits granted by pacted aetherbeasts, or Aethercores, are not merely reflections of the animals they resemble but manifestations of their primal essence. To pact with an aetherbeast is to inherit both its strengths and its instincts—from the resilience of a tortoise to the stubbornness of a mule. But not all primal traits are transferable. This is the meeting point between the archmage and its Aethercore.

—Fletch Gellutad, Master Channeler, Clergo

A pair of attendants stood just outside the ring etched on the ground, their eyes fixed on the glowing runes encircling its edge. Magic pulsed lightly along the perimeter, the energy radiating toward Callum's feet as he stepped into the center. Across from him, Draven had his fists at the ready, prepared to strike as soon as the battle began.

The rules weren't very complicated.

Injuries would be healed, no killing, and there were several ways to forfeit a bout, from simply giving up to passing out. "The goal is to see how powerful you actually are," Master Cruedark reminded them. "Those of you that placed lower in the entry exams now have a chance to prove yourselves. Those of you that are legacy candidates also have something to prove. And finally, those of you that ranked somewhere in the middle have a chance to test yourself against someone who was perceived to be more powerful than you."

Master Cruedark gave the signal and Callum and Draven instantly melded. Callum activated his Armorcore and Draven took to the sky with a pair of blackened wings. Callum's Tempest Fang swirled in his hand and released a spiral of wind, which Draven quickly avoided as he bashed into Callum.

"Fallen heritage," Draven said as he lifted Callum and slammed him down.

Callum again tried to strike him with the wind sword only for Draven to land an incredibly powerful punch directly to his chin, one that would have broken his jaw had it not been for the protective wings created by Callum's Armorcore.

Callum hit Draven with Zephyr Strike at point-blank range, which tossed the duke's son sideways, where he smacked into the protective barrier keeping them inside the ring. He followed this up with two quick swipes of his Radiant Claws, sending blazing slashes of burning light in Draven's direction.

The ground beneath Callum's feet filled with red mana, which produced numerous arms that latched onto him. Callum was not able to break free.

As Fen shouted in his head, Callum struggled to tear himself away from the arms, muscles made of magic bulging as it seemed like he would be pulled *into* the ground.

<Radiant Inferno, or I'll do it!> Fen bellowed, his words finally making sense.

Draven leaned in close as the arms continued to pull at Callum, hands coming to his neck, fingers stretching over his face, nearly digging into his eyes. "You have no idea what you are doing. You showed up on a whim, you barely know of your own legacy. The only reason you have been accepted to the Great College is because of your stubborn farm boy toughness. A backwoods noble, if you can even be called that."

Rather than listen to the warlock's monologue, Callum focused his power, charging it and preparing to give everything he had to break free of Draven's hold.

Just as Draven started to laugh, the warlock going on about Callum being poor and stupid, Callum released a blast of pure light that landed behind Draven, swelled, and tore through the warlock's mana creation.

It struck Draven off his feet, scraping him against the ground until he once again slammed into the barrier protecting the ring.

The arms that had been holding Callum down relaxed. He fell to the ground only to jump back to his feet, fists at the ready as his wind sword formed in one hand and a lance in the other.

The barrier around them dropped and Callum's ears popped.

"I haven't given up!" Draven shouted to Master Cruedark, who stepped through and got between the two of them.

The big, bearded combat master slowly looked from Callum to the duke's son. "Callum, stay where you are. I'll find you another opponent.

Draven, you're being reassigned. We're here to challenge ourselves, and whatever is happening here *isn't* the point of these exercises." He scanned the students, most of whom had turned to the fight between Callum and Draven rather than focus on the others that were happening. "Victrin," he called to the tall redhead man whom Callum had once faced in the Entry Duels. "No, actually, Theogar."

Callum glanced at one of the men who had been hanging around Draven earlier. A smirk formed on Theogar's face as he entered the ring.

"I have it," Theogar told Draven quickly. He nodded at Callum. "I hope you're ready."

Callum steeled himself. He could feel his energy waning, aware that using a charged Radiant Inferno took its toll. He would have checked Soul Sense had it not been for Master Cruedark stepping by him, leading Draven away.

"I need to see you after class," Master Cruedark told Callum privately.

Callum was just turning back to Theogar when the other student summoned an Armorcore lined in mana spikes. This was followed by a Weaponcore flail. He exploded toward Callum, who would have taken the brunt of the attack had it not been for his own Armorcore, which surged into action, protecting him.

Try as he might, Callum was unable to get a solid strike in. He was too frazzled from the lack of sleep, low mana levels, and the way Draven had taunted him. Not to mention the fact that he was now supposed to meet with Master Cruedark after class.

But he also wasn't one to forfeit.

Even with his exhaustion, Callum dug deep as he conjured his lance and hurled it at Theogar just as his opponent dropped to all fours. Theogar brushed off the attack as the spines pressing out of his form grew larger.

It's his Aethercore, Callum thought as Theogar bolted toward him. *A porcupine?* He dodged Theogar's first charge, but had to hit the protective barrier to do so.

The two continued like this until all the other matches were called. By the end, Callum was barely able to stand. He gritted his teeth and settled his gaze on Theogar, who was now limping yet still poised to strike.

Callum thought that the duels were over, that he had made it through what was increasingly starting to feel like a gauntlet, but it turned out that this was just the first duel of the class.

Soon, he was dueling against a blonde-haired woman with tan skin named Demandra Corin who had a pacted koi fish. Demandra never said anything as her fish appeared in the air above them and released glittering bits of scaly mana that all exploded.

He kept near the outer edge of the ring and attempted to hit her from a distance, but her koi fish swooped down to block every attack. The fish actually *absorbed* Zephyr Strike by simply opening its mouth and inhaling, then did the same with Callum's lance.

The koi fish released more of its explosive scales, and Callum had to dive to avoid them.

He rolled and came back up, his speed increasing as he charged at Demandra using his Shatterlight Bear Powercore. He burst right through the koi fish, which tried holding back but was unable to as Callum finally struck Demandra, the two colliding with the protective barrier around the ring.

Callum didn't know what to expect, but he certainly didn't think his attack would be strong enough to completely knock her out. He actually felt bad as Master Cruedark's attendants carried her out of the ring, yet there was no time to catch his breath as Quinn stepped into the ring.

"Hey," Quinn said apprehensively.

"Hey," Callum replied, fighting the urge not to smile at his friend. "I didn't think I'd be up against you."

"Let's just do our best."

"Agreed."

<Just treat it as any other sparring match,> Fen told Callum privately.

He did just that, and while Quinn was able to get a few licks in by melding with his Darkmoor cat, it was clear that he wasn't going to put up much of a fight. Quinn forfeited and Callum's next opponent stepped into the ring soon after. He remembered Artur Filin from the ceremony and the way he had brought his hands into a prayer position in front of him after being given his rank.

"Farm boy," Artur sneered, revealing his true colors, "Draven has told me all about you." A pair of long dragon necks rose from his shoulders. They were coupled with gleaming armor that flowed in layers, horns pressing out of the mana epaulets on Artur's shoulders.

<We might need Radiant Fire here . . . >

If I do that, Callum thought, *I won't have anything in the tank for the next round.*

<We'll see his moves first,> Callum said, going with strategy over simply jumping into the fray.

<Right. And yes. That's a brilliant idea.>

Artur's moves, while intimidating, seemed centered around his pacted aetherbeast. One of the dragon heads spewed a fiery mana and the other bolt-sized projectiles. The wings of Callum's Brightflame Armorcore protected him from the projectiles, and he was fast enough in his meldform to avoid the flames.

Where are his Powercores? Callum thought as Artur continued to alternate between these two aetherbeast attacks.

Finally, Artur tried something different as he slammed a fist into the ground, sending jolts of mana in Callum's direction that he was unable to avoid. The mana shocked him, momentarily freezing Callum in place.

<*I'll distract him!*> Fen unmelded and rushed toward Artur.

The fox jumped into the fray with a fiery strike against one of the dragon heads.

As Fen slipped away, prepared to attack again, Artur produced a Weaponcore that resembled a curved dagger. He slashed at Fen, who returned fire with his Radiant Claws.

"I'm back!" Callum shouted as he was finally able to free himself from his frozen state.

Fen melded with him instantly and Callum rushed forward, dodging an incoming blast of mana from one of the dragons and hitting Artur with a surge of wind. It was the kind of direct hit Callum had been hoping for all along. Callum had aimed at Artur's knees and the attack blew him back, his top half falling forward.

One of the dragons spit mana fire at Callum, yet he had sidestepped its area of effect and conjured his blade. Gusts of wind traveled up to the hilt of his weapon and back to the tip as he kept the sword pointed at Artur.

Callum thought he had his opponent pinned until the double-headed dragon came alive, unmelding and careening toward Callum. It swept him up, the aetherbeast's serpentine body tightening around him as it drove Callum straight into the ground before his Brightflame Wings could break the dragon's grip.

Blackness seeped in, followed by a sudden rush of light as Callum hit a second wind, his stamina rapidly regenerating.

He broke free of the dragon's grip and slammed it into the barrier around the ring. His wind sword appeared in his hand yet again, and Callum beat at the aetherbeast in a frenzy that forced the dragon to return to Artur.

Callum rushed to his opponent and delivered a direct, mana-powered punch to Artur's stomach.

It was only after delivering the punch and watching Artur fly twenty feet and smack into the ring's barrier that Callum realized what he had done. He had channeled wind into a solid blow, one that sent a ripple of mana twisting forward.

And even though Artur wore an Armorcore, Callum could see that his strike had broken through. He saw the flash of shock in Artur's eyes, one that caused the other man to stagger backward. Barreled over, his two enraged two dragon heads back on his shoulders and gnashing their teeth at Callum, Artur took a final step forward and collapsed.

<Callum?> Fen asked as the world started to blur around Callum. *<Stay with me here.>*

"I'm here," he said, but his voice sounded distant, like someone else was saying it.

Callum didn't fully pass out, but he barely remembered Artur being taken out of the ring as the attendants reset for another fight.

"I believe that's enough," Master Cruedark said, his big form moving into Callum's periphery. "Take a knee and recover. You've pushed yourself enough."

"I can keep going," Callum said as he felt his stamina creep up, a *third* wind coming to him.

"I don't doubt it. But today isn't the day to push yourself that hard. You did prove my point, however, and I would like to thank you for that."

"I did?"

"Yes, and I'll explain everything once the rest of the fights are finished. For now, join the other students and don't forget, I want you to stay after class to speak with me."

Callum gulped, and as he did, Fen's voice came to him.

<This is a good thing. Maybe now you can ask someone who actually knows what they're talking about when it comes to the Archive of Destiny.>

CHAPTER 34

The Archive of Destiny is our kingdom's greatest repository of knowledge. The World Ledger and all the Fusion Ledgers are linked to it, providing instant access to both historical and arcane knowledge. May it fuel the collective knowledge of our world for this age, and every age to come.

—Hugo Thirdson, Duke of Aveiro and famed orator

Master Cruedark watched as his attendants walked around the ringed battlegrounds. As the runes dimmed, the mana traveled toward a central node, fizzled, and vanished. The other students had all left, leaving Callum standing awkwardly, awaiting further instruction.

"Are you familiar with leylines?" Cruedark asked him after his attendants, who Callum had assumed were upperclassmen, stepped through the portal and departed.

"Not exactly."

"But you are familiar with mana springs."

"I am."

"That's right, in the King's Forest." Master Cruedark nodded his chin at the Heart of Creation, which was visible in the distance. "The ward protection and other magical properties of the Great College are connected to the Second Heart of Creation through leylines. This is something that was done long ago, and it has protected New Albion. There are other leylines across the kingdom, and many initially started as a mana spring."

"I see," Callum said, uncertain what the master was hinting at.

"Like an idea, one spring can connect to the next, forming a conduit of mana that, if harnessed correctly, can do something magnificent like this," he said as he swept his hand toward the rings. "But for that to happen, there has to be a connection, the springs must work together. And so goes the life of an archmage that graduates from the Great College, those tasked with protecting the Valestra Kingdom. It certainly is an interesting thing to consider, and yet another testament to the mana of our world. Mana should be harnessed correctly. This brings me to my next point.

"Both you and Draven were certainly at each other's throats today. While competition is good, trying to kill each other is not. I don't know what is going on with you, but you don't seem the type to take things to that level, even if you are competitive. I can't say the same for the duke's son. So what is it?"

"What is what?"

"Did you and your friends drink too much ale last night? Have you been pushing yourself too hard? You weren't exactly sloppy today, but I can sense something is wrong. And the powers you exhibited, especially the one where you channeled all of that mana, while remarkable, can easily lead to burnout. You know what happens when your reserves are fully extinguished?"

"Not fully," Callum admitted.

"Then let me ask you: What do you think happens?"

"I don't know. I'm guessing it isn't good."

"No, it is not. *Hollowing* is what happens if your Mana Reserves drop past the critical point. It is quite rare, but I have seen it happen when students push themselves too hard. It can also occur when facing off against certain aetherbeasts, generally ones with Life Affinity or Death Affinity. Either way, the results are brutal. I know because I have had this happen to myself, just once, and I was lucky to make it out of that situation alive. You experienced a version of it yourself in the Attribute Trials."

"I remember," Callum said.

"If Hollowing takes place, the only way to recover is with an external mana source. It does not feel good and using a power like Radiant Inferno unchecked could lead to that. Have you checked your reserves? Low, yes?"

"Yes," he told Master Cruedark after checking.

"There are six states, and you are aiming to remain somewhere in the top three: Full, Steady, and Half-Full. Once you get below Half-Full, you reach Low and then Hollowing. If you go above Full, you can reach an Overcharged state, but that is not something you need to be concerned about just yet."

"I see. I'll rest tonight." Callum ran his hand through his hair. "Actually, I was wanting to ask you something."

"Yes?"

"The Archive of Destiny."

Master Cruedark just stared at him blankly for a moment. "What about it? The Archive of Destiny is in the Great Library. You can't really miss it."

"Yes, I was planning to go there next—"

A rare, knowing smirk appeared on Master Cruedark's face. "Before you head there, and certainly before you do anything else, I need you to do something for me."

"Yes?"

"First, I need you to promise me that you will take care of your power and that you will pay closer attention to your reserves. Had you tried Radiant Inferno again, you likely would have bottomed out. I don't need that. You don't want that. I don't need it because it reflects poorly on my instruction—even though, I should say, all your classmates already know about Hollowing. You don't want it because you're on academic probation and word that you Hollowed will get around."

"I promise."

"I'm not done. You need to start getting better sleep, especially if you want your Mana Reserves to naturally replenish. Yes, there are other ways to replenish your reserves, which you will learn about during your time here at the Great College. But every good day begins with a good night of sleep. So you're going to start there."

"Understood."

"But there's something else. Near the entrance of campus, tucked away in the first hallway on the academic offices, is a small restaurant that serves food augmented by mana. Have you heard of Master Weaver Arjun Bonjardim?"

"I can't say that I have."

"His recipes are still practiced to this day, made with cutlery that is similar to your new Weaponcore. That's an interesting one, by the way," he said as he looked Callum over. Callum knew that Cruedark could see his stats. "Weaponcore of the Tempest Fang. And where did you get that?"

"The Emporium."

"Is that so? There aren't as many unique Weaponcores there as one would think."

"My friend knew someone who wanted to trade," he told his instructor as he thought of Birchwen, the shardcrafter who he was starting to realize had given him quite the deal.

"That makes sense. Well, it's a good one, and, just so you know, there are others that are equally as good if not better. You will be able to cycle them out, and they can very much become a part of your core loadout as long as you have space for it. That is what makes what we do unique. You could move up the ranks and have several Aethercores and a dozen weapons if that's your build style. Or, you could simply have one Aethercore and all Powercores. I have seen someone who focused mostly on Armorcores, which, as you have already experienced, have their own benefits. You could even just be someone who strips everything down for component shards."

"I never thought of it that way."

"There's so much to learn. Even I stumble across something new on a weekly, if not daily, basis. That is the advantage of being here at the Great College. Anyway, you should get going." He produced a coin. "Have a meal at the small café I told you about and present this to them. Do that first before you go to the library."

"Understood." Callum took the large copper coin and bid farewell to Master Cruedark. After traveling through the portal, it took about fifteen minutes to reach the entrance to the Great College. He found the café in question, which was so tucked away that he didn't think anyone would have noticed it without prior instruction.

Callum expected Fen to comment on what had happened, but other than saying that it was smart not to reveal everything about the demonic attack to the combat master, the fox kept quiet.

He stepped through an arched doorway and found a dark-haired woman with a gloomy demeanor seated on a stool behind the counter. He gave her the coin, she gestured for him to toss it onto a ceramic plate, and then she motioned for Callum to take a seat at an old wooden table. He was just about to say something when she stepped away.

"I guess she already knows what I want."

<I don't think you have a choice.>

No, I do not, Callum thought as the woman brought him what looked like a simple meal, just some meat and vegetables over a bed of rice. But then he noticed that there were no utensils.

She stepped away, and he was about to say something to her again when she simply lifted a finger in the air letting him know that she would return. The woman did so with a small wooden box held in her hands, one that glowed with mana.

She placed the box on the table. "Enjoy."

"How does this work, exactly?"

"You should eat your food while it's hot, that's how. I will be by once you are finished to collect the silverware."

Even though he had seen mana glowing around the box of silverware, he assumed that the food would be what replenished his Mana Reserves. Yet in reaching for the silverware, Callum realized that the charge was coming from the cutlery itself. By the time he was finished with the meal, he checked his reserves to see that they were completely topped off.

"How was it?" the woman said as she approached again.

"It was great, I think. I really had no idea what to expect."

"Most don't. It's nice meeting you." And with that, she took the cutlery from him, placed it in the wooden box, and stepped away.

<The Archive of Destiny,> Fen said as soon as Callum stepped out of the café.

<We can finally enter the Great Library.>

<Indeed.>

As Callum stepped out of the administrative building, it suddenly struck him that he didn't know exactly where the Great Library was. With such a sprawling campus, he got the feeling it would take him some time to really get an understanding of his new environment.

Luckily, he saw Victrin walking by, and remembered the man with the pacted Lightning Elk that he had defeated in the Entry Duels. Victrin offered him a quick wave as Callum approached. "You don't happen to know where the Great Library is, do you?"

"It's there," Victrin pointed to the other side of campus, "with the spire on top. On the outside, it kind of looks like a cathedral."

"And the Archive of Destiny is there?"

"It is. At the bottom of the Veiled Spiral."

"Thank you," Callum said.

"Hey," Victrin called them once it started to move on, "good work today. I'm sure Master Cruedark told you otherwise, but you held your own against . . ." A slight smile formed on his face. "You know what, never mind. But good work, and perhaps we'll face each other again in the near future."

<See?> Fen asked once Callum moved on. *<He doesn't like warlocks either.>*

<You think that's what he meant?>

<I'm certain of it.>

After a walk that sent him around a sunken courtyard where students were having meals, Callum reached the Great Library.

Just as Victrin had said, the library resembled a cathedral due to the spire over its entrance. Upon entering, Callum found that there were vaulted ceilings decorated with images from battles that had taken place during the Great Demonswar. *My forefather is somewhere in these images*, he thought, *but there's no time to look for him now.*

Aside from the pressing matter of reaching the Archive of Destiny, Callum was too overwhelmed by the sheer size of the space and the visual nature of a spiral staircase that headed down into the ground. It was partially covered by a semitransparent veil that ran all the way to the ceiling.

"That must be the Veiled Spiral," Callum, said as he approached the stairwell, which also led up to a second story filled with study knocks, the walls lined in ancient tomes. Callum headed down the stairs as several students passed him on the way up, many carrying scrolls or books tucked under their arms.

He felt a pull almost immediately as he reached what would normally be a basement, the space filled with more books than he had ever imagined.

After stopping to admire it for a moment, Callum continued down to the next floor, which seemed twice as large as the one he had just been on and featured large worktables spread among the bookshelves, many of which were twenty feet high and required ladders to reach the top.

Yet again, he felt the tug of what he knew was mana, something beckoning him forward.

Another floor down, then another.

It felt as if he had descended into a new world, one made of crisp parchment and bound by leather, of mana and arcane secrets, ink and history.

He reached the bottom floor and finally found what he was looking for, even though Callum didn't know exactly what that was. The object before him resembled a massive mana shard that had runes covering every corner of its surface. The shard's size rivaled that of a carriage. It rested atop a pedestal adorned with intricate gold filigree, which gleamed with an otherworldly brilliance.

Callum took a step closer to the Archive of Destiny, ignoring everything in his periphery as Fen spoke to him.

<*Touch it.*>

The Radiant Fox's voice seemed distant, like it was coming from the far side of a great precipice.

Now in a trancelike state, Callum reached a single finger toward the giant crystal and was immediately engulfed by a blinding light.

CHAPTER 35

Proposal: With the numerous abandoned campuses across the kingdom, especially with the change of borders and the consolidation of archmage education into key cities, I believe there may be a solution that could benefit both our students and the Valestra Kingdom as a whole. By using the previous campuses, many of which have fallen into ruin, as training grounds and as locations to hide Powercores that could better a student's chances at survival, we will kill two birds with one Powercore. Yes, I wrote this note to you while I was drunk, and yes, it's still a grand idea, Rufus, you must admit that. Let's explore it further in our meeting next week with the Council.

—Letter from Dayanne Jadedark, Mastress Weaver,
to Rufus Blain, Master Channeler

The light that flashed before Callum faded, his vision blurring back into focus.

"Where am I?" he asked as his focus shifted to a man standing in front of him in heavy armor, his face obscured, light shining from beyond and partially enveloping him. "Who are you?"

Fen, who stood next to Callum, slowly looked up at the man and tensed. A beat later, the fox shot forward.

"Callum!" Fen shouted.

Suddenly, Callum understood what was happening, even if it didn't make any sense.

The man standing before him, his features still obscured and backlit by the eerie light was unmistakable—Callum Stross, the Demonslayer. His broad shoulders and the gleaming edges of his armor exuded power and an overwhelming sense of foreboding, a true legend seemingly in the flesh.

"It's you. It's really you!" Fen said as he circled around the man excitedly.

"No, and yes. Yes and no. I'm so very happy to see you, Fen. Incredibly happy. I am also incredibly disheartened." His shoulders lowered and he seemed to sink into himself. The Demonslayer brought a hand to his chin and kept it there for a moment as he looked down at Fen, and eventually over to Callum. "So it worked. I have been reincarnated."

Callum touched his chest. "As me?" *But I'm . . . me*, he thought. *I'm not him.*

The Demonslayer suddenly looked much larger, towering even as he continued to keep one hand on his chin and turned to Fen. "No, I'm not you, Callum. I'm a construct of the Demonslayer, your forefather. I have his memories, to some extent, and I understand what is going on here at the Great College. I believe, and this is from years of observation, that my existence is tied into the leylines that exist between the Archive of Destiny and the Second Heart of Creation."

Callum remained unsure about the being that stood before him, but at least there was a sense that he didn't have to live up to expectations, that it wasn't the *real* Demonslayer. "So, you aren't real," he finally said.

"No, I am not. But I am here for a reason. I have been dormant for all these years, watching the kingdom flourish and the knowledge held here in the Great College, in the Archive of Destiny, expand. I've also seen the kingdom put itself closer to calamity as it takes a great risk in embracing Demoncores."

"I feel the same way," Fen said as he returned to Young Callum's side and sat next to him, tail lightly tapping against what should have been the ground. "Warlocks are making headway. But how could he know? How could the original Callum pull this off?"

"I will now speak to you as if I were the Demonslayer."

"Understood," Fen said.

"At that time, long after I sealed you away, I devised a way to leave behind a series of triggers that would need to be activated before my Soul Sense triggered my reincarnation. Are you familiar with portals?" he asked Callum directly.

"I am.

"In the way that a portal can move someone from point A to point B, a variation can also transfer a portion of someone's soul. But this doesn't mean that that person will have the original person's memories, nor will they necessarily exhibit any of their traits. That is what I did. I set that up first, and stored my soul upon my death within the Second Heart of Creation itself. You've seen it?"

"I have," Callum said.

"It is constantly updated with the happenings of our realm through the World Ledger, yet it cannot act. This was one of the changes we made when the original was destroyed. The Second Heart of Creation is a powerful conduit of mana, and it can absolutely absorb the intensity of an aetherstorm, no matter how strong, but it can no longer attack as it once could. As more demonic aetherbeasts have appeared, their influence growing, it has taken notice."

"Where are these demonic aetherbeasts coming from?" Callum asked.

"They are coming from a different world, one not unlike ours. Aetherstorms can trigger their appearance because of a storm's ability to shred the integrity of our world and the magics that keep it intact. The Cult tried their damnedest to use this fact and the destruction of the original Heart of Creation to merge the worlds. And if it hadn't been for me, the Demon King would have pulled this off some five hundred years ago."

"What were the triggers?" Fen asked. "The ones that sparked the transfer of soul?"

"There have been numerous smaller ones over the years, but they have been insignificant compared to recent developments. One of those developments is the sheer cleverness of the demon's coming through and the way the Cult has harnessed their powers for the last two decades, creating new Demoncores, some that other kingdoms have started to use."

"The Geshwine Empire," Callum said.

"They know of us, of Callum and me," Fen told the construct. "One of the first things I discovered after Awakening was that one of the buildings on the farm was filled with Corruption. Are you saying that this had nothing to do with me?"

"I don't know exactly when that Corruption would have been placed there, but it was meant to disguise you, and to curse the Strosses."

"My . . . mother?" Callum asked.

"Corruption can have many victims," the Demonslayer construct said without elaborating. "And while the Heart of Creation is designed to stop demonic influences, there have been cracks over the years, and through those cracks, and with the right knowledge of Ledgers, someone could certainly plant the seed of demise. Which sounds like what happened at the Stross family farm."

"We were attacked by a demonic aetherbeast last night," Fen said.

"I would expect nothing less at this point," the construct said. "They know you are here, and they must know that something happened at the farm for that to have taken place. A Stross hasn't attended the Great College for ages. For you to suddenly show up with a Radiant Fox, of all pacted aetherbeasts, must have really put them on high alert. And it would make sense that they would try to assassinate you now, while you are still weak."

Callum didn't like the sound of this and balled his fists at his side. He was stronger now than he had ever been in his entire life, able to wield a sword made of wind or conjure a lance of light. When he melded, he felt like he could lift a house, or punch through a solid stone wall.

I'm not weak, he thought.

"I agree," Fen said, surprising Callum. "He needs to be much stronger and his family's recent history has prevented him from truly taking the reins. And I mean this with no offense, but we are much further behind the other students, some of whom have been training for this all their life, like Princess Selene. When I first arrived in your life, you had no other plans, really, than to help your father on the farm and eventually take it over. Am I wrong?"

Callum begrudgingly nodded his head. It was true, but he kept coming back to everything that had happened since, to a point where he didn't even recognize his old self. What had been his goal? Had he really planned to stay on the farm in Weatherby forever and hope for a better harvest? In a way, it was like his entire life had been a blur, up until the fateful night that he tried to hide in the East Manor.

"What of the Demonslayer's other Aethercores?" Fen asked.

"They were all released of their pacts upon the Demonslayer's death. Rata, the Sand Wolf of Aveiro, is dead; Astel, the Goddess of Dragons, remains with her kind; Lisalen, the Brightflame Phoenix, is pacted with King Morninglade; and finally Killeas, the Gryphon Vanguard of Fates, hasn't been heard of for some time. He is out there, somewhere."

Callum blinked a few times as he processed what the construct had said. He remembered the statue that had all the pacted aetherbeasts around the Demonslayer, and Callum could now put a name to their carved faces.

Is one of them really with Selene's father? Crazy! he thought.

Fen spoke again, sadness in his voice: "So Rata is no longer with us. Just hearing that name brings back so many memories. Such a loyal aetherbeast, and perhaps the scariest I have ever encountered."

"You remember?" Callum asked the fox.

"Vaguely. Like a scent, a name can trigger memories once thought lost. But it is good to know the others are still in existence. I find myself most curious about Killeas. When you reach the next Rank, Callum, you can take an additional Aethercore, forge another pact. Killeas would be a sure choice."

"If Killeas is locatable," the construct said. "Neither the Second Heart of Creation nor the Ledgers are able to keep track of Aethercores that have unpacted, in the same way that it doesn't know how many wild aetherbeasts there are, demonic or otherwise. No, you are going to need to get stronger and quickly. You have six Powercores currently, and as a Conjurer you are allowed up to nine."

"Right, but I'm not going to be able to find anything like that around here. I would need to buy them or go to the King's Forest," Callum said. "I could get shards there, and sell them to buy better cores here at the Emporium."

The Demonslayer's construct leaned in a bit closer, and while Callum still couldn't make out its face, he had a sense it was grinning. "What if I told you there is a way for you to get cores here. They will not be easy to find, however. The Great College has a challenge system in place for those that wish to improve rapidly. I suppose you could consider them something like scavenger hunts, but they are much more than that. They are designed to force students to think in different ways and challenge themselves."

"I knew the campus was large, but is it really that large? Are there really cores hidden here?"

"Remember when I asked you earlier about portals? That was for a reason. I was put here to help you get stronger. And it is not your fault that you are at your current power level, it is the fault of, well, your family, really. The choices that were made to bring the House of Stross from founders of the kingdom to farmers on the outskirts. But this is nothing to be ashamed of. You had nothing to do with that. You are here now, and you have an excellent guide in Fen."

"So where do I find these hidden cores?" he asked, eager to get started.

"The branches of the Great College used to extend all the way across the kingdom. And, like the portal you took to the training grounds and the portal the Soul Pythia used during your Attribute Trials, there are portals that can take you to these abandoned campuses. But I must warn you, many of these campuses have been completely overrun by aetherbeasts. Some are in locations where there was once war, and others are close to the borders of opposing kingdoms, which can create other issues. Those would be too difficult for you to tackle now, but in a few months, you would surely do well exploring them."

"Where should I start?"

"Yes, tell us," Fen said, matching Callum's excitement.

"You should start with sleep. Actually, you are sort of sleeping right now. You passed out when you touched the Archive of Destiny. This isn't the first time that someone has done that, you know. But as to where you should start, you should start with sleep, and I have something to help you with that."

"You do?"

"Have you seen the statue of your namesake?"

"I have," Callum told the construct.

"Approach the statue and place your hand on Rata's paw. You will see that others have done this in the past, it has become somewhat of a superstition said to create better luck on exams. Or, it was, a hundred years ago. That practice has fallen out of popularity, but you will see the paw. Place your hand on Rata's paw and you will receive something that any student could desperately use, and something the Demonslayer especially enjoyed."

"No hint?" Callum asked after the construct paused.

Fen laughed. "I'm in suspense as well. I guess we can visit the statue after we wake up."

"These other campuses, any suggestion of where I should go first?" Callum asked. "And how would I get to them? And what about these hidden cores? Is there a list, or something?"

"There is. It is commonly held knowledge, actually. You can pick it up on the upper floor of the Great Library. Every student can get the list, but only those that are really trying to challenge themselves pursue it. As for which abandoned campus you should go to, that is a bit more complicated. You can ask the help desk on the upper floor, but these Powercores are hidden for a reason; they are not registered in any Ledger, meaning I couldn't tell you exactly where they were. But people talk, students have assumptions, and there are some locations that seem to produce more cores than others. So you can get that information there. Where will you be staying tonight? Surely, you aren't going to be staying in town considering the assassination attempt on your life."

"My dorm room isn't ready yet, so I will stay in the princess's suite."

"Oh?"

"She has become somewhat of a friend, I think," Callum said.

"A good friend to have considering her father is pacted with the Demonslayer's phoenix. Perhaps you can request an audience."

"I don't know if we're *that* close yet," he told the construct. Callum's eyes bulged slightly at the thought of meeting the king. *What would my father think about that?*

"It's a starting point. Get the item left by your predecessor, and before you do that, pick up a list of the hidden cores."

"Understood."

The construct clasped his hands together. "While you have a long way to go, you've proven in a short amount of time that this is a journey that you were destined to take. I can say for certain that the Demonslayer would be proud of the man you are becoming, proud of the way that you have maintained the strength of his soul, yet also apprehensive about what is to come. Because there's a reason you're here now, standing before me. You may visit me again in the future, once you have reached the next Rank. Until then, good luck, Callum. May you prevent the Second Demonswar, and may you once again restore honor to your family."

CHAPTER 36

The storage of constructs within the Archive of Destiny is a practice that harkens back to the construction of the Second Heart of Creation. Often, the constructs left can dispel a simple message, a time-woven recording of something the creator hopes to pass on to their descendants. Yet it is said that other constructs can do much more than that, and are able to guide the course of their bloodline from the beyond.

—Henry Evo, Master Convoker, Clergo,
and former Chief Historian of the Great Library

Callum sat up slowly, his body aching as he realized he was on a simple straw mat. Not far from him loomed the massive shard known as the Archive of Destiny, its runic surface glowing. A student who had just rolled up a scroll turned to Callum.

"Good, you're finally up. Next time you feel the urge to touch the Archive of Destiny, don't," the woman said. "At least not until you let someone nearby know so we can prepare to catch you if you are granted a vision. I'm assuming that's what took place?"

Callum offered her a terse grin. "Sorry about that."

"In any case, I hope it was insightful. If you are looking for the current list of hidden cores, you will want to head to the top floor of the Great Library."

He squinted at the woman. "How did you know—?"

"It's a common thing that these constructs tell students in their visions. You aren't the first to hear it is what I'm saying here. But each person's vision is different, and I hope the rest of it was something useful to you."

"I see. Um, in that case . . ." Callum got to his feet, gave her a short nod to hide his embarrassment, and headed up the stairs.

<First the list, and then we see about the statue,> Fen said. *<And don't worry about what happened before in the Archive. It must happen all the time for them to have mats.>*

Callum let out a deep breath. *<Maybe you're right. I need to get to my history class, too.>*

<And then you get to spend some time with the princess, since you'll be staying in her suite.>

<We'll see about that,> Callum said as he headed up the enormous spiral staircase. He passed several levels before he reached the entry floor, then traveled up two more flights to arrive at the top of the Great Library, where doors led out onto a terrace.

After a quick look around, Callum approached a desk that had a pair of students behind it, both of whom busied themselves reading books, noting things on pieces of parchment. He waited until one of the students, a man with dark hair and a patchy goatee, looked up at him and asked, "May I help you?"

"I was looking for a copy of the list of hidden cores."

As if he had been asked the question a thousand times, the man opened a drawer and got out a strip of leather that had been branded on both sides. "Before you ask, they keep the current list on leather because students often bring it with them on their excursions. This isn't an exhaustive list of every hidden core. That changes once a year, or whenever the current list has been fully discovered, which is rare."

"And the locations?"

"I should add the answer to that question to my spiel. Anyway. There are *rumors* as to where the Powercores are located, but that's all they are, really. They are hidden because they are hidden. Yes, that's one way to phrase it. I can tell you that when someone finds one, that information is accessible in the World Ledger. As the semester progresses, you'll hear more and more about these rumored locations. Take that all with a grain of mana. They are rumors, after all."

"Got it." Callum folded the leather strip and placed it in the pocket of his overcoat, figuring he would look it over later. He left the Great Library and headed in the direction of the statue of the Demonslayer surrounded by his pacted aetherbeasts. He found the statue and then eyed Rata the wolf, the aetherbeast's stone paw darkened by myriad hands that had been placed on it over the years.

<Let's see what happens when we touch it,> Fen said.

Callum scanned his surroundings to make sure no one was watching him. There were students seated on stone steps not far from the statue, but they seemed to be having a deep conversation and hadn't noticed him.

<Alright, then.> He placed his hand on the paw and the statue trembled. Callum heard a sudden click followed by a gasp of air that sounded like it had been trapped for ages. A slot on the side of Rata's other paw opened, producing a glowing orb that immediately rushed into his hand.

Empowerment of Rejuvenation
Type: *Support*
Grade: *Legendary*
Infusion Requirements for Grade Increase:
0/30 Vigor Shards
0/40 Resilience Shards
0/10 Mind Shards
Effect: *When bound to one's Soul Heart, this core aids in rejuvenation and mana recovery with as little as one hour of sleep.*

<This is amazing,> he told Fen as he examined the orb.
<Indeed!>
<The only problem is its Grade. Legendary means that at my current Rank, it will only operate at twenty-five percent. Still, a stronger, more rejuvenating sleep is certainly something that I could benefit from.>
<Especially once you start looking for the hidden cores.>
<Especially.> Callum turned in the direction of one of the academic buildings. Soon, he found himself seated in the front of an older woman with a big belt tied just above her waist. Mastress Shaper Aena Gilford started with an introduction on the history of Aethercores, which naturally turned to a conversation about the Demonslayer.

"Have any of you seen our campus's statue of the Demonslayer?" Mastress Gilford asked at one point in her lecture. "It was sculpted for Callum Stross's mausoleum, yet he preferred an anonymous burial, so the statue was placed here instead."

Callum thought about this later as he walked with Quinn, who had offered to lead him to the princess's private residence. *I might need to find that mausoleum . . .*

"Our first day is officially over," Quinn said with a yawn.

"Coming to a close," Callum said, "that's for sure."

"And I know we didn't talk about it earlier, but you did well in the combat class, especially considering your exhaustion from last night. I had my own matches to compete in, but I got this feeling that Draven and his friends were especially interested in you."

"I noticed," Callum said.

"You are related to the Demonslayer and Draven is a warlock. Not exactly a meeting ground there, even if things are changing. I'm sure your forefather would have a few things to say about warlocks."

<*You can count on that,*> Fen told Callum quietly.

"But I think you would have beat him," Quinn said. "Unless he cheated. I guess we'll have to wait for a rematch, if Master Cruedark allows that to happen."

They reached the gate to the princess's private on-campus estate. After some discussion with the guards, they were led into a foyer, where Sir Trindade approached, wearing a set of armor with chainmail covering his arms. "Apparently, she wasn't joking," he said instead of greeting the two.

Quinn pointed a thumb at Callum. "About him staying here? No, the Princess wasn't. I was there."

"In any event, we will speed up the completion of your dorm," Sir Trindade told Callum, "because you certainly can't stay here for long. It is highly unusual for another student to stay in the suite, but you are technically from one of the first noble families, even if your family's influence has all but disappeared."

"Right," Callum said, realizing once again that everyone seemed to know who he was descended from.

"I have it from here," Sir Trindade told Quinn. "You may go—"

"What about the princess? Is she around? I figure we could have a meal."

"She's busy," the guard said.

"Doing what exactly?"

"Come again?"

Quinn smiled. "You said she was busy. Busy doing what?"

"You know I am not at liberty to discuss that with you. I can tell you that she's not here and she won't be until much later." Sir Trindade returned his focus to Callum. "She will not be joining you for a meal either; you will take that in your room. Alone. Your things are in there."

"They already came from the tavern?" Callum asked him.

"You think we aren't capable of making haste? Her Ladyship explained what happened, which is very curious. I have already filed a report and noted it in the World Ledger. But I'm afraid to say nothing will come of it. It is nearly impossible to trace where a demonic aetherbeast originated."

"I could take a wild guess," Quinn said.

Sir Trindade settled his gaze on the stout young student. "Anyone can take a wild guess, but that is not how we operate. Unless there is something else, I will lead Callum to his room now."

"But—"

Callan turned to Quinn. "I guess I'll see you tomorrow."

"Try to get some rest tonight."

Once Quinn was gone, Sir Trindade motioned for Callum to follow him. The two traveled down a long corridor with a marble floor, their footsteps echoing. Busts lined the corridor, and the walls were decorated with grand paintings featuring what Callum assumed were previous members of the world family and their pacted aetherbeasts.

"Does there happen to be one of King Morninglade?" he asked.

"That one." Sir Trindade gestured to a painting of a man seated on a throne in what looked like a jungle. Behind him, making it look as if he had wings, was a phoenix.

<That must be Lisalen,> Fen said. <I don't remember much about her, but it does make sense that she pacted with the royal family. Perhaps the soldier knows.>

"Lisalen," Callum said, "the phoenix. Do you know how long she has been pacted with the royal family?"

"Since the end of the Great Demonswar," Sir Trindade said. "She was gifted to the king's family by your distant relative, the Demonslayer. You know, when I studied here, I wrote a paper on your forefather. Anyway, shall we?"

"Please," Callum said.

Sir Trindade stopped at the end of the long hallway and took a few steps down into a space with several rooms. He chose one of the rooms at the back. "Sure. These will be your quarters until the dorm is complete." He opened the door for Callum. "Your meal will be served in an hour."

"If the princess does come at a reasonable time—"

"She will not, and if she does, Her Ladyship will not have time to meet with you," he said in his normal stilted way. However open to a conversation Sir Trindade had been just moments earlier, he seemed to have abruptly changed.

"I didn't mean it like that," Callum told him. "I just wanted you to thank her for me."

"That is something I can most certainly do. Good night."

Callum stepped past Sir Trindade and into a basement room with light coming through rectangular windows at the top. It seemed more like a servant's quarters than a guest bedroom, but it was large, all of the linens were freshly pressed, and, upon sitting on the bed, Callum noticed that it was quite soft. "This will do."

Fen appeared, his glimmering form taking shape with a spar. "You would think they would give us one of the nicer rooms up top, but I believe Sir

Trindade when he says that this is unorthodox. Selene is betrothed to the duke's son, after all, and in politics, perception often outweighs the truth. Let's see the hidden list of Powercores."

Callum got out the leather list. There wasn't anything written about the hidden cores aside from their names, but their names gave him a sense of what they would be able to do:

Galeform of the Thunderhowl Wolf
Empowerment of Spiritfire
Antler Break of the Froststag
Weaponcore of the Sunsteel Ram
Armorcore of the Twilight Drake
Spiked Lunge of the Direwolf Stalker
Poison Hiss of the Ashen Viper
Empowerment of Blightwing
Armorcore of the Ironspine Panther
Lunar Sweep of the Shadowbound Crane

"These all sound incredible," Callum said after he'd read the list aloud to Fen.

"They do indeed. And the sooner we can travel to one of these distant campuses and join an excursion, the better. We'll need all the Powercores we can get."

CHAPTER 37

Even someone not trained in the arts of mana should be able to understand their soul and their place in the world with a simple spell.

—Fae Allure, contemporary of the Demonslayer and archmage who unlocked the Soul Sense ability for everyone in the Valestra Kingdom after forming an aetherforge with a Nightgaze Owl

The days that followed were as intense as they were fascinating. Callum attended his classes and assisted in the rebuilding of the barn that had been destroyed in his fight against the demonic aetherbeast. As his room renovations dragged on, he got used to the quarters he was staying in at Princess Selene's place, even if he only saw her once.

<*It's like she doesn't even go to school here,*> he told Fen one day on his walk back from his Manavitality class, which was increasingly becoming one that would be quite impactful.

Mastress Lucerne was the instructor for the class, the same strange woman that had overseen the Attribute Trials. The Soul Pythia, as she was known, wore a hood over her head, one that had a way of obscuring her eyes. Yet from what Callum could tell, her features weren't shifting like they had been in the Aeternal Tabula. Her explanation on the first day, which many of the students had dismissed with boredom, lingered in Callum's mind for some time after the class:

"Every archmage is limited by the size of their core. Yes, like a Powercore, an Armorcore, a Weaponcore, and especially an Aethercore, each of you has a similar mana repository in your soul that has limitations. This is why we use the Soul Sense. It is also how native magics and cores can be used by someone who isn't pacted. This limits, of course, what they can do, but it is all still possible."

Mastress Lucerne continued: "Your current Rank, viewable in Soul Sense, is the way to very quickly understand the current size of your core. This is why, as an example, a Conjurer can have nine Powercores, Armorcores, or Weaponcores and one Aethercore. It is based on the size of your soul, if it helps you think of it that way. Although it is much more technical than that. As many of you know, each core is further classified to let you know its inherent power limitations based on your current abilities. This is why a Conjurer can only use a Legendary Powercore at twenty-five percent of its maximum efficiency, because it is all your soul can handle considering what is already being stored there. Now, we come to my point: How does one strengthen their own core?"

Callum took note of everything Mastress Lucerne said. The question had been at the back of his mind for some time now, especially after experiencing low power levels and learning what could happen when someone reached a critical reading.

"I will list the ways to strengthen your core first, and then we will spend the rest of the semester better understanding how to get the best results from these varying, but often complementary options. The first way is through meditation and focus. This should be self-explanatory, and I'm aware that some of you have come from boarding schools that had meditation courses. But we will still spend time going over these, as if you're new to the subject.

"The second is through mana cycling. Practicing the art of mana cycling allows an archmage to absorb ambient magical energy and bring it into their system. A healing Powercore amplifies this, as do certain Attributes. The third way to strengthen your core would be through simply using it. Yes, every time you use a power, it has a way of enhancing the potency of not only your core, but the power itself. There have been numerous studies done testing this with fireballs and aetherbeasts granting Fire Affinity. I suggest you take a look in your free time. The fourth way to strengthen one's core would be getting stronger Powercores. By switching out cores, you can help augment your own abilities and strengthen your core.

"We have two more ways to discuss," Mastress Lucerne said as she glanced around the room. "And then we can start with meditation theory. The fifth way would be through what is known as symbiotic resonance. The longer you are with your pacted aetherbeast, the stronger bond you will form. Add another Aethercore and this has a compounding effect. Finally, there are ways through alchemy and visiting mana springs or, more likely, ley lines, that can boost your core and even move you to the next Rank."

The instructions that followed were things Callum thought about one autumn night as he prepared to meditate. After lighting a candle and watching the flame settle into a tear shape, he began inhaling slowly to the count of five and exhaling the same way.

As he drew deeper into a meditative state, he imagined the dormant mana in the air around him and noticed these effects in the flame, which began to split into two like a snake's tongue. This happened much faster than it had in his previous attempts, and he noted that he was getting better at tuning in to the mana that existed all around him.

Callum's focus broke and the flame returned to its thin tear shape.

"Strengthening your core this way takes a lot of practice," Fen told Callum.

"The other ways sounded easier, that's for sure," Callum said.

"Yes, who wouldn't want to simply use one's power to grow one's power? But as Mastress Lucerne alluded, all of this is done in an augmentary way. The best archmages use a combination of these techniques to improve themselves."

Callum leaned back against the bed. He didn't feel tired. He rarely did now that he had Empowerment of Rejuvenation, but he did feel the weight of receiving so much information in such a short amount of time.

Aside from Manavitality, the history class, and the combat class with Master Cruedarkhe also had Elemental Mana and Its Principles, taught by Master Shaper Luso Alpen, a disgruntled middle-aged man prone to rambling.

The only issue with his ramblings was that they came off as code at times, the nuggets of wisdom encased by stories and anecdotal thoughts that made it all hard to parse. Even so, a lot of the information from the class made sense to Callum:

"You can't fully use a Powercore tied to Shadow Affinity if you are pacted with a Flaming Turtle of Western Albion, everyone knows that," Master Alpen said in an offhand comment. "But what if you fused a Shadow Affinity Shard in the same way you would, let's say, an Empowerment of Deftness Shard? What then? Is it theoretically possible to use a Powercore to its full potential based on *your* Rank, even if you aren't attuned to this Elemental Mana? The answer is yes."

The only problem with this new bit of information was that it had been sandwiched by a thirty-minute lecture on the local politics of swamp farmers of Western Albion and a rant on faulty construction in the Belldrum District, which made Callum wonder if the story had something to do with the fire Telluride had told him about.

Next time I come into contact with a Powercore I can't fully use, maybe I will hold onto it. As he sat in his bedroom recalling his day, Callum thought back to his time in the King's Forest and the numerous shards he had received. *Maybe I could have even used the Veil of the Gravewind Hawk. I had Shadow Affinity Shards at the time . . .*

"I think I'm ready to go again," he told Fen as he sat up straight and focused on the flame.

"By all means." Fen's voice tensed before he said, "Wait . . ."

Callum jumped to his feet at the sound of a knock on the door. But then he relaxed to some degree. "If it was another assassin, they probably wouldn't knock."

"It's me," Princess Selene said as she opened the door and stepped into the room.

Callum stared at her dumbfounded for a moment. "Princess?"

Comfortable as ever, she sat on the ground in front of the candle. The princess was dressed in what Callum assumed were her night robes, which were black with white frill, most of the fabric covered in fine needlepoint stitching. "Are you going to sit?" she asked as she looked up at him.

"Um, sure," Callum said as he took a seat again, his back against his bed. "Are you alright?"

"Do I look ill or something?"

"No, nothing like that. I just figured I would have seen you by now. This is going to sound strange."

"Yes?"

"You do go to school here, right?" Callum grinned at her, which seemed to relax Selene to some degree.

"Yes, I do. I will begin attending classes next week and I have a team of tutors that help me. I also have two notetakers in each class."

"Notetakers?"

"They blend in with the other students. I have two because they are tasked with taking notes on different things."

"Like?"

"You have a lot of questions, don't you?"

"No offense, Your Ladyship—"

"Call me Selene."

"No offense, Selene, but you did just show up in my room in the middle of the night."

"It's hardly the middle of the night. That won't be for another two hours. I see you have been learning," she said as her eyes fell to the candle.

"Everyone here seems like they're ahead of me."

"That's because they are. But that doesn't mean you won't do well. You are, after all, a relative of the Demonslayer. So I wouldn't worry about people being ahead of you," she surmised. "You'll get there, and soon."

"I'm still on academic probation."

"I know. And I think that will change too." Selene clenched her eyes shut for a moment and let out a deep breath.

"Are you okay?"

"My father is preparing me for the role I will eventually take as Queen of the Valestra Kingdom. You are familiar with the Badlands?"

Callum thought of what he had learned of the Badlands in a recent history class. He had heard the term before, but the Badlands were so far to the east of Weatherby that he never really gave them much thought.

"The Badlands separate our kingdom from the Geshwine Empire," his history instructor, Mastress Aena Gilford had explained a day ago. "The Geshwine Empire, as many of you know, was the first of the neighboring kingdoms to embrace Demoncores. While we technically have an alliance with them, this has led to skirmishes in the Badlands, which is ripe with aetherstorms, and even what is known as Beast Tides."

The flame between Callum and Princess Selene flickered.

A short smile formed on her face as the fire formed into a burning orb that resembled a Powercore. "It's been a while since I worked with a flame."

"Nice," Callum said under his breath.

The flame returned to its tear-shape.

"Anyway, there have been developments in the Badlands. It's no secret that we are trying to find a diplomatic solution because my father is not ready to fully embrace Demoncores, regardless of the duke's influence. My grandfather was the one who formed the alliance between our kingdom and the Geshwine Empire in the first place. I was sent alongside a pair of Beast Masters to see to these negotiations."

"Beast Masters?" Callum asked, the first he'd heard this term.

"You won't see them here at the Great College unless there's some sort of demonstration. We are both Conjurers at the moment, right?"

"Correct."

"And there are seven Ranks of progression that most people take."

"Right. The next one would be Wielder. I want to reach it so I can get another pacted aetherbeast," he said.

"Don't we all. A Beast Master is someone who has gone far beyond the final Rank. They have partially melded with their Aethercores, as in a permanent meld. Even the best teachers here, like Master Convoker Patrjohn Granadam, Magistor of Gilded Radiance, are technically at the seventh Rank."

"Meaning he's a Convoker."

"Correct. Now, he has specializations, hence the rest of his title. But a Beast Master is someone that has gone beyond that, and I'm not talking in an academic way. They are truly monsters, but they are *our* monsters with loyalty to our kingdom. Does that answer your question?"

"Which one?"

Both laughed. Princess Selene covered her mouth with a hand. "Sorry, we should keep quiet. But that was funny. You do have a lot of questions, and rightfully so. To answer at least one of them: that's where I was, at the border with them hoping to solidify peace before we find ourselves wrapped up in a war. Since the Badlands are a disputed region, the war would initially take place there, but that could have profound mana effects that we're hoping to avoid."

"What do you mean? Aetherstorms?"

"Worse. Beast Tides."

<There's that word again,> Fen said to Callum.

"What is a Beast Tide exactly?"

"You have experienced an aetherstorm before, right?"

Callum's terrifying experience in the East Manor came to him. "I have."

"Think that, but multitudes worse. The problem with war at the mana level, which is what would happen if the shaky alliance between our kingdom and the Geshwine Empire crumbled, is it will not only lead to the things that are typical in war, like famine and death, it will also lead to environmental destruction."

"I see. What now?"

"Now? We wait and see if our efforts to convince them have worked. I believe we made a very good case as to why we should be exceedingly careful with where we go next, and what we do in the Badlands. But that's not the only reason I came to your room tonight."

He gulped. "It's not?"

"It's your last night in my suite. Sir Trindade told me your dorm will be ready tomorrow, and I wanted to see if you knew about this." She produced the hidden core list, hers also on a piece of leather.

"I have one as well."

"Good. I'm not quite certain where all of them are yet, but once my notetakers—"

"What do your notetakers have to do with this?" Callum swallowed hard. "Sorry to interrupt, Your—"

"—Selene. I know because one of my notetakers is tasked with taking notes on the lesson, and the other on the students themselves and what they say." The same smirk she'd given him earlier appeared on her face. "The most valuable thing to anyone everywhere in any stretch of time or place is information." Selene pointed to one of the listings. "I want this one,

Armorcore of the Ironspine Panther, but I'll settle for any of them, really. What about you?"

"I don't know what they do."

"Well, this one is self-explanatory, even if I do know a little about it. A combat master I had when I was a child used it, and the armor was quite good. Not only does it create an incredibly strong protective shield, it gives you a mana tail that you can sweep at enemies."

"That sounds awesome."

"It will be. I trained with it before." She peered at him quietly for a moment, Callum uncertain what she was thinking. "How much have Quinn and Marcella told you about me?"

"What do you mean?"

"My notetakers said that the three of you have become close. They said that two recently helped you rebuild a barn."

"Yes?"

"I'm wondering how much you know about me and my situation."

"You mean about your arranged marriage?" Callum watched the shift on her face upon hearing this, the expression of disdain so strong that he pressed back a few inches as if she were going to lash out at him.

She didn't. "Yes, I'm supposed to marry Draven in the coming years. It is absolutely something I do not want to happen. But I don't really have a choice at the moment. I am the only heir, and this was set up long before I really understood what it would mean. He's a warlock."

"You were the first to tell me that."

"The duke's family has ties with the Lands of Grimbald, not far from Weatherby."

"I've never been, but I have seen their caravans before."

"They're not really of concern to me because my family has an alliance with Grimbald as well. What concerns me is the Geshwine Empire, and the duke, Draven's father, seems to think the only way we will be able to maintain our power is to match theirs now that they have legalized the usage of Demoncores. It is still early. This only happened in the spring, but . . ." she trailed off for a moment.

"But?" Callum asked when she didn't continue.

"The Great College, the most prestigious college in our kingdom, now has someone who is openly a warlock on campus. And not just anyone, the duke's son, whom I happened to be betrothed to." She could barely hide her disgust. "Even a year ago, this would have been unheard of."

"No one seems to mind or say anything, at least from what I've seen."

"That's because of the power of my father. The duke is using his friend-ship with my father and our future nuptials to coerce his way into bringing this into the open. People don't know how to react to it, but since it is com-ing from the King, and despite the fact I'm totally against this, they don't say anything. They just blindly accept that a warlock is here."

"Have you spoken much to Draven? He seems—"

"Like an asshole? He wasn't always like this. I used to play with him when he was younger. But he has changed, especially over the last two years. I hardly recognize him anymore."

"And his red eyes."

"Yes, those. That feature is new as well. I keep asking people if I'm the only one that thinks a warlock walking around with red eyes is a good thing, but no one has a good answer for me. But anyway, I came to say I was sorry for my absence. I was hoping to have at least a few meals while you were staying in my quarters."

"It's not your fault. You have princess jobs to do."

She gave him a funny look. "Is that how you would define them?"

"Is there something else I should call them?"

"I suppose there isn't." She put the leather list away. "I should go. Sir Trindade likes to check on me regularly, and if I got caught in here, well, nothing would really come of it, but it would be a pain to deal with. I'll keep my eyes and ears open about the hidden cores. Once I'm certain of a loca-tion, I'll let you know."

"Thanks," Callum told her as he respectfully got to his feet.

Princess Selene seemed like she was going to say something else but said no more. Instead, she left quickly and Callum was once again alone in his room with Fen, who appeared next to him.

"Ah, the weight of legacy," Fen said as he watched the flame. "The Gesh-wine Empire did not exist during my time, but if it had, and if it had given in to the influence of Demoncores, I'm certain your forefather would have had something to say about it. He would be livid to find the world shifting into darkness and embracing warlocks. But I digress. The alliance may be stable for now, but my gut is telling me it won't be for long."

"You're probably right," Callum said.

"It's good to have a literal princess with spies on our side. We're going to need all the help we can get, especially since there is a warlock on campus and the duke is clearly up to something. We just don't know what yet."

CHAPTER 38

*A weighted stone, an iron bar, an uneven ground that shapes your
stability—there are always new ways to sharpen your skill.*

—Pervus Sinbad, Master Convoker and Chief Combat Instructor of
the Great College from Year 465–490

The following day, Callum and Marcella moved into their dorm rooms. Quinn, who had a room one floor down, helped Marcella with her things while Callum took stock of his new dorm.

"It's so big," he said as he placed his bag on a wooden table pressed against the wall. He said the same thing every time he reached the room for the next few weeks, never quite sure what to do now that he had so much space.

His room had a window that provided a view over a courtyard where students often studied and met late into the night. The bed was just about the most comfortable thing he had ever laid upon, and since everything had been refurbished, the room's smell became a constant reminder of how good he had it.

As his friendship with Marcella and Quinn deepened, and the three rarely seeing Princess Selene, Callum threw himself into his studies. His history class often moved into discussions on noble families and their histories, which could turn contentious, given the nature of Callum's classmates. He kept his head down during these discussions, especially given his relation to the Demonslayer.

His Manavitality class, taught by the mysterious hooded Mastress Lucerne, continued to be one of his favorite classes. Recently, they had a discussion on Hollowing, the Soul Pythia detailing a time in which it had happened to her in the Badlands:

"You can get overconfident, you know, once you have been at this a while," she told the students. "You get a feel for it, and that is something you should absolutely trust, but confidence can often be a silent killer. For me, I was incredibly lucky to be there with other archmages, one of whom had a second party healing ability that came with his pacted gerbil." There were a few snorts. "You laugh, but had he not been there, I wouldn't be standing before you today. That gerbil saved my life."

Later, this led to a discussion between Marcella, Quinn, and Callum on the possibility of learning about the future powers they might get as they increased the Grade of their Aethercores.

"Traits differ," Quinn explained. "So there's no real way of knowing."

"Surely, there's a record," Marcella said.

"I was told by my tutor that you can actually find out past traits exhibited by Aethercores, but she recommended *not* doing that because it can lead to false hopes."

"So you're saying there's no telling if Tuck will get a cool healing power?" she asked in reference to his pacted Darkmoor Cat.

"Who knows?"

Callum later learned in his Elemental Mana and Its Principles class that new traits were often exhibited based on the person and their pacted aetherbeast's response to their soul.

"This is why," Master Alpen told them, "we once used the term *aetherforge* to describe pacting. The meld itself is a forging of two souls, the mage's and the aetherbeast's, into something entirely new when melded. This compounds at higher levels, for those that don't go the academic route and are destined for the Beast Master trajectory."

Callum's biggest surprise in the days that followed came during combat class, when Master Cruedark asked him to stay after. "It will just be a minute," the big man told Callum as the other students turned back to the gateway that would portal them back to the Great College.

Callum waited patiently, unsure what he had done to warrant another discussion with the large man.

<Relax,> Fen told him, <*he probably just has a pointer or two.*>

Once the students were gone, Master Cruedark turned to Callum. "Follow me." He led Callum to a series of stones that had been arranged so people could sit on them and watch the matches take place. A forest of trees noted for their golden fall leaves lay beyond the seating area, giving the space an otherworldly feel. "Please sit, and feel free to summon your fox."

Fen appeared, and Callum looked up at the combat master. "Did I do something wrong?"

"No, nothing like that." Master Cruedark brought a hand to his chin as he looked down at Callum. "You are doing the best you can with what you have picked up by watching other students and your time in Weatherby. You worked on a farm there, right?"

"I lived *and* worked on a farm. My family's farm."

"I see. And that would explain your overall size and the boost to Might that none of the other students have. What they have that you don't is—"

"Training," Fen said. "We're aware. I am unable to train him myself as well as I'd like. While I can influence his movements and certainly do from time to time, there is an instinct that must come from the human I have pacted with, not that Callum fully lacks this. It just isn't ingrained in him as it has been for some of the others who have been at this for years."

Master Cruedark looked from the fox to Callum. "Correct, which is one of the reasons your appearance here at the Great College has been remarkable in its own right. You are still on academic probation, but you have already shown yourself to be brave and fearless. The problem with being brave and fearless is not knowing how to distinguish between the two. Plenty of students are brave, and plenty turn into archmages who know when to be fearless, but there is a fine line, believe it or not, and I want you to learn to be fearless in a calculating way."

"What do you mean?" Callum asked.

"You have four classes now, right?"

"Yes, sir."

"In that case, you will begin apprenticing under me four nights a week. This means you will need to have a big lunch because you won't be able to eat again until much later." He lifted his hand above his head and his massive Weaponcore hammer appeared, which he rested on his shoulder. "We can start now."

Callum's fists clenched at his sides as he tried to psyche himself up. *He wants me to . . . fight him?* He stood. "Yes, sir."

"That would be the first lesson I want to impart on you," Master Cruedark said as he looked down at Callum's clenched fists. "You absolutely should use all your power in a fight, but you also need to keep things loose and be more fluid with your movements. I haven't quite noticed a rigidity that needs much correcting, but it is something people can develop and it's something you should note. The future trials you will face, especially against mages much stronger than you, and later, truly powerful aetherbeasts and even mages from the Geshwine Empire, will push you to your limits."

Callum relaxed a little. "I think I understand. Remain loose."

"Exactly. First, we will work on refinement. Later, we can talk combat strategy. I've seen in some of your fights that you have figured out ways to use Fen as a diversionary measure. This is good. We will work with that more, and we will work with other ways to meld and unmeld in a moment's notice that can produce profound effects. Finally, weapon training. That is another thing we need to work on, Weaponcore or not, it is important for you to have a foundation. Let's get started. How long before your next class?"

"An hour and a half. I was going to grab a meal."

"This will take an hour and you will have plenty of time. Come on."

For the next hour, Master Cruedark showed Callum the correct way to hold and summon his Tempest Fang to maximize time. He gave Callum pointers on his stance, and exercises to do in the morning that would work on the *side muscles*, as he called them, which were necessary to swing a weapon.

"Students often can't comprehend what a ten percent boost in strength tied to your natural muscle mass can do in a fight. Whereas before, you were able to strike an opponent hard, perhaps hard enough to break through their Armorcore if they were wearing one or kill them if they were an aether-beast, now you can deliver a truly devastating blow."

The big man's Weaponcore disappeared and mana armor hardened around him. It was the thickest mana that Callum had seen yet, so thick that he couldn't see through it as he usually could with other Armorcores.

<He should have given us an Armorcore like that!> said Fen, who had once again melded with Callum.

"I want you to strike me in two ways and feel the difference," Master Cruedark told Callum as his hammer vanished. "The first time, I want you to come at me in the way you would have normally, if I were an opponent standing in your way. Disregard everything I told you. Just attack."

Just attack, Callum thought as he went for it. Even if he struck Master Cruedark's armor with a sword made of wind, it still felt like he had punched his fist into a brick wall. He stumbled back, shocked at the combat master's protective strength.

"Ah, I failed to mention my armor has a repellent nature to it, one that causes some damage to whatever is striking it. How did it feel?"

Callum's sword disappeared and he shook his hand out. "Not great."

"The number of times that has come to my aid are hard to quantify. It's why a good Armorcore is so important. Even better to be able to switch them out later on, too, depending on the situation. Now, try again, and this time pay attention to your stance and the way you swing your arms. Remember what I said earlier: a Weaponcore is an extension of your raw power now cast in an indestructible medium for maximum delivery. You can hit something with all your Might and *then* some—that ten percent I mentioned—but you have to do it right. There has to be muscle training behind it, and your stance matters."

Callum moved into the stance Master Cruedark had described.

He pictured himself charging forward and striking in the same way. It was somewhat impractical, and a real enemy would never provide an opening like this allowing him to strike with all his power, but he could see in his first attempt that there was something to it.

I can adjust to this, he thought as he stepped back, his hand hurting again.

"Remember to strike *past* me not *at* me," Master Cruedark said. "And this is just single-handed now, another thing to note. We'll shift to double-handed later, but you will probably find yourself needing your other hand for things, especially if you get an Armorcore shield like this." He produced a massive shield made of hardened mana, one that stood at least six feet tall. "Some Armorcores come with their own shields, most do not."

"So it's a Shieldcore?" Callum asked.

"Sure, you could call it that, but most people just call it an Armorcore shield. Anyway, try again, like I showed you," Master Cruedark said as the shield faded away. "And remember, I'll give you something you can use later to strengthen your actual core and practice swinging your sword."

"A wooden sword?"

"Why would I give you that?"

"I've trained with one before."

"Ha. I'll give you weighted bars of iron. They're short but heavy. You can use them in your dorm to practice your swings and do other exercises to build your core, like holding them out in front of you. But I digress, attack me."

Callum did just that, going at the combat master again and again until his muscles ached and his brow was covered in sweat. Master Cruedark laughed at the way Callum finally dropped his arms when they finished.

"That was something," Callum said with a deep breath out. Even though he felt tired, he also felt good, energized in a strange way. *Was I just mana cycling?* He recalled a deeper discussion in his Manavitality class about cycling mana while in combat.

This led him to immediately check his Mana Reserves to find that they were full.

"See? I told you it can be exhausting," Master Cruedark said. "Yet it seems you have discovered something."

"Was I really cycling mana?" Callum asked.

"Yes and no. Truly cycling mana isn't a trait a student usually exhibits this early on, at least not in combat. There can be elements of that, but proper form and striking in the way I showed you actually use less energy overall. How? You're not exerting yourself in the same way as you were when you were fighting without form."

"I think I understand."

"There is a mental aspect as well, which tests have shown help to conserve mana. So that's what I mean by *yes and no*. You weren't cycling mana, but you experienced something akin to it." He looked to the gateway beyond, the portal that would lead back to the Great College. "You should have time to grab a quick bite. Might I suggest a sandwich? Your next class starts soon. And tonight, meet me at the same gate so I can give the weighted bars and a bit of instruction. I want you to start training with them. You're going to need everything you can muster soon, especially if a detail the administration has been working on pans out. I still don't see how they're going to pull it off, but politics was never my thing." He shrugged. "I'll see you tonight, Callum."

CHAPTER 39

Portals differ from the rigid doorways of this world.

—A quote from *Soul Pythias of Yore*
by Mastress Weaver Emlee Sawbend

A week of training with Master Cruedark and using the weighted bars he gave Callum had yet to fully pay off. *At least it doesn't feel that way,* Callum thought as he ran a hand over one of his biceps, not sure how long it would take to notice the effects.

Each weighted bar was about the size of a baton, which allowed Callum to either use them together or place his hands around a single bar and move it like it was one large sword. He didn't know how much they weighed but they were certainly heavy and when working with them, he always built up a sweat.

Another thing Master Cruedark taught him was to hold both weighted bars together in front of him for as long as possible, either keeping them together or with his arms outstretched, which was precisely what he was doing late one night when he heard a light rapping at his door.

He assumed it was Marcella.

She had stopped by a few times to chat due to her restlessness. According to her, the people of Aveiro often stayed up much later than those who lived in the northern part of the kingdom. That and she liked to gossip.

There was another knock.

<*I suppose we will be interrupted, then.*> Callum finished his set and dragged his feet to the door, taking his time. The moment he pulled it open he nearly stumbled back, startled by the cloaked figure standing silently on the other side. "P-princess?"

"It took you long enough." Princess Selene pushed into the room as if she owned the place and pressed the hood of her cloak off her head. "My notetakers heard something." Selene looked from Callum to the weighted bars and then to his biceps. "You were working out?"

"Training. Master Cruedark has been teaching me four nights a week."

"Ah, that explains it then . . . And good, he'll have you caught up in no time. Though . . . those bars aren't particularly fun to train with."

"You've used them before?"

"More times than I can count. Here, I even came up with a trick to help pass the time while I worked with them." She approached the bars and picked them. "Ugh, these are much heavier than the ones I used, but I think I can still do it."

Princess Selene twirled them for a moment, which created a slight humming sound. "Looks like I still got it."

"Looks like it."

Once she set the bars down, Princess Selene returned her focus to Callum. "Get ready."

"Ready for what?"

"Right, I didn't tell you that part. Sorry. My mind has been racing as of late. I believe I may have located the Armorcore of the Ironspine Panther. Someone says it is here."

"Here? As in the Great College."

"Yes and no. And this person has provided good information in the past."

"Where would it be?"

"I should explain. There are hidden portals around the Great College that lead to some of the abandoned campuses. If you look carefully, or you get the right information . . . Just let me show you." She produced a piece of parchment. "I've narrowed it down to three obvious or not-so-obvious places. There are the catacombs, but I don't think they would place the portal to this Armorcore there. Too easy to find."

"How so?"

"The catacombs are too predictable a location, that's what I'm saying. Then I thought perhaps it has something to do with the Great Library. There are wings jutting off the Veiled Spiral that are closed off to students, you know. And that might actually be an option. But then I learned of the portrait storage building and some recent activity there. You know, the big marble building that also houses a museum."

"I don't, actually. And what kind of activity? Is this stuff your notetakers have picked up?" he asked, recalling that she had one for actually taking notes and one for spying. "And didn't you say you'd be in class with us?"

"I did and, as usual, things came up. But back to the museum. It's on the other side of campus, surely you've seen it."

Callum thought of how large the campus was, how it felt as if he discovered a new building or nook almost daily. "The grounds of the Great College are larger than the village I come from."

She considered this for a moment. "I haven't really thought of it like that, but that does make sense. Weatherby is certainly quaint. But we can talk about that later. I believe the portal we will first need to find is there, in the museum. If it is not, we can always dig deeper into the library. So, are you in?"

Fen appeared. "Of course, we're in. But what about you? Where is your guard?"

"Sir Trindade thinks I'm sleeping."

Fen glanced from Selene to Callum. "And if he gets caught out with the princess? What then?"

"I can handle that. Get dressed, Callum. I'll wait outside." To illustrate she meant business, Princess Selene placed her hood back over her head and stepped out.

"What do you think?" Callum asked Fen once she was gone.

"A secret excursion sounds like the perfect way to test all you have learned recently. Plus, we may be able to learn more of what she has been up to."

"Good idea."

After donning his cloak just like the princess, Callum followed her to the other side of campus. Selene kept to the shadows, reminding Callum of how a barnyard cat would sneak around at night hunting mice.

The princess doesn't seem like an assassin, he thought as she pointed out a particular shadow for him to stand in as a pair of students walked by, *but she certainly moves like one.*

The pair reached a building crafted in marble, a stately, three-story structure with a gated entrance and ornate carvings adorning the windows. She motioned to the entryway, which was wide enough to fit a carriage and easily twice Callum's height. "We won't be able to get in that way," she whispered. "But that's not an issue. Come on."

She led him around back and stopped in front of what looked like an ordinary wrought-iron fence, one that stood nearly ten feet tall. Selene placed her hand on it and guided her fingers over the metal until she found something.

Click.

A hidden door presented itself, allowing for a smaller, inner gate to be open with relative ease.

"How did you know?" he asked her.

"I'm used to these kinds of buildings. There's always an entrance hidden somewhere for certain types of escape and to bring in things like catering, believe it or not. There's likely an underground passage we could have taken, but those can be harder to locate, and I have no idea how long that would take. And yes, if we had the right Powercores, we could have used them to fly over the fence and land on the other side. But that risks triggering a ward, which would bring archmages here faster than you can imagine."

She stepped through and Callum did the same.

<The princess has the knowledge of a thief. Heh. Makes sense,> Fen said as they approached the back door. His point was further illustrated as Princess Selene used a hair clip to pop open the door.

She summoned a small triangle of mana, which oscillated in front of her.

"What's that?" Callum asked, the two of them now in semidarkness, their faces illuminated by the glowing green triangle.

"It's a core that can detect hidden mana. We just need to find the storage rooms. Let's keep going." She headed up a winding staircase to the second floor. After passing by a few busts and then entering a room with the ceiling painted in motifs Callum had never seen before, they came to a room labeled storage.

<Easy enough,> Fen said as the door creaked open, and they entered a large, dark space filled with paintings stored on vertical racks—open frames that allowed each piece to be quickly slotted in or pulled out. The triangle of mana hovered over the stored paintings and stopped at one about halfway down at the end of the row, where it sparked and faded.

"Let's check it," Princess Selene said.

Callum got on the other side and helped her remove the painting from its slot. As soon as it was out, it became abundantly clear that this was no ordinary portrait. In place of a painting was a murky substance that soon solidified, revealing a stretch of field lit by moonlight.

Princess Selene dipped her hand in to confirm.

"How do we get inside?" Callum asked as he felt the slight pull of mana.

She glanced around. "We prop it up against that wall and crawl in. We'll come back the same way."

"And if anyone discovers the painting is down?" he asked as they propped it up.

"We'll be back before then, come on." Princess Selene crawled into the portrait, leaving him alone in the storage room with Fen.

<That was unexpected.>

<All of this is unexpected,> Callum said as he crawled in after her.

The portal opened onto a large field illuminated by a starry night. Callum recognized the plants immediately.

"Do you know what it is?" Princess Selene asked.

He approached a stalk and pulled it in closer to him. A sad smile formed on his face as he thought of his father and how far he had come since he had left the farm. "It's a kind of wheat that grows wild in the northeast. The beard is white and fuzzy, like a sheep."

She cocked her head, her gaze sweeping over Callum as the moonlight reflected off her eyes. "Did you call it a *beard*?"

"I did." He touched the fuzzy white on the head of the wheat. "It protects the kernels. See?"

Princess Selene touched it and nodded. "It's almost fluffy."

"It is. But it doesn't grow in Weatherby. The soil isn't right. My father talked about this variant several times. It came through town once and we went to see it. I thought it looked like snow."

"How old were you?"

"I must have been ten or eleven. It was a while ago. Anyway." Callum released the stalk. He turned away from the princess as he was overcome with a bit of sadness thinking of his father. *If you could see me now . . .*

"Ecaris," Princess Selene said. "Give us a look, will you?"

Her pacted aetherbeast took shape, the creature towering once she stood on her hind legs, allowing her to see over the tops of the stalks. "We are half a mile away from the campus," Ecaris said, her voice soothing and graceful.

"Then that's where we will go. If the rumors are true, we will find the Armorcore there. Both of you be ready," Selene said with a firmness that showcased that she was used to giving orders. "And any shards we find along the way are yours," she told Callum. "I meant to tell you that earlier."

"You're sure?"

"It's only fair. All I'm interested in is the Armorcore of the Ironspine Panther. This might be an all-night affair, but I'm fine with that. As long as we are back before the sun is up. Ecaris?"

"Yes?" the bear asked as she dropped down to all fours.

"Can you keep track of where we are and how to get back here? To the portal? You're better than me at it . . ."

"Of course, I'll remember." Ecaris started through the field of wheat, the stalks of which parted around her as if they were trying to move out of her path.

"That's one way to do it," Callum said. "I seriously thought we were going to have to push through on our own, which isn't as easy without a hand scythe."

"I didn't consider that," Selene said as they followed the path created by Ecaris, "but this works too."

"It does."

"And are you excited?"

"For?"

"To test your refined skills in the field. Fighting your peers is one thing, even if you've been training with Master Cruedark. Not to say that he isn't knowledgeable. He's very good at what he does."

"He mentioned that something was coming up but he was really vague about it."

"What's that?" she asked.

"Something about an event that would require some politics. That's why I'm mentioning it to you."

"Ah, that. Yes. Well, I suppose it would be best for the official announcement rather than telling you here. I am privy to certain information, you know, information that I cannot share."

Callum looked ahead as Fen followed Ecaris, the fox's tail was lit with mana and bouncing happily along. "So you can't tell me anything?"

"No, unfortunately, I cannot."

"Can I ask you a different question then?"

"You don't need to ask me if you can ask me questions unless they are personal, Callum."

"I don't know if it's personal or not. It is something that I've, um, heard rumors about. With some recent incidents I've been a part of, I figured it was worth asking."

Ahead, Fen's ears perked up.

"Go on," Princess Selene said cautiously.

"The Demon King. Has he been . . . reborn? Has something happened?"

"That's quite the leap."

"I figured if anyone knew, it would be the royal family."

"We are more worried about the Geshwine Empire and their use of Demoncores at the moment. We believe these have amplified the diminished voices of the Cult of the Black Dawn, now at its weakest point since its inception. Does that answer your question?"

Not exactly, Callum thought, but he also had a sense that it was the best answer he would get from the princess.

"Moving on, or moving backward, is there anything you are interested in on this semester's hidden core list?"

"I don't know what they do," Callum told her. "At least the ones that aren't obvious."

"In that case, I will pick one for you."

"You will?"

"Yes, after we get mine, we can look for yours. It will keep me distracted. You don't understand."

"Understand what?"

She turned to him, a flash of desperation in her eyes. "I need distractions. My life can be quite heavy sometimes."

"I'll bet."

"But I'll think about it, and once I see how you are shaping up here, I'll pick one for you. Do you want it to be a surprise or not? Never mind that, surprises don't allow you to plan. So I'll just tell you what I think is best before we finish up here tonight. Deal?"

Callum found himself nodding at the Princess. *She sure knows how to convince someone*, he thought, which reminded him that this was precisely what she had learned to do since she was a child. The difference in their lives was something he hadn't really considered, but hearing the way she spoke and operated was certainly telling. And as always, it was a reminder of how different Callum was from his classmates.

"Yes?" she asked again, once he didn't say anything.

"Sure."

"Not much further," Ecaris called back to them after she stood on her hind legs again.

"Great." Princess Selene beamed a smile over at Callum. "Time to put all of our cores to good use."

"How many abandoned campuses have you visited?" he asked once they reached the end of the wheat field.

"Just one, but it was overrun with aetherbeasts, and Sir Trindade was with me. This time, it's just you and me."

CHAPTER 40

The grandeur of the Valestra Kingdom lies not in what remains,
but in the faint and lovely whispers of what it once was.

—Bregor Gaston, poet

Callum and Princess Selene approached an enormous set of stairs covered in cracks and moss. Both Fen and Ecaris melded with them, the two aetherbeasts vanishing in a flash of mana.

<Better to conserve power this way,> Fen told Callum, who continued to examine the abandoned campus, which seemed to be erected on an enormous hill. There wasn't much Callum could see from his current vantage point, the steps too steep for him to gauge the layout of the campus. He could tell it was absolutely massive, though, because the steps alone were just about the longest set he could ever remember encountering.

"Why were these campuses abandoned again?" he asked Selene as they started up to the top.

"Various reasons that could range from the location—if it is near the Geshwine border—to if there was a particularly bad aetherstorm in the vicinity. Usually, but not always, our forces can deal with the fallout from an aetherstorm. If archmages can't, specialists like Beast Masters can. But sometimes, a storm is so strong and so impactful that it entirely changes a place. I've toured areas like that."

"You . . . have?"

"Several times," she said in her typical nonchalant way. "The sheer damage a powerful aetherstorm can do is something that people living in New Albion can't seem to fathom due to the Second Heart of Creation and the way it protects our capital. And they certainly couldn't fathom a Beast Tide, which has a tendency to produce massive demonic aetherbeasts."

"How large are we talking?"

She continued up the steps for a moment, lost in her thoughts. "Bigger than Ecaris. Bigger than the one you killed in the King's Forest, the Gravewind Hawk."

"Seriously?"

"I am not one to lie to a friend," Selene said before moving on.

She thinks of me as a friend? Callum caught up with her, hoping for clarity, yet he didn't get it as they reached the top of the steps and were presented with an enormous campus half in ruin. Several of the larger buildings resembled cathedrals and the quad was cratered like there had been a huge battle. The statues surrounding the campus were toppled, and some of the pillars holding up the front entries of the buildings were scattered about as if a giant had casually swept a hand through the campus, knocking things over as if they were toys.

<What an utterly dismal sight.>

Selene spoke again: "As to where we should start . . ."

"What about the Powercore you used back in the museum?" Callum asked, remembering the floating triangle and its strange green glow. *It was certainly helpful there!*

"We'll use it, but it can attract aetherbeasts. We'll need to be prepared." She reached into a pouch on her belt and produced a pair of shards for Callum. "Might and Deftness. You know what, take one of these as well." She gave him another crystal. "Vigor."

"Take them all at once?"

"You've never done that before?"

"I've only used shards like this during harvest season," Callum said. *They're expensive*, he thought as he looked down at the shards she had given him. "And the ones I got in the King's Forest—" he paused.

"Yes?"

"Should I call it, um, Your Father's Forest?"

She looked at him crossly. "Yes but also no."

"In that case, the ones I got in the King's Forest, I either traded, or used for my Powercores."

"That makes sense. I try to use shards as often as I can in duels or in situations like that."

"And everyone is like that?" Callum asked. "Sorry if that's a stupid question."

"You mean the students you've been facing off against in your classes? Yet another yes and no answer. The richer students can afford it, but they don't do it every time. Why waste a shard? But it does happen, and it's not exactly against the rules. You'll want to have some shards available in the future. They don't last long, so use them sparingly. And I meant it when I said take them all at once. There is a compounding effect when you do so. It's not a lot, but you'll certainly feel it."

"So do it now?"

"Wait until we reach an aetherbeast where we could use a little boost."

"Got it."

Princess Selene produced the green triangle of mana. It started to whirl and turned toward a building just past the quad.

"This one can sense other mana sources," she explained, "sources that have been cloaked. Whatever it is leading us to will certainly be something more useful, but you need to be ready. You'll see what I mean when I say it can attract aetherbeasts. If the campus wasn't so large, I wouldn't use it here. But this will make finding the core faster. Plus, it's dark and this will give us light."

"And if we come across Corruption?"

"Surely, Fen will know what to do. All pacted aetherbeasts can convert corrupted mana into something useable. It's one of the ways that they can later recharge your Mana Reserves. I'm going to guess that Mastress Lucerne didn't tell you that part yet."

"She did not."

"These first semester classes are usually refresher courses of things many have learned from tutors or in preparatory schools. As with everything, there are levels. Come on, let's see what's inside."

Princess Selene started toward the building. The green triangle of mana illuminated the path ahead, which wrapped around an old stone bench that had been partially overtaken by thick roots. After a short walk they came to an entrance, and Callum was surprised by a partially crumbled stairwell that led to the second floor.

The two soon entered an open space partially concealed by a roof that was mostly held together by vines. Large parts of the walls had crumbled, the night's sky allowing Callum to see through several rooms.

The triangle floated ahead and they carefully followed it.

<Do you feel it?> Fen asked Callum as they entered an interior space missing a huge chunk of the ceiling, as if a great beast had flown out of it.

"I definitely feel something," Callum said as Princess Selene looked up at the hole.

"We're getting closer to something," she said as they continued on into a wide corridor where they were immediately ambushed by the same kind of corrupted mana imps Callum had once faced in the East Manor of his farm.

His Weaponcore in hand, Callum beat back the imps while Princess Selene slashed them away, the two making quick work of their opponents.

Empowerment of Mind Shard

Callum put the shard in his pouch. He was just about to move on when he thought of something. "Have you ever used a Mind Shard before?" he asked her.

"Yes. It helps with focus and it can be nice for studying. But it is also quite useful in the field. I would describe it as expanding your awareness."

"Good to know." With his current ability loadout, Empowerment of Rejuvenation was the only one that could use a Mind Shard for upgrade purposes. *Certainly worth considering,* he thought as they continued through the corridor.

"Incoming—!" Princess Selene swept her cloak aside, revealing light plate armor, as a four-legged aetherbeast exploded into the corridor.

Part wolf but with massive wings and a forked tail, the aetherbeast exuded a demonic presence. Its snout was lined with multiple glowing eyes and blackened mana tendrils rose and flickered ominously from its form. The beast shrieked and lunged for Princess Selene, who produced a trident Weaponcore that Callum hadn't seen her use before.

She kept the aetherbeast at bay as Callum rushed into action with a surge of wind. His attack cut through the beastly aetherbeast's shoulder and hit a wall, which sent stones tumbling and dust falling from what was left of the ceiling.

"I've got it!" Princess Selene dropped to all fours herself and bolted toward the monster, her pacted bear's form creating a thick shield around her that almost entirely obscured her body.

She slammed into the creature and it stumbled backward, allowing Callum to hit it with an amplified attack from his claws.

<Let's finish this!> Fen shouted as Callum moved in with his wind sword and Selene with her huge bear paws, which she used to smack the aetherbeast left and right as Callum snuck in fast and sneaky attacks that felt different than they had before.

What's this . . . ? Their combined strength soon overwhelmed the aetherbeast, but not before it was able to send its mana tendrils into the ceiling and bring down what was left of the roof.

"Watch out!" Callum rushed toward Princess Selene, determined to shield her from the falling tiles and planks of wood. But it was the princess who saved him as Ecaris protected them with her huge bear form.

Air Affinity Shard

"Don't you have an Armorcore?" Princess Selene asked Callum as the dust had settled.

"I do. That was sudden enough that I didn't think about it."

"We all make mistakes," she said, her eyes bulging slightly. "Only sometimes, those mistakes cost us our lives. Remember that."

"Thanks," Callum told her as they moved on, where he tried to swallow the embarrassment he felt. Part of the reason he hadn't activated the Armorcore was because of the sheer power he had felt in using his Weaponcore. He could tell something was different, and he hadn't even used a Might Shard to get there.

The training I'm doing with Master Cruedark might actually be paying off, he thought, *but all the training in the world won't help if I can't focus.*

To better focus, he went ahead and used the Mind Shard. His Soul Sense flashed information before him explaining that it would be active for thirty minutes.

He blinked a few times as his awareness expanded. He couldn't quite see around corners, but he got a sense of what was to come as they reached a decrepit dining hall, where they found goblin aetherbeasts feasting on corrupted mana.

The two made quick work of them, and Callum received a Death Affinity Shard from the goblins.

"I get what using an Attribute Shard does," he told Selene as their aetherbeasts cleaned up the Corruption, "but what about using a Mana Affinity Shard? I'm aware that it can help one overcome a gap, if they don't have an affinity is what I mean, but what if I have affinity? What if I used an Air Affinity Shard with Fen?"

"Then your meldform would be that much stronger. It's another way archmages who can afford to freely use Affinity Shards use them. But not me, not when I don't need to. I'm aware of what I am and the wealth my family has. I have access to any shards I want. The only thing that really keeps me from upgrading everything to its max level is my own Rank; or rather, I should say all of my Powercores are at their max, but they only operate at the Conjurer Rank."

"I see."

"What I'm saying is I know how valuable these things are. I know that many in our kingdom will only ever use Attribute Shards a handful of times and they are a great store of wealth."

"They are," Callum said, remembering how his father kept the shards they did manage to get under lock and key. They used Deftness Shards during harvest and that was pretty much it.

"In my opinion, Mana Affinity Shards are extremely valuable. They're necessary for upgrades, and while it isn't cheating to use them in a duel, I don't think enhancements help illustrate a person's true potential," Princess Selene said. "Let's continue."

They came to the end of the abandoned dining hall, passed through a place where students once washed their hands from the look of all the shattered porcelain, and arrived at what Callum assumed was meant to be a study space. There were still tables here, many of which had been overturned. Enormous chandeliers drooped from the ceiling, and there was glass everywhere.

"One of the things I really hope to do in the future is clean these places out," Princess Selene said as they traveled under an arched stone doorway that led into a courtyard overgrown with plants. With the way vines hung from everything, it looked like a jungle, and their path forward was no longer as clear, even with the wide-open night's sky above.

"Aren't these campuses meant to be training grounds?"

"Yes, but certain abandoned campuses are in key locations that I would like to once again bring into our kingdom. Imagine a place like this actually thriving again. Imagine the village that would surround the campus on top of the hill, the businesses that would exist, the farms beyond. What if it could be restored? If not," she brushed some of the vines aside, "it could at least be stripped for its parts. There is a lot of wood here that is still good. The stone is also good, carved with techniques we no longer use."

"What do you mean?"

"I had a private tutor who insisted I learn some things about architecture." She pointed at one of the bits of stone overrun by the foliage. "He knew I wouldn't be building anything, and at the time I thought he was crazy, but now it makes sense—the architecture of our kingdom tells us many things. It displays the differences in regions and what is possible, the differences in techniques over the years, and how we have used Powercores and Aethercores to enhance our capabilities. Think of Marcella's home of Aveiro, and all the color and white sandstone."

"I've never been there."

"Aveiro is lovely. You will have to go some day. A campus like this, one that seems ancient, one that seems like it would take a hundred years to construct, can be built in a handful of years."

"Really?" Callum remembered the stairs they had taken at the start of the abandoned campus and the way the cobblestone had been arranged near the entry gate, each piece placed with precision and care. *It makes sense, especially if the builders had enhancements*, he thought as she brushed aside some more vines. "I think I get it," he told after they took a set of outer stairs down to an overgrown courtyard.

"Studying this could even help me protect the Royal Treasury when there are issues that need to be resolved, like an aetherstorm coming through. Destruction is often twofold. There is the initial wave, and then there's what comes after, from desperation to exploitation."

Even though Callum knew her intelligence made sense considering her upbringing, he continued to develop an appreciation for just how well-rounded it was. He had seen Selene fight, but to hear just how deeply she thought about things gave him a sense of what kind of leader she would be.

And to think she's betrothed to Draven . . .

This part didn't make any sense to Callum. If they really did get married, what would it mean for the Valestra Kingdom? She clearly had good intentions in her heart, but having a warlock as her husband would complicate things. *And that's not including the potential legalization of Demoncores*, Callum thought as they took a small set of steps that led to a fountain filled with large purple flowers.

While he hadn't fully learned about the potential of Demoncores, Master Alpen, had spoken a little about them in Callum's Elemental Mana and Its Principles class:

"One thing we all have to be weary of," Master Alpen had said, "is what I like to call the known tenants of Demoncores, be they demonic Powercores, Aethercores, Weaponcores, or Armorcores. The first is corruption of the soul, which should be self-explanatory. There is also the potential for spiritual rot, which can lead to a gradual decay in one's moral compass. Then there is desecration, which most of you would recognize as *Corruption*. And finally, there is the addictive allure of demonic power and the way it can transform someone over time."

That would explain Draven's red eyes, Callum remembered thinking at the time.

<*What's that?*> Fen asked, snapping him out of his reverie.

Callum looked ahead to find Princess Selene examining a crater. It wasn't smoking, but the impact looked recent. Not only was it covered in soot, but there were claw marks cut into solid stone.

A flash of concern traced across Princess Selene's face, which was lit yet again by the green triangle of mana.

"That bad?" Callum asked.

"Only an enormous aetherbeast could do something like this, a demonic one. It would make sense, especially this far out. But I honestly didn't expect we would encounter one."

"What makes you think it's demonic?"

She pointed at black marks burned into the stone that looked as if someone had lashed it with a fire whip. "These are from the tentacles that the more powerful demonic aetherbeasts often have. They use them to suck dormant mana, corrupted or not. The tentacles grow larger over time, and they weigh them down to some degree, leading them to drag the tentacles on the ground."

Callum looked around again. Even though their surroundings were lit only by moonlight, making the tentacle marks hard to see, it was clear that there were many of them. In focusing on them again, he started to notice a pattern, something he might not have picked up if it hadn't been for his Empowerment of Mind Shard.

There were two possible paths for them to explore, but only one had the markings. "We should go this way," Callum said, even though Selene's triangle of mana had drifted toward the opposite direction.

"You think?"

"There are more of the markings that way."

She stepped into the dark and observed them. "Huh, I didn't see that." Princess Selene looked up through another arched entryway that opened onto a set of stairs that led into another wing of the enormous building. "The beacon is saying it's this way, but it has been wrong before. And . . ."

"And?"

"And, if there is a demonic aetherbeast in the other direction, it's better we handle it." A grin appeared on her face. "I hope you're ready to get your hands dirty, Callum."

CHAPTER 41

Another hour exploring the abandoned campus proved to be fruitful. Callum and Princess Selene faced off against a number of lesser aether-beasts, some demonic in nature, others simply attracted to the dormant mana that sat heavy in the air over the campus.

Empowerment of Deftness Shard
Empowerment of Vigor Shard
Empowerment of Regeneration Shard
Light Affinity Shard
Fire Affinity Shard
Life Blade of the Spring Ferret Weaponcore

This is definitely an interesting one . . . Callum thought as he examined his newest core. Even though he wouldn't be able to truly use the Weaponcore because he didn't have Life Mana Affinity, it was still a really good one, a piece that Callum would be able to strip of its shards.

Life Blade of the Spring Ferret Weaponcore
Type: *Accessory*
Grade: *Rare Weapon*
Infusion Requirements for Grade Increase:
0/10 Light Affinity
0/20 Life Affinity
0/10 Deftness Shards

Affinity Requirements: Light or Life
Effect: When bound to one's Soul Heart, this Weaponcore gives the user access to a Life Blade, which both injures and saps mana from an opponent.

Callum looked up at Princess Selene, who was now focused on a set of stairs leading to closed double doors. "You're sure you don't want it?"

"I don't use Life Affinity. Ecaris is Earth and Light."

Callum thought of his Shatterlight Bear Powercore, which also used Earth and Light Affinity. "This is really good," he said as he pressed the core into his chest since he had a few available slots. "To be able to both deal damage *and* sap mana would be really helpful in a fight."

"Indeed. And don't forget—we agreed that anything that we find aside from the Armorcore of the Ironspine Panther is yours. You could strip it of its parts or give it to Marcella. Harold, her pacted heron, uses Life Affinity. She would probably trade you for it or pay you in shards or spare cores."

"I think I'll do something like that or save it. I don't know when I'll move to the next Rank, and I don't know if the next aetherbeast I pact with will use Life Affinity, but a power like this would be very useful."

Princess Selene looked ahead at the large wooden double doors. Her green mana triangle floated in front of it, spinning. "Whatever we were tracking earlier isn't in there."

"There are no markings, and how would it get in anyway? Also, your Powercore is active again." Callum was referring to her mana-seeking triangle and the way it had slowed earlier when they took a different path, as if it sensed they were going the wrong way. Now, it spun rapidly, a clear sign that they were onto something.

"Mana works in mysterious ways," Princess Selene said. "I'll get the door open. You and Fen be ready to rush in. There's no telling what's on the other side."

A sudden rush of power twisted around Selene—her shoulders bulking up, her mana form growing in size as she melded with Ecaris. Together, they easily pushed the doors open, revealing a large, ritual-like space filled with stacks of books piled on top of one another.

A dark swell of mana appeared in the middle of the space, its outline almost human. As tendrils draped from it, the dark form rose into the air, features obscured, aside from glowing yellow and red eyes that cascaded randomly down the front of its body.

"Your Attribute shards!" Selene said as she went for hers as well, the princess taking all three at once.

Callum activated his Armorcore and did the same. He felt an instant boost, from his strength to his stamina, speed to dexterity. He rushed forward, intent on trying a few test attacks with his claws when new forms pressed out of the blackened mana painted across the ground.

The sight of what looked like other archmages, albeit ones completely drenched in dark mana, threw Callum off guard.

Other . . . students?

He stepped back as Selene rushed forward, now on all fours, the princess slamming into one of the lesser constructs.

Inspired by her action, Callum attacked with blasts of wind and followed up with a few fiery slashes with his Radiant Claws. More constructs pressed out of the pools of dark mana, these armed with things that resembled Weaponcores.

<Watch out!>

The first opponent lunged for him with a staff, but Callum was protected by his Armorcore. Another fired dark bolts of mana at Selene as she tore through it.

Callum summoned his own Weaponcore and drove it into a construct in front of him. Another rushed at him with its staff held high. Callum batted the attack away, only to be blasted by a ball of dark mana that sent him flying backward.

Thanks to Fen, he landed on his feet, turned, and drove his wind sword through another of the constructs. Glancing ahead, Callum caught Princess Selene fending off two while another bubbled out of a portal behind her. He tossed a lance made of light at the newest construct, destroying it.

Meanwhile, the strange mana being they had first seen upon entering the chamber hovered above, guarded by an orb of mana that was increasingly purple, like it was absorbing the mana in the air . . .

The edges of the sphere frayed.

<It's going to blow!>

"Selene, watch out!" Callum moved toward the closest thing that would provide cover, which happened to be one of the enormous stacks of books. He dove behind it just as the sphere of mana exploded, hurtling lightning-shaped bits of mana around the chamber. Rather than fizzling out, they twisted around like homing arrows until they found their targets.

Callum's Armorcore protected him from most of the bolts, but a few got through, sending a strange shock through his system. He felt as if his blood pressure had suddenly dropped.

Even with the adrenaline, the intensity of their opponent and its constructs, Callum felt a biting weariness, a sense that his energy had been zapped.

He knew better than to throw himself into the fight again, at least not without checking his Mana Reserves. Callum blasted another construct with wind, used Soul Sense, and saw his Mana Reserves were Half-Full.

How? It must have something to do with its earlier attack. It has to be that. I shouldn't be at the halfway point. It's like the Weaponcore I just got; the aetherbeast's attacks are able to absorb mana!

Fen picked up on this as well. *<Every time it releases its corrupted power, it takes our mana. I don't know how many more of those attacks you can take. Maybe two. Maybe. If you get to low, we're doomed!>*

<I won't let us get there!> Callum thought back. A stack of books blew out of the way as Selene fired on the sphere protecting the aetherbeast using her trident Weaponcore. The blast it produced was the thickest stream of mana Callum could remember seeing, able to easily sear through anything in its path and tear into their opponent.

Hoping to follow up her attack, Callum conjured a lance and tossed it at the aetherbeast. Then he summoned his Tempest Fang and cut into it, which seemed to stagger their opponent. The aetherbeast fell to the ground.

He locked eyes with Princess Selene and nodded.

The two rushed toward their opponent, only to be blown back by a sudden rush of wind mana that sent Callum into a stack of books and Selene into a wall.

Callum hit the stack hard, the ancient tomes falling on top of him, burying him beneath their weight. He would have been crushed had it not been for his Armorcore, which protected him as he pushed the books off. As soon as he was back on his feet, Callum was struck by one of the constructs, which pummeled him with a club-like weapon. His armor continued to protect him, yet he could still feel the impact, which felt as if someone had swung a log at him.

Winded, Callum cut the construct away with his sword and then shifted his focus back to their main opponent, who rushed back in the air, a spherical shield taking shape over its muddled body.

If it explodes its shield again, it will take more of our mana. How do I . . . .?

<Should we hit it with Radiant Inferno?> he asked Fen.

<That could work. But we need it to be on the ground before it does that. It's protected in the sky by its shield, and using an inferno will take a ton of your reserves.>

"We need to deal with the aetherbeast!" Callum shouted at Selene, who had started to cut down more of the constructs.

Selene grunted a response, pulled back, and once again went for her trident Weaponcore. She hurled it through the air, her weapon piercing the aetherbeast and pressing out of its back before returning to her hand. This brought their opponent back to the ground and disrupted the formation of its shield.

Callum started to charge Radiant Inferno while Princess Selene fended off more of the constructs *and* managed to hit the demonic aetherbeast a second time.

Almost there . . .

Radiant fire poured from Callum's palm, hit the ground and exploded into a frenzy of flames that ignited the aetherbeast. He thought they had it; he thought it would only take another strike or two to kill the creature. But then the aetherbeast rushed into the air again, its shield forming instantly as all the constructs were sucked back toward it, the humanlike mana constructs slapping together and strengthening the aetherbeast's spherical shield.

"Take cover!" Callum shouted at Selene as their opponent charged its attack for another few seconds. The demonic aetherbeast released all the charged power at once, which blew back some of the stacks of books and managed to bring down several of the bookshelves.

One of the bookshelves would have crushed Callum had it not been for the wings attached to his armor, which instantly grew and batted it away, allowing him to roll to the side.

Shit! His vision blurred and he suddenly felt weaker than he could remember feeling in weeks. Callum knew his levels were low; while he had avoided much of the aetherbeast's mana explosion, he had still been hit by some of it, enough to push his Mana Reserves closer to Hollowing.

Think, Callum, think!

He had learned ways to recharge, but he still had a ways to go with cycling, which would be ideal in a scenario like this.

"I'm going in!" Selene called to Callum as he took cover behind a bookshelf, where he noticed corrupted mana.

Fen, I need Fen. That's it!

<I need you to get mana for me,> Callum said quickly.

<Are you sure? If it hits you in your unmelded state it could kill you!>

<I'm certain. Hurry!>

Fen's form appeared next to Callum. The Radiant Fox began absorbing the corrupted mana as quickly as he could while Princess Selene fought the demonic aetherbeast.

Callum watched her spear it again with her trident, which returned to her hand as she charged past. She was struck by a thick tendril of mana, which slammed her into one of the mountainous stacks of books. Before

Callum could call to her, she recovered and came back up with her claws, which sent wave upon wave of sharp mana in the direction of the demonic aetherbeast.

"How are we looking?" Callum asked Fen, who continued to absorb corrupted mana.

"Almost there!"

Hang on, Selene! Callum glanced around again to see her thrusting her trident toward the aetherbeast, which was yet again forming a shield around its body. If it exploded its mana shield again, Callum knew they were done for. *If I'm near Hollowing, she's either at Low or Half-Full. We won't make it. We—*

He felt his power surge as Fen returned to him, the meld augmented by the Attribute Shards Callum had taken and what the fox had quickly absorbed.

<Here's our chance!>

Callum knew he could pummel the aetherbeast with wind, his Radiant Claws, or his lance. He could slam into it with his Shatterlight Bear, or he could summon his wind sword and hit the aetherbeast with an augmented Zephyr Strike or a full-on attack. There was one other option. *<Do we have enough for one last Inferno?>*

<Risky, but I say we go for it!>

Callum started to charge. He braced himself as he heard the princess continue to fight, wishing he could jump back in, yet aware that it took a moment for Fen's trait to work.

"Selene!" He called after he reached the threshold. Callum stepped around the stack of books, his palm stretched in front of him. "Get ready to hit it with everything you have!"

The spherical shield protecting the demonic aetherbeast pulsed, mere seconds away from exploding when Callum released a searing blast of mana that landed before the shield, exploded, and scorched the monster within.

Selene moved as the aetherbeast hit the ground, striking it multiple times with her amplified claws. Callum came in beside her and delivered the final strike with his wind sword. Mana fizzled all around them as the demonic aetherbeast let out a death rattle and finally expired.

Shards rushed toward Callum.

Empowerment of Might Shard
Empowerment of Might Shard
Empowerment of Regeneration Shard
Empowerment of Regeneration Shard
Shadow Affinity Shard

Death Affinity Shard
Sphere Shield of the Doomlight Shadecaller Armorcore

"I'm going to guess by the look on your face that you didn't receive the Armorcore of the Ironspine Panther," Princess Selene said once the dust had settled.

"Shards and something called Sphere Shield of the Doomlight Shadecaller Armorcore."

"A Shadecaller . . ." Princess Selene crouched as Ecaris left her, Fen doing the same so the two could absorb mana.

"Do you know what that is?" Callum asked as he caught his breath, which was much easier than it should have been because of the shards he had used.

"I have read about them, or heard about them." Her eyes twitched. "One of the two. What does the Armorcore do?"

Shield of the Doomlight Shadecaller Armorcore
Type: *Demoncore Accessory*
Grade: *Sublime*
Infusion Requirements for Grade Increase:
0/20 Shadow Affinity
0/20 Death Affinity
0/15 Vigor Shards
Affinity Requirements: *Shadow and Death*
Effect: *When bound to one's Soul Heart, this powerful Armorcore produces a hardened shield with Shadow and Death properties.*

"It produces a shield with Shadow and Death properties, whatever that means," Callum told her. "So it's a shield. Master Cruedark mentioned these."

"It is. As for what it does? My best guess is it would mean that wielding the shield can cause fear through the Shadow properties, and reduce your enemy's willpower or, essentially, power, through the Death properties. It's also something that, if we're being honest, a normal archmage wouldn't wield openly."

"Like a warlock?" Callum asked as he scanned the description again and saw that it was listed as a Demoncore Accessory.

"Precisely. You should sunder that one. Do not sell it because it will only end up in the wrong hands. You could keep it, but you're not a warlock, and you don't have access to Death or Shadow Mana."

"I am in agreement with the princess," Fen said as he came around, brimming with light from the mana he had absorbed. "Best to sunder something like that because I seriously doubt, or should I say, I seriously forbid, we go down the path of a warlock."

"They aren't as bad as you may think," Princess Selene said carefully. "While I don't necessarily agree that Demoncores should be widely used, and I don't know where I stand on simply allowing the Crown to use them because doing something like that always leads to turmoil with citizens and, somewhere down the line, deceit, I do believe they have their place. The Geshwine Empire is using them freely now, but they do not have the same training we have here."

"Like at the Great College," Callum said.

"Exactly. Our kingdom has spent the last five hundred years perfecting and understanding what it means to aetherforge, to be pacted. We have made incredible advances that I doubt your forefather, the Demonslayer, would have ever thought possible. We have done so by fundamentally coming to understand what we are able to do with mana and with our pacted aetherbeasts. One could argue that Demoncores aren't even necessary—there is always a workaround without using corrupted mana."

"So a non-demonic Armorcore shield that does something similar?"

"Correct." The princess turned her focus to the green triangle of mana. "There's always a workaround. It just might take longer to find or forge." She let out a sigh. "Well, this has certainly been an interesting detour, but we still don't have the Armorcore of the Ironspine Panther. There are just a few hours left before we need to go back. I say we head in the opposite direction, the one that my scout here originally pointed out."

While the green triangle wasn't exactly sentient, it did seem to tilt upward a few hairs, as if it were lifting its chin in confirmation that it had been right all along.

"Sounds good to me," Callum said as he checked his Mana Reserves, which were at Half-Full. "Hopefully, we don't encounter anything like that again."

"Agreed. If we do, I'm afraid we will need to come back another night." Selene grew flustered. "But let's not let it come to that. Ecaris," she called to her bear, who was searching around between the fallen stacks of books, "let's keep moving."

CHAPTER 42

Portals aren't set in stone. They hold no allegiance to certainty.

—Oliven Ladas, Master Convoker, Magistor of the Fire Wyrm, and
Dean of the Great College from Year 400–431

The other path wound its way through a garden filled with more crumbling statues, some of the pieces reminding Callum of the great ale barrels that were occasionally transported from the lands of Antiqua through Weatherby. The biggest by far was a sculpted head that was nearly the height of a two-story building, lying on its side and missing the jewels that had once been fused into the man's curled hair.

"Bandits tend to take over places like this," Princess Selene said. "It's sad, really, but not surprising. Over the past hundred years, thanks to pressure from the Royal Court, funding to protect relics like these—old Great College campuses and such—has pretty much dried up. The same goes for other places in the kingdom that used to stand as symbols of glory."

Callum thought of the dead soldiers he had come across in the King's Forest. *Would they have died if there had been more men to protect the path? Perhaps.* He remembered the Gravewind Hawk and how large it had been. *Even a large group would have problems without an archmage . . .*

"Why aren't there more archmages protecting places like this?" Callum asked, asking the next logical question that came from his memory of the King's Forest.

"Archmages, nearly always from noble families, aren't required to serve if they don't want to. If we are ever in a war, they can all be conscripted, but many go on to do things that aren't military related. Some become lecturers, researchers, historians, poets, bards, or they are elected to the Royal Court. Some simply go back to their lives. There are those that become Beast Masters, who usually head to the front lines, the best of whom usually are employed by my family. But that selection process is very difficult. There are those that transition into trades by becoming shardcrafters. Others simply get the education afforded to a noble and go on with their lives, whatever that may be. There is one catch, however."

"Yes?"

"Only a few of the roles I've mentioned are able to keep their Aethercores. The archmages will still retain the affinities they bonded with, but they won't have full access to cores in the same way they would with their aetherbeasts."

"What do you mean?"

"The strength of a Powercore is augmented by your Aethercore, your pact. At best, Powercores will only operate at about thirty percent of their true power if a person isn't pacted with anything. So something like a fireball would still do damage, but it wouldn't do the same damage as it would do if, say, the archmage was pacted with a Fire Swine."

Callum laughed. "A fire pig?"

"You laugh until you see one in action."

Callum imagined a flaming pig and snorted. When he was younger, Rhane took care of their neighbor's pigs for a summer, which quickly became Callum's job after his father slipped in the mud in the pigsty and vowed never to look at a pig again. True to his stubborn nature, they stopped eating pork after that.

I wonder if he's had pork since I left, Callum thought as they reached the end of the statue garden.

Princess Selene looked out at an amphitheater, much of the seating crumbled. "Can you imagine listening to a lecture here? It must have been so grand."

"Why do you say that?"

"Do you see us getting lectures outside at the Great College?"

"Master Cruedark has his combat classes outside."

"Yes, in other locations that you travel to through portals. The Great College doesn't have outdoor lectures because of New Albion's weather."

"It's been fine so far."

"You haven't experienced a New Albion winter, have you?"

"I can't say that I have."

"The first snow should be soon. And after a few months of that, spring comes, which is gorgeous until the rains start up. Those last until summer, which is dry and pleasant, but the college isn't in session. *The fall starts, leaves fall, snow comes, rains drench, summer suns, begin anew.* Have you heard that poem?"

"No," he told her honestly. The only poem he could remember hearing in Weatherby was a rhyming prayer for a good harvest.

"It's not the best, but it is memorable, and it's about the weather of New Albion. Anyway," the princess looked ahead to her floating green triangle, which had reached the bottom of the amphitheater, "our adventure continues. I hope the information my notetakers were able to get is right. At least you got some shards and cores out of it."

Definitely, Callum thought as they passed the amphitheater. They walked along a pathway that was once covered by a stone pergola, now just a few slabs of marble still suspended above them. *And that means I can send a little money back to my father too.*

He quickly scanned his current core loadout to see if there was anything that he would be able to upgrade without spending too much. He first focused on Inner Light, which Callum felt wasn't yet strong enough to truly make a difference.

This one needs four Empowerment of Regeneration Shards and three Light Affinity Shards. I currently have three Regeneration Shards and one Light Affinity Shard.

As they walked, Callum fused the shards he had into the core, meaning that Inner Light would now only need one more Empowerment of Regeneration Shard, and two Light Affinity Shards.

That is certainly something I could trade for, he thought as he turned to the Charge of the Shatterlight Bear. *It needs five Light Affinity Shards and five Empowerment of Might Shards, ten in total. I currently have two Empowerment of Might Shards, but I think I'll hold onto those for now in case I need them.*

From there, Callum looked at Gift of the Luminous Lance, which needed a whopping eight Light Affinity Shards to upgrade. *Between this and the Shatterlight Bear, I should probably do this one first because of how much I use it. It's strong and gives me range. Once I run out of Powercore slots, I might need to take the Charge of the Shatterlight Bear out anyway.*

He thought of the two cores he had just received, the Shield of the Doomlight Shadecaller Armorcore and the Life Blade of the Spring Ferret Weaponcore.

There are clearly stronger cores out there. But Inner Light and Gift of the Luminous Lance will be the best to upgrade with the shards I can get from trading and sundering.

His plan solidified, Callum refocused on the princess and her large bear, who were walking up a long set of stairs. He thought they were about to reach another building, but was surprised to reach a platform with a pedestal that hoisted a pair of glowing stone swords crossing one another at the tips.

"Another portal," the princess said as her green triangle picked up its spinning speed.

"How do we use this one?" Callum asked, unsure where he was supposed to pass through. The portals he had encountered so far had all had enough space for him to either crawl or walk through.

"I've seen ones like this before. If we get any closer, it will activate." Princess Selene paused, as if she were considering how she should frame what she was about to say next. "My family has portals as a means of escape. The only issue with a portal far away from the Second Heart of Creation, is that they're harder to power this far out."

"But we portaled here, to the field."

"Yes, but the power of that painting's portal is still being fueled by the Second Heart of Creation and the dormant mana it picks up from the air, especially when aetherstorms approach New Albion. It does happen, you know, several times a year. You'll probably experience one this fall. It's remarkable, really, seeing the Second Heart of Creation completely absorb the power of the storm."

"And why aren't there other Hearts of Creation? Why just the one?"

"There could certainly be lesser ones, but after the Great Demonswar, it was decided that they would be much harder to guard in other places."

Fen appeared, fox swishing his mana tail as he examined the two crossed swords. He looked up at Princess Selene. "So you're saying you don't know where this particular portal goes, and you don't know what is fueling it?"

"Yes, that's exactly what I'm saying. But my beacon seems to think it is the way to go and I don't see any other option."

"What if it sends the two of you somewhere far, somewhere that you won't be able to return from?"

Selene shook her head. "I have yet to encounter a one-way portal. They weren't designed that way."

"I don't know," Fen admitted. "The science behind portals is something that wouldn't have been toyed with in my time. That is how you open the door to the Demonsrealm."

"From everything I've learned, that door remains sealed," Princess Selene said in an even tone. "If the two of you prefer, you can stay here."

"No, we're going with you," Callum told her. "We've made it this far."

The princess considered this with a soft harrumph. She approached the portal and reached her hand to it, her body pixelating away.

"I suppose if we have to find our way back to New Albion, then that's what we'll do," Fen said once she was gone. "We can't let her go alone. All of this is so risky!"

Fen's right, but . . . Callum approached the portal and felt its magnetic pull. *It's exciting, too!*

Soon, he stood before an enormous waterfall illuminated only by the twilight. Princess Selene, who had been admiring some lily pads with light blue flowers, turned to him. "Good, the portal is still there."

Callum looked back to see the same pair of stone swords, crossed at the tip and radiating with power. "Any idea where we are?"

"By the change in temperature I'd guess somewhere in the southwestern part of the kingdom." Princess Selene cast her hand forward and a beam of mana took shape near the portal, marking the exit point. "Shall we?"

Callum looked around. All he could see was a waterfall and a chiseled cliff face that had no paths leading up. But then he noticed the faint green glow coming from behind the waterfall.

"It's back there?"

"Something is back there," Princess Selene said. "But it looks like we'll need to get a little wet to reach it." She removed her cloak and tied it around her waist. She took off her finely stitched leather boots and hiked up her pants. "What are you waiting for?"

Callum did the same. Once his boots were tucked under his arm, he waded out into the water and followed the princess to the far side of the waterfall. The sound was so loud, the splash of water in his face so distracting, that Callum hardly noticed the slight chill of the water. All he could think about was that wherever they were, it felt like they were the only two people in the world, even if they also had their pacted aetherbeasts.

And he liked that. The princess had a unique charm about her. Selene was adventurous and smart, and just about the most well-rounded person he could remember meeting when he accounted for her fighting skills, her understanding of diplomacy and history, and the fact she rarely reminded him of her royal status.

He suspected someone like Draven was the exact opposite, someone who took their wealth and status for granted. *I can't believe she will be forced to marry him . . .*

"Fun," Princess Selene said as they slipped around the falling water and came to a small opening carved into the stone. Her green beacon hovered before it, spinning yet again.

"I can go ahead," Fen said as he appeared next to Callum. "It's better to send me in and let me see what I can uncover first."

"Not a bad idea, a fox in a hole," Princess Selene said. "And if it's too small for us to fit through later, if it tapers, you can just return, and we'll figure out something else."

"I'll let you know what I find." Fen disappeared into the hall, leaving Callum and Selene on a ledge, the water falling behind them.

Callum's skin pricked as he sensed movement. He turned and his Tempest Fang appeared in his hand as an enormous aetherbeast fish took shape, one that looked like a catfish with long, drooping whiskers, the water parting around it.

"Wait," Selene said as she stuck her arm out to stop Callum. "This one would have attacked us in the water had that been its intention."

"That . . . that makes sense."

Hello," Princess Selene told the aetherbeast, which continued to hover, its dark eyes boring down on the pair. "We are in search of something."

The catfish considered them for a moment. "You have an aetherforge?" he finally asked.

"I do, and she is with me now."

"And you?" the fish asked Callum.

"A Radiant Fox. He is exploring the tunnel."

"And what is it you seek?"

"The Armorcore of the Ironspine Panther," said the princess.

"If you want the Armorcore you will need to do something for me."

"Name your price," Princess Selene said.

"A small aetherstorm deposited corrupted beasts in the pool above, which feeds the waterfall. You are young magelings, are you not?"

"Magelings?" Selene asked. "You mean students."

"An old word for that, yes. If that truly is what you are, then handle the Corruption for me, and I will reward you with the Armorcore. You can also leave the way you came, or I suppose you could threaten me for the prize, but that wouldn't be very wise of you."

"We don't mind helping," Callum said. "We just need a way to get to the top of the waterfall, that's all."

Several of the aetherbeast's large whiskers curled, almost as if he was smiling at them. "I don't believe that will be a problem."

Fen came out of the hole, the fox becoming skittish the moment he saw the catfish aetherbeast.

"It's fine," Callum told him. "We've come to an understanding."

CHAPTER 43

If mana exists everywhere, and an aetherstorm can call forth terrifying beasts, some with ties to the Demonsrealm, I ask you, what else can be aided or corrupted by mana?

—Amindra Dew, Mastress Weaver, Archona of Ontaria

Princess Selene waded into the water, which came up to her knees. The waterfall was behind her, far enough away that she and Callum weren't sprayed by the mist it produced. "Here?" she asked the catfish aetherbeast, who continued to float nearby, whiskers curling as it watched the two of them curiously.

"That should be fine," the catfish said.

Callum stepped up next to the princess. *This should be interesting*, he thought as he gave her an uncertain look.

Watery mana rushed all around Callum, twisting around his legs and sliding beneath his feet. There was a sudden shift as a platform of mana rose from the water and carried them to the top of the falls.

Amazing, Callum thought as he was presented with an enormous lake, one that would have certainly been deep had it not been for the way they now hovered on top of the waves. The catfish aetherbeast brought them to a shore, and Callum was able to see the start of a swamp beyond.

"You will find the Corruption there, deep within the bog."

"We will return once it has been cleared," Princess Selene said with all the confidence in the world. She placed her boots on the shoreline, Callum noting that the lack of footwear didn't seem to bother her in the least. "I'd rather not get my boots dirty," she explained.

"That makes sense."

"Sir Trindade will know. We can wash the mud off, obviously, but the leather will remain wet." She rolled up her pant legs a bit more. "This will likely be fun and messy. Ecaris, Fen?" Both appeared at her call. "Good. Be ready. Keep the snakes away. We only have about an hour or two before we need to head back to the campus."

They said goodbye to the catfish aetherbeast and continued along the shoreline. The lake's dark, reflective surface gave way to the murky shallows of a swamp, the air growing heavy with the pungent scent of damp earth. Princess Selene trudged ahead as if she had walked along the edge of the swamp numerous times, occasionally making a strange face whenever she squished something questionable.

While Callum didn't have any experience in a swamp, he had spent plenty of time outdoors, where he usually felt comfortable, even in the heat of a Weatherby summer or the profound stillness of night on the farm during the winter.

It's not exactly the same, but I'll get used to it, he thought as he ignored the cold mud beneath his feet.

A snake slithered into the water and Fen pounced. "That one was rather large," he said as he turned back to Callum.

Ecaris found this amusing, laughing at Fen as she went back to traveling along the shoreline.

"This is all so elaborate," Selene said as they continued walking.

"What do you mean?" Callum asked.

"The list of hidden cores is provided by the Great College, meaning it was someone's job to come out here and set all this up, likely an upperclassman or someone entering a mastery course so they could become an Archon or an Archona. Someone arranged all this with the catfish aetherbeast, who must call the area home. I suppose we could have fought the catfish for it, but this is a better option."

"And what does that mean exactly, an Archon?" Callum had seen the title the last few weeks at the Great College but hadn't pressed anyone for clarity.

"An Archon or an Archona is a person who has completed two mastery courses after graduation. It's usually followed by their birthplace. If you became an Archon, you'd be an Archon of Weatherby. The next level would be Core Lector or Core Lectora. This is a person who was an Archon who has since mastered the ability to create Powercores. This would simply follow your name, Callum Stross, Core Lector."

"And the final would be Magistor?" Callum asked, thinking of Master Patrjohn Granadam, the Dean of the Great College.

"Yes, Magistor and Magistra, the final title one can receive and generally noted by their preferred or first pacted aetherbeast. If you reached this level, you would be Callum Stross, Magistor of the Radiant Fox. But all of this stuff is purely institutional because academics like to classify things. Beast Masters are more powerful, generally . . ."

"Found one!" Ecaris chased a snake into the water, Fen bounding along after her. The fox suddenly froze, his ears going erect.

"Something is ahead," Princess Selene said as she summoned her Armorcore.

Callum did the same, mana hardening around him.

A wingless demonic aetherbeast that resembled an oversized baby bird exploded out of the swamp, corrupted mana rippling off its form. It released a series of tendrils on its back, which rushed toward Ecaris, who swatted them away.

Fen returned to Callum, the two melding in an instant as he drew his Tempest Fang and rushed toward the aetherbeast. Beside him, Princess Selene did the same with her trident.

Rather than aimlessly beat at the tendrils, Callum went at them with precision, remembering Master Cruedark's lessons as he weaved his wind sword in and out of the air, severing darkened tentacles.

Bits of Corruption flashed around him, yet Callum remained protected by his Armorcore. A sudden rush of mana to his right told him that Selene and Ecaris had also melded. The Princess threw herself into the fight and struck the demonic aetherbeast, the two rolling into the swamp.

<Hold back!> Fen shouted as they splashed into the low-level water, Princess Selene quickly getting the upper hand, only to be thrown off by a sudden pillar of mana that exploded out of the aetherbeast's stomach. She flew to the right, right into the swamp, the splash of her armor loud enough that Callum used the distraction to his advantage as he moved in with a wind attack, and followed this up with a powerful jab from his Tempest Fang that finally killed the aetherbeast.

Empowerment of Mind Shard

"You good?"

"I'll be fine," Selene said as she got to her feet, the princess sopping wet. She wrung out the ends of her cloak, teeth chattering a bit as she spoke: "Not great, but fine."

"You're cold—"

"I'm fine."

"Take my cloak." He removed it from his shoulders as their two aetherbeasts went to work absorbing corrupted mana.

"I don't need it."

"Princess," Callum said with a firmness he wasn't used to using with her as she shivered. "Take it."

They exchanged cloaks, the princess instantly wrapping his around her body while Callum did his best to wring out as much water as he could from her's before placing the cold, wet cloak on his shoulders.

"Will you be fine?" she asked.

"Always," Callum said, which was true when it came to things like dealing with the cool temperature. There had been a few winters where they had to ration firewood, especially the years that Miss Barrowsly had lived near their farm. The old woman had been unable to afford firewood, and while Callum chopped plenty for her, there just wasn't enough wood on her property to fuel her needs. To make sure she stayed warm, Callum and his father adjusted. They wore thick blankets and took care of her as best they could. Miss Barrowsly was always thankful, and always ready to greet them with a hearty stew.

He thought of that stew now as they headed deeper into the swamp, where he saw the telltale signs of mana ahead. Not only was there a glow, Callum noticed there was a pull on his chest, one he was becoming increasingly familiar with.

The next two demonic aetherbeasts they took down were small and reptilian, goat-sized with long tails split that in two and were capable of producing tendrils. They dropped another Death Affinity Shard and left behind a lot of mana for Ecaris and Fen to gather. More aetherbeasts followed, none of which dropped shards.

The two came to a strange tree that had grown out of the swamp, and both Ecaris and Fen immediately became alert upon seeing it. A strange, sour scent wafted from the tree. Its branches stretched out like twisted claws.

"Can it be?" Fen asked with a growl.

"A corrupted aethertree," Ecaris said. "This is what has been poisoning the swamp."

"To me," Princess Selene said to Ecaris as her Armorcore hardened around her.

Ecaris melded with the princess, Fen doing the same with Callum.

"I've never heard of such a thing," Callum said as he took in the sight of the tree, which had a dark, purplish glow to it. A spiral of gold occasionally twisted up its trunk, as if it were taking big breaths of air, its lungs and veins expanding.

"Before you take a step closer, be prepared for it to attack you from below and above."

"Below?" Callum asked the princess.

"It's roots. It will use them as weapons. Same with its branches. I'm surprised we haven't reached that threshold yet. We must be close. Do you think you can reach it with your lance from here?"

"No, I can't. If you cover me, I can hit it with Radiant Inferno," Callum said. "But only once. I don't want my reserves to dip below Half-Full."

"Then let's save that for the finisher. This is it," she said, her voice raising, "we deal with this, we return to the catfish, we get the hidden core. Our best bet is to reach the tree before it can attack us with its tentacles."

"You mean its roots and branches?"

"It will be both."

"Run toward it?"

"As fast as you possibly can," she said, readying herself.

Callum summoned his Armorcore of the Brightflame Falcon, which twisted around him, forming a hardened mana shell. His Tempest Fang in hand, he glanced at the princess, nodded, and took off running toward the tree.

He saw her racing beside him, Selene on all fours, the ends of her borrowed cloak beating in the wind she caused from her powerful charge. Mana roots tore themselves from the swamp, slinging mud and brackish water as they tried to swat the two away.

Fen took over, the fox making Callum's body jump with such precision that Callum was glad they were melded. *I could never have made that jump!* he thought as a root ripped out of the swamp directly in front of him. He sliced through it with his sword just as the princess was about to reach the aethertree.

To cover her, Callum produced a lance of light from his palm and fired it at the tree as a distraction. He twisted, ducked beneath a swinging branch, and blasted another spiny branch with wind. As the princess continued to hit the tree with huge blasts of mana, causing its limbs to shake wildly, Callum severed more of its roots.

A quick check of his Mana Reserves showed Callum he was at Half-Full, and reminded him that he needed to be careful. *Let the Princess do most of the fighting; come in at the end with the finisher!* Callum thought as he did just that, attacking repeatedly from the outskirts. He kept his focus on the roots that were trying to attack Selene, trying to cut them off every time.

<Incoming!>

Before he could act, a root swept Callum away and hurtled him into the swamp.

Fen helped with the landing, yet it still hurt. Callum could feel pain in his bones, his nostrils flaring at the intense smell of the water. He looked ahead to see Princess Selene wielding her trident. She was in a form that he hadn't seen her take before, one split evenly down the middle, the right side of her body human and protected by an Armorcore, the left side of her body bearlike, her big claw batting anything that got near her while she charged up her trident.

She tossed the trident into the center of the aethertree, and dodged left as a sharpened root tried to take her head off. Selene came up poised and ready to go as Callum began to charge his own attack. *I need to get closer and build up as much power as I can for Radiant Inferno!*

Selene hit the aethertree with her trident and portions of it exploded, which tore a few chunks out of the tree. The Weaponcore reappeared in her hand, and she used it to keep more of the roots at bay.

<I wish she had told us about that power!>

The princess's focus inspired Callum as he drew more of his mana into Radiant Inferno. Stepping back to charge a bit more, he hit the threshold he was becoming increasingly familiar with and lobbed a searing bolt of mana at the trunk. The aethertree ignited with a swirl of mana, its limbs and roots shrieking in agony.

A slew of prompts followed.

Empowerment of Resilience Shard
Empowerment of Resilience Shard
Empowerment of Regeneration Shard
Empowerment of Regeneration Shard
Empowerment of Regeneration Shard
Earth Affinity Shard
Light Affinity Shard
Roots of the Willow Aethertree

Roots of the Willow Aethertree
Type: Ability
Grade: Exalted
Infusion Requirements for Grade Increase:
0/15 Light Affinity
0/15 Earth Affinity
0/5 Resilience Shards
Affinity Requirements: Light or Earth
Effect: When bound to one's Soul Heart, this core allows a mage to summon the mana roots of an aethertree to surprise, bind, and attack your opponent.

"That's amazing," Callum said, his eyes fixed on the Powercore. Despite being caked in mud and soaked to the bone, the rush of adrenaline kept him oblivious to the discomfort.

"What did it give you?"

"Roots of the Willow Aethertree. Basically, I'd be able to use roots to attack or bind someone."

"And the Grade?"

He checked again. "Exalted."

"Meaning you won't be able to use it at its full power, but at least it would be over sixty percent. Do you have the affinity to use it?"

"It says Earth *or* Light Mana. I have affinity to Light Mana from Fen's Aethercore."

"Ah, in that case, you can use it." Selene flicked some water from her hands. "But it won't be as strong as it would be if you had access to both."

Like Charge of the Shatterlight Bear . . . Callum went ahead and fused the orb into his chest. "This means I have nine now," he said.

"Nine, the limit for a Conjurer. You can always take one out if you need to and hold onto it," Selene said. "But this is good. We have completed our mission, and all we need to do now is collect. You don't mind if I wear your cloak a little longer, do you?"

"Of course not," he said. "Please, princess, wear it."

"*Selene.* And I will. But we'll have to switch once we get back to campus. Mine has the royal seal on it."

Callum reexamined the wet cloak and saw the seal just over his shoulder. "That could have been bad."

She laughed. "It really could have. Come on, then."

They returned to the start of the waterfall, where they found their boots. Even after washing his feet in the water, and giving them a moment to dry, it felt strange putting boots on again, strange to once again be stepping into the civilized world after such a strange excursion with royalty. *What a night,* Callum thought as the catfish aetherbeast appeared.

He hovered out of the water and bent toward them, his form growing in size, large whiskers drooping. "You have done it."

"You didn't tell us it would be an aethertree," the princess said.

"I honestly didn't know if you would make it that far."

She gave the aetherbeast a skeptical look. "The Armorcore, as we discussed."

"Yes, come with me."

Callum felt the aetherbeast's influence spread around him and float both of them over the side of the waterfall. It brought them back down to the large pool below, which began to part on both sides as they landed on the shoreline.

Is there going to be a treasure chest or something? Callum wondered as the water continued to part.

A massive bass leaped from the wall of water, landing heavily in the open space and smacking its lips. The fish flopped awkwardly for a moment on its side before spitting out the Powercore with a wet, guttural sound.

"Good," Selene said as the orb rushed to her hand. "Armorcore of the Ironspine Panther, perfect." Her eyes lit up with delight. "Thank you," she told Callum. "And thank you," she told the catfish. "It was a journey, that's for sure."

"I can tell," the catfish told her. "And you know your way back?"

Princess Selene looked in the direction of the portal they had taken to reach the waterfall.

"Ecaris does," she finally said. "We can find our own way back."

CHAPTER 44

Royal Decree: By command of His Majesty, Death Affinity Shards should now be turned into the Crown for secure processing. All shard transactions are cataloged in the World Ledger, and any attempts to illegally conceal or withhold such shards will result in immediate investigation by Royal Authorities. Let this serve as a reminder that the safety of the realm depends upon strict compliance with this decree.

—Decree announcing the collection of Death Affinity Shards

Callum meant to practice mana cycling the next morning, but he became engrossed in distributing shards instead. He put an Empowerment of Regeneration Shard and a Light Affinity Shard into Inner Light, leaving him just one shard remaining before it was upgraded.

"Almost there," he said, knowing that whatever he did, he would be sure to trade shards he couldn't use to upgrade his healing power. "Now, to your Aethercore."

Fen, who sat under the window, looked at Callum and projected his voice. "Yes, let's see what we can do . . ."

Callum fused an Air Affinity Shard, an Empowerment of Deftness Shard, two Empowerment of Resilience Shards, and two Might Shards he had received into Fen's Aethercore.

The Earth Affinity Shards he had went into Roots of the Willow Aethertree. Callum figured he could sunder the core later if he decided he needed the mana. He fused the Empowerment of Mind and Empowerment of Vigor shards into his Rejuvenation Powercore. He also set the single Fire Affinity Shard he had received into his Armorcore of the Brightflame Falcon, leaving him a handful of shards to sell or keep for later.

"One Shadow Affinity; four Death Affinities; and one Life Affinity shard to take to the Emporium. I believe I'll save the two Empowerment of Regeneration Shards to either use or fuse into Inner Light once I'm able to upgrade it."

"Not a bad plan at all," Fen said. "The faster we can heal, the better our chances of survival will be."

"I also need to sunder the Shield of the Doomlight Shadecaller Armorcore and see if Marcella wants the Life Blade of the Spring Ferret." Callum recalled that this particular Powercore allowed someone to sap mana from an opponent, yet required affinity to both Light and Life Mana to use it. "That's a good one."

"Indeed," Fen said. "And what an adventure last night turned out to be. You gained quite a bit from it, and you made a friend."

"The princess?"

"No, Ecaris, her bear." Fen laughed. "Yes, the Princess. And as for the Demoncore, perhaps you should pay Telluride a visit over anyone at the Emporium. Not that Birchwen didn't make us a fair offer last time."

"Good idea, tonight, then."

"The princess will likely insist you visit the city with her guard."

Callum didn't like that part. The only time he'd been able to sneak out since getting his dorm room had been on their little adventure the previous night.

"But at least she cares," Fen said when Callum didn't respond. "And now she has more reason to care, thanks to your help finding the hidden core that she wanted. There are few people better to have in debt than a literal princess."

"True."

"And she did mention she'd find one of the hidden cores for you, so who knows? Maybe she'll show up some night, ask you to don your cloak, and the two of you will visit another abandoned campus."

Callum looked across the room at his cloak, which was still drying with the other clothing he had worn last night. "We'll see."

As the day continued, Callum couldn't shake his memories of their trip, how they had crawled through the painting, and how strange it had been to return to New Albion.

Even two months ago, something like that would have been impossible. Now . . . Now I just have to ask myself, how many of these things have been happening over the course of my life? How many things that I missed? Are there portals like that in Weatherby? Is there more hidden at my farm?

During his lunch break, he wrote his father a letter, which he planned to send with a little money.

Father,

I have adjusted well to life here at the Great College and I've made a few friends. I am still on academic probation, like I told you in my previous letter, but I don't think I will be for much longer. The other students have proven to be more prepared than me, but I have started taking private instruction from Master Cruedark, whom I told you about in my last letter. I don't know when I will visit Weatherby and the farm, but I look forward to seeing you and the village again.

After detailing a little more about his classes, Callum folded the parchment and put it in his pocket with plans to send it after he had sold off some of the shards.

He attended his Elemental Mana and Its Principles class led by Master Alpen, who spent most of his time telling the tragic story of a man who tried and failed to use Life Mana to resuscitate his dead brother. The man then used Death Mana when that didn't work, which got him banned from the community due to the taboo against the nature of necromancy.

"I did not think that was what we would be talking about today," Marcella said as she joined Callum and Quinn after class. "Although I won't lie, since I have an affinity with Life Mana I have often wondered what it would be like to have affinity with Death Mana as well."

"It's not as crazy as it sounds," Quinn told her. "You could keep your pact with Harold and gain a new Aethercore at the next Rank, perhaps a Shadow Weasel—"

"Stop it."

Quinn laughed. "It exists."

"I think a Shadow Weasel is more of Draven's style," she said as she nodded at the duke's son, who'd already given Callum and the other two a dirty look. He joined his friends and left. "What about you? What do you have going on for the rest of the day?" she asked Callum. "You don't have to train with Master Cruedark today, do you?"

"Not today. Actually, I need to head into the city," he told Marcella.

"Oh?"

"What do you plan to do in the city?" Quinn asked Callum.

"I need to have something sundered and I need to trade and sell some shards."

"So the Emporium first, then dinner?"

"Telluride, then the Emporium, and then dinner," Callum said. "Plus, this." He produced the Life Blade of the Spring Ferret core and gave it to Marcella, who examined the orb, her dark eyes wide with surprise. "I thought you might be interested."

Quinn examined it next. "Where did you get this?"

<Careful,> Fen reminded Callum. <The princess never said you could reveal what the two of you did last night. Although, I suppose, it would be better to tell them than running around with the secret, especially if the two of you were ever witnessed together.>

"You got it when you went with the princess last night, right?" Marcella asked, beating Callum to the punch.

<I didn't expect that!>

Callum gawked at the tall woman from Aveiro, whose jewelry gleamed in the afternoon sun. "You knew?" he asked.

"Of course, I knew. Selene is a friend. How many times do I have to tell the two of you that she's my friend? Anyway, we have breakfast occasionally. Or, rather, she has someone show up at my dorm and bring me to have breakfast with her, like she did early this morning to tell me about your little excursion."

<Proceed.>

Callum grinned at the voice in his head. "Well, then you know. That's how I got it."

"She didn't say what you got, only that I would like it. I suppose she was teasing me in that way. I was wondering when you would ask if I wanted it. And the answer is yes. I also have some things that could be sundered, so perhaps we could make a trade. What do you need?"

Callum knew that he needed a single Light Affinity Shard to upgrade his healing power, but the core he had just given her was worth much more than that. The problem was he didn't know how much more valuable. Marcella was his friend, so he didn't want to ask for more than it was worth. *But I know it's a good one . . .*

Quinn seemed to pick up on his inner thoughts. "Easy. We can get an estimate at the Emporium."

"Or I can make you an offer right now," Marcella said, challenging Quinn's suggestion. "You use Fire, Light, and Air Mana, right, Callum? I happen to have some Light Affinity Shards, and an Airspear Weaponcore that I can't use. I could give you that; you could sunder it, or I could sunder it and give you the components."

"People from Aveiro—"

"Don't say we're pushy with sales," Marcella told Quinn.

"Why do I need to say it when you are proving my point?"

"It's a fair offer and you know it." Marcella leaned forward and beamed a smile at Callum. "We can do it now or you can wait and find out in the city. Normally, there'd be a penalty with something like that, but now?"

"A penalty?" Quinn asked her.

"What if it is worth less than I have offered here? You come from a family of merchants, as do I. You know how business works, even if it is your brother who will be running it."

"I suppose it is a fair trade," he admitted to her.

"It's more than fair. Would you like to see the Powercore?" she asked Callum. "If you aren't interested in using it, which you might be, sundering it will surely net you more Air Affinity, and perhaps some Attribute Shards as well. Something to keep in mind. Well? Would you like to see it?"

"Sure."

Now that she had officially taken over the negotiations, Marcella produced an orb of light and handed it to him. "This, plus the Light Affinity Shards I have. That's my offer for the Life Blade of the Spring Ferret."

Callum examined the orb she had given him:

Piercing Air Spear Weaponcore
Type: *Accessory*
Grade: *Common Weapon*
Infusion Requirements for Grade Increase:
0/10 Air Affinity
0/10 Vigor Shards
Affinity Requirements: *Air*
Effect: *When bound to one's Soul Heart, this Weaponcore conjures a spear made of air capable of both piercing your opponent and blowing them off their feet.*

This could actually be useful, he thought as Fen spoke quietly to him.

<You really need to reach the Wielder Rank so you can have fifteen Powercores and two Aethercores. Then, we could easily add this to our repertoire. If we wanted it now, we would need to take something out, perhaps the Charge of the Shatterlight Bear. You have quite a bit infused in that core, but Telluride could sunder that.>

That's true, Callum thought as he used Soul Sense to see what he had already infused into the Powercore in question:

Charge of the Shatterlight Bear
Type: Ability
Grade: Common
Infusion Requirements for Grade Increase:
5/5 Earth Affinity
0/5 Light Affinity
5/10 Might Shards
3/3 Resilience Shards

That's thirteen shards I could redistribute, he thought. *And the Piercing Air Spear will be easy to upgrade.*

"If you want to test it, you can," Marcella told him.

"No, this will work," Callum said.

<*I agree. While you currently have Gift of the Luminous Lance, which has come in handy, it isn't an actual Weaponcore like your Tempest Fang is. Having something with range, a literal spear, something that won't fizzle away and is also able to blow your opponent off their feet, would be to our benefit. Worst case scenario: you strip it for its shards later.*>

Callum extended his hand to Marcella. "I will take the Powercore and the Light Affinity for the Life Blade of the Spring Ferret. Deal?"

Marcella extended a hand to him and Callum shook it, noticing for the first time just how long her nails were, and how she had glued jewels onto them. He gave her the core and placed the Piercing Air Spear into his chest after removing the Shatterlight Bear orb. While he did so, she produced the Light Affinity Shards, which she kept in a pouch that had been decorated with elaborate beadwork.

"Just give me a moment," Callum told the two of them once they were finished up. "I need to do something."

"We'll wait for you at the entrance," Quinn said. "And since we're going with you, I don't think you will need Princess Selene's guards. We'll let them know."

"Lucky," Marcella teased. "I wish I was important enough to have guards joining me in the city."

"You always say that," Quinn told her as they moved on. "And every time, I roll my eyes."

"One day, you'll laugh."

Callum took a seat at a stone bench and went about upgrading Inner Light by fusing a final Light Affinity Shard into its orb.

<*This is smart,*> Fen told him. <*Healing will become crucial later one.*>

Callum walked to the entrance of the Great College, traveling past the Ordelarium. <*I still am unable to heal someone else.*>

<*Not yet, but as Master Alpen said today, upgrading Powercores past the Uncommon Grade can sometimes spawn new features. If not, perhaps you'll get a Powercore later that allows you to heal someone else. Then you could sunder Inner Light and use its shards to augment your new core. Either way, this is progress. Good progress.*>

Callum met Quinn and Marcella at the entrance to the Great College and the three headed to Telluride's barn in Stadacona that they had helped rebuild.

Callum entered the barn and could instantly smell the shardcrafter's pipe tobacco. He called out his name and Telluride came from a back room with a curious look on his face. "Ah, guests," he said instead of hello.

"Quinn Vendrick and Marcella Faite, whom you met before," Callum told the shardcrafter as he gestured at the two students.

"I remember. I suppose you're here for sundering," Telluride said. "Or is this just a friendly visit?"

"I have something I figured I should bring to you first for sundering. A Demoncore."

Telluride cleared his throat. "Ah, in that case, let me get my table. It's not often that I encounter a Demoncore."

"But you can sunder it, right?" Quinn asked.

"Of course, I can, but it might not produce anything, and there can be complications. Either way, it is good to destroy. Come with me."

Telluride led them to the room where he sundered and had them all sit on cushions around his low table. Once he was in position, he examined the Shield of the Doomlight Shadecaller Armorcore, his brow furrowed. He set it in the groove on his table and pulled some shards from a pouch at his side. "Life Affinity," he told them. "It could be risky sundering this without the boost."

"That is quite the expensive boost," Marcella said.

"Life Affinity isn't cheap, but believe me, you do not want to be corrupted with Death unless you have an Aethercore that can process it," Telluride explained as he squeezed the Life Shards tightly in his hand. A glow filled the interior of the barn and settled into a halo around them. "Let's begin."

He examined the Demoncore, his eyes focusing on it as he pressed a single finger to the outer surface of the dark orb of hardened mana. It sparked, the color draining from the room as he pressed his finger even further. A sizzling sound was followed by the orb splitting into several pieces. Telluride let these shards drop onto his board, where many of them broke again. He counted them up. "Not as much as I would have hoped, but not bad. Ten Death Affinity and Nine Shadow Affinity shards. Five Vigor. As payment, I'll take the Death Affinity; you can take the others." Telluride slid the Vigor and Shadow shards over to Callum. "Was there something else you needed me to sunder?"

"Charge of the Shatterlight Bear," Callum said as he produced the glowing orb. "I was close to upgrading it, but I got something that I think will be more useful today, another Weaponcore."

"Courtesy of me," Marcella added.

"Good, good," Telluride said as he took the Powercore from Callum and examined it. "You're sure you don't want to keep it? Even if you are fully loaded out, you can always use another Powercore by removing one you have currently loaded up."

"I need the shards," Callum said.

"Then let's see what we get." Telluride rubbed the orb in his hands for a moment. He held it over one of the grooves on his shardcrafting board and the Powercore cracked, producing a number of mana crystals, which he quickly counted up. "Five Earth and three Light Affinity; five Might Shards and four Resilience Shards."

"Thanks," Callum said. "What do I owe you?"

"No need for payment. The Death Affinity from the last core will suffice. What about the two of you? Anything?" he asked Marcella and Quinn.

"None at the moment," Marcella said.

"Unless you're in the market to trade some shards," Quinn added.

Telluride cracked his knuckles. "You will have better luck at the Emporium."

"What did you want the Death Affinity Shards for, anyway?" Marcella asked him.

"I'm actually planning on destroying them, but that takes some time and concentration. The problem with Death Affinity is that the shards are often used by people dabbling with Demoncores, people like warlocks. So generally, when I get them, I destroy them."

"In that case, let me give you the four I have on me," Callum said as he got his shard pouch out again. "I would have just traded them at the Emporium."

"That's a possibility as well," Telluride told him, "and the reputable dealers will just destroy them or turn them in to the Crown."

"Hold on," Fen said as he appeared in a flash of radiance. "The Crown is collecting Death Affinity Shards?"

"Not publicly, no, but it is something they've asked for." Telluride stroked his beard for his moment and his eyes bulged. "Wait!"

"Don't you see?" Fen asked.

"I can't believe I didn't see it myself!"

"See what?" Marcella asked Telluride.

"The duke. His name was signed on the decree asking for shardcrafters to either destroy or turn in their Death Affinity Shards for compensation. Considering his son is a warlock . . ."

Fen started to pace. "I don't like the sound of any of this. We should ask the princess about it."

"She's traveling at the moment," Marcella said.

"Where to?" Callum asked, surprised she hadn't mentioned it to him.

"Actually, to your neck of the kingdom. Weatherby. She has something to do in the lands of Antiqua."

"Why didn't you tell us earlier?" Quinn asked Marcella.

"I didn't think it was important. And Her Ladyship is always up to something. I suppose we will have to wait for her to get back before we can ask what's going on. She may or may not tell us, but it's worth asking her."

"I don't see why she wouldn't tell us, or at least Callum on account they met last night," Quinn said. "She has been honest until this point."

"To your knowledge," Marcella told him. "But you must know by now that there are secrets you must maintain for the security of the kingdom, at least, I would assume this is the case."

"It is rather suspicious, the Crown collecting these shards," Telluride said as Callum handed over the Death Affinity Shards, "but at least the three of you are connected, much more than I am, anyway. Let me know what you find out, but if you get any more of these shards, you can certainly bring them to me."

Fen seemed even more troubled than usual. "The Cult of the Black Dawn is active, and warlocks are among us. It must have something to do with the Demon King and the reopening of the Demonsrealm."

"We don't know that," Quinn said. "I hate the fact that it feels like there's so little we can do about it."

Telluride leaned back. "I know it can feel that way, but there's still time, and there's always hope. These things don't happen overnight until they do." The space swelled with silence for a moment before he finally spoke again. "All you can do up to that point is prepare. And really, who knows?

Maybe none of this is as bad as it seems. Maybe all of these signs are false positives, or perhaps it has something to do with the Geshwine Empire and their legalization of Demoncores, which will lead to a war but not necessarily the Second Demonswar. Maybe this is simply the Crown trying to get ahead of it." He produced his pipe from his pocket. "It's hard to tell. Yet I can say this: however thick the fog, the truth cuts through in time."

CHAPTER 45

*What a Beast Tide leaves behind is not a battlefield but a scar, the
land eternally forced to remember its sudden fury.*

—Sir Eligus Ruthsep, Duke of Livingston

A week without a word from Princess Selene didn't seem all that
unusual. Callum busied himself with his studies and his personal
practice, and noticed that he was getting better at absorbing dormant mana.

Still not enough to fill my Mana Reserves quickly, but it's a start, he
thought one night after purposefully burning off mana in one of the training grounds to see how quickly he could recover.

With the Shadow and Earth Affinity shards he had traded for at the
Emporium, plus the remains of what he had received from Marcella, Cal-
lum upgraded Gift of Luminous Lance and his new Piercing Air Spear
Weaponcore. He went ahead and fused the Empowerment of Might and
Resilience shards into Fen's Aethercore, and the two Regeneration Shards
he had into Inner Light. He also got some money from trading at the
Emporium, which he sent back to Weatherby with the letter he'd written
for his father.

Callum also received more shards from a trip he took with Quinn and
Marcella to another of the abandoned campuses, on the hunt for a hidden
core that Marcella had grown interested in.

While they didn't find the hidden core on their excursion, Callum did
net some Air Affinity Shards to put into Fen's Aethercore. He also had
picked up a few Might and Vigor shards, which he decided to hold on to for
the time being so he could use them in his next excursion.

He didn't know when that would be, but he expected it would be soon,
especially with what Master Cruedark kept alluding to during their private
lessons, which lately had revolved around his spear Weaponcore.

"Big announcement incoming," Cruedark reminded Callum with a gruff laugh. "What can I say? I'm terrible at keeping secrets, but I guess I'm good enough to not reveal everything." His tone changed back into the firm lecturer voice that Callum was familiar with: "Remember what I told you yesterday, a spear is about reach and balance. It all starts with your grip, your foundation. I know it feels strange."

He was referring to the air at the tip of the spear that continually cycled down the shaft. It took some getting used to.

"Got it." Callum adjusted his grip around the Weaponcore and remembered another piece of advice that the combat master had given him: *Hold it too far back, and you lose control. Grip it too close to the tip, and you lose power.*

Cruedark continued: "Remember, a spear is not about brute force. It's not like my hammer. There is nuance here. And ignore the fact that your Weaponcore has magical powers. Thrust when an enemy comes in close, sweep to keep them at bay, and don't forget to redirect a strike rather than block it head on. Let's see."

He stepped aside and conjured a pair of aetherforms that he had recently started using with Callum. They reminded Callum of the constructs that the Doomlight Shadecaller had conjured.

The aetherforms came at Callum with swords made of hardened mana. He swept the legs out from beneath the one on the left and blocked a strike from the one on the right, just as Master Cruedark had taught him to do.

"Steady stance, lad. That was good, but had they been better swordsmen, the second one would have been able to deliver a strike strong enough to take you off balance. Reset and let's go again. Maintain the line on the tip of your spear. And remember, small adjustments with their hands can make all the difference."

After more training, Master Cruedark turned his attention to how to properly throw the spear. "You have the Gift of the Luminous Lance, which you have used for a ranged attack. I've seen it myself."

"I have."

"As you may have suspected, you are able to do something similar with your Weaponcore. Once a Weaponcore solidifies, the tangible nature will make the sensation different, and you will need to use your physical strength to throw it, only to then be aided by the spear's Air Affinity. Your body must align with the throw and you must not throw from your chest."

Master Cruedark conjured a spear-like weapon twice as large as Callum's. The weapon was adorned with mana claws that moved with a sentient fluidity—opening, closing, and smoothing into a form that resembled a hand miming a duck's face.

<That is quite the Weaponcore!> Fen said as Master Cruedark got into position.

"Remember what I said, Callum: your body must align with the throw. Plant your feet firmly, one foot forward, the other back for stability. With your lance and its mana-nature, you can put all of your melded farm boy strength behind it. Heh. But be careful with that. Think of it less like trying to toss a battering ram, and more like sending a paper crane flying through the air. Have you ever made a paper crane out of parchment?"

"No, but I understand what you are saying."

"Good." He demonstrated the way to toss the spear. "Focus on the arc and let momentum and the air that fuels your spear do the work." Master Cruedark finally launched his spear. Much to Callum's surprise, the claws at the tip opened and quickly spun, creating a propeller at the front that naturally increased his weapon's speed. "I can throw farther," the big man said once it landed a good fifty yards away, "but that will do for now. Your turn."

Following his directions, Callum practiced launching his spear until he got the hang of using the natural wind boost created by the weapon's affinity. He couldn't send the spear quite as far as Master Cruedark, but by the time Callum had to head to his next class, he was getting the hang of it.

"Not bad," Master Cruedark said, "you really do learn quicker than most. I think that will come in handy in the coming weeks . . ."

<There he goes again, hinting at something,> Fen said as they moved on. *<But I wonder what it could be.>*

Callum was late to his history class, which had a guest lecturer from the Great Library who went over details about the Archive of Destiny. None of the information was new to Callum, but he took notes anyway. The fact he was still technically on academic probation was always at the back of his mind.

After class, Marcella and Quinn caught up with him. Marcella was barely able to contain her excitement.

"Come out with it, already," Quinn said, who had apparently been teased by her announcement before class.

Marcella looked around. They were near a quad where students studied, not far from a portal that went to one of the training grounds. "Follow me . . ."

She moved toward the portal. Callum expected her to slip through to the other side, yet she stopped in front of it, scanned the area again to be sure no one was near, and then motioned them closer.

<*What does she want?*> Fen asked Callum.

<*No telling,*> he said as he approached Marcella.

She clasped her hands together, and some of her bracelets clanked down to her wrists. "I had breakfast with the princess again."

"She's back?" Callum asked. "I haven't seen her for a while now."

"Keep your voice down!"

"No one is around," Quinn reminded Marcella. "I mean, there are students over there, but unless their aetherbeasts have a listening skill. You know what? Let's just step through the portal." He gestured to the arched doorway, which led to one of the numerous training grounds accessible from the Great College.

"Maybe a better idea. See you two on the other side." Marcella stepped through, Callum and Quinn following suit. They appeared in an enormous space that was currently empty. Rain clouds hovered above and it was much more humid here than it had been back in New Albion. "Good. We're alone."

"So, you had breakfast," Quinn said.

"I did, and the princess has some good news for us. Especially you, Callum."

"Me?"

"No, the other farmer-turned-fighter from Weatherby."

"What about us? Start there," Quinn told her as they gathered around a statue of a tiger holding a massive sword in its mouth.

"Apparently, there is an excursion every year for royals, and they get to curate their party. This year we have Princess Selene, Draven, and Victrin. The princess, the Duke of Karna's Son, and the Duchess of Ontaria's son."

"That's who he is?" Callum asked.

Marcella stared at him blankly. "You didn't know?"

"No—"

"Seriously?"

"It's fine," Quinn told both of them. "That part doesn't matter. What matters is this: each of them gets to pick three people to go on a trip. Princess Selene has picked us."

"She did?" Quinn asked, growing excited. "Why? I mean, that's wonderful. But also, aren't these excursions—"

"Dangerous? No more dangerous than the one we went on. Or perhaps equally dangerous. But stop interrupting me. There's more. Selene has learned that there should be a hidden core in this location, one that she thought you would like, Callum. There might be a few complications . . ."

"Yes, what's the catch?" Quinn asked, slightly exasperated now. "There's always a catch."

"The excursion is in an area not far from the Badlands. Are you familiar with the Sunless Peaks?"

"I am, actually," Quinn told her. "My father was interested in setting up a location in Livingstone but decided against it due to the conditions of the region. It's in the mountains," he told Callum, "at a higher elevation than other places in the south so it is cold there."

"According to Selene, the site of the abandoned campus was recently devastated by a Beast Tide. The storm tore down most of the structures, exposed a massive sinkhole, and left a mana spring behind. But that's not the crazy part. Beneath the campus, hidden in a vast network of caverns, are the ruins of an ancient city. So first, the core. Since it was planted near this campus, it is buried somewhere down there."

"Which one?" Quinn asked her.

"Weaponcore of the Sunsteel Ram."

"Ah, I don't know what that does exactly."

"Selene claims it would allow Callum to wield a pair of rams horns as blades."

Quinn looked at Callum. "Does that sound like something you're interested in?"

"I'll certainly give it a shot!" Callum said as he imagined himself wielding two heavily curved blades. *I wonder what Master Cruedark will think about it . . .*

"Moving on," Marcella said, "as you both very well know, a Beast Tide is stronger than an aetherstorm, which I'm going to assume means that the aetherbeasts left behind are powerful, perhaps demonic in nature. According to Selene, a team of Beast Hunters has already swept through the area. They arrived as soon as the storm subsided because of its proximity to the Badlands."

"They don't want demonic aetherbeasts moving into the Geshwine Empire's territory," Quinn chimed in.

"Precisely. So we should be fine. Plus, Master Cruedark will be there, and you know they won't let the princess go without some assurances of additional protection."

"Do you know who Victrin and Draven are bringing with them?" Callum asked her.

"I don't. I would assume Draven is teaming with his groupie *nobies* he has surrounded himself with—Theogar, Petyr, and Artur. No idea about Victrin, though. He's friendly enough but often keeps to himself." She rubbed her hands together in a conspiratorial way. "Either way, exciting times ahead! We have potential treasure, we have a potential mana spring, and we have potential shards. Shards galore."

CHAPTER 46

*No map can chart the wonders and potential perils of an expedition
in the Valestra Kingdom.*

—Sir Gildrus Sarave, famed adventurer

The next morning, Callum met Quinn and Marcella at one of the smaller dining halls, where he found the pair seated outside. Marcella was drinking a hot cup of tea while Quinn was nibbling at a butter and sage nut scone. They both had large backpacks with them, which immediately drew Callum's eyes.

"What?" Marcella asked as she followed his eyes to her pack. "We might be there for two days. All you're bringing is a small shoulder bag and a cloak?"

"That's really all I need," Callum said as he took a seat.

"Look at you, the picture of restraint." Marcella set her teacup down. Callum noticed that she wasn't wearing any jewelry, or none he noticed until she shifted forward and he saw the glint of a necklace. "I've never done something like that, you know."

"Neither have I," said Quinn, who wore a thick winter jacket that had caused beads of sweat to appear on his forehead. "But this isn't our first excursion," he reminded Marcella. "We had the trip to the King's Forest. And there's also last summer."

"Last summer was hardly an excursion. We were at the beach while our parents discussed the shipment of salted fish from Aveiro to New Albion."

"How could I forget the salted fish," Quinn said. "The warehouse we stored it in still smells."

Marcella finished her tea and stood. "The princess should be ready by now."

"We'll catch up with you," Quinn said. "She's never ready on time," he told Callum after Marcella had started off. "But it's not Selene's fault. There's always some last-minute thing she has to attend or deal with. I still can't believe they're letting her go out alone."

"Sir Trindade must really trust Master Cruedark."

Quinn took another bite of his scone, chewed, and finally swallowed. "I wouldn't go that far. But who knows. It really is hard to tell what goes on behind the scenes. I wish it were as easy as sending Tuck out to do some spying for me, but they would know. There are wards that can find even the stealthiest aetherbeasts. Anyway. Let's go. Marcella has me feeling like we're going to be late."

Callum and Quinn met Marcella outside Princess Selene's suite, where they found her pacing back and forth. "I was wondering when you would come," she said. "I'm clearly early."

"She'll be ready when she's ready," Quinn assured her as he adjusted the straps of his backpack.

"How are we going to get there exactly?" Callum asked. "Is there another portal?" *Perhaps a hidden one?* he thought, recalling his last excursion with Selene.

"Sir Trindade," Quinn told Callum.

"What about him?"

"You didn't know?" Marcella asked. "Sir Trindade can open portals. He's a Convoker, although I've never seen what he's pacted with. Did you really think they'd let some random soldier protect the second-in-line to the throne?"

Callum shook his head. "I never knew what he was capable of. He doesn't have the same title as the others."

"That's because he's knighted," Quinn said. "Once a person is knighted, their other titles don't matter as much. All the 'Master Convoker Jon Albion, Core Lector, Clergo,' is academic stuff."

"Selene went over that with me," Callum said as the door to her suite opened.

The princess stepped out in armor, her golden gorget catching the light as she moved. A rich, fur-lined cloak was draped over her shoulders and her light blonde hair had been braided to cover both of her ears, the braids meeting at the back of her head. Like Callum, Princess Selene had a small bag slung over her shoulder.

"Good," she said. "You're here."

Behind her, still inside the suite, Sir Trindade continued speaking to the staff while the princess looked Callum, Quinn, and Marcella over. "This should be exciting." She turned her focus to Marcella, excitement in her eyes. "Did you tell him about the hidden core?"

"I did."

"I'm certain it's there. But finding it will be harder with the destruction from the Beast Tide."

"Do you think the others know about the core?" Callum asked her, referring to Draven and Victrin and their teams.

"Maybe not. Likely not," she said. "We all have our motives, and Draven's lie in finding some of the stranger powers he can. That and being the first to reach the mana spring."

"Draven will be looking for Demoncores," Marcella told Selene.

"Not always, but yes. Although, with Beast Masters sweeping the area, I don't know how many of those will be there. With Victrin, I can't be sure of his interest in the area. His mother, the duchess, is on the court, but I rarely see her since most of my duties involve dealing with the Geshwine Empire. Ontaria is to the west, and they have a great relationship with not only their sister cities in the lands of Antiqua, but the people that live in the smaller villages around the city. So I can't say for certain what ulterior motive he may have, if he has one. It could be hidden cores; it could be shards; it could be simply exploration and the mana spring. These ruins that were uncovered are ancient. They existed long before the Demonswar. There's really no telling."

Quinn raised a finger in the air. "We'll come back to the Draven's motives later because that's something we wanted to talk to you about." He cleared his throat and switched subjects. "Can you believe that there are hardly any history books about the time before the Demonswar? And only a few can understand the written language they used at the time. Just five hundred years ago."

"It has changed rather rapidly, but there are those on the court who are able to translate, and some aetherbeasts can help as well. One of the Soul Pythia's duties is to respond when sites like this are discovered," Princess Selene said as she watched Sir Trindade approach.

"Well? Are you all ready?" he asked in a stilted way. "And you are certain, Your Ladyship, that this is who you would like to bring with you. I can always accompany you, you know that I have a bag—"

"I will be safe. I have already assured you and Father of this multiple times. Master Cruedark is there, and we will be joined by Rhea Whitecloak."

"Who?" Callum whispered to Quinn as Princess Selene continued to argue with the soldier.

"She's one of the ones training to become a Soul Pythia," Quinn said. "You probably saw her when you did your Attribute Trials."

Callum thought back to the Attribute Trials. He vaguely remembered Mastress Lucerne being joined by two younger women, but he couldn't recall what they looked like. In truth, he had been too distracted by the trial to pay much attention to anything else.

"I believe we are ready," she told Sir Trindade in a friendly tone, yet also firm enough to let him know that the matter was no longer up for discussion.

<*It goes without saying,*> Fen told Callum, <*but I will do so anyway: if the warlock gets the urge to misbehave, we will put him in his place. Or at the very least, I will, and you can blame me.*>

Callum almost told the fox that they should try *not* to get into a fight, but then he didn't really know what would happen in another direct confrontation with Draven. *I need to be ready. I still don't know if he's the one that helped orchestrate the attack on the bar,* he thought as Sir Trindade stepped away and traced his finger through the air.

For a moment, Callum thought that Sir Trindade was about to physically draw a portal, but what happened next caught him completely off guard.

I'm falling—! He felt a sudden shift as the ground vanished beneath his feet followed by a bright flash that brought him from Princess Selene's suite to the top of a towering cliff, one that overlooked an enormous sinkhole with spires rising out of it. They were in the mountains now, where a dense cloud shrouded much of the sinkhole. The jagged landscape bore unmistakable evidence that something incredibly powerful had torn through the expanse. And there was a sudden pulsing, deep in his core that Callum's heartbeat immediately matched.

Mana was in the air.

He looked ahead to find Master Cruedark wearing a fur vest with a hood, his bare arms exposed. The students joining him were all wearing thick overcoats, the kind Quinn wore.

"It's *so* cold," said Marcella, who instantly drew her arms over her chest.

"I told you to wear something warmer," Quinn said.

"You didn't say it would be this cold!"

"Sir Trindade, please escort Marcella back to my suite where she can get one of my winter jackets," Princess Selene said without taking her gaze off Master Cruedark and the students that stood around him. "Will you be fine, Callum?"

"I'm good," he said as he shifted his cloak over his shoulders. A smirk traced across his face as he thought of his father, how Rhane had been right yet again in suggesting he buy the piece. Callum didn't exactly run hot, but the cold didn't really bother him, and the cloak worked perfectly.

"Please don't approach until I'm back with you all," Marcella said.

"Of course not," Selene told her. "We will join Master Cruedark as a unit."

Sir Trindade opened a new portal, the knight stepping out of reality alongside Marcella as if they had passed through an invisible doorway. This left Quinn, Callum, and Princess Selene across from the others, who were about forty feet away.

Callum tried not to look at them, especially the way Draven glared at him, the warlock's red eyes intensifying. Quinn nervously cracked his knuckles while Princess Selene stood as if she had all the time in the world and there weren't people waiting on her.

Fen said something, which finally caused Callum to glance ahead to the other students. <*You should be aware of who has joined Victrin and Draven.*>

"I know them," Callum whispered back to the fox.

Joining Draven Blademark were Theogar Desde, who from what Callum knew, had a pacted porcupine. There was Artur Filin, who had a double-headed dragon, and Petyr Norwood, who Callum had watched once in a sparring match. He was unsure what kind of aetherbeast Petyr had, but he knew that it gave the slightly silver-haired man a tail when he summoned it.

Victrin Righexa was joined by Lynnafer Sunsouth, who had a pacted badger. There was also Godric Rush, who had a pacted simian, and Demandra Corin, who Callum had once fought in Master Cruedark's class. He remembered her pacted koi fish, how it had used shimmering scales as an attack. He was also aware that he had beaten her, and she hadn't spoken to him ever since . . .

"Better," Marcella said as she joined them, the woman now in a coat made of rabbit fur with a hood. "Wait. Is that Demandra? Ah! Yes, it is! It would make sense that she's teamed up with Victrin. They're dating."

"They are?" Callum asked.

"She's from Aveiro, too. But we're not friends or anything." Marcella leaned in a bit closer to Callum. "She's been a noble a lot longer than I have and there may be a little jealousy there with the fact that I'm friends with you-know-who."

Really? Callum watched the blonde-haired woman shiver as they approached, her arms clutched over her chest. As if she had spotted him looking at her, Demandra raised an eyebrow at Callum, but didn't say anything as Master Cruedark rubbed his big hands together and began speaking: "Good. Everyone is here. Your goal over the next day or two is to explore the ruins below with the hope of finding the mana spring and obtaining shards and cores, if they are available. Rhea Whitecloak, you will join Princess Selene's party."

"Understood," Rhea said as she stepped over to the princess and turned back to Master Cruedark. Rhea wore a thick overcoat with a fur hood and red prayer beads that were wrapped around her left wrist.

"Good." Master Cruedark glanced past Sir Trindade, who stood anxiously awaiting a word with him. "Haldir Pyke, you will join Draven's party."

Haldir, who stood nearly seven feet tall with broad shoulders, grunted a response and stepped over to Draven's side. The two men locked eyes and nodded at each other as Master Cruedark turned to the final upperclassman who had joined him.

"Galadriel Tarly, you will join Victrin's group."

A faint smile formed on the red-haired woman's face. "Understood," she said as she clasped her hands together over a blackened chestplate.

"Your expedition teams are now complete," Master Cruedark told them. "If there are any issues, Rhea, Haldir, and Galadriel have been instructed to immediately bring me to the conflict."

"They can all create portals?" Godric asked.

"They can use portals, yes. Your safety is of the utmost importance to our institution. An excursion like this doesn't happen every year," Master Cruedark said as he stroked his beard. "The last one was . . . how long ago? It must have been three, no, four years ago. What I'm trying to say is opportunities like this don't come often. So in that regard, happy hunting." He swept the same hand toward the misty valley below. "Sir Trindade and I will be standing by, but I'm going to assume qualified candidates such as yourselves won't need our assistance. Good luck, all of you."

CHAPTER 47

A lot was lost. People thrived before the shadow of the Great Demonswar fell upon the Valestra Kingdom.

—Xander Callow, Master Channeler, Clergo,
and famed Demonswar Historian

There were many ways Callum could think of to scale down the side of the cliff, yet before he could suggest anything, Rhea conjured a portal and motioned for them to step through it.

"I really hope I get a Powercore that lets me summon a portal," said Quinn, the first to step through. He was joined by Marcella, who turned back to Callum and gestured for him to keep up.

"Where would you even go?" Marcella asked Quinn.

"Wherever I wanted to," he said as Callum joined them.

She snorted at the reply. "I was hoping for a more specific answer."

They were now somewhere in the mist below, unable to see the cliff face. Princess Selene was the last to step through the portal, but only a minute or so behind, which told him that she was likely dealing with Sir Trindade a final time.

The portal sealed and the four friends turned to Rhea.

"Is there a particular way that we should be—" Before Quinn could finish his question, Princess Selene called forth the Powercore that allowed her to track mana anomalies.

The green triangle spun a few times and then drifted down a pile of rubble, where it stopped as if it were waiting for them to follow after it.

"So we follow that," Quinn said. "I guess."

"We have a hidden core to find," Selene said as she moved on. "I don't know what exactly is down here, especially with the recent Beast Tide, but we shall soon see. Rhea?"

"I am not to interfere unless I need to, Your Ladyship," she said in a soft voice.

"In that case," Quinn said, "I have some questions about becoming a Soul Pythia."

"Later," Rhea said as they started down the rubble. They reached the bottom, where they found Princess Selene crouched and running her fingers over carefully placed cobblestone, the white and black stones arranged in a zigzag pattern that Callum had never seen before. He imagined it would have been beautiful, had it not been for the way everything seemed to drop off just beyond the sinkhole's outer rim.

Standing there for a moment, Callum could see in his mind's eye what the Beast Tide must have looked like, the swell of mana stronger than any hurricane. It also made him wonder if the people that once worked at the campus had any idea of what was beneath it. *An ancient civilization, one that existed long before the Demonswar. Did they know?*

It made him feel small.

But it also gave him a sense of destiny, an idea that he was still toying with. All of this had happened for a reason, from Fen's appearance to Callum joining the Great College to the attack by the demonic aetherbeast. Things were falling into place in a way that was perplexing on the one hand, yet, considering his namesake, made sense on the other.

It's just a matter of time . . .

"It looks like the stairs to an old reservoir," Princess Selene said after they had walked for a few minutes around the outer rim of the sinkhole. They had yet to see Victrin or Draven's expedition groups, a reminder to Callum of the size of the campus and the sinkhole.

"Is that what that is?" Quinn asked as Tuck appeared. "An old reservoir?" The Darkmoor Cat hopped down the steps as Quinn pointed to brick that had been stained green over time from moss. "Ah, that would be the roof that sat over the reservoir, and that was probably the water line. How's it looking down there, Tuck?" he called to his cat.

"It's certainly an entrance," the cat called back to him.

Fen appeared, joining the cat at the base of the stairs.

Marcella exchanged glances with Princess Selene. "Should I send Harold out just to see where the others are?"

"No, I'm not really interested in what they are doing at the moment."

"Makes sense." Marcella carefully took the stairs down, followed by the princess, and then Callum. Rhea stayed at the back, as she had before, quiet as they followed Selene's green triangle deeper into the ancient reservoir. They reached the end, which was partially covered by the roof above.

Callum all but expected to be forced to get down onto his stomach and crawl on.

A sudden gust of wind blew past him, which caused Rhea to come forward. She summoned a trio of floating orbs that glowed brightly. They pressed forward into the darkness, revealing a great pit below.

<The wind is coming from down there, it seems.>

<Apparently so.> Callum thought back to Fen. He couldn't tell how deep it went, but the drop in temperature and the echo of air made it feel vast and hollow.

"Stay alert," Princess Selene said, interrupting a conversation between Marcella and Quinn.

"Sorry," Quinn said.

As they moved deeper into the opening, their paths continued to be lit by the orbs that Rhea had created, which settled over their heads. Ahead, Fen and Tuck pressed on, their silhouettes outlined by shifting glimmers of mana.

"That's strange," Quinn said once they came across some basements from the abandoned campus that seemed to have punched through the ceiling above their heads. There were wooden boxes and boxes of uniforms, some of the clothes scattered about.

"Wait!" Tuck jumped to the side, Fen doing the same as the clothing itself came alive. The uniforms, seven in total, twisted quickly, flinging the ends of their clothes like they were weapons.

"Aetherwisps!" Princess Selene said as she quickly melded with Ecaris, her pacted bear.

Beside her, Marcella did the same with Harold, which gave her a set of wings and beak-like protrusion on her face made entirely of mana. "Let's see how they respond to this!" She sent one of her wings out and fired sharp feathers at the seven dancing uniforms.

Callum drew his Tempest Fang, his power strengthened once Fen returned and melded with him. He exploded toward the aetherwisps, Callum noticing an instant increase in his speed and power. His wind blade was strong enough to strike one of the uniforms down, where Tuck made quick work of it, the pacted cat clawing it to shreds. A shard flew toward Quinn for this.

Whoever gets the kill, gets the shards! Callum thought, which checked out with his experience with the Gravewind Hawk.

With this in mind, he moved on to the next aetherwisp, easily cutting it down. He spun into another, his strike amplified to the point that the wind blew the aetherwisp backward, killing it instantly and sending a crystal toward him.

Empowerment of Mind Shard

They finished the rest of the aetherwisps and Fen returned to Callum.

<That would explain what we once fought in those ruins, that suit of armor. I don't recall there being such a thing when I was pacted with the Demonslayer.>

Tuck strutted over to Quinn. The Darkmoor Cat sat, his tail lashing against the ground. "Aetherwisps are so fun to chase."

"You would say that," Marcella said as she stepped toward a naturally formed corridor that seemed to be the only viable path out of the sunken room. "Come on, we have more to explore."

Princess Selene caught up with Callum a few minutes later, after they passed under a strange archway, the orbs over their head lighting the way. "Fascinating location, isn't it?" she asked.

"Definitely."

"It beats trudging through water like last time."

"That wasn't so bad," he joked.

"I'm glad I didn't catch a cold."

"It's an entirely different world down here. That's for sure," Callum told her as the passage around them narrowed.

"It is. I've explored other caves in this region before, with a Beast Master from Echospire."

"You have?"

A light smile appeared on her face. "As you know, I try to sneak out when I can. Wait." She paused in front of a stone that Callum realized was shaped like a pillar. The orb of light over his head allowed him to see the intricately carved details on the stone, much of which had started to crumble away.

Rhea approached, her sudden appearance nearly startling Callum. She had been so quiet that he had forgotten she was there. "May I, princess?" she asked as Marcella and Quinn continued walking, the two alternating between a discussion and an argument about the origins of a New Albion delicacy.

"By all means," the princess told her.

A mouse with a long tail formed in Rhea's open palm. It scurried up her arm and stopped on her shoulder. It was faint, but Callum could see a slight radiance coming from the mouse as it focused on the old stone pillar.

"What can you tell me about it," Rhea said, her face twitching. For a brief second, it seemed the whiskers appeared on her cheeks. Callum also was certain that Rhea's face had morphed and resettled, her eyes widening and dimming, her brows arching and nose growing smaller before it all snapped back to her normal features as the mouse started squeaking.

<Her pacted mouse seems to be communicating with her through . . . squeaks,> Fen said. *<It does not speak the common tongue?>*

Callum noticed the squeaks and the way they made Rhea's face shift.

Is the mouse . . . controlling her? No, it's showing her something, he thought as her pupils grew in size.

The mouse vanished and Rhea turned to Princess Selene. "Your Lady-ship. May I?"

"Please, do. And you may call me Selene."

"I am still a Soul Pythia in practice, one who will specialize in Memo-rycore creation, which means I do not yet have full access to the World Ledger. I can tell you this, however, based on the visions Jeronymo gave me: The settlement beyond was once the seat of a mountain kingdom that has been erased from much of the record. It was destroyed by a great snow-storm with an aetheric origin. Those that remained moved into a deep cav-ern and rebuilt their society here, but they were unable to sustain it."

Princess Selene considered Rhea's words for a moment: "I see. Once we return to the Great College, report your findings to Mastress Lucerne so it can be added to the World Ledger. I will make sure that the Crown sponsors a trip for you, Auralia, Mastress Lucerne, the College's top historians, and protection. It is important that the current Soul Pythia and her two trainees record what we can from this discovery."

"Hey!" Marcella called to them, her voice echoing through the narrow passageway. "Are you all coming? You're going to want to see this . . ."

Callum didn't know what to make of the sight once they traveled through a passageway that opened onto a ledge overlooking the ruins of an ancient civilization, the buildings crafted from thick stone, much of it intact. At first, he wondered how he could see so clearly in the cavern's depths. But then he glanced up and realized that the snow and ice from the ground above refracted sunlight through cracks casting a pale, ethereal glow over the abandoned city.

"There," Quinn said.

It was at that point that Callum spotted an aetherbeast watching them from what was left of one of the ancient rooftops. He squinted, trying to take in its features. "A Subterranean Panther," Rhea said. As Callum turned back to her, he noticed the mouse on her shoulder again. "This will prove challenging for the three of you."

"We have to figure out a way down first," Princess Selene said as her tri-angular beacon floated onward, directly toward the panther. Much to their surprise, the beacon's movement startled the aetherbeast beyond, causing it to slip away into the ruins.

"I guess it's shy," Marcella said.

Selene called her green triangle back to her. "We'll deal with the aether-beast first and then continue our search for the hidden core. Rhea?"

"Yes?"

"Once we reach the ruins, gather what information you can. While we search for the panther."

"As you wish."

CHAPTER 48

Aetherwisps are tricksters of the unseen until they anchor themselves to an object. Mind where you sit, lads!

—Master Weaver Octavious Reyalds, Archon of Morefell

Tuck appeared next to Quinn and started searching for a way down the cliff. "If you all weren't human, this would be much easier," the cat told them, his tail hiked up in the air.

Marcella produced a pair of wings, turned to them, and fell backward off the edge. She glided up a few moments later before landing in the ruins below.

Quinn rolled his eyes. "If I wanted to, I could meld and basically hop down myself."

"Could you?" Selene asked.

"I could!"

"I'd like to see that."

Tuck, who had been searching along the edge of the cliff, looked back to them. "No need for that. There's a path here. It is a bit narrow, but I'm sure you'll be able to handle it." The Darkmoor Cat hopped down to it, his mana-filled form providing just enough light for them to see where to go next. The orbs that Rhea had created also lit the space as they made their way down. Finally, they reached Marcella at the ancient settlement.

"This place is amazing," Selene said as she looked up at a set of stairs carved into the stone, one surrounded by a pair of buildings that still had paint on them.

"It was all preserved," Callum said as Fen appeared. The fox moved to the top of the stairs and used his vantage point to jump to one of the roofs. Tuck did the same; rather than search around like Fen, the cat approached the edge of the roof, sat, and looked down at them.

"Where would you like to set-up?" Princess Selene asked Rhea.

"I could do so here or at the top of the stairs. Any space should be fine, and if I can sit here longer, it will give the three of you time to explore. There is certainly activity in the area."

"I can sense it as well."

Upon hearing this, Callum quieted and tried to see if he could notice any difference in his surroundings. It may have been stronger had it not been for the distraction that came with being in a party of several people. *It makes sense why Rhea would want to stay behind*, he thought as he looked back to the top of the stairs to see Fen racing down toward him. "What—?"

"Aetherwhisps incoming!" The fox shouted as he leaped into Callum.

Callum took a step back, surprised at Fen's intensity.

But then he heard the rumbling at the top of the stairs, the sound of stone scraping on stone.

Rather than climb to the top, Marcella jumped, her melded wings easily bringing her to the roof. By the time the others joined, Princess Selene now armed with her trident Weaponcore, Marcella had already engaged a couple dozen terracotta planter pots.

"Try not to destroy them all!" Selene said.

"How?" Marcella cried back. "They're attacking us!"

Tuck jumped from the rooftop and took down the first enchanted pot. He melded back with Quinn, who produced a pair of claws and sprouted a mana tail that Callum hadn't seen before. *Why didn't he use that when we fought in Master Cruedark's class?* It soon dawned on Callum as he saw Quinn rush ahead that perhaps his friend had been going easy on him. Quinn could fight. Or at the very least, Quinn could fight pots.

The hefty young man jumped into the fray with such alacrity that Callum actually stepped to the side to watch him smash pot after pot. It was only after Fen shouted for him to get in there that Callum joined the battle.

The first pot shattered easily with a wind attack. Near him, Princess Selene melded with her bear and charged ahead on all fours, bounced off the side of an ancient wall, and landed in the middle of the pot army. She performed a spin attack that broke at least six of them.

They just keep coming! Callum thought as he destroyed another pair of pots and received an Empowerment of Deftness Shard. As his friends grappled with the pots, Callum scanned the buildings and noticed that many of the enemies were coming from an opening that was large enough for a horse to fit through.

"Let's investigate," he told Fen as he too dropped to all fours and bolted toward the large doorway. He jumped over a pot, landed behind it, and simply grabbed it from behind and tossed it into another pot. Ahead, Callum saw that shelving with more pots, which came alive, jumped to the ground, and hobbled toward the opening.

He stepped aside and charged up Radiant Inferno, intent on destroying rows upon rows of pots with a single blast.

<Let's see how many we can get!> Fen said once he understood what Callum was doing.

"That's the plan!" Callum focused everything he could into a sphere of mana, which hit the ground near the pots, swelled and exploded.

Empowerment of Regeneration Shard
Empowerment of Deftness Shard
Empowerment of Deftness Shard
Empowerment of Mind Shard
Light Affinity Shard
Fire Affinity Shard
Fire Affinity Shard
Earth Affinity Shard
Earth Affinity Shard
Death Affinity Shard

Fen appeared and quickly investigated what was left of the pots. "Not bad for a single attack. Not bad at all."

CHAPTER 49

Not only am I asking you if it is possible, I'm telling you that it is. Possession by an aetherbeast is a paradoxical state pairing a surge of unimaginable power with a rapid erosion of self, a soul rewritten, tarnished.

—Combat Master Convoker Faylen Smigg

As Callum stood in the building once filled with pots, the shattering sounds outside faded. *Looks like they've finished up*, he thought, crouching to examine one of the shards—a terracotta piece etched with ancient script. He understood now why Princess Selene wanted to preserve as much as possible.

"So that was you," Marcella said, stepping into the workshop. Her eyes scanned the broken shelving. "There were a lot."

"There were."

"Get a load of shards?"

"I did."

"Nice. Wait, what's that?" Marcella moved to investigate an opening in the far wall. She stuck her head into the opening, her curiosity quickly turning to awe. "Hey, there's a passage leading out the back of the building to . . . Whoa. I wasn't expecting this. You have got to see this."

Callum hurried over and joined her, stepping cautiously into the passage. Beyond it lay an inner courtyard, the space covered in moss that clung to the cracked stone walls. At its center stood a crumbled fountain, its once-ornate carvings weathered by time. Around the fountain were several partially mummified bodies, their desiccated forms frozen in various poses of reverence. Some knelt, others reached toward the fountain as if pleading or worshiping in their final moments.

Fen slipped past Callum, starting his own investigation. "Strange."

"So that's what happened," Quinn said as he came upon the scene. "Good thinking. You destroyed the source of the aetherwisps."

"That wasn't the plan," Callum told him, "but it seemed to work."

"Sometimes, that's all that matters," Marcella said.

Princess Selene emerged into the courtyard, her attention quickly drawn to the bodies surrounding the fountain. "Perhaps a sacrificial ritual?"

"Something like that," Quinn replied.

"I wonder if we'll find more of this." Selene glanced around. "There don't seem to be any cores here, at least not visible. Let me try something."

She accessed her beacon, the green triangle hovering for a moment before turning back toward the room they'd just come from.

"We should keep following it, but cautiously. It seemed to spook the panther."

"And Rhea?" Marcella asked.

"She's at the bottom of the stairs trying to glean anything she can from the area. We won't venture too far from her. If we stay on the main path, we can simply turn back to reach her." Selene stopped under an arched entrance. "Shall we?"

The four left the courtyard by way of the workshop entrance, heading deeper into the maze of closely packed buildings where more aetherwisps floated about, though not nearly as many as earlier. They quickly dealt with the wisps and explored what appeared to be a bathhouse, its layout reminding Callum of the bathhouse in Weatherby.

"Are we really going to camp down here tonight?" Quinn asked as they entered their fifth courtyard filled with partially mummified bodies.

"Ghosts aren't real," Marcella said.

"I didn't say they were. It's just creepy."

"We'll find a spot outside the city," Selene assured him. "Perhaps near the cliff we entered from. I'm surprised we haven't run into the others—this place is enormous."

"I can always send Harold up," Marcella offered.

"Later," Selene said. "If we find them, we may have to compete—especially with Draven's group. He's very competitive. I'm not as familiar with Victrin or his motives."

"He's always been nice to me," Callum added.

"His life hasn't been easy," Selene replied as they reached a town square. There were no bodies here, but debris from a landslide littered the area, and several statues lay crushed by massive stones. "Duchess Righexa of Ontaria had several suitors who caused trouble for their house when Victrin was younger. From what I've been told—"

The scream that interrupted her wasn't something Callum heard; it was something he *felt*, as if the ground itself had shrieked, the sound reverberating through his bones. They exchanged glances as the orbs of light above them vanished.

"Rhea," Quinn said hurriedly.

"Let's go!" Callum shouted, already sprinting toward her.

The group melded and took off together in the direction of Rhea's last known location. They rushed into the gloom below, where they found the Subterranean Panther, its sleek, form crouched low and coiled with latent menace. Its yellow eyes gleamed in the dim light as it turned toward them, an unsettling intelligence burning in its gaze.

The beast loomed protectively near Rhea, as though guarding its prize. Her transformation was a chilling sight to behold. The woman stood motionless, her fists clenched tightly at her sides, head bowed, hair obscuring her face. Manabound spider legs had erupted from her back, their glossy, segmented lengths curling over her shoulders and wrapping around her torso in a grotesque, intricate Armorcore. The shimmering carapace seemed alive, pulsing faintly with mana as it hugged her body.

Jagged blade extensions jutted from her knuckles, sharp and lethal, glinting menacingly in the faint light as her hands twitched with restrained violence.

Princess Selene was the first to break the silence, her voice steady but urgent. "Callum, you and I will handle Rhea. Quinn, Marcella—focus on the panther. It's controlling her. If we take it down, we save her! If not . . ."

She trailed off, leaving unspoken the truth hanging heavy in the air. The stakes were clear: they had to stop the panther before its hold on Rhea became permanent—or worse.

But didn't Beast Masters clear this area? Callum thought as the panther melted into the shadows, leaving Rhea poised to strike.

<*That's how it avoided detection!*> Fen said.

"Same plan," Selene said, "Quinn, can you track the panther?"

"Yes, *we* can," he replied, his eyes turning entirely black. "Come on, Marcella!"

Following Quinn, Marcella flew over Rhea, who barely flinched as she stood ready to confront Callum and Selene.

With a quick breath out Callum summoned his Tempest Fang only to be swept aside by a spiral of mana before his Armorcore could react. He slammed into an ancient wall, vines of light tightening around his armor. *They're not just holding me back—they're absorbing my mana!*

Selene engaged Rhea with her trident as Callum focused on breaking free. *What if I try this? It won't work at full power, but it should be enough.* He used Roots of the Willow Aethertree.

Thick roots of light erupted from the ground, ensnaring Rhea. She responded by summoning more manabound spider legs, which lifted her off the ground.

Callum summoned his spear and rushed forward, using the weapon's reach to his advantage.

"Break her Armorcore!" Selene shouted.

"Got it!" he yelled back.

The enhanced speed from his meldform made it easy for Callum to dodge a spider leg and jab his spear into Rhea's chest. Her Armorcore fizzled, but she retaliated with a blast of mana that split into three bolts. One exploded near Callum, knocking him off balance and tossing him through a slab of brittle wood straight into an old cellar.

Callum was back on his feet in seconds, checking his Mana Reserves to find they were listed as Steady. He looked up at the top of the cellar.

<We can make it!>

Callum jumped, grabbed the edge, and pulled himself back up. Selene was striking Rhea repeatedly, her form jarring Callum enough that he nearly stumbled back into the cellar.

What the hell? he thought, struggling to comprehend what Selene had become. She had melded with Ecaris in a way he hadn't seen before—her form still visible, but her movements were sharper, almost predatory. This wasn't just a surface fusion or a coat of glowing mana. It had solidified—her body and Ecaris's essence converging into something entirely new.

She wasn't channeling power anymore. She was the power.

Callum couldn't make sense of it—the raw aggression, the speed, the way she dismantled Rhea's defenses and shattered her Armorcore without hesitation. Now she stood over Rhea's collapsed form, breath steaming in the cold air, her expression burning with fury. "Selene—?" Callum asked.

She looked at him, her eyes flashing with burning fury that vanished almost as quickly as it had appeared. Selene stumbled to the side, shoulders heaving as she fought to catch her breath.

Beside her, Rhea moved unnaturally. The Weaponcore blades pressed from her knuckles again, and she stood as if being manipulated by an invisible force.

"No!" Callum surged forward and skidded to a halt, stepping aside as both Selene and Rhea collapsed.

He stood there, staring at the two fallen bodies, unsure what to do as Fen rattled off ideas.

<Maybe she was possessed again? Maybe the panther did something through Rhea? Or the princess used an attack we didn't know about?>

Callum tuned Fen out and crouched in front of Selene. She lay on her side, blinking slowly as she reached a hand to him.

"Are you alright?" he whispered.

"Callum Stross . . ." Her voice was barely audible as she squeezed his hand. "I think . . ."

Marcella landed, startling Callum. "And we're back. One Subterranean Panther down. Wait. What happened to the princess?"

"I don't know. She—"

"I'm fine," Selene said abruptly, pushing herself to her knees as if nothing had happened. She locked eyes with Callum. "Don't worry about me. Let's check on Rhea."

Quinn arrived, slightly out of breath. "That was intense. But it dropped a good Powercore—Shadowmeld of the Subterranean Panther. I can use this, you know. Shadow Affinity."

"I already told you it was yours," Marcella said. She joined Selene in helping Rhea up. The Soul Pythia–in-training looked dazed, her jaw repeatedly dropping open until Marcella gently corrected it.

"Anyone know what's wrong with her?"

"Her Mana Reserves were stripped by the panther," Selene said. "I've seen something like this before."

"Do you think she's Hollowing?" Quinn asked. "I hope not!"

"She's close," Selene replied. "She needs to recharge and then . . ." Her expression hardened. "We might need to take her back to Master Cruedark. That would be the responsible thing to do."

"It would," Marcella agreed. "But there's a hidden core we need to find, and the mana spring too, so . . ."

"So?" Quinn prompted. "What are you suggesting?"

"We keep going," Callum said, catching something in Selene's expression. "And we don't leave Rhea behind again. She can return later with Mastress Lucerne to further study this place."

"Agreed," Selene said.

"Are you serious?" Quinn asked. "You want to continue on after something like this. We should at least camp for the night."

"If we do that, we may lose valuable time," Callum said.

"I agree," Marcella added. "We could use Life Affinity."

"You have shards?" Quinn asked.

"I have one," Callum said.

"Good. Give it to her," Marcella instructed. "And if things get bad, I can fly out and get Master Cruedark and Sir Trindade." She motioned toward the ceiling above them, where light filtered through the ice in shades of blue.

"And circle back to the cliff he's on?" Quinn asked, catching on.

"Exactly. I would send Harold to look for the mana spring, but he might attract the attention of the others."

"So we stay," Quinn said, coming to grips with it.

"We stay," Callum told him.

"We can vote if you want," Selene offered.

"Not necessary," Rhea rasped. "And I'm sorry. It's my fault for letting the influence overcome me. I can't portal us back yet, but if we stay, I can cycle mana and stay out of the fight. The shard will help. Thank you, Callum. Thanks to all of you for coming to my aid. This is . . . embarrassing."

"Not a problem," he said, handing her the shard.

"And don't be embarrassed," Quinn said. "I've done way worse, and I'd do way worse to find a mana spring. I think that made sense."

Rhea offered him a crooked smile. "The mana spring is one of the main reasons I joined this excursion, you know. It's why others like me joined as well."

"I assumed as much," said Selene. "A mana spring left behind by a Beast Tide could be astronomically powerful."

Callum looked ahead at the ancient ruins. "Then let's find the mana spring before the others do. If the Powercore is along the way, we'll grab that too."

CHAPTER 50

Mana has a way of reflecting the soul of its wielder in the same way a person's actions reveal their true character. It is not the power that can corrupt, but the intent.

—Hesa Sharron, Duchess of Ridgebarrow and famed orator

Callum's group moved on once Rhea had recovered enough to create the orbs of light again. The Soul Pythia–in-training remained at the back of the group, while Princess Selene and Callum took the lead. "Be ready to use some Attribute Shards," the princess reminded them.

I'd better see what I have . . . Callum checked his inventory: two Mind and Vigor shards, three Deftness and Might shards, and one Regeneration Shard. *It'd be nice to have Resilience Shards if we're going to pull an all-nighter . . .* he thought as Quinn and Marcella discussed their own supplies. Callum moved a Might, a Vigor, and a Deftness shard to within easy reach, just in case he needed quick access.

<Smart,> Fen told him. <*That will give us an edge in most fights.*>

"Where should we go now?" Quinn asked as they came to the bottom of a hill, where they found a half-buried anchor stone. Callum stepped over and examined the thick iron ring bolted in the stone's center and its reddish-brown surface. Despite the decay, the stone hinted at its former use as a tethering point for livestock.

Selene accessed her beacon again. The green triangle hovered before her, dimmed, then brightened as it began to move forward.

"Will it lead us to the mana spring or to the hidden Powercore?" Marcella asked.

"It doesn't really know the difference," Selene replied. "It just gravitates toward power."

"So it could be anything," Marcella said as the triangle led them toward a cobblestone road covered in dust and flanked by towering walls—the kind of walls Callum expected to find outside a fort.

"Anything, yes. But whatever it is will be powerful."

Later, as they moved onto a new path, Fen and Tuck unmelded and climbed to the rooftops.

"Let us know if you see any flashes of mana," Selene told them.

"Certainly," Fen replied as Tuck hopped onto a balcony and wove through the crumbled stone balusters.

After traveling around a sunken hearth, the group reached another courtyard, this one free of mummified bodies. They paused for a moment and Rhea took a seat on the fountain's ledge.

"It's getting darker," Quinn said once everyone had settled.

"That's how night works," Marcella quipped.

"Funny," he retorted before turning to Rhea. "I know I won't be invited on the expedition, but I'd love to see what's uncovered when this place is fully explored. Do you think the city's as big as New Albion?"

"Maybe," Rhea replied. "Depending on where you're going, it can take days to cross New Albion because of all the smaller towns it has annexed. Maybe that's what happened here."

Fen reappeared. "We've found something ahead."

"What is it?" asked Callum, who had been tracing his hand over what looked like a weathered obelisk.

"Imp-like in nature but smaller, floating, with tentacles. A lesser aether-beast, for certain."

"It sounds like a tendriling," Rhea said.

"I've seen one before," Selene added, calling her beacon back. The green triangle of mana fizzled away. "They're dangerous in numbers. If you saw one, there are more. We'll need to find their hive."

"Jeronymo can help with that," Rhea offered, summoning her mouse. It wiggled its nose and darted off.

Callum instinctively glanced at Tuck, who sat near Fen licking his paw. He half expected the pacted cat to chase the mouse but was reminded that these creatures weren't like other animals. *Not like the cats on my family farm*, he thought.

"How should we handle the tendrilings in the meantime?" Marcella asked. "Until we find their hive, I mean."

"They're fast and hard to catch. If you have a ranged Weaponcore," Rhea said, "or a projectile Powercore, you might be able to hit them."

Radiant Claws and Zephyr Strike should work, Callum thought as he waited for Jeronymo to return. The pacted mouse emerged from a hole Callum hadn't noticed and sat in front of Rhea. She twitched slightly as the mouse relayed its findings.

"He says the hive isn't far—over a fence and in a ditch. Most of the tendrilings are on the other side of the fence for now."

"We'll tackle the ones already out, then move onto the hive," Selene decided.

"If you do that, the hive might alert others in the area," Rhea warned. "They have a way, you know."

"We split up?" Callum suggested. "Two of us take the tendrilings, while the others hit the hive."

"Will we be able to see each other?" Quinn asked. "I don't want another situation like last time."

Rhea consulted Jeronymo again. "We'll be much closer," she assured him.

"In that case, who wants hive duty?" Marcella asked.

"I'm best suited for the tendrilings," Callum said.

"Same," Selene agreed.

"Same teams as last time, then," Marcella concluded. "Jeronymo, lead the way."

"And make it a path humans can actually follow," Quinn added.

The mouse looked to Rhea for confirmation before setting off.

"That's our cue," Marcella said.

Fen melded with Callum, Tuck doing the same with Quinn, as they squeezed through a partially open door. The group passed through an ancient granary with massive clay containers and nearly petrified wooden barrels, everything with a thick layer of dust on it. A stepladder led them to a platform that exited onto a raised ledge, where faint beams of opaque light came through the cracks, giving the space an eerie stillness. Peeking over the wall, they finally spotted the tendrilings.

The creatures were unlike any aetherbeast Callum had seen before—tentacles three times the length of their jagged, spherical bodies, anchored by something resembling a slitted eye.

"Let's distract them," Selene told Callum. "We'll join the rest of you once we finish."

"Remember," Rhea warned, "they're fast. Much faster than you might expect. Some can even burrow into the ground and ambush you. Be careful when you approach."

Callum and Selene slipped over the wall and dropped to the ground below. Selene immediately summoned her Armorcore, and Callum followed with Brightflame Falcon. His senses seemed to sharpen as they crept along the ancient stone wall, Selene leading the way.

They reached a natural opening and Selene peered around the edge.

Zap!

A bolt of mana struck the brick, sending dust into the air. It was all the prompting they needed to move quickly through the opening. They rushed the group of tendrilings, Callum using a wind strike as he'd planned. His first attack splattered one of the aetherbeasts, causing the others to swarm toward him.

Dropping to all fours as Fen took control, Callum lunged forward and delivered a powerful strike, his manabound claws shredding a tendriling glowing with mana. He pivoted, expecting to face another, but was instead struck in the face.

A tendriling wrapped its tentacles around Callum's head, driving him backward into the ground before his Armorcore could react.

He pried the aetherbeast off, but not before feeling a burning sensation that left him gasping, sucking in the air that had been stolen from his lungs. *I can't let that happen again!* he thought, glancing at Selene as she dispatched another tendriling with her trident. *Did she see that?* Callum scrambled to his feet and swallowed a wave of embarrassment. *Maybe not.*

Summoning his wind sword, he surged back into the fight, killing another tendriling that dropped an Attribute Shard.

Empowerment of Resilience Shard

A larger tendriling lunged at Selene, who had shifted into her bear form. She crushed two of the creatures by grabbing hold of the larger one and smashing it onto the smaller. Callum took advantage of the opening, using his Piercing Air Spear to strike a tendriling that was farther away. He felt a surge of satisfaction as the wind from his attack took out another.

"Just a few more!" Selene called.

One tendriling flew dangerously close to Callum's face, but he swatted it away and stomped on it.

Empowerment of Regeneration Shard

Not bad!

Selene finished another tendriling off by driving her trident into the ground, where she intercepted it as it tried to burrow and attack her from below. The final tendriling moved to attack, but Callum brought it down with a lethal funnel of wind, leaving behind a trace of corrupted mana.

"Ecaris, Fen, please clean up the corruption," Selene instructed.

Her pacted bear shifted away from her as Fen unmelded from Callum, his tail flickering with light.

"That was a good exercise in dealing with airborne opponents," Fen remarked. "The Great College could benefit from a scenario like that."

"We'll face much more at the College," Selene assured him. "I guarantee it."

"I expect nothing less from the institution founded by the Demonslayer," Fen replied, his head held high as he joined Ecaris.

Selene stepped up beside Callum. "Good work back there."

"Thanks," he said, glad she hadn't noticed how the tendriling had latched onto his face. *Or if she did, she's not mentioning it.*

The princess glanced toward the cavernous ceiling, where the light filtering through frozen veins of ice was rapidly dimming as day turned to night. "And Quinn was right earlier—it'll be night soon."

"At least we have Rhea's orbs of light."

"That will certainly help."

A loud explosion echoed through the cavern, sending bricks from the ancient wall tumbling to the ground. Callum and Selene turned toward the direction Quinn, Marcella, and Rhea had taken, just in time to see a plume of smoke and hear a startled yelp.

Callum's heart raced and, without hesitation, he took off toward the explosion.

CHAPTER 51

Dormant mana drifts like a formless wind toward the edge of existence, aimless as driftwood on a foreign shore.

—Kay Fife, poet

Callum and Selene used their meldforms to clear the ancient wall, where they found Marcella bent over laughing while Quinn's cat riffled through the smoke.

"There's nothing left of the hive, Tuck," Marcella told the cat. "You can stop now."

"It's still worth looking," Tuck replied. "And I will stop when I feel it's appropriate!"

"What was that explosion?" Selene asked Rhea, who stood a few feet away, her hands nervously clasped behind her back.

"My apologies, Your Ladyship."

"Selene."

"Right, Selene. It was an explosion that I should have anticipated. There was mana in the hive, and hitting it triggered . . . well, you heard it. As I said, the calamity is my fault. I have experienced something familiar before and—"

"Could there have been another way?"

"Yes," Rhea said hurriedly. "And I would have gladly interfered if it would have prevented the explosion."

"Maybe it alerted the others," Callum said. "That was loud."

"Yes," Quinn said, a troubled look on his face. "It could alert other things as well. Are anyone else's ears still ringing?"

"Mine are," Marcella said, "but it wasn't *that* loud."

"I beg your pardon—"

"Have you been to a Coral Celebration in Aveiro? No? Fireworks all night, song and dance, more alcohol than you can imagine. You can't escape it, especially the fireworks. It sounds like that," she said, turning her focus to Selene. "Where to now?"

Selene accessed her beacon, the green triangle of light spinning for a moment before settling, tilting south and then slightly west. "We keep going. It will lead us somewhere, and Quinn is right—we might have attracted unwanted company with that explosion."

Tuck popped out of the smoke and sat. "Shall we?"

"He acts like he's in charge," Marcella said to Quinn as they moved on.

"He is a cat, you know . . ." Quinn told her.

The group came to an area where massive slabs of stone had fallen, with rock pillars extending all the way to the surface above. Tuck and Fen climbed one of the rocks to investigate, while the others shared a quick meal of dried fruit and meat that Rhea had brought along.

"I know some of you have Sustenance cores," she said, "but real food is always nice."

"I couldn't agree more," Quinn told Rhea with his mouth full. He quickly swallowed, embarrassment washing over him. "And your Mana Reserves? How are you feeling?"

"Better. The Life Affinity and Marcella's powers helped. I should be portal-ready soon," Rhea said. She locked eyes with Selene and looked away. "Just in case."

As he chewed a piece of dried meat, Callum glanced up at the natural opening above. Snow swirled, and starlight sparkled beyond. *I wonder what Tuck and Fen are getting into up there . . .* The scale of the sinkhole still took him by surprise as he turned back toward the center of the ancient settlement, unable to see much beyond another wall.

He refocused on Selene's beacon, which hovered near one of the large slabs of stone. There was an opening they could travel through, their next logical path forward.

He scanned for any signs of Draven's or Victrin's groups. Callum even tried closing his eyes, attempting to tune in to the dormant mana in the air. *If I could ever actually do anything like that,* he thought. He couldn't discern any differences beyond the constant pull of the mana spring nearby until . . .

Can the others not feel it?

Callum's heart quaked. He glanced at Selene, who was looking up to where Fen and Tuck had gone. As usual, Marcella and Quinn were too busy talking to notice, and Rhea had joined their conversation about the southern part of the Valestra Kingdom—a frequent topic of conversation for Marcella.

Callum stepped over to Selene. "I think we're close. We're close, right?"

She turned to him. "What do you mean?"

"I don't know. It feels stronger here—the pull of mana. I remember it from the last mana spring in the King—I mean—your father's forest."

Selene grabbed Callum's wrist, startling him. She pulled him away from the others, who continued talking, oblivious to what she was doing. "Good work." Selene released his wrist, focused her breath, and slowed her breathing. "And you're right. It's faint. I'm surprised you can feel that."

"I was trying to sense for the others when it came to me," Callum said.

"I would say it's our destiny to find the mana spring first but things don't always work that way. Everyone!" she called out. "We should keep moving. Callum and I both think we're close."

"To the Weaponcore or the spring?" Quinn asked.

"Likely the mana spring, but perhaps the Weaponcore too. I've spent considerable time with Beast Hunters. If they cleared this area—which they most certainly did—they would have found the Weaponcore. My guess is they moved it closer to the mana spring as an additional bonus for whoever finds it first."

"You really think so?" Rhea asked Selene.

"I'm certain of it. Consider it an added incentive. We'll continue following my beacon, and we should probably pick up our pace. Just because we can't hear the others doesn't mean they aren't near. In fact . . ."

"We're being too loud, aren't we?" Quinn asked.

"I didn't want to say it," Selene replied, "but yes. Less conversation—we are so close. To what? I don't know. But to something."

"Then back into the unknown it is," Marcella said, as Fen and Tuck returned.

They passed under rocks that had fallen on top of one another, forcing them to duck their heads down. The passage grew tighter, the uneven arrangement of stones creating a narrow, jagged archway, their footsteps echoing faintly in the confined space.

Quinn wasn't the only one who gasped when they pressed out of the other side. Marcella brought a hand to her mouth, while Rhea and Selene stared in wonder for a moment.

A bridge made of stone? Callum thought as he looked out at the expanse. *Impossible.*

The landslide that destroyed most of the abandoned campus above had produced a massive slab of stone, jagged and uneven, which formed a treacherous path across an underground canyon. The stone pathway was weathered smooth in some places, rough and jagged in others, creating tripping hazards. The canyon below swallowed light and sound as the wind howled through the abyss, and a deep cold rose from its depths, all of it a testament to nature's chaotic will.

How deep does the chasm go? Callum thought as he scanned the darkness.

"This must be why we can't sense the mana spring," Selene said as she recalled her beacon, which seemed to be confused.

"Ah, I get it," Quinn said. "There's nothing to extend the mana influence aside from this . . . rock bridge? How would you describe this?"

"I would describe it as a good reason to summon Harold," Marcella said, calling upon her pacted heron. The graceful bird appeared, hopping onto the stone bridge as light swirled around his tail feathers.

"Why, hello there." The heron bowed gracefully to Marcella.

"Cute, Harold."

He looked up at her. "I thought you would like that."

"What's down there?" she asked as though she were embarrassed. "Before we cross, we need to know what's at the bottom."

"I see. I could take Tuck with me," the heron suggested.

"Yes, that's a good idea. Tuck." Marcella motioned to Quinn. "Well?"

"He doesn't like being carried by Harold."

"It doesn't hurt him," she said. "We've been over this before."

Tuck appeared, the cat instantly straightening his tail in defiance. "We could send the fox."

Fen flashed into existence next. "I have no problem going if it is required for the mission."

"You would say that," Tuck muttered.

"No, you're better at this," Marcella told the cat. "And it's dark down there. You were born for this mission."

Tuck licked his paws. "I was born in the Darkmoor Swamps during an intense aetherstorm." He sighed, his whiskers relaxing slightly. "But if you insist."

Harold swooped down, grabbing Tuck by the scruff of his manabound neck and dropping over the side of the long, stone slab.

Straight into the abyss, Callum thought, walking to the edge. A flutter ran through his stomach as he peered over, watching the light Harold and Tuck produced vanished into the shadows.

There was no telling what they would find . . .

CHAPTER 52

To command through mana is a delicate manipulation of threads that once pulled reveal a path where corruption and control intertwine.

—A quote from *The Darker Aspects of Mana, Third Edition* by Master Shaper Friedkin Oleksander

The wait grew excruciating. *What's taking Harold and Tuck so long?* Callum thought as he peered into the swelling darkness of the underground canyon. He gauged whether he had the courage to walk out on the slab of stone that had fallen, creating a natural bridge.

It looks fairly stable . . .

As he examined the slab further, he was reminded of a tree that had fallen across a dry creek bed on Miss Barrowsly's property. Callum remembered secretly playing around the fallen tree when he should have been helping her with something. He couldn't recall what the task had been, but it probably involved moving things around. She always needed help with things like that.

That tree was much less stable than the stone looks to be, Callum thought as he tried to spot any fissures. "Rhea, can you send Jeronymo to check the stone for any big cracks?" he asked the older student.

"Good idea," Selene chimed in. "I can also send Ecaris. She would be a good test for something like this."

Both the pacted bear and mouse appeared and began their inspection, Jeronymo racing ahead while Ecaris progressed more cautiously.

"I still don't see them," Quinn said, shading his eyes with his hand as he looked down into the darkness. "Tuck really doesn't like flying, you know."

"He'll be fine, Quinn," Marcella assured him, standing much closer to the edge than the others. "He's a tough cat."

Jeronymo returned first, bouncing along excitedly as Rhea relayed his thoughts. "He says there are cracks along the stone, but it seems stable. Ecaris agrees."

Callum looked ahead at the large aetherbear, now at the opposite end of the slab. She turned her head back to them and nodded.

"And where it leads to," Selene said, "what can we expect there?"

"Not much, actually," Rhea replied. "There are ledges, but most of the other side has been destroyed by the landslide. Jeronymo could slip through the cracks, but if the mana spring is there, it'll be nearly impossible for us to reach."

"Let's hope that's not the case. Wait!" Marcella pointed at a flash of azure light heading their way, chased by what looked like a wave of shadow large enough to engulf a house.

"We have company," Selene said as her Armorcore formed. Callum felt the mana around him tighten as Harold landed, Tuck dangling from the heron's beak.

"A bull!" Tuck shouted as he bolted toward Quinn.

The rush of darkness that followed wasn't as strong as Callum had expected. It felt more like an aftereffect, a remnant of something yet to come.

Harold, who hadn't melded with Marcella, explained. "There's a bull aetherbeast down there—if you can even call it that. The corrupted mana has triggered natural demonic tendencies."

"So it's not from the Demonsrealm?" Rhea asked.

"No, we don't believe so," Harold replied. "But it has absorbed enough power to naturally break down the barrier between the realms. A rare occurrence, really."

"So we need to kill it," Marcella said.

"Why didn't the Beast Masters deal with it?" Rhea asked.

"It might have been smaller then," Selene said.

"Could they have left it as a challenge?" Quinn asked.

"Depends on the Beast Master," Selene said knowingly. "Is the mana spring down there?"

"We believe so," Harold answered.

"Then that's where we must go," she told him before turning to the Soul Pythia trainee. "Rhea, did Jeronymo notice if the ledges on the other side of the stone bridge lead down into the canyon?"

"He didn't explore that far down. I can send him again, if you'd like."

"Yes, do."

Rhea summoned Jeronymo as Fen appeared. "I'll assist," the fox said, joining the mouse. The two quickly moved out onto the stone bridge.

"What about a fly around?" Marcella asked. "Say the word."

"If we're going to fight a corrupted aetherbull, we should do so as a team," Selene said. "Agreed?"

"Definitely," Quinn said. "Tuck won't stop talking about how massive the thing is."

The light surrounding Fen and Jeronymo faded in the distance. It soon returned with a flicker that quickly grew in brightness as the two aetherbeasts appeared again.

"Yes," Fen said, excitement sparking through his mana. "There is a way down, and the climb shouldn't be too hard. We should all be able to manage it."

"In that case, we just need to cross the stone bridge," Rhea said as Jeronymo melded with her again.

"I'll go first," Callum volunteered. "I've done something like this before."

<You've crossed an underground canyon hosting an aetherbull?> Fen asked as Callum stepped out onto the stone slab.

<Something like that,> he told the fox as he remembered Miss Barrowsly's fallen tree.

Callum ignored the sounds below, alternating between a banshee-like howl and the harrowing quietude of an endless expanse. *One step at a time,* he reminded himself, even though it wasn't exactly a balancing act. *The stone is nearly five feet wide, plenty of space to walk.*

Still, Callum kept his arms out wide. He stepped carefully around the cracks Jeronymo had found, the glowing orb above providing just enough light to see ahead.

When he finally reached the other side, Callum looked back across the stone bridge and waved at the others. *<How do we get down?>* he asked Fen.

The fox appeared, a beacon in the darkness. "Here," he said, motioning his snout toward the ledge. He hopped down. "There's enough space for one person at a time. You should be able to climb down by dangling from the edge and dropping."

"Nice." Callum glanced back to see Selene crossing the stone bridge next, followed by Marcella, Rhea, and finally Quinn, who dropped to all fours in his meldform for better balance.

"What? Cats are agile," Quinn said as he joined the others.

Fen, now on the ledge beneath them, acted as a guide as the group descended carefully, ledge by ledge, taking their time reaching the canyon floor.

As they neared the bottom, Callum felt certain the biggest obstacle still lay ahead. The darkness around them seemed to consume the light from their orbs and aetherbeasts, which dimmed through their descent.

At ground level, they stared into the shrouded blackness beyond. A rattling sound caught Callum's attention. *Marcella's jewelry?* he wondered, glancing at her. She stood poised to strike despite her slight shiver.

Callum accessed Soul Sense and saw that he had one Light and one Death Affinity shard, and two Fire and two Earth Affinity shards. *Light and fire. I should be ready to use them just in case.* Callum hadn't experimented much with taking Mana Affinity Shards before, but knew using one might be required in the challenges ahead.

"I'm heading in," he said after a quick glance at Selene. Callum moved into the gloom, Tempest Fang at the ready, Armorcore glowing faintly around him.

<I sense something will happen soon,> Fen told him. *<But you are prepared. You are getting better, you know.>*

Callum acknowledged the compliment with a grunt as he smashed the Might, Vigor, and Deftness shards he had ready to go in his free hand. The others followed suit, and Callum felt the sensation of augmented power. It wasn't like melding—he had already done that with Fen. This was an instant, noticeable change. His steps felt lighter, and his muscles tensed with newfound strength.

The boost was exactly what Callum needed.

In a move that would have been impossible in his normal state, Callum stepped aside just as the aetherbull exploded out of the darkness. He managed to hit the monster's upper leg with his wind sword.

Its upper leg! Callum thought, registering just how large the aetherbull was.

Jumping back, he fired Zephyr Strike at the charging creature as Marcella performed a similar move, producing a sharp, feathery burst of mana that sparked brightly enough to briefly illuminate the area.

He only got a glimpse, but Callum caught sight of the princess running on all fours toward the aetherbull. She launched herself into the air and passed right in front of it, distracting the monstrosity as Quinn rushed in to hit it from the side with his claws.

A skeletal mana wing, sharp as a scythe, exploded out of the aetherbeast's back and stabbed into the ground. Quinn barely scrambled away in time. Callum dismissed his sword and summoned his spear, moving in to jab at the aetherbeast and give the others a chance to regroup.

Another scythe-like wing tore out of its back, this one lined with writhing tentacles. Tuck separated from Quinn and leaped toward the aetherbull, aiming for a quick strike before remelding. The tentacles ensnared Tuck in an instant, the cat writhing in agony as mana swelled around him.

<It's draining his energy!> Fen alerted.

As both Selene and Marcella moved in, Callum activated Roots of the Willow Aethertree, sending light-filled roots toward the aetherbull. The roots wrapped around its legs, pinning it in place, as Selene and Marcella delivered coordinated strikes.

Jeronymo ultimately freed Tuck. The mouse darted in and chewed through the tentacles with astonishing speed, releasing the cat.

"Thank you!" Quinn called out to everyone.

"Don't let your aetherbeasts attack it directly," Rhea warned. "Use Weaponcores and ranged powers. And keep it grounded!"

Keep it grounded? Callum wondered as he hit the aetherbeast with his Luminous Lance. A closer look at its skeletal wings revealed the answer: *The beast can't truly fly, but the bladelike tips of its wings are gathering shadowy mana. That must be how it feels like it's everywhere at once!*

A sudden flash of power to Callum's left nearly caused him to stumble. He glanced right to see Draven and his group had arrived.

"Hell no!" Marcella shouted as Draven's mana wings—glowing with a strange darkness—folded back. A bright red greatsword appeared in the warlock's hands. Behind him, Theogar Desde, Petyr Norwood, and Artur Filin summoned their Armorcores, ready for combat. Then there was Haldir Pyke, the towering older student wielding a massive flaming axe.

"We have it from here," Draven said, his eyes darting between the seething aetherbull and Princess Selene. "Step aside, Your Ladyship."

CHAPTER 53

An archmage's true self is revealed not in quiet study, but in the chaos of calamity.

—Caison Biterolf, poet

Draven rushed forward and launched into the air, his opening strike driving the aetherbull into the ground with a resounding crash. Callum expected the others who had joined Draven to also move in and attack, but they all held back, as if they were under orders to let Draven handle it.

For a fleeting moment, it seemed like he might succeed.

Draven had the upper hand as he severed one of the bull's grotesque skeletal wings. His red eyes flared with delight as he moved in for his finishing attack, only for the monster to throw its neck back and sprout a pair of curled horns from its skull. It used them to slam into Draven, driving him straight into the ground.

"What are you waiting for?" Selene shouted at Draven's party. "We have to do something!"

Haldir Pyke merely stared ahead, while the others avoided eye contact.

Why aren't they doing anything? Callum didn't need to glance at Selene, Quinn, Marcella, or Rhea to know they had to act. *We all do!*

A burst of wind scattered some of the lingering dust that veiled much of the surrounding battle. The move gave him another glimpse of Draven, the warlock now clad in an Armorcore with a beak-like helm. Draven's relentless blows rained down, each strike more forceful than the last. Yet the aetherbull endured, its horns swelling grotesquely as tentacles began to emerge from its form.

Fen's power surged through Callum and together, they hit the bull with a sweeping gust of mana-infused wind. Selene rushed past and delivered a fierce strike, her meldform more bear than human.

"It's not working!" Callum yelled at Draven, who attempted another attack with his red sword. The warlock leaped back to avoid the scythe-like wing that came crashing down. He dismissed his weapon and unleashed a flash of yellow fire from his palms, which engulfed the bull and sent the aetherbeast into a frenzy.

The creature swatted Selene aside, reared back, and slammed its hooves into the ground, creating fissures sprawling toward the canyon walls. Tumbling rocks and slabs of stone landed all around, and dust filled the air. Callum was able to taste the stone as he instinctively moved toward where he had last seen Selene.

He found her lying on her side, arm cradling her head, Marcella and Rhea already at her side. Quinn stood guard in his meldform, complete with cat ears, claws, and a sparking mana tail.

"Is she . . . ?" Callum asked.

"I'm handling it!" Marcella cried, her hands glowing faintly with white mana. "She's just unconscious. She'll be fine in another minute."

"I'm going to conjure a portal," Rhea began.

"No," Marcella told her. "At least let us see what Selene wants."

Callum looked back toward the bull as more clashes echoed through the canyon. The first to fly out of the dust was Artur Filin, his body arcing through the air before crashing heavily into the ground nearby. He groaned and clutched his side as he managed to stagger to his feet.

Artur's aetherbeast—a double-headed dragon no larger than a rabbit when not melded—appeared beside him. The student took a shaky step forward, determination flickering in his eyes as if he intended to rejoin the fray.

"Princess—" Marcella began, but Selene interrupted her with a raspy cough as she pushed herself upright.

"I'm fine," the princess insisted as she reached for Callum's hand. He helped her up, her gaze already fixed on Rhea. "Not yet," she said. "No portal." Then with all the fire that Callum had come to expect from her, the princess turned her attention to Artur. "Why?" she demanded.

"He doesn't want us to kill it, Your Ladyship," Artur admitted.

"Why not?" Selene asked, her voice sharp and unyielding, her form radiating Ecaris's ursine power and an aura of authority.

Artur's tiny dragon shrieked and melded back into him.

"Tell me what he's planning," Selene ordered.

"He wants it," Artur finally said, his eyes bulging.

"Draven has Malrif—that raven has been in his family for generations."

"He's close to his next Rank. What I'm saying here is Draven wants the bull as his second aetherbeast. If he can get it to critical mana levels, he has an ability to temporarily enslave it."

"Enslave it?" Selene's voice laced with disgust.

<A warlock ability, surely,> Fen said to Callum, matching her disdain.

"And he would keep it enslaved until he could force-meld with it?" Selene pressed.

<Force-meld?> Callum thought.

"Warlocks—" Artur stammered.

"I don't care if the darker aspects of mana are part of a warlock's nature! I don't care if his father convinced my father these practices are worth exploring!" Selene pointed at him. "We will not play a part in this."

An explosion shook the ground, sending a spiraling flash of mana upward. It struck the stone bridge above, bringing it down in a matter of seconds. A deafening roar consumed everything, followed by a shifting gray as dust swirled in dense clouds. Huge chunks of rock rained down, the ground trembling with the force of the collapse.

<It's all coming down!> Fen shouted as he took control and used amplified strikes to blast stones out of the air. He moved Callum away, separating him from the rest of his group. The dust became instantly suffocating, coating Callum's throat and filling his lungs with grit. Shapes loomed in and out of the thick fog of debris as he tried to make sense of where he was. There were shouts, followed by a flash of fire.

I have to find the others! Callum sucked in a deep breath and raced ahead, tearing through the cloud of dust to find Theogar unconscious, his peer being dragged out of the battle by Petyr. Haldir Pyke stumbled toward Callum and collapsed, the big man's fire axe sizzling out.

"Where's Draven?" Callum asked Petyr, his ears still ringing.

Petyr didn't reply, the man too shaken to speak as his breaths came in shallow, uneven gasps. The oppressive darkness seemed to close in around them, marked by the faint echoes of a battle beyond. Quinn pushed out of the gloom, his meldform casting an eerie shifting silhouette of light.

"Callum!"

"I'm fine," he said as he registered the concern in his friend's eyes. "Help him."

"Yes, I can . . . I can help him to safety!"

"Good. And Haldir too." Callum pointed back to where he saw the other student.

"Got it!"

"Where are Marcella and Selene?" he asked, every breath rasping as though the air had turned to ash.

"Marcella's helping Artur," Quinn said. "Selene and Rhea have already started searching the rubble."

"Good. I—"

"Callum?" Quinn interrupted.

"Yes?"

"Don't do anything stupid. Or too risky."

"I won't," Callum replied.

"I'm serious," Quinn said, true concern in his eyes.

Callum placed a shaky hand on Quinn's shoulder, he opened his mouth to make a promise, but the words wouldn't come out.

"You can't give me your word, can you?" Quinn asked.

"I can't, but that's not because I don't want to."

Callum let Fen take full control. Together, they rushed toward the epicenter of the crash, where a jagged portion of the bridge jutted from the ground like a fractured pillar, its edges sharp and imposing. Dust still hung in the air, swirling around them in the faint light of the orb over Callum's head.

Callum heard Draven shout from the other side. He pressed forward, running his hand along the weathered surface of the rock wall as he searched for a way through.

Just as he was about to move on, Callum's fingers brushed against a fissure. "This is it," he whispered. "This might be the only way to break it."

<Radiant Inferno?> Fen suggested.

Callum checked his mana levels to see they were at Half-Full. *If I use Radiant Inferno, I'll drop too low.* He heard more muffled clashes beyond the stone. *But what choice do I have?*

"Let's do it!" Callum stepped back, charged for a moment, and launched a spinning sphere of mana at the fissure, hoping it would penetrate deep enough to break the slab. A shower of light followed, which only widened the crack.

"I can cycle and try again," Callum said, checking his levels. "I can try—"

<There has to be another way!>

Callum had just started running his hand along the rock again when Selene appeared.

"Callum," she said, a mixture of fear and excitement on her face. "We need to hurry. Rhea has given us all of five minutes to handle this before she brings Master Cruedark here."

"How do we get through it?" Callum asked. "I already used my strongest attack."

"My Weaponcore."

"Your . . ." he gave her a perplexed look. "Your trident?"

"Step aside." Selene produced the weapon, which glowed with an intense golden hue. "It has an overcharge capability. I'll be able to break the stone, but you might have to take it from there. I have other things I can use, but this is my most powerful attack, and using it comes with a recharge period."

"Got it." Callum took two Affinity Shards from his satchel, a Fire and a Light, and quickly consumed them . . . He felt a twist of new power within him, one that he hardly recognized as manabound claws formed on his hand as he prepared to attack. "I'm ready when you are," he told the princess, doing all he could to contain the power swelling within him.

CHAPTER 54

Leylines are the veins of our kingdom, their origins traced to mana springs able to shape and shield everything they touch.

—Master Weaver Duke Strider Vellor

Princess Selene thrust her Weaponcore trident forward and unleashed a searing flood of mana so intense that Callum had to shield his eyes and turn away. The effect was immediate: the massive slab of rock fractured with a thunderous crack, fissures tracing across its surface. The air vibrated with the force of the trident's release before the entire structure collapsed like a stage curtain, sending up another choking cloud of dust and debris.

This time, Callum didn't hesitate.

He surged forward, his momentum carrying him through the dust-filled breach, where he came upon a scene that sent a chill down his spine. Draven hovered over the aetherbull, his sword at his side. A single, twisted rope of energy extending from the palm of his hand had wrapped its way around the bull's neck. There was a madness in the warlock's red eyes, a madness that quickly shifted as the bull lurched forward, the winglike scythe on the beast's back able to break Draven's hold by slamming him into the ground.

The bull reared onto its back legs, intent on crushing Draven when Callum shot forward, wind spiraling around his arms and hands. He blew the aetherbull off-balance, landed before it, and was just summoning his Tempest Fang when the bull drove its horns into the ground, producing a wave of mana that flung Callum and Draven backward.

Still energized by the rush of power, Callum sprang to his feet and was just starting back toward the battle when a low groan stopped him dead in his tracks. He looked down to see Draven partially covered in dirt and rocks, his head fallen to the side, eyes closed.

I can't leave him here like this. Callum expected Fen to say something, but the fox remained quiet as he crouched in front of Draven and helped the other student up.

Draven was conscious, but barely. That was the first thing Callum noticed when the warlock took a step forward, his eyes still closed. It was like he didn't want to admit defeat, like he knew who was rescuing him, even if, to Callum's knowledge, Draven had never actually checked to see who was hauling him away from the fight.

A few moments later, Princess Selene reached Callum, her expression tense. "I'll handle him from here," she said firmly." There's not much time. Cruedark will be here in any minute. If we want, if *you* want to tackle this thing yourself, Callum, now is your chance."

Face it alone? He glanced down at Draven as the warlock stirred and blinked.

"Selene?" Draven muttered, his voice weak. He shoved Callum aside in a feeble attempt to stand on his own, stumbled, and fell again.

"That's enough of you," she snapped, her tone cold. "I'm helping you out of obligation, not choice. Callum, go—if that's what you want." A faint, knowing smile formed on her face. "I'll catch up if I can."

Callum turned back toward the place where he had last seen the aetherbull. *Quinn said not to do anything risky . . .* he thought as he peered into the wreckage, which was shrouded in shadow and dust.

<We're going to do this, yes?> Fen asked.

<Of course, we are.>

<It was what the Demonslayer would have done, you know.>

Callum took off, his power surging once more, amplified by the shards he had consumed. He tore through the swirling mist of dust and found the aetherbull, its massive form seething with rage, yet also clearly wounded. The bull lashed out, sending tentacles screaming toward him. Callum met them head-on with his wind sword, slicing through the onslaught with precise swings.

He sent his Tempest Fang away and summoned his spear instead. Callum ran toward the aetherbull, intent on putting everything he had into driving the spear through its body. The aetherbull's horns flared with energy, elongating in an instant. Rather than deflect his attack, the horns twisted forward like serpents, ensnaring Callum mid-strike.

<No!>

With a violent thrust, the beast hurled Callum into a jagged pile of scree. The impact reverberated through his body, even with the protection of his Armorcore, rattling his bones, and leaving him momentarily dazed.

Gritting his teeth, Callum clawed his way out of the rock pile and summoned his sword. As the aetherbull charged again, its horn arcing toward him like a spear, he swung his blade with all his might, severing the incoming horn in a clean strike. The beast let out a deafening roar of agony. Its massive hooves struck Callum square in the chest, launching him backward.

The force of the blow drove Callum deep into another pile of rock, where he was quickly engulfed by the stones. The sharp edges bit into his Armorcore as he sank into the debris, the sheer weight of the stones threatening to crush him. He struggled against the shifting mass, but as more stones tumbled down, they created an unlikely cocoon, a tight yet protective barrier that shielded him from the crushing force.

I'm trapped beneath the rock! Gasping for breath, he braced himself for his next move, his mind racing as the aetherbull stomped closer. Callum gulped as the realization sank in. <*What do I do?*> he asked Fen, tight with fear.

The orb Rhea had created hovered nearby, its light dimmed by a large rock partially concealing it. Callum could barely see the jagged stones surrounding him, the small gaps between them offering only slivers of light.

<*I've . . . I'll admit, Callum, I've never been buried like this before,*> Fen replied, his voice uncertain. <*It seems that if we move, we might dislodge the stones protecting us from being crushed. Perhaps . . .*>

Fen's words were cut short as the aetherbull slammed into the pile with the force of a battering ram. The impact sent a shockwave through the debris, shifting the rocks violently. Callum's protective cocoon lurched, dragging him downward as more stones tumbled from above.

What's happening? Callum thought, his body jarring with every shift.

The pile of stones he was buried in groaned and cracked as the bull's relentless attacks continued, forcing Callum deeper into the unstable mass. Then, with one final heave, the aetherbull's remaining horn tore into the pile, dislodging an enormous slab of stone.

The slab gave way, and Callum slid through a sudden gap, tumbling into a hidden cavern below. He landed hard, the air knocked from his lungs as he rolled to a stop.

"Where . . . ?" he started to ask.

Around him, soft blue light filled the space, one that made Rhea's orb glow with intensity. At the cavern's center, a radiant mana spring shimmered, its surface rippling with raw energy.

What is this place? Callum thought, staring at the spring in awe.

<*It's the mana spring!*> Fen said, his voice steadier now and tinged with excitement. <*The aetherbull's attack forced you down here. This is a rare chance, Callum! Recharge here while you can!*>

"There's something else . . ." Callum said as he peered at the apex of power. He could hear the bull above, its furious roars reverberating through the stone. Dust and pebbles rained down as it continued to hammer against the cavern's ceiling, trying to reach him.

With Fen's help, Callum crawled forward and found a Powercore, which had been placed on an anvil-shaped stone before the mana spring.

Weaponcore of the Sunsteel Ram
Type: Accessory
Grade: Rare Weapon
Infusion Requirements for Grade Increase:
0/25 Light Affinity
0/25 Might Shards
Affinity Requirements: Light
Effect: When bound to one's Soul Heart, this Weaponcore allows a mage to produce a pair of curved Sunsteel Ram swords capable of amplifying their power when the blades are crossed.

"What Selene said was true," Callum whispered. *A Beast Master placed this. The hidden Powercore is with the spring.*

Callum didn't have a chance to react further as the light from the spring surged forward, the brilliant wave of energy cascading toward him. He extended a hand toward it, palm open, as if trying to shield himself or perhaps embrace what was coming. The magical warmth pulsed against his skin, not like the heat of fire but a soothing, vibrant energy that seemed to hum with life itself. It flowed around him in shimmering tendrils, wrapping his body in an almost tangible current of power. For a moment, he couldn't tell where the spring's power ended and his own began.

You have reached the Wielder Rank.
Your Powercore capacity has increased to fifteen.
Your Aethercore capacity has increased to two.

Callum quickly checked his Powercores to see some of the changes. Zephyr Strike, Inner Light, and Empowerment of Sustenance had leveled up, each of them reaching the Rare Grade.

Using Soul Sense told him his Mana Reserves were back to Steady, Callum now with plenty of power.

<We have to get back up there!> Fen said with excitement.

Callum fused the Weaponcore of the Sunsteel Ram into his chest. He triggered his new Weaponcore, conjuring two curved blades, which were defined by thick ridges along their edges that resembled ram horns. "Nice." As he examined the two massive blades, he suddenly knew what he should do next. He sent the swords away.

"It's ironic, you know," he told Fen as he looked to the stone overhead, his gaze tracing along the fractures and contours. He was already piecing together where he would need to strike to bring it all down and carve a path to take on the aetherbull. "We started in a subbasement of the East Manor, and now we're here, buried once again."

"Only this time, you have the power and clarity to face what lies ahead."

Callum used his final Fire Affinity Shard. "Radiant Inferno. And this time, let's make it count."

CHAPTER 55

The invisible thread that weaves life, magic, and the very fabric of our world into existence is mana. We are all part of that storied legacy.

—Maxim of the Great College of New Albion

A charged Radiant Inferno, amplified by the Fire Affinity boost, erupted from Callum's hands. It blazed through the rock above at an angle, producing sparks of light and mana fire. The explosion that followed sent shockwaves rippling through the air as dust and stone cascaded down toward the mana spring.

<That's it!> Fen said as Callum stepped back.

The debris settled into a natural slope, glowing faintly in the light of the spring below.

Callum steeled himself and bolted up the scree, his movements a blur of speed and precision. Each step felt weightless, as though the mana from the spring still coursed through him, propelling Callum forward. The heat from the Radiant Inferno lingered in the air, crackling faintly around him, as he closed the gap with the aetherbull, who still seemed to be processing the explosion that had just taken place.

Callum unleashed a spiral of wind, his form cutting through the swirling dust like a gale. The force of his attack connected with the aetherbull, driving it back with a guttural roar.

He drew his Tempest Fang and slashed at its incoming horn, deflecting the bull's momentum. The beast reared back and slammed its hooves down, shaking the earth. Callum dove left, rolled, and came up with another epic blast of wind mana.

<It's falling back!> Callum told Fen as he summoned his two new Weaponcore blades, their forms gleaming with raw power, and cleaved forward. Remembering that their true potential was unlocked when crossed, he drew

the blades together. As they met, a surge of energy fizzled between them, and Callum unleashed a V-shaped wave of blistering light at the aetherbull. He backpedaled a bit and then hit the beast with another devastating attack.

<We can end this!>

<I have to be careful,> Callum told Fen as he performed another of these attacks. *<I haven't used two swords before!>*

Even with one of its skeletal wings severed, the bull jumped and took to the air, shadow trailing around the creature like a flock of birds. *Light and Fire Affinity versus Shadow*, Callum thought as he charged after the creature, which had started to flee. *I can do this!*

He went for another attack with his new Weaponcore but then dismissed it in a flash, summoning his spear instead. *<Give me everything you have!>* he commanded Fen, his voice a blend of desperation and resolve.

Just as he had practiced with Master Cruedark, and sparked by a surge of energy from Fen, Callum rushed forward, two hands on the spear, and closed the distance in a blur of motion. He plunged the spear into the aetherbull's side, puncturing its thick, hardened mana exterior.

The beast let out a terrifying bellow, its massive form trembling as Callum bore down with all of his weight. He pushed the spear deeper as his entire body surged with Fen's energy. His Weaponcore flared with light and the bull's tentacles writhed with violence.

The aetherbeast slid, kicking up stone and bringing Callum with it to the floor as the beast collapsed under its own weight. Callum staggered back, chest heaving as the creature released a final raspy breath. It was done.

Empowerment of Mind Shard
Empowerment of Might Shard
Empowerment of Might Shard
Shadow Affinity Shard
Shadow Affinity Shard
Shadow Affinity Shard
Death Affinity Shard
Death Affinity Shard
Onslaught of the Thunderhoof Shadowbull

Onslaught of the Thunderhoof Shadowbull
Type: Ability
Grade: Sublime
Infusion Requirements for Grade Increase:
0/35 Light Affinity

0/35 Shadow Affinity
Affinity Requirements: *Light or Shadow*
Effect: *When bound to one's Soul Heart, this core grants the wielder the ability to summon the power of a shadowbull to unleash a spectral charge that scatters enemies with an unstoppable force and is capable of toppling structures.*

"Toppling structures?" Callum said as he caught his breath. Sweat dripped from his brow, mixing with the dust caked on his skin.

<*We could use something like this.*>

"Agreed." *A charge attack has proven useful in the past*, he thought, recalling his Shatterlight Bear ability. *But being at the Sublime Grade means I won't be able to use its full potential. But toppling structures . . .*

As the world around him settled, corrupted mana still tingling in the air, Callum pressed the new Powercore into his chest. *What a fight . . .*

He could hear the others racing toward him now, yet it still took them a moment to move through the rubble. The first person he saw was Princess Selene, the orb over her head lighting her path as she locked eyes with him. Rather than slowing down, she quickened her pace, and for a moment Callum was certain Selene was about to throw her arms around him. She stopped abruptly, mere inches from where he stood, her eyes locked on him.

"Ecaris," she said, gathering her wits, "Fen, please handle the Corruption."

"As you wish," Fen told her upon taking shape near the bear.

Quinn and Marcella joined them, their faces alight with excitement and a mixture of relief and pride. The tension they carried seemed to melt away as they caught sight of him.

"Callum!" Quinn said, his voice brimming with relief and joy. "I knew you could do it!"

"And the others?" Callum asked when he didn't see Draven or any of his group.

"They have portaled back to the Great College," Quinn said hurriedly. "And Victrin and his group left way earlier, apparently. They didn't intend to camp overnight."

Marcella came forward and hugged Callum, surprising him. She pushed away and punched his shoulder. "You crazy farm boy! I really thought you had taken on too much." Her eyebrows twitched. "Hold on. The mana spring is near. I can feel it."

"It's that way," Callum told her as he pointed toward the rubble.

"How did you . . ." Marcella began, but the question remained unfinished as Rhea and Master Cruedark joined them, the latter wearing an expression of uncharacteristic uncertainty.

Even though it was cavernous, it was as if the air was suddenly sucked out of the space, leaving an oppressive silence in its wake. Master Cruedark's sharp gaze swept over Callum, his brow furrowing as he turned his attention to the wreckage beyond. He was soon joined by Sir Trindade, who carried an uncertain look on his face as he took in the aftermath of the fight with a scrutinizing eye.

"Callum Stross," Master Cruedark began, his tone measured. "What you did here today . . ." A grin broke across his face, lifting the ends of his beard. "What you did here today exemplifies what the Great College strives to achieve in its archmages. From aiding your peers to charging into a situation that could have gotten you killed. All of it." He nodded as he spoke, his conviction deepening with each word. "You embody the kind of student we hope to train. You have not only proven yourself worthy of being removed from academic probation, something I'll see to when we get back—"

"Really?" Callum asked, overcome with relief. He hadn't even realized the pressure academic probation had been putting on him until Master Cruedark mentioned that he was off it.

"Truly. You, and if I'm being honest, all of you," Cruedark said as he motioned toward Rhea, Quinn, Marcella, and Princess Selene, "risked your lives to help your peers. Your courage and resolve have not gone unnoticed. Your reward will be first access to the mana spring. But that's not all." He paused and glanced at Selene's guard. "While Sir Trindade and I . . . actually you know what? I'll let him tell you."

Sir Trindade stepped forward and cleared his throat. "While we were waiting, we received word that a tournament between our kingdom and the Geshwine Empire has been approved, the first of its kind in nearly a hundred years. This will pit the best of the Great College against the finest from their college, the Crimson Sigil."

A tournament? Callum's thoughts raced as murmurs broke out among the group.

Once they quieted, Master Cruedark explained further: "What you have done here today proves to me that you have the gumption to compete in this tournament. Of course, there will be qualifying rounds—your peers deserve their chance—but I have no doubt that some of you will earn your place among our champions." His smile widened, radiating pride. "Now, the mana spring awaits. See what it has to offer, and then we will return to the college. There is plenty to do between now and the start of the tournament."

As the group turned toward the mana spring, Callum felt the weight of the announcement settle on him. *A tournament? Against the Geshwine Empire's best?*

ABOUT THE AUTHORS

Luke Chmilenko is the bestselling author of the *Ascend Online* series and other fan-favorite fantasy epics, including *Iron Prince* and the Hat Trick and Shattered Reigns series. He has become a cornerstone of the LitRPG and progression fantasy genres, known for crafting vast worlds and delivering high-stakes magic and combat. Luke lives in Ontario with his wife and two daughters, splitting his time between writing, gaming, and plotting new stories faster than his hands can keep up.

Harmon Cooper is the bestselling author of nearly one hundred books across the LitRPG, cultivation, and progression fantasy genres including the Pilgrim, Cowboy Necromancer, Cozy Abyss, Shadowborn Exile, and War Priest series. He began writing LitRPG in 2015 and hasn't looked back since. Born and raised in Austin, Texas, Harmon lived in Asia for five years before relocating to New England and ultimately settling in Portugal.

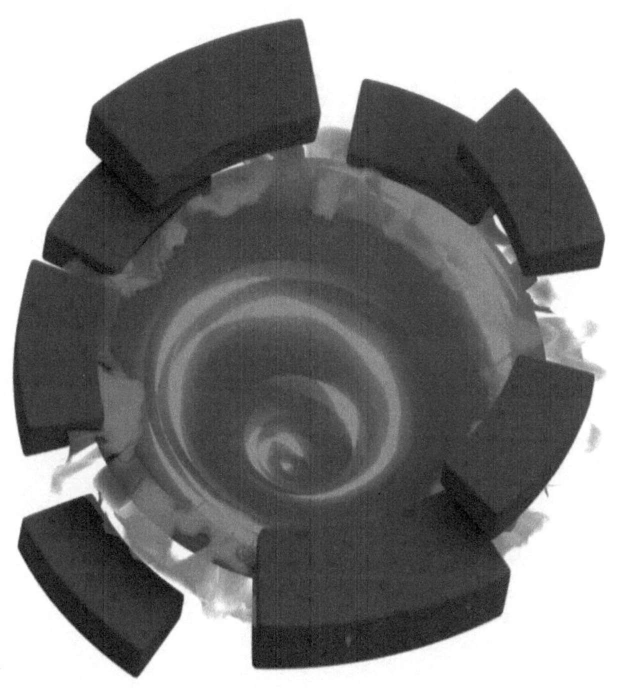

RESPAWN YOUR CURIOSITY

follow us on our socials

podiumentertainment.com

@podiumentertainment

/podiumentertainment

@podium_ent

@podiumentertainment